From the day he was found in a carrier bag on the steps of Guy's Hospital, Andy McNab has led an extraordinary life. As a teenage delinquent he kicked against society. As a young soldier he waged war against the IRA in the streets and fields of South Armagh. As a member of 22 SAS he was at the centre of covert operations for nine years, on five continents. During the Gulf War he commanded Bravo Two Zero, a patrol that, in the words of his commanding officer, 'will remain in regimental history for ever'. Awarded both the Distinguished Conduct Medal and Military Medal during his military career, McNab was the British Army's most highly decorated soldier when he finally left the SAS. Since then, he has become one of the world's bestselling writers, drawing on his insider knowledge and experience. Besides his writing work, he lectured to security and intelligence agencies in both the USA and UK, he works in the film industry advising Hollywood on everything from covert procedure to training civilian actors to act like soldiers, and he continues to be a spokesperson for both military and literacy charities.

You can discover more about the author at www.andymcnab.com

FOR VALOUR

When a young trooper is shot in the head at the Regiment's renowned Killing House at the SAS's base in Hereford, Nick Stone is perfectly qualified to investigate the mysterious circumstances more deeply. But less than forty-eight hours later, a second death catapults him into the telescopic sights of an unknown assassin bent on protecting a secret that will strike at the heart of the establishment that Stone has spent most of his life fighting to protect. And now with the clock ticking, Stone hurtles from the solitude of a remote Welsh confessional to southern Spain, in an increasingly desperate quest to uncover the truth about a chain of events that began in the darkness of an Afghan hillside, and left a young man haunted by the never-ending screams of a dying friend.

Books by Andy McNab
Published by Ulverscroft:

ANDY McNAB

FOR VALOUR

Complete and Unabridged

CHARNWOOD
Leicester

First published in Great Britain in 2014 by
Bantam Press
an imprint of Transworld Publishers
London

First Charnwood Edition
published 2018
by arrangement with
Transworld Publishers
A Random House Group Company
London

A catalogue record for this book is available
from the British Library.

ISBN 978–1–4448–3646–2

Published by
F. A. Thorpe (Publishing)
Anstey, Leicestershire

Set by Words & Graphics Ltd.
Anstey, Leicestershire
Printed and bound in Great Britain by
T. J. International Ltd., Padstow, Cornwall

This book is printed on acid-free paper

PART ONE

1

Lake Sommen, Östergötland

Thursday, 7 May 1992
17.17 hrs

I eased open the front door with a little help
from a couple of strips of steel wire and tapped
the six-figure sequence into the panel beside it to
disable the alarm system. Colonel Chastain had
given us the code — he had friends in high
places and I guessed serious cash would have
changed hands somewhere along the line.

A scrubbed-pine kitchen, dining area, snug,
and huge open-plan living space stretched across
the ground floor. Then upstairs, four bedrooms,
all with en-suite bath and shower, the master,
with a big fuck-off four-poster, one for the kids
and two for guests.

The half-sunk basement contained a gym
packed with state-of-the-art equipment, a ping-
pong table and a sauna, along with the working
parts — gas and electricity supply, washing-
machine, tumble-drier, all that sort of shit.

The windows down here were covered with high-
tensile brushed-steel security mesh. I undid the latch
on the one beneath the wooden steps that led up
to the side entrance and left it for later. I reckoned that if we were going to turn the house into
a fire-bomb, this was where we'd light the fuse.

3

Even in the engine room the owners had gone for the designer look. I found a well-stocked toolbox in a cupboard beneath the polished granite work surface, then took a close look at the jamb, rebate and frame of the door that led down from the house.

To start with, Harry worked quickly and silently alongside me. As the minutes ticked by, though, his muscles became tighter, his movements less fluid. He was well aware that we couldn't leave any sign of making entry, but I could tell that all he really wanted to do was rip the place apart.

It was probably a mistake to take a last poke around the main living area. The furniture — stainless steel, glass, oiled wood and leather — was arranged with clinical precision. It felt like a showroom. Everything in its proper place.

The silver-framed family portrait was what tipped Harry over the edge. About two feet wide and eighteen inches high, it stood in pride of place between a pair of shiny candlesticks, beneath a window that looked out across the mirror-flat lake. The Saddam Hussein clone at the centre of the group was grinning from ear to ear. With a beautiful blonde Swedish wife and a couple of olive-skinned kids hugging him like their lives depended on it, he had a lot to be happy about.

But, close up, you couldn't help noticing that Jahmir Koureh's smile didn't reach his eyes.

I'd only seen it happen once, very briefly, during our six-week stay in Baghdad's Ba'ath Party HQ — when he'd leaned in to fasten his pliers around my one remaining wisdom tooth and wrenched it out of my gum to add to his trophy collection. He had never bothered with anaesthetic. It stopped him getting maximum satisfaction from his work.

There was a low growl to my left. 'I swear it, Nick, I'm going to kill that fucker with my bare hands . . .'

Harry looked like he'd seen a ghost. His skin was stretched across his forehead and cheek-bones like cling-film, and beads of sweat had started to bubble up at his hairline. His knuckles whitened beneath his clear polythene gloves as he gripped the chair-back beside me.

Fair one.

I'd thought I'd managed to bury the memory of our Gulf War captivity, but I couldn't stop the metallic taste of blood and bile leaking onto my tongue again now. And whatever damage Koureh and his mates had done to me, it wasn't a patch on what they'd done to Harry Callard.

2

I hadn't expected tea and biscuits after we were captured by the Republican Guard in the north-western Iraqi desert a year ago. We'd made casualties of quite a few of their mates as we'd fought our way to the Syrian border. I could see they weren't in carnival mood when they dragged me out of the storm drain where I'd been hiding since first light, and wasn't surprised that they filled us in every chance they got en route to the interrogation centre.

Once they had stripped and blindfolded us in our cells, they banged our heads on the floor until they turned into over-inflated footballs. Then they climbed aboard us with their boots and lengths of four-by-four. They were kids, really, angry at the world, angry about the length of time it was taking to grow their bum fluff, and seriously pissed off with the enemy who had suddenly appeared in their backyard and ruined their day. I didn't even mind when they made us eat our own shit — it was better than another beating.

But the cool dudes with the perfectly chiselled Saddam moustaches were something else again. They knew a thing or two about pain. They knew what really seared your bone marrow and broke your spirit, and they carried on dishing it out long after the usefulness of any information we might have carried had expired.

6

While we spent the whole interrogation period trying to conceal our true identities, Koureh seemed keen to boast about his. 'Are you a Londoner, Nick? Of course you are. I can tell by your accent. When you and your friends were robbing corner shops in Catford, I was studying dentistry at your King's College Hospital. My fellow students used to call me Jammy.'

I noticed then that he had shark eyes. Even when he was cracking a funny they never reflected the light.

I filed away every fragment of int I could lay my hands on. Who knew when I might need it? And the rest of the time I tried not to give them the satisfaction of knowing what they were doing to me hurt like fuck.

There was no foolproof recipe for survival. We all developed our own strategies. The lads with wives and kids tried not to think of home: it took their eye off the ball and made them vulnerable. Some did mathematical calculations in their head. Trev made up his own crossword clues; he might have looked like a Neanderthal, but he could do pretty much any puzzle — general knowledge or cryptic — in under fifteen minutes.

We all did our best to keep the banter going. Richie Rothwell stumbled back from one of Koureh's sessions, gobbed up a mouthful of blood and splintered enamel and rasped, 'At least they can't make yer pregnant.' Whenever things went to rat shit I kept that gag alive in my head. It probably kept me alive too.

At first, Harry tried to join in the fun and

games back in the cell, but we could all see that he was in shit state. He didn't have any more crusted blood, pus and mucus on him than the rest of us, but you could see that they'd messed big-time with the inside of his head.

Some days, after Johnny Sawbridge died, he did nothing more than squat on the floor, barely making a sound, rocking backwards and forwards, like he was a small boat on a heavy swell.

3

I had hoped this Swedish job might help Harry draw a line under the whole Gulf nightmare; but I was already starting to regret bringing him along.

I reached out and touched his shoulder. He recoiled and skittered back across the uncluttered pine floor like I'd zapped him with a Taser. But this wasn't the time or the place.

'Mate, we've got to move . . . ' I gathered him up and aimed him towards the front door.

As we emerged, the evening sunshine glinted off the water beyond the crescent of firs that fringed the dentist's lakeside spread. We'd come here via the slow road from Tranåas, so knew his nearest neighbour was more than three Ks to the north of us, but I was still glad of the trees, especially now that Harry was starting to lose it.

We needed to conceal ourselves, to sort out what was going to happen next, and our scrape was just about perfect for the job. We had a juniper trunk and a big lateral branch at our backs and plenty of cover in front but a clear view of the house and the track that approached it through the forest. We could also see enough of the lake to our half-left to give us all the warning we needed of an imminent Viking attack.

I kept up a gentle monologue as I steered Harry back to the LUP (lying-up position). 'Deep breaths, mate. We're nearly there. Tea,

9

sticky buns, evening paper . . . ' I thought it might help remove some of the tension from his shoulder muscles, maybe even bring a smile to his face. But he hardly reacted, just stared back in the direction we'd come, jaw clenched, the veins on his neck standing out like whipcord.

Koureh's Stockholm practice obviously wasn't short of business if his weekend place was anything to go by: steeply raked, slate-tiled roof; traditional dove-grey clapboard walls; bleached blue shutters standing to attention each side of massive picture windows that overlooked the water. His sundeck was the size of a tennis court, which left plenty of room to stretch out on the stainless-steel and cream canvas steamer chairs once you'd dragged yourself out of the hot tub. The nickel-plated hurricane lantern on the glass-topped dining table looked like the nose cone of a small space rocket.

I knew that all this five-star luxury was making things even worse for Harry. What kind of God let Koureh bring his designer family, and the occasional upwardly mobile receptionist, to this slice of Scandinavian Paradise when a lot of good lads still hadn't recovered from his wartime dental treatment — and at least one we knew never would?

He blinked a couple of times and finally managed to tear his gaze away from the window where we'd been admiring Koureh's happy snaps. The sweat was still pouring off him big-time, but his skin was looking better. He wiped a sleeve across his forehead. 'Nick, I'm sorry. I lost it for a minute back there. I keep

10

seeing Snakebite's body lying in the corner of that interrogation room . . . '

'I know. Not good.' It was the smell that had got to me. They'd only taken him out and buried him a day or two before the maggots saved them the trouble. 'But you've really got to try and cut away . . . '

It was easier said than done, of course.

Harry had taken his mate's death hard. They'd been inseparable since Northern Ireland. They'd even been alongside each other when a toadhead pitviper had bitten Johnny on the knob in Colombia. We took the piss out of them both severely about that, of course. It was what friends were for.

4

We weren't expecting our target to make an appearance for twenty-four hours or so. I hoped that would give Harry enough time to calm himself down and start thinking beautiful thoughts again.

Using the cover docs supplied by Chastain, Trev and I had flown in to Stockholm separately and spent the last eight days putting surveillance on the target until we reckoned we knew pretty much every detail of his routine. Apart from the practice, he basically had five regular stopping-off points: their apartment, St Erik's Hospital, the kids' school, Mrs K's office and the local communal pool.

Harry had arrived via Copenhagen. He'd paid cash for a six-year-old Merc estate with Danish plates and brought it over on the Helsingøor-Helsingborg ferry. I'd RVed with him at Tranås yesterday morning.

Trev was fluent enough in Swedish to be kept warm on long winter nights, so it made sense for him to stay with the target. His job was to keep the trigger on Koureh until he slid behind the wheel of his steel-grey Saab 900 convertible tomorrow night, then give us the standby as it headed south for the weekend. The wife and kids always came down in the Volvo estate after the Saturday-morning swimming lessons.

My only real worry — aside from Harry going

into meltdown — was that our man in the white tunic might take advantage of the opportunity to show his latest receptionist the view from his super-king-size duvet before his nearest and dearest joined him. We weren't in the business of killing real people.

Fuck it, we'd have to cross that bridge when we came to it.

Right now I wanted to get some calories down our necks, and visualize what we'd do when Koureh showed.

I dug into my daysack for water and scoff. Neither of us had fancied the idea of fermented herring, so our choice was a fairly simple one — Swedish meatballs or Swedish sausages. We didn't bother heating them, just necked them straight out of the can. I left his pack of Camel Lights where they were. It was a disgusting habit, and we needed to keep the place sterile.

I glanced at Harry from time to time as we ate and drank. He'd got some colour back in his cheeks and was having a go at normal. And normal for Harry wasn't all bad. Some of the girls around Hereford thought he was a dead ringer for the blond guy in *Thelma & Louise* — Brad somebody. I could never remember his name.

All was good — well, getting better — and soon we'd put our feet up, to lie back and enjoy the sunset. The mosquitoes weren't due for another month in this part of the planet, so there was nothing to spoil our day.

That was when the radio sparked up and Trev came on the net.

5

Trev was one of the world's great improvisers, but he really hated being taken by surprise. So I could always tell when he was feeling the pain, even over the net. And right now he was feeling it big-time.

'Mate, I've fucked up. I do not have Bravo One . . .'

Our comms operated on a frequency-hopping system, so they were pretty secure unless you used the handset to call your mum and she kept you on the line, but it still made sense not to ID names.

'The appointment diary was full to bursting until around now, and all day tomorrow, so I went for a brew. When I got back, the wagon wasn't there.'

I didn't ask him whether he'd zipped through a couple of crossword puzzles while he was waiting, but I would later.

Trev brought us up to speed. He'd rung the receptionist and asked for an emergency appointment; apparently he even knew the Swedish for 'root canal'. She'd told him Mr K had left for the day, and wouldn't be back until after the weekend. That was bad news for us, but probably good news for her. As the shadows lengthened, Stockholm was going to be a lot more comfortable than this bit of Östergötland.

Trev had checked out Koureh's city apartment

14

and the four other known locations, but he wasn't at any of them. So we had to assume the target was heading in our direction. His drive was about three and a half hours from the capital, which meant we had to get our finger out.

I put the empty bottle and sausage cans back into my daysack and took out the alarm clock we'd bought at a Clas Ohlson hardware store in Tranås. Next out of the sack were the Swan Vestas. You could spark these things up on the zip of your Levi's, but the coarse sandpaper striker that ran along the side of the box was what I needed. I cut the strikers off two boxes and tucked them into the left-hand pocket of my bomber jacket. The clock and a bunch of loose matches went into the right.

I told Harry to take up position behind the treeline. Good-looking or not, I still reckoned it would be a whole lot safer for both of us if he stayed out of sight while I went back inside and messed around with Koureh's pipework. And if anyone came along the track that led to the house, I wanted to hear about it from Harry first.

I told him to do his owl call if he spotted any incoming threat. It was one of his favourite party tricks.

I could see he was chuffed, but a bit worried too. 'What if you confuse it with a real owl?'

I gave him a big grin and clapped him on the cheek. 'No chance of that, mate. It sounds more like the siren on a New York fire truck. That's why I suggested it.'

I got to my feet and moved a few metres back for a piss before doglegging towards the lake to check for movement on the water. I didn't want a summer cruise party or even a lone kayaker as an audience when I slipped into that basement. A pair of osprey circled lazily above the trees on one of the nearby islands, but nothing and no one else was invading their space.

I picked up a forked stick a couple of feet long on my way back through the trees and slipped on my gloves as I walked out onto the immaculately trimmed lawn.

Five minutes later I ducked beneath the slatted platform at the top of the steps up to the kitchen doorway. Dew had started to form, making the gravel pathway surrounding the house cold and slightly slippery to the touch. I could feel my shirt and jeans dampen as I got down onto my belt buckle.

The window I'd unclipped earlier was hinged at the top and wider than it was high — so big enough to allow a lad in Timberland boots and a bomber jacket to gain entry if he didn't want to keep using the front door. The frame stood proud of the casing by about a centimetre where it met the sill. I gripped both sides of it with the tips of my polythene-covered fingers, prised it open and wedged the forked stick in one corner to keep it in place.

Then I turned and slid inside, feet first.

6

Harry and I were travelling light on this job. We always did. The Swedish police might routinely carry pistols and keep Heckler & Kochs locked down in their wagons, but they didn't like anyone else doing it, especially if they were in-country without a formal invitation. The same went for slabs of high explosive and rolls of det cord. So when you were aiming to bring the rafters down on a guy who didn't deserve to keep enjoying his Jacuzzi, you had to make do with whatever came to hand.

It was still light enough outside for me to see clearly without having to risk a torch beam blitzing a darkened window. First up, I pulled the toolbox out of its cupboard. Judging by its contents, none of the family wasted much of their time on DIY. Every gadget was in mint condition, even the pliers. Maybe Koureh was saving them for someone special.

I selected a small hand drill, a clear plastic packet of bits, a roll of double-sided tape and a very shiny adjustable spanner, then took a cloth from a neatly folded pile.

The boiler gave a sudden rumble as I placed the spanner and the cloth on the floor in front of it, then resumed its soft murmur. I put the roll of tape and the hand drill on the top step beneath the entrance from the house, and extracted the Swans, their ignition strips and the alarm clock

17

from my bomber jacket. I lined them all up and screwed a drill bit the same diameter as a match-stick into the chuck.

I slowed my breathing and opened my mouth to quieten the roar of the blood-flow in my ears, then turned the door handle and pulled it back far enough to be able to listen for movement above me.

Nothing.

I wasn't expecting any, but these routines always made me feel a bit more secure. Now I could just get on with the job.

The tape rasped as I peeled two or three inches off the roll and fastened both the ignition strips alongside each other on the bottom of the door. Leaving it ajar, I drilled five neat holes in the sill, as tight as possible to the point at which the leading edge of the strips would cross the threshold. I pushed it closed and tapped a Swan into each hole until only its little red head was visible, then checked that we'd be guaranteed a strike.

I blew the coil of wood off the bit, slid it into its packet, and put it and the roll of tape back in the toolbox before returning to the boiler.

Like pretty much everything else in the place, this bit of kit belonged on Planet Zanussi. Its gleaming aluminium casing was a world away from the rusty enamel monster I'd grown up with on our estate in Bermondsey, but it needed to be fed in much the same way. I spent a minute or two following the pattern of the pipework leading in and out of it, then took a couple of paces back, slowed my breathing, opened my

18

mouth and listened some more.

Still no noise from the rooms overhead.

I moved back to my entry window and went through the same routine.

Again, nothing. No owl. No New York fire truck siren.

Then, in the distance, a sound like a squeaky wheel.

I slowed my breathing further. After a moment, I heard a soft, sad echo. So, not a wheel. The osprey was calling to its mate.

I went back to the boiler and wrapped the cloth around a pressure joint by a right-angle bend. If anybody was in the mood to examine it closely enough, I wanted this thing to look like it had sprung a slow leak, and that meant leaving no scratch marks on the brass. I tightened the jaws of the spanner over the freshly wrapped nut, gripped the moulded, rubber-sheathed handle and applied some gentle pressure. It was rock solid.

I tried again, with a bit more muscle. Same result.

The third time, it gave.

I loosened the spanner, removed the cloth, crouched down and leaned my ear right up close to the joint. There was a whisper of gas, like air leaving a radiator valve if you could be bothered to do the rounds with your little brass key when the cold weather arrived.

The digital time display read 19.57. There was probably a scientific formula for this, but I had no idea what it was. I just wanted Koureh's basement to fill with enough gas to make a nice

19

big bang the moment he opened that door.

Natural gas was lighter than air, and dissipated relatively easily. The house had been built in the thirties, so it wouldn't take long for it to find its way up between the floorboards. The trick was to make sure the mixture was right — more than five per cent by volume but less than fifteen, or it wouldn't ignite. I gave the nut an extra twist for luck, replaced the spanner and the cloth where I'd found them and shut the cupboard.

I wound the alarm clock, primed it to go off in a couple of hours, and left it on the slab of highly polished granite nearest to the doorway. It didn't exactly go with the Georg Jensen gear in the rest of the house, but if Koureh hadn't already lit himself a cigar upstairs or come down here to pop his boxers into the washing-machine or do a session on the treadmill, it would ring loudly enough for him to throw open the door to see what was going on.

At that point the strikers would brush the match heads and we'd have ourselves a serious bonfire. If all else failed I'd creep back onto the sundeck, light his Gucci hurricane lantern, lob it through the glass into his living room, then do a runner.

As I hauled myself out of the basement window and lowered it back into place, the silence of the pine forest was suddenly broken, and the cries I heard now had nothing to do with the ospreys.

7

Harry was sprinting across the lawn, brandishing the world's biggest branch and shrieking like a banshee as the crunch of tyres on gravel announced the arrival of a wagon at the front of the house.

He'd obviously decided to bin Plan A. Plan B seemed to involve hurling himself straight at the target's vehicle with the intention of clubbing him senseless.

Plan B wasn't the best plan in the world. Then again, maybe it wasn't the worst. When I'd slithered out from underneath the steps I could see that Koureh had his roof down. But he wasn't about to sit there admiring the sunset while some crazed lunatic got up close and battered him around the head.

As Harry stormed onto the driveway, Koureh adjusted his steering, floored his accelerator pedal and rammed his attacker mid-thigh.

Harry cartwheeled off the front wing like a rag doll. He landed in a heap on the gravel, gave a low moan and scrabbled around with his fingernails, like a lobster trying to escape the cooking pot. He wasn't going anywhere fast.

Koureh braked hard and threw the Saab into reverse. It took me a second to realize that he was more intent on finishing the job with Harry than getting out of my way. I caught up with him as the nearside rear tyre missed his victim's head

21

and bumped across his lower torso, and launched myself into the back seat as the front tyre followed suit.

Koureh spun the wheel to throw me off balance, but before his right hand could yank the gearstick into first I scrambled up and wrapped my right arm around his throat. I wrenched him out of the driving seat, away from the pedals and wheel. The wagon stalled and juddered to a halt, and I brought my left hand up to grip my right wrist and tightened my hold.

The only sounds now were the ticking of the engine and Koureh's frantic snorts as I hauled his shoulders over the back of his seat. He shot out his legs, trying to jerk his head and body backwards to unbalance me.

His hands came up, flailing wildly, trying to loosen my grip, but it wasn't happening. It took another couple of minutes for Plan C to achieve the result A and B had aimed for. I let Koureh's body slide back into his seat and clambered out over the side of the wagon.

Harry wasn't moving. I knelt beside him. There was no exterior bleeding. His legs were splayed and swelling. His pelvis was shot to pieces and both femurs were broken, but no bone fragments had pierced the skin.

I had no idea of the extent of his internal injuries, but I'd have been surprised if his spleen and kidneys had got off scot free. I shoved two fingers into his neck. His carotid told me some stuff inside him was still working. His heart was pounding like a jack-hammer.

He opened his eyes, but not much. I could

have blindfolded him with dental floss.

'Is he dead?'

I eased his head towards the Saab to let him see what was slumped against the driver's door.

'Nice, Nick . . . nice . . .'

He groaned as he turned back to me and glanced down at his injuries. 'Not brilliant, eh?'

'Seen better.' I switched into reassuring mode. 'But I've heard some very good things about those Swedish doctors.'

He gave me a sort of smile. 'I've heard some very good things about those Swedish nurses.'

'Dream on, mate.' I pulled a face. 'They've got no time for ugly fucks like you.'

He knew as well as I did that going to a Swedish hospital was out of the question. Some things took too much explaining. I thought about claiming that it had been a hit-and-run; at least that was consistent with his injuries. But he'd be bedbound for weeks, so however quickly we extracted from this area, we'd still be in the country. And in the shit.

Right now his job was to stay right where he was. He knew that. He had to hold tight and take the pain until I could get him out of there and work out what to do next.

'Mate, don't go walkabout, OK?'

He tried to roll his eyes. 'As if . . .'

The light was fading when I returned with my forked stick, the radio handset and Harry's daysack, but it was still enough to see that he'd managed to raise himself onto his elbows and got some of the light back in his eyes.

'I'm not going to say sorry again, Nick. I

needed him to know it was us.'

'Fair one.' I tossed the stick onto the Saab's passenger seat. 'But do us both a favour, eh? The next time you decide to go on a kamikaze mission, give me some warning. If I'd known what you were up to, I wouldn't have wasted all that time trying to turn Koureh's dream house into a party-size Molotov cocktail.'

'There won't be a next time.' His lip trembled. 'The jobs are over, mate. We both know that.'

It was on the tip of my tongue to remind him about his six-year-old son, but now wasn't the time. 'Let's worry about that shit later.'

I zipped up his fleece, shrugged off my bomber and covered his top half with it to try to keep some heat in him.

'Right now I need to sort the Saab and the body. Then I'll be back with the Merc ASAP to pick you up and reconnect the gas.'

I pulled out some water before tucking the daysack between the back of his skull and the gravel. 'I'd light you a Camel, but you know they're not good for you. You'll have to make do with some of this instead . . .'

When I raised the bottle to his lips, he wasn't interested.

'No, mate . . . My drama. I fucked up.'

I put it down on the gravel beside him in case he changed his mind.

8

I ran over to the Saab, triggered the boot release, then hoisted Koureh out of his seat and into the boot. I opened the driver's door and tried the forked stick for size in the foot-well. Then I got in behind the wheel, shifted into neutral and switched on the engine.

About fifty metres back along the track there was a turning to the right, which led through the trees to a clearing where we'd left our Danish Merc. By the time I got there it was nearly dark o'clock.

I parked up and walked to the end of the rocky outcrop, which stood like a diving platform above the edge of the lake. One or two lights glimmered on the far shore.

When we'd arrived there at midday the water had been crystal clear to a depth of ten metres, yet I still couldn't see the bottom. It looked like oil now. It seemed a good place for my version of a Viking funeral. Koureh was going to have to do without the flaming longboat and the drinking horns, but he didn't deserve any of that shit anyway.

I turned the Saab's engine on again and reversed about twenty metres. These wagons were front-wheel drive and weighed over a ton, so I needed a bit of a run-up before hitting the launch pad. I put it into second and, keeping my left foot on the clutch and my right on the brake, wedged down the accelerator pedal an inch or two with my stick. Then I lifted both feet, gripped the top of the steering wheel, lifted my arse and stepped back onto the nice soft leather.

The Saab gave a brief shudder and moved forward, gathering speed. I kept the wheel in place. As soon as I was sure it was going fast enough and wasn't going to stall, I vaulted sideways over the driver's door, hit the dirt and rolled. Just not as well as I'd hoped. I'd have a couple of bruises of my own in the morning.

9

The exhaust system grated against the rock and the engine whined as the front wheels left the ground and spun freely in the air, but the wagon already had enough momentum to complete its journey.

I scrambled up in time to see it hit the water, wallow for what seemed like a lifetime in the pale moonlight, then plunge nose first to its grave. Thank fuck Koureh hadn't gone for the Monte Carlo yellow paintwork option that was all the rage with Saab freaks this year. Steel grey would match the lake bed nicely.

I kicked over the tyre marks with my Timberlands and rubbed fistfuls of dirt into the scars left by the undercarriage on the rock edge. It wasn't much, but it was the best I could do, and we'd be long gone before the local *polisen* sent in their divers.

I fired up the Merc and headed back the way I'd come. I stopped short of the house to pick up my daysack. I'd already checked that our scrape was sterile. It wasn't complicated — we hadn't even been there long enough to take a shit.

Before going on round the front to pick Harry up, I folded down the rear seats to leave him as much space as possible. My plan was to put some distance between us and the lake, then get Trev on the net and tell him that Harry needed to be casevaced. I didn't care what strings the colonel was going to have to pull, or how far I'd have to drive, I just knew that if we put Harry Callard in the care of a Swedish medic our cover would be blown, and if we didn't, he would never see his son again.

But for the second time that day, it appeared that Harry had a different plan.

As I shut the tailgate, there was a lightning flash — the kind that seared white spots on your retinas — followed by the world's biggest thunderclap, and a pressure wave that blew me off my feet.

10

Iraqi troops had set fire to seven hundred oil wells as part of their scorched-earth policy during their retreat from Kuwait in January 1991. We'd seen all that shit happen as our Chinook ferried us across the Iraqi border — pillars of flame reaching into the night sky. Now I knew what it was like to see one up close.

The heat was already too intense to take the direct route, so I skirted the blaze until I could get a clear view of the front of the house. My bomber jacket, the radio and Harry's daysack were still where I'd left them, but he was no longer lying on the gravel driveway.

I raised a hand above my eyes, palm outwards, so that I could focus more clearly. One of the big picture windows that looked out over the sundeck had imploded and its shutters hung off their hinges. I reckoned its twin was about to go too.

A few shards of glass still clung to the frame as the fire raged inside. The dove-grey paint blistered on the clapboard. The canvas smouldered on the steamer chairs, and the decking beneath them was starting to crackle. I couldn't see any sign of the Gucci hurricane lantern.

I moved closer, until the heat on my bare skin let me know that enough was enough, and the charred body I could now see lying beneath the smashed pane confirmed what I'd already begun to suspect. Somehow Harry had managed to drag his broken body onto the deck, sparked up the nickel-plated lantern and launched it through the double glazing like a missile.

I gathered up my bomber and the gear he'd left behind and legged it to the Merc. When the municipal fire brigade turned up, I didn't want to be here to make them cups of tea.

11

Abergavenny, Monmouthshire

Sunday, 14 June
15.30 hrs

Father Martyn lived in a stone-built cottage on the Welsh border, between Hay-on-Wye and Abergavenny. The front of it was covered with flowery shit and his door was always open to the left-footers in the Regiment, plus one or two others who weren't fully paid-up members of his club.

Me and God had had a few close calls, but we still weren't on first-name terms. That didn't seem to matter to Father Mart. He'd always been part of the Regiment's furniture, the secret sounding board for people who needed to get stuff off their chest. I'd gone to see him after Snakebite's death in Baghdad, and I needed to see him again now.

I'd been back from Sweden for more than a month, and I was still having difficulty shifting Harry's image from the screen inside my head. It wasn't as if it was the first time I'd seen a corpse, or what fire could do to a man's skin. I'd witnessed more charred bodies on ops than I could count. Flashbacks were a symptom of post-traumatic stress disorder, but I didn't do PTSD. I probably wasn't smart enough. I just

31

kept seeing the look on Harry's face when he said there wouldn't be any more missions.

'Cut away' was the advice I'd given him when he'd lost it with Koureh, because cutting away had been my answer to every problem as far back as I could remember. I'd done it after a mate of mine fell off a factory roof when we were playing soldiers on my seventh birthday. Maybe I'd even done it before that, when my stepfather lost it with my mum and she turned up at the breakfast table wearing sun-gigs.

But cutting away didn't always work.

I told Father Mart as much as I needed him to know about Harry's death over a brew at his kitchen table.

He had his wise face on beneath the beard. 'And?'

'And I guess I feel responsible in some way. I'm not sure he would have come if I hadn't persuaded him . . . '

'Trevor and Harold were also close, weren't they?'

I nodded.

'Does Trevor feel the same?'

I hesitated for a moment. 'Not sure. But he must feel something. He's looking after Harry's boy.'

Father Mart sat and listened at times like this, maybe put a hand on your shoulder, looked you straight in the eye, said a few very simple words and somehow made you feel a whole lot better than you had done when you came into the room. Right now he leaned back and steepled his fingers. 'It sounds to me as though Harold knew you'd beat yourself up. And this was his way of trying to tell you not to.

'He knew the risks. He could have said no, when you asked him to come. But he didn't, did he? And it was his own decision to sacrifice himself to keep you both safe.'

He placed his palms flat on the table and leaned towards me. 'If it had been you on the gravel instead of Harold, would you have come to the same decision?'

I didn't have to think too hard about that one. 'Sure. It's a straight numbers game, isn't it? One down, the rest stay standing.'

Father Mart's right forefinger came off the table and jerked towards me, like he was about to accuse the woman next door of being a witch. 'Exactly!'

I'd thought these guys were supposed to be filled with the Holy Spirit.

'So, if it had been you instead of Harold, would you have wanted him to feel this bad?'

'No.'

'Then why are you?'

I racked my brain for an answer.

'In your own time.' He waved at my brew. 'Please, drink your tea.'

Father Mart never stood in judgement, even when a stewards' enquiry didn't go his way. He never pretended to have the answer to the mysteries of the universe. And he hadn't tried to become the dad I'd never had, or any of that shit. He wasn't in the business of miracle cures either. He concentrated instead on reminding dickheads like me what was what, and hoped they'd get the message.

PART TWO

PART TWO

1

East Grinstead, West Sussex

Monday, 23 January 2012
23.15 hrs

I flew in on the late-evening easyJet from Zürich and took a cab from the Gatwick South Terminal rank to the Church of the Most Holy Redeemer.

The Catholic Church didn't advertise its garaging facilities, but Father Mart had mentioned a mate with an empty lock-up when I'd needed to get to the French Alps at warp speed in March last year and was trying to find a place to drop my dark blue Porsche 911.

I had only seen Father Gerard for about ten minutes at that point, before I'd had to leg it, but knew immediately that he was my kind of priest. I wasn't surprised. Father Mart chose his racing mates wisely.

I expected the wagon to be up on bricks after all this time, but it was sitting outside the rectory with a warm engine and a very smiley Father Gerard in the driving seat. He bounced out to say hello, and took me on a guided tour of the bodywork, in case I hadn't spotted the showroom shine. 'I took her for a little spin, after you called to let me know you were on your way . . . '

Judging by the sparkle in his eye, that little

white lie was going to cost Father Gerard a few Hail Marys. I was prepared to bet good money that his flock had sought spiritual comfort on a regular basis at Lingfield and Plumpton, and that he'd have needed the Porsche to help him spread God's word as far afield as Ascot and Cheltenham too.

As I swapped places with him, he told me that Father Mart sent his blessings, and needed me to drop by his cottage.

I asked when. He gave me a slightly pained expression. 'Tomorrow morning, Nick. If you could manage it . . .'

2

Abergavenny, Monmouthshire

Tuesday, 24 January
11.17 hrs

Father Mart wasn't on my speed dial. He didn't need to be. His job was to be around whenever he was needed to do God stuff. But I had dropped by once every few years to say hello. It didn't seem to matter whether the gap between visits was months or years, the welcome was always the same.

Sure enough, he was standing on his doorstep to greet me, as if I'd only nipped down to the corner shop to replenish his stock of Yorkshire Tea five minutes ago. But when I'd parked alongside his mud-streaked Land Rover and walked up the path I could see he was far from happy. His handshake was as warm as ever, but his gaze was troubled and the skin was taut across his temples.

We went through the usual rituals, and I took the piss about his beard having turned white enough for him to take a part-time job as a Tesco's Santa if business got slow. Then, as soon as he'd fixed us both a brew and motioned me towards my usual chair at the table opposite his Rayburn, he started to let me know what was on his mind.

39

'It's Trevor. He needs your help.'

It was clear from his tone and uncharacteristically brisk delivery that Trev wasn't simply going to bimble along to Father Mart's kitchen and share our plate of Hobnobs.

'When?'

'As soon as possible.'

'Where?'

'He's calling later. He'll let us know.'

I necked some of my brew and munched a biscuit. 'Any other clues?'

'Things aren't good at Credenhill.'

'Trev doesn't have anything to do with Credenhill any more. As far as I know. He left the Regiment about twenty seconds after I did.'

'He does now. There was an accident. An incident. Call it what you will. In the CQB Rooms. One of the lads took a bullet.'

I shrugged. 'Sad. But not a first.'

The Counter Terrorist Team refined their covert entry and hostage rescue techniques in the Close Quarter Battle Rooms — which meant live firing as well as showing off your favourite moves from the martial-arts catalogue. These places had targets and rubber-coated walls to absorb the rounds, and could be adapted to cater for almost any scenario — fast rope, heli drop, you name it.

It wasn't somewhere you just minced around in designer headphones and a pair of orange Oakleys, loosing off a few shots with a Desert Eagle to impress the chicks. We trained and trained and trained there, with flashbangs and all sorts of shit, in every conceivable environment.

40

We'd be in blindingly bright light one minute and total darkness the next, and a lot of the time the 'enemy' was shooting back.

I'd been on the team the day Prince Charles and Princess Di came by for a demo and one of the lads accidentally set fire to her hair. Ever since the Gulf, the Big Dogs had given themselves hernias trying to stuff the Special Forces genie back into the bottle. But that was easier said than done. The invitations for day visits, dinners in the mess with sports personalities and benefactors — even the media — still muddied the waters.

At the same time, all serving members of the Special Air Service now fell under the thirty-year rule, and you couldn't even mention their presence in hi-vis conflicts without having your bollocks chopped off. I'd heard that the new director of Special Forces, Major General Steele, was so determined to reinstate the invisibility cloak that he'd threatened to do the operation personally, with a rusty razor blade.

Father Mart didn't seem sure when Trev's call would come through, so I scribbled my iPhone number on his notepad and said I'd head down to Hereford and see if they had a vacant room at the Green Dragon, maybe knock on Trev's front door.

That was when I knew this thing was really serious. He gripped my arm with surprising force and told me that Trevor wasn't at home, and not to go anywhere near Hereford for the time being — at least, not until he had had a chance to put me in the picture.

We were outside, admiring the pattern of frost on his potting shed, when his phone rang. Father Mart dashed back into the house and picked up. Steve Jobs hadn't changed his life: he still put his trust in Bakelite and circular dials. And God, of course, but they probably contacted each other direct.

He emerged about thirty seconds later. Trev obviously hadn't been in the mood for a chat. 'The Bolthole. Tomorrow at fifteen hundred. He said you'd know what that meant.'

'Nothing else? Should I be wearing a red carnation?'

At last, a wry little smile flitted across his face. 'He said you should wait there until he decides it's safe to make contact. And don't bring your Porsche, or your telephone.'

I couldn't stop myself laughing. 'My *telephone*?'

3

The Bolthole had probably saved our lives, back in the day. I visualized the route I'd take to get there as Father Mart rustled up whatever was in the oven. I was a lot better at sorting myself out in advance, these days, than I had been then.

Trev and I had done a lot of our training for Winter Selection in the Black Mountains. The idea had been to sharpen up our endurance, stamina and determination, and while we were running uphill and downhill in clear weather, we felt quite pleased with ourselves. When the weather closed in it was a different story. The day-trippers stayed in the pub and we were in the shit.

It got seriously cold eight hundred metres up in the Brecon Beacons, and you could easily freeze to death lower down when the wind blew. We'd all heard the stories of the lads who'd lost their way when the snow started to fall, then got exhausted, bogged down or injured, and never made it back. Legend had it that one of them was frozen so stiff the rescue crew used him as a sledge to get back down the mountain.

We'd made a shitload of stupid mistakes, and taking off that morning in combats, T-shirts and thin waterproof tops was right at the top of the list. The mist closed in as we summited Waun Fach and the blizzard quickly followed. It wasn't long before we knew we were in trouble.

My watch hadn't had a temperature gauge,

but my fingers and toes told me it was getting way below zero. One of the first signs of hypothermia was mental confusion, but some would say that was what we'd been suffering from in the first place. The only sane thing we'd done was pack bivvi bags, rations and a hexy stove in our Bergens.

Somehow we managed to make our way down, trying to get out of the killer wind, and stumbled upon a cave. We had no idea where.

It wasn't until the following afternoon that the conditions cleared enough for us to get our bearings. Trev had originally nicknamed our refuge the Elephant's Arsehole, because of the shape and colour of the stones that flanked it, and because it was large enough inside to shelter a couple of idiots, but I guess he couldn't bring himself to say that to a priest.

'A penny for your thoughts, as my mother used to say . . . '

I looked up from the plate of lasagne he'd put in front of me. I'd almost forgotten he was there. 'Sorry. Miles away.'

'No apologies necessary. It's always good to see you smile.' He was smiling too, but I could still see the tension behind his eyes.

'Don't worry about Trev. He hates surprises, but there's no one in our game who can deal with them better than he can.' I told him a couple of silly stories about us getting into scrapes in Colombia and Trev taking charge.

He gave a chuckle. 'And what about *you*, Nicholas?'

It wasn't the question itself that caught me

off-guard, but the fact that only one other person in my life ever used all three syllables in my name, and she was the woman I'd left behind in Russia thirty-six hours ago.

Anna hadn't come to Domodedovo airport on Sunday to wave me goodbye. We'd agreed that if I was going to carry on being a bullet magnet, it would be better for her and our five-month-old son to stay well away from the target area. And, besides, neither of us had wanted to prolong the agony.

Cutting away was never going to be easy. I'd seen them safely tucked into their gated community on the Moscow margins, given them both the warmest hug that I'd ever given another human being, picked up my grab bag and got into the cab.

I'd left some stuff there, partly because I'd always liked travelling light, and partly because it helped convince me that I wouldn't be gone for ever. I still wanted to be with her and our son, but we both knew they'd always be safer when I wasn't around. Her words still echoed in my head: *I don't think you pick fights, Nicholas. But they sure pick you . . . You were the kid who always got into fights at school and didn't know why . . .*

I heard myself starting to leak the story to Father Mart as the wind rose outside and began to chuck the odd fistful of hail against the windows. 'You remember the blonde one from Abba?'

'With or without the beard?'

'Funny. The one with the cheekbones and the sad smile. That's Anna. We met in Tehran. At an

45

arms fair. She was an investigative journalist. The campaigning kind. Working for a Russian indie. She wanted to make the world a better place. Then she joined *Russia Today* and went out to Libya to cover the uprising.

'As soon as she got pregnant, everything changed. And when our son was born, we could no longer ignore the fact that a dad in my line of work is a bit of a liability . . . '

'Does your son have a name?'

'Nicholayevich. But I think she'll probably shorten it to Nicholai. Except when she loses it with him.'

That wry smile reappeared from somewhere beneath the Father Christmas face fuzz. 'As a tribute to Count Tolstoy, of course.'

'You're not wrong.' I felt myself smile too. 'She started me on *Anna Karenina*, then had me reading *War and Peace*. Even the *Peace* bit. And going to art galleries and concerts and shit . . . '

My leak had become a bit of a flood. I paused for a moment and looked at him, embarrassed. 'Any minute now you'll have me on *Piers Morgan's Life Stories*.' I picked up my glass of water. 'And I can't even blame the Communion wine . . . '

His eyes sparkled. 'We'll have you in that confessional yet, my boy.'

Much later, I got my head down on Father Mart's sofa and thought some more about what I'd left behind. I didn't care about the things, but I did care a lot about the people. That was a new one on me. It was also one of the reasons I'd had to leave.

4

Father Mart's lean-to was filled with the same kind of crap that real people had in their garages, only more of it, but he somehow managed to find room in there for my motor as well. I stuck my head out of his Land Rover as he pulled down the door. 'I'll try to bring the Popemobile back in one piece. Fingers crossed.'

He came alongside the driver's window and I gripped his hand. 'And if you need any help taking the Porsche for a spin, Father Gerard's your man.'

I crunched the old Defender into gear and pulled out onto the road. It rattled a bit, but it would look after me nicely as the temperature dropped. The truth was I loved these wagons. Whatever you threw at them, they were up for it. I'd driven the 109 in Belfast as a Green Army squaddie. I'd thrown a Series IIA Pinkie — stripped of doors and windscreen and tooled-up with smoke grenades, twin GPMGs and a Milan wire-guided missile launcher — around the Middle East.

Father Mart's 110 didn't have the firepower of the Pink Panther, but it wasn't covered in the outrageous so-called 'camouflage' paint either. As Trev hadn't needed to tell me, nobody in this neck of the woods would give it a second glance.

First stop was an outdoor equipment store in Abergavenny. I parked in Frogmore Street and

47

was one of the first punters through the door when they opened. I was already kitted out for a Russian winter, so I didn't need any extra clothing, but I wasn't about to go for an action replay of our pre-Selection adventure.

I gathered up an ice axe with a nice sharp pick, a folding shovel and a pair of crampons with the kind of claws that would have been at home in *Jurassic Park*. I added a first-aid kit, two boxes of hexy blocks, matches, a mess tin and a water flask. I already had a pocketful of Father Mart's Yorkshire Teabags, so all I needed now were some protein bars, in case it was a while before he could conjure up my next full English with all the trimmings. I bundled the whole lot into a daysack.

I threw in a spare pair of socks and some discounted waterproof gaiters for luck, then paid cash at the checkout. That always brought a smile to the face of every trader, particularly since the Crash, but it wasn't the reason I did it.

American Express used to boast that flashing their plastic said more for you than cash ever could, and that was why I hadn't used a credit or charge card for as long as I could remember. Even before my stint as a deniable operator with the security services, I'd never fancied my movements being traced via my financial transactions. And I hadn't enjoyed those embarrassing moments at the supermarket checkout when my payment wasn't authorized.

I'd picked up a turbo-charged debit card during my Zürich stopover that meant I could turn my back on all that shit. It was a sleek black thing without any embossed numbers, which delivered money from my Swiss account at any ATM worldwide. Because the link between me and my bank vault was routed through a randomly selected, ever-changing configuration of about twenty-six separate servers, the very sharply suited gnome who'd handed it to me in its little velvet pouch claimed that my privacy was guaranteed.

Next up was a visit to Go Mobile. The NSA had been tracking cell phones for nearly a decade, which meant GCHQ and any number of bad guys had too — you could even trace an iPhone with your iPad, these days — but I'd decided to ignore Trev's instruction twice over. My iPhone was zipped into an inner pocket, but I wasn't sure which network would have the best signal on the hill. I bought a Samsung G3 and three pay-as-you-go SIM cards, each with a different network, as back-up in case everything went to rat shit.

I'd been caught in the open without comms more than once when the weather closed in, and it was never a good day out. And the GPS systems on these gizmos were now reliable enough to save me having to unfold an Ordnance Survey map every ten minutes and bring out a compass.

A shaft of sunlight burst through the swirling grey cloud as I slung the sack into the wagon and aimed us in the direction of the main to Brynmawr. There was an internet café fairly close to the centre that had come in useful to me from time to time. It also served the best

Americano outside Colombia. Words like Wi-Fi, Twitter and Instagram didn't yet feature in Father Mart's vocabulary, and I needed to check stuff out.

The patch of blue sky had headed east by the time I got there. I made my way past a line of plastic fliers, emblazoned with giant daffodils, which flapped their 'Welcome' message in the strengthening breeze.

I was met by a beaming Welshman and the smell of frying bacon as soon as I opened the door, so added a pig roll to my coffee order. A large one. I'd only recently had breakfast, but I had time to kill, and you never knew when you might need some extra calories. I was also pretty sure that for an hour or two I was going to be a whole lot warmer in there than I would be for the rest of the day.

The Welshman handed me my change and waved me across to a row of keyboards and computer screens. And, yes, he was happy for me to crack the Samsung straight on the charger and bin the packaging.

I shrugged off my Gore-Tex jacket, bunged it over a chair and loosened my fleece.

The first site I tuned into was ARRSE, the unofficial Army Rumour Service. It gave squaddies the chance to do what they did best: honk about everything and everyone.

The SAS references, not surprisingly, had more to do with the number of ferrets we had to bite the heads off to pass Selection than what actually went on behind closed doors. Halfway down the postings on the News Forum someone claiming to be SBS (user name: Coldfeet) asked if anyone had heard about a fuck-up behind the wire at Credenhill. He'd been met by a storm of abuse from the party faithful, mostly accusing him of Small Bollock Syndrome. A Crap Hat wondered if one of the Boys in Black had got tangled up in his abseil rope; another thought he might have dropped his ice cream. There was no reference to the CQB Rooms.

Elsewhere, a girl called Rosie with a Good Sense Of Humour was looking for Fun Times with A Hero In Uniform, and the Old and the Bold queued up to applaud Guy Chastain's posthumous VC. The colonel's boy had sacrificed himself to save the lives of his men on an op in Afghanistan, and the old man had sparked up a fund-raising campaign for a statue. I didn't know quite what to make of that. On the one hand, I'd have loved a dad who cared enough to keep my memory alive. On the other, I'd always believed that, in war, shit happens.

I scanned the headlines on the *Telegraph* and *Sun* sites, and the *Mail Online*, but there was nothing much there either. A page-three girl, who called herself Victoria Crossley, claimed to have had a Brazilian in the shape of the legendary medal. The caption writer said that he'd be happy to share her firing position anytime.

I stopped to take a sip of the Americano, then gave my full attention to the pig roll. As the fat seeped out between the layers of bread and dribbled over my fingers, I thought life didn't get much better than this.

5

You could drive to Grwyne Fawr Reservoir from Abergavenny through the Mynydd Du Forest, but I never put my trust in cul-de-sacs without good reason. And Trev hadn't invited me up there to draw attention to myself. I turned left onto the Crickhowell road, and the remnants of last night's hail crunched beneath my tyres as I skirted the western edge of the Black Mountains. There was snow on the high ground, and the sulphurous tint to the light promised more before the day was gone.

I pulled off the main some distance short of Talgarth and wound my way up the back lanes, through patches of woodland. I parked not far from the church at Llanelieu. I'd first spotted it when Trev and I had found our way out of the Elephant's Arsehole, and gone back later when I'd started getting excited by medieval history. God no longer paid St Ellyw's formal visits, even on Sundays, and it had never been on Father Mart's beat, but I figured his wagon wouldn't be out of place there. And I wanted to see if the loft was still painted blood red.

The 110's rear door gave a squeal of complaint as I went back to sort out my kit. That was when I noticed the graffiti. In the coating of mud beneath the Defender label someone had added 'of the Faith' with a wet fingertip.

I decided against taking my Russian tank

commander's hat. I'd bought it from a stall when Anna and I had been wandering around an open-air market near Gorky Park. The sheepskin earpieces made it the warmest thing I'd ever owned, but if you wore that kind of gear outside Eastern Europe you just looked like a dickhead or a Chelsea fan.

I threw the shovel and all the other shit that I'd bought into the daysack. I might not need any of it, but I'd spent a fair chunk of my adult life running around with thirty-five-kilo packs on my back so it was hardly going to slow me down. I fastened the gaiters, tightened the straps on the sack, grabbed my ski gloves and was ready to put one foot in front of the other.

My first objective was the bothy beside the stream that fed the reservoir. I didn't go straight there, but I didn't zigzag like a lunatic either. Trev was playing Secret Squirrel, but as far as the rest of the world was concerned, I was a well-equipped walker in search of the best vantage-points from which to enjoy the breath-taking scenery.

Once I'd left the sheep grazing in the churchyard behind me, there was no sign of another living thing on the hillside. I stepped from tussock to tussock, their tufts of grass crisp with frost beneath my Timberlands. We used to call them baby's heads when I was a squaddie, and I could never quite shake the image from my mind.

★ ★ ★

The bothy was a tiny stone-built affair with a slate tile roof, tucked into the hill above a weir. During the summer it virtually disappeared from sight among the greys and greens and browns of the surrounding landscape. Today it stood out against the dusting of snow.

There was no smoke leaking from the chimney above the wood-burning stove, so I decided it was a good moment for a brew. I filled my flask from the stream and scooped up some more water with my brand-new mess tin.

Once inside, I broke a chunk off a hexy block and watched it bring the water to the boil. Being out of the wind with some of Father Mart's Yorkshire Tea inside me was all I needed right now, so I wasn't about to frighten up a roaring fire. I might do that if I had to later. I wasn't sure I'd make it back past the reservoir before last light, but there was a track that I could follow all the way along the ridge.

I fished out the Samsung and tried each of my new SIM cards in turn, selecting the network with the best signal, and tapped its number under 'A' in my iPhone address book. There was plenty of room for it. I never kept anyone's contact details. The few I needed were already safely tucked away inside my head, and I didn't need to advertise them. Old habits died hard.

I'd always thought these mountain refuges were brilliant. Some of them were originally constructed for itinerant workers during the Industrial Revolution. Now they offered shelter to dickheads like me and Trev if we took the trouble to find them on the map before setting out — or bumped into them by accident when we'd somehow managed to dig ourselves out of the shit.

We'd celebrated our escape that night by carving our initials into the mortar beside the chimney, as you do when you're a thoughtless little prick who's glad to be alive, but someone had got busy with the Polyfilla and whitewash long since, and covered them over.

As I sat and listened to the swollen stream cascading over the rocks outside, I wondered which route Trev had chosen for today, and what had made him so jumpy that he couldn't just meet for a brew in Hereford.

6

Trev was a bit excitable at times, but he didn't fuck about. And he was always there when you needed him. Before the Gulf we'd mooched around in Colombia together. In the late eighties and early nineties it had been responsible for providing the lion's share of America's multi-billion-dollar cocaine supply, and for fuelling a fearsome percentage of indigenous fatalities. The year we went, there were three thousand drug-related killings in one town alone — which was why the locals were almost as keen to nail the cartels as the DEA was.

A bunch of us had piled into a Hercules C130 and headed down there via Newfoundland. Once we were in country, we debussed into cattle trucks.

Our initial task was to train the Colombian militia, then to help them wipe out as many drug-manufacturing plants as we could ID and locate. Since it took two hundred kilos of leaves to produce one kilo of coca paste, the DMPs were thrown up as close as possible to the growing areas.

They were mostly hidden in jungle, heavily guarded, and criss-crossed by tunnels and escape routes, but our biggest obstacles were corruption and wholesale slaughter. A 12,000 per cent mark-up from production cost to street value buys a lot of informers, and in a world where you were either on the payroll or dead, fully operational DMPs had more often than not turned into ghost towns by the time we got to them.

Fair one. We were just visiting; the militia had to live there. We didn't have to worry about our wives being raped and killed, and our kids being hosed down on the way to school. We had to become more proactive, and strike without warning.

Me and Trev spent weeks on hard routine, kitten-crawling through the undergrowth with a bunch of lads who all seemed to be called José or Miguel, coated with cam cream and mozzie rep, sweat leaking from every pore. Our combats were covered with so much slime we could no longer see the camouflage pattern.

We pinged a complex under the canopy not far from the Darién Gap and moved in for a close target recce, our bollocks and armpits stinging in the jungle heat. There was a heli pad, a processing plant, storerooms, a long, low-roofed Nissen hut where the coca paste was laid out on trestle tables to dry, and accommodation for the white-eyes — the Europeans and North Americans who took care of the chemistry — and the muscle.

Destroying the place wasn't exactly going to bring the Medellín cartel to its knees, but our guys had enough PE4, clackers and det cord to do the business, and I could see Trev's eyes brighten at the prospect. He moved towards me on his elbows and toecaps and leaned in close to my ear. 'Why hang about?' He hated surprises, all right, but he didn't mind dishing them out.

I nodded. Why indeed?

We surrounded the site, deployed cut-off teams to stop any runners reaching their boats or vanishing into the foliage, and blew it apart. The best news of all was that we didn't take a single casualty. The Josés and the Miguels were all going to make it back home for tea and sticky buns. The bad guys weren't so lucky. One boy legging it off the premises with his finger locked onto the trigger of an AK-47 got on the wrong end of a cut-off team, and a white-eye took a round in the chest.

I hauled the boffin out of the dirt, dressed the wound and threw him into the first Huey on the pad. I was rewarded with a blast of hard-core Marseille abuse. Trev chuckled. 'Mate, looks like we've wrapped up the French Connection.'

I blamed myself for what happened next. I sat on my Bergen in the middle of what was left of the DMP, still enjoying the joke, as another wave of anti-narcotic police helis screamed in. The ANP lads were quartering the place, seeking out and destroying the stocks of precursor chemicals before burning the whole installation to the ground.

I'd got a brew on, but not quickly enough for Trev. He was stomping around behind me as I waited for the water to boil. 'I'm gagging for some Tetley's, Stoner. Pull your finger out.'

He was still having a moan when I heard a commotion off to my right. The ANP had unearthed two guys who must have hidden themselves during the attack.

They legged it towards the canopy, desperate to get back into cover before they got shot, and I was directly in their way. All mad hair and staring eyes, the one with a gollock headed straight for me. As he raised the weapon I dropped the mugs, and, still on my arse, pushed back on my Bergen to dodge the blow.

I knew I hadn't moved fast enough. His blade was so close I could see my face in it. Then blood blossomed from two neat holes, one in his forehead, the other in his neck, and he dropped like liquid. A nanosecond later another couple of 9mm rounds were pumped into his mate. The whole thing was over almost before I heard the Browning's report.

As I straightened, I heard an animal snarl beside my ear. 'You going to finish making that brew, or what?'

7

I exited the bothy and tabbed south-west, well past the point where the Grwyne Fawr stopped behaving like a stream and started being a full-on river, then flanked the northern edge of the reservoir. An hour or so later I scrambled up through the gorse onto the path that curved across the top of the huge stone dam.

It towered above the next stretch of the valley, and the sight of it never failed to stop me dead. The times we'd been here since our first Waun Fach adventure, Trev and I used to go straight into Guy Gibson mode at this point. It was impossible not to. Mostly we'd whistle 'The Dam Busters March', just like every other tripper. Before we'd deployed for the Gulf, we'd taken it a stage further and danced around on the parapet, pretending to be the German sentry in the Carling Black Label ad, keeping a never-ending succession of bouncing bombs out of our imaginary goalmouth.

We weren't the only ones to behave like idiots here. Prince William and Prince Harry got a serious bollocking for abseiling down the front of it without the right kit when they were teenagers. The Royal Protection Squad had been given a king-size slapping as well.

But there was no one around now.

The first new flakes of snow began to fall as I passed the strange chunks of overgrown concrete that flanked the dam's eastern approach. It made the spooky metal gates that creaked open beneath the overhanging fir trees seem even more like something out of a Dracula movie.

I stepped out onto the walkway and into the wind. The block-house at the halfway point seemed empty. I wasn't surprised. I guessed that most of its functions were automated now. I stopped beside it and looked over the rail, as you do when you've come to admire the view — first at the reservoir stretching back the way I'd come then down the almost vertical drop on the opposite side, where Tiggy Legge-Bourke and the princes had come to have some fun.

I didn't have to pretend to be impressed. The water spilled through the arches at my feet, sluiced down the century-old stonework and boiled white when it rejoined the river a hundred and fifty feet below.

I moved out onto the track on the far side of the dam, aiming half left. A loop right about a mile further on would take me into the gully that ended at the Bolthole. The snow was heavier now, but the light was still good. I slipped off a glove, unzipped the breast pocket of my Gore-Tex jacket and took out my iPhone. I wanted to check how much time I had before my RV with Trev.

I hadn't even sparked it up before a voice said, 'Stoner, you dickhead, I thought I'd told you to leave that fucking thing behind.'

8

Grwyne Fawr Dam, Powys

Wednesday, 25 January
14.00 hrs

The voice came from the shadow of the trees to my right.

I kept eyes on the screen, not on the place I thought Trev might be hidden. 'I wouldn't need it if I was tucked up somewhere nice instead of out here playing hide and seek. What's all this about?'

He told me to make like I was checking out Google Maps for a minute or two, then keep walking uphill, around the western edge of the coppice, until I reached a clearing. He'd meet me there.

We finally met up twenty minutes later. Trev looked like he'd rewired his brain and gone feral. He was in full-on Rambo mode — field parka bristling with pockets and pouches, cam cream from the neck up, the lot. I felt like a shop-window dummy alongside him.

'So, is this a change of plan, or was this always the plan?'

His brow rippled like corrugated iron. 'As you may have noticed, Stoner, when you were mincing around on the parapet, the weather is closing in. And the more I thought about it, the less I fancied the idea of spending another night cuddling up to you in a snow hole.'

He clapped me between the shoulder-blades and guided me back, under cover of the canopy, to a hide that was so well concealed among the interwoven branches of a cluster of firs that you'd have needed an infrared camera to find him.

'And this, ladies, is something I prepared earlier ... ' He ushered me inside a cross between an A-frame shelter and a tepee. The braces were tied in place with twine and sheathed in cam netting. A mixture of twigs, pine fronds, leaves, undergrowth and moss gave it the kind of haphazard appearance that deceived the eye until you were almost standing on top of it. It must have taken him ages to construct.

'Fuck, Trev, how many weeks have you been out here?'

'I'm not staying anywhere long right now, Stoner. Must be the hedge monkey in me.'

I cracked a smile. 'Join the club.'

He was doing his best to make light of it, but the strain showed if you knew where to look. Trev was a big, tousle-haired bear of a man with sideburns that were still stuck in the seventies and in no hurry to leave. He didn't change his style for anyone. Never had done. But if things began to get to him, he'd rub the pad of his thumb rapidly across the stubble under his chin. It made him the world's worst poker player. And he was doing it now.

'Well, we'd better not hang around, then, eh? You can start by telling me why you're up here playing Grizzly Adams.'

'Mate . . . I could really use your help. I don't know what you've heard on rumour control about what went down at Credenhill, but there's been a drama . . . '

'All I know is what God's messenger told me: man found dead in Killing House.'

He gestured towards a couple of logs and we squatted in the gloom beside a neatly rolled bivvi bag and a Rocketpak Bergen. I could make out a selection of Meals Ready to Eat and their flame-less ration heaters neatly stashed in one of its side pouches.

The glint in his startlingly blue eyes told me that the banter was over. 'A kid took a round in the head during training.'

'When?'

'Two weeks ago. Eleventh of January.'

'How?'

'That's the million-pound question. They're claiming a negligent discharge. I don't believe a word of it. If it was that simple, why the blackout? DSF has pulled the shutters down tighter than a duck's arse. That's one of the things that bothers me.'

'What are the others?'

'I could give you a list, but here's the headline: the lad being blamed for it is under lock and key at Barford, and I'm certain he didn't pull the trigger. It's a stitch-up. And as soon as I stuck my nose in where it wasn't wanted, they tried to fuck me up.'

'Mate, you know I'll always go the distance for you, but what's this got to do with me?'

'He could be facing a manslaughter rap. He needs us to get him off the hook, Nick. And you've been out of sight long enough not to be caught up in it.'

'Caught up in what?'

He shifted position on his log, but his eyes never left mine. 'Whatever shit is happening behind the wire. I don't know what's going down, but they're killing their own because of it.'

There were a whole lot of things here that didn't add up. 'How can you be so sure he didn't do it?'

'Because I've known this lad since he was yay high.' Trev placed the flat of his hand about six inches above the ground. 'Virtually adopted him when we got back from Sweden in 'ninety-two.'

Now I knew where this was heading.

Trev nodded. 'Yup. It's Harry's boy, Sam.'

I took a couple of deep breaths and watched them billow in the chill air as I exhaled. 'We all fuck up from time to time, Trev.'

His eyes blazed and his thumb pad went into overtime. 'Do me a favour, Nick. I know Harry lost the plot for a moment back in Swedeland. But this is twenty years later, and I haven't.' He gripped my arm. 'OK, so I wasn't absolutely sure from the word go that someone else pulled the trigger in the Killing House, but I am now. You want to know why I've gone native?'

He looked like he might start frothing at the mouth any minute now. I nodded.

'Because some bastard left a claymore in my front hall. An MRUD, for fuck's sake. If Icarus

65

hadn't gone ape-shit, I'd be history.'

'Icarus?'

'My dog.'

9

Unlike a conventional anti-personnel mine, the MRUD wasn't disc-shaped and didn't have to be buried underfoot. In its plastic convex casing, it looked like an iPod sound dock on legs, or a drab green scale model of the Grwyne Fawr Dam.

They could be mounted on the ground, in trees, or on your target's hall table. Some of the American versions had 'FRONT TOWARD ENEMY' embossed on their face, so even the grunts knew which way to point them.

Trev, ever the linguist, had once told me that MRUD was the acronym for *Mina Rasprskava-juća Usmenog Dejstva*. When I'd scratched my head and looked stupid, he'd written it down and explained that it basically meant 'directed fragmentation' in Serbian. And from what I'd seen of them in Bosnia, they did exactly what it said on the tin. Triggered by a command wire, det cord, manual detonator, booby-trap fuse or bog-standard electrical power source, nine hundred grams of explosive blasted hundreds of steel balls in a sixty-degree arc, with a lethal range of about thirty-five metres.

I wasn't surprised he looked miserable. 'So you must have rattled the bars on somebody's cage . . . '

He gave his thumb a rest and sucked his teeth instead. 'I've got some ideas about that, but even

67

the Old and Bold are keeping schtum, and I've been knocking pretty hard on every door I can think of. I paid Chastain a visit at Downton Abbey. Thought he might be able to shed some light on it, maybe push a few of the right buttons . . . '

'And?'

'Her ladyship gave me a brew and some homemade flapjacks, but he was away somewhere, putting the world to rights.'

Trev was silent for a moment. This scenario had really rocked his world. 'You know what's getting to me most, Nick? I'm not sure whose side *anyone* is on right now, top to bottom. And I don't want to huff and puff about an Englishman's home being his castle, but when your own semi becomes the battle space, what's the world coming to? You, Father Mart and the dog are the only people I can trust.'

I gave him a grin. 'I suppose there's one consolation . . . '

'Don't tell me.' He managed to give me half of one in return. 'At least it can't make yer pregnant?'

We repeated the old catchphrase in unison.

'Is anyone else getting fucked over?'

He shrugged. 'But I've tucked Sam's girlfriend out of harm's way, just in case. With a babysitter, obviously.'

'Does Sam have any ideas?'

Trev shook his head. 'Haven't seen him. I was planning a trip to Barford before someone took liberties with the message on my welcome mat. I reckon going there now would be the same as holding up a sign to whoever's behind this drama saying, 'Shoot him. And then shoot me as well.' '

We spent the next ten minutes or so sketching out some basic operating procedures — division of labour, where and how we were going to connect, the places we needed to go, the people we needed to see. There were some new names I'd heard about but never met, and some old ones from the past we hoped we could still rely on. Ken Marabula and his nephew Fred were on the list, and Al Gillespie.

I told him he was always welcome to stay with me if he didn't have somewhere better to go.

He was impressed. 'I didn't know you had a UK base, Stoner. You've only been back from Moscow five minutes.'

'It's not a base, exactly. It's the back seat of Mart's wagon.'

That little gag earned me a clip across the ear. Some people are never grateful.

I didn't ask where he'd hidden the girlfriend. I didn't need to know right now. And I was starting to think about my journey back. I could still use the bothy as a stopover, but I fancied picking up the Defender ASAP and putting in some distance. Maybe Trev's angst was contagious.

We unfolded ourselves and exited the shelter. I gave him a man-hug as soon as it was possible to stand fully upright, then turned to leave via the side of the wood by the dam, the point furthest from the clearing where I'd come in. I expected Trev to disappear from sight again, but he stayed with me.

'I'll kiss you goodbye at the treeline, Stoner. I'm getting a bit stir-crazy in there. I can't even lose myself in a crossword.'

Snowflakes swirled above the reservoir in the strengthening wind, and had started to drift against the stone balustrade. We paused for a moment at the edge of the coppice, but a moment was all an experienced sniper needed.

10

I heard the weapon's report a nanosecond after its round lifted off the top of Trev's head, just above the eyeballs, like a soft-boiled egg.

I dived to my left, then wriggled back into the undergrowth on my elbows as a massive crater appeared in the trunk of a conifer a couple of feet above my head. I made like a snake and slithered deeper into the bracken, leaf-mould and shit beneath the canopy.

There was no need to check Trev's pulse first.

Two more shots tore lumps of bark out of a beech two metres to my right. I only stopped and turned when I reckoned I had a good few trees between me and whoever was squeezing the trigger.

He'd have to assume I was switched on enough not to stick my head up out of cover any time soon, so that meant he'd have to come after me. He wouldn't want to leave any loose ends. And I was now a loose end.

The snow was building, but we were a long way short of a blizzard, and the sky had that strange, special-effects type glow that you sometimes got before the light faded completely.

Did he have thermal-imaging kit?

I guessed I'd soon find out.

Right now I'd have to expect the worst and hope for the best. Either way, I figured that he'd stay where he was until nightfall, taking advantage of the height of his firing position.

Two more rounds confirmed it. He was putting them into the likely cover in case I was hiding there. It was a no-brainer. At worst I'd have to run for it and present him with a target. At best he'd get a kill. You always missed with the shots you never took.

Then all I could hear was the whistling of the wind.

I stayed where I was. I reckoned he would too. The snow had started to make it almost impossible for me to scan the far hillside with any confidence, but his options were limited. He had to stay below the mist that was now shrouding the ridge and above the treeline if he was going to maintain eyes on my escape routes.

When I was a kid in Bermondsey, one old granddad used to sit outside the corner shop on Tanner Street, letting the dandruff settle on the shoulders of his moth-eaten tweed overcoat. Every time I passed, he'd point at the hoarding around the hole in the ground between two terraced houses across the street and mutter, 'Doodlebug . . . '

I had no idea what he was waffling about — until I stopped one day and he told me about Adolf Hitler's V1 missiles raining down on London in 1944, and how you knew you were safe until the engine cut out. In the silence that followed you just prayed the thing wasn't going to land on your head.

That was how I felt about the silence now.

11

The leaves and pine needles I was buried in were cold and damp and dank, but I didn't much mind. Better to be here in the shit than back there in Trev's blood.

I ran through my options.

I couldn't go back across the dam, or along the west side of the reservoir. In both cases I might as well have painted a target on my forehead or between my shoulder-blades and shone a spotlight on it.

The fact was that whichever route I chose, running away was out of the question. He'd simply follow, and kill me. If not today, tomorrow. Or some time next week. He no longer had a choice.

I didn't want to mess around. If this lad knew how to handle himself, I had to bring him towards me, channel him to a place of my choosing, my killing ground, and finish him.

I wouldn't interrogate him first. That only happened in the movies. I might lose the fight to contain him. And I only picked fights I knew I could win. Besides, I didn't expect him to be carrying a photographic driving licence with name, address and details of his recent speeding fines, or a wallet full of business cards and restaurant receipts. And even if he knew who'd sent him after Trev — which he wouldn't — there was no way he'd reveal it with his dying gasp.

I burrowed further inside the coppice until I

was in deep enough cover to stand, and made my way back to the hide. I stayed long enough to take a good look through Trev's Bergen. I was pretty certain I wouldn't find a weapon. He hadn't had a pistol on his belt, and if he'd been in the mood to bring one along, he'd hardly have left it in his luggage.

I wasn't wrong, but it would have been madness not to check.

Trev hadn't wanted to load himself down any more than I did, so there was nothing much in the forty-litre compartment that I didn't already have. In the side pouch I'd already spotted, he only had enough rations to keep him going for the next two or three days. Then I unstrapped the other pouch and hit the jackpot: lightweight AN/PVS-7 night-vision goggles complete with eye-cups, single-tube scope and head-strap.

I put the NVGs into my daysack, then added a couple of MRE packs and their flameless heaters. Who knew when I might need them? I wasn't sure when I'd have my next chance to hydrate either, so I poured half the contents of his water flask down my neck.

I paused for a moment at the edge of Trev's clearing, slipped off my right glove and sparked up Google Maps on the iPhone to set my bearings. It took a while to work out where it was, then told me pretty much what I already knew. I'd be in cover until I went past the south-western corner of the wood.

I didn't have to stay close to the trees; despite the rate of incline, I wouldn't be visible for about the first half of my journey between here and the ridge. Then I'd have to cross about forty metres of open ground, like a rat up a drainpipe, before I could duck below the crest and head right for the gully.

That forty-metre stretch was where things would get complicated. I wanted my sniper mate to spot me, because I needed him to know what path to follow, but I didn't want to give him enough time to get a lead on me, then squeeze the trigger.

Judging by the mess it had made of his head, the round that had killed Trev had had a lead knocker in its base, or my new best mate on the other side of the valley was using polymer tips.

Stopping power and flatter trajectory, even in a high wind, meant that the polymer option was fast becoming the good old boys' favourite during the Midwestern hunting season: it could separate an elk from its antlers at three hundred metres. And they didn't just make them in Nebraska: the Lucznik munitions factory in Radom, a hundred Ks south of Warsaw, kept the Eastern European market well supplied.

Wherever it came from, one of these fuckers wasn't just going to give me a superficial flesh wound. It would either miss completely or take a big piece of me with it.

I put the iPhone back in my jacket, replaced my glove, visualized the next twenty minutes of my life, and stepped out from beneath the canopy.

By the time I'd got halfway towards the open ground I was beginning to regret having left my Russian tank commander's hat in the Defender. The temperature had dropped big-time, partly because the day was drawing in and partly because of the wind-chill. My cheeks and the tips of my ears started to burn with cold.

The US Military Field Manual once spread the word that a human being lost between 45 and 50 per cent of his body heat through his head. In truth it was probably closer to 10, but anyone who took comfort from that had probably never been out on the Black Mountains in sub-zero temperatures. The fact remained that driving snow turned your hair rapidly into an iceberg and frostbite hurt like shit, then made bits of you drop off. And since the head was where most people's brain was located, it messed with your cognitive functions, and thus with your reaction time. So, if I'd just been out on a ramble, I'd have zipped my ears as tightly as possible into the Gore-Tex hood folded beneath my jacket collar. But in a strong wind the fabric rippled as loudly as an America's Cup jib sail every time you moved, and whenever someone big and ugly was creeping up behind me, I wanted as much warning as possible.

I'd stick my neck out as long as I could bear it.

We were fast running out of daylight by the time I reached the start line of my forty-metre dash, but there was now enough of the white stuff on the ground to give my sniper mate a big green dot to aim at, thermal imaging or not. In these conditions I'd never know how close his misses were, unless they zinged past my ear. But so what? A miss was a miss.

I was no Usain Bolt, but I took off for the ridge good style.

After twenty-five metres I felt I'd hit my stride. After thirty-five a searing pain wiped out my leading ankle and I was hurled sideways, like a sack of shit.

12

I had no idea whether my ankle could hold my weight, but wriggling the last five metres to the ridge on my belt buckle was not an option. At least I knew it hadn't been on the receiving end of a polymer tip. If it had, there'd be nothing left of me beyond a soggy stump at the southern end of my gaiter.

All I'd done was hit a baby's head at a bad angle, and rolled.

As I reached forward to haul myself up, my eyes were still close enough to the ground to see another tussock disintegrate in front of me. It was all the encouragement I needed. Crouching low, I angled right, then left, then right again, scrambling like a prop forward through the opposition on a wet day at Huddersfield. I don't know if it made me a more difficult target, but it was good for morale, and when I dived over the ridge I felt the kind of elation I guessed a rugby player must have felt when he crossed the try line seconds before the final whistle.

I gave myself a minute or two to catch my breath and flex my ankle. As soon as I knew it was in reasonable working order — no sprain, no snapped tendons — it was time to move on.

Fuck knows why, but I once let a shrink wire me up to some magic piece of machinery — the all-singing, all-dancing version of a lie-detector — and try to put me through the mental wringer. He used every trick in the audio-visual book, from showing me pictures of people being chopped up with machetes to the kind of porn films they screen 24/7 in German hotel rooms.

My vital signs had hardly fluctuated.

In any situation that demanded my full concentration, I routinely tuned out any external interference, but I allowed his conclusion to filter through right now because it always made me smile. 'You're a psychopath, Mr Stone. But in a good way.'

Hot on their heels, Anna's words also echoed in my mind, what she'd said about me not looking for a fight.

Well, I was looking for one now.

I reckoned Sniper One still wouldn't break cover until he had to. Neither would he be staying where he was on the off-chance I'd suddenly pop back into view like a fairground target and invite him to have another crack at me.

He'd be busy hoisting the weapon's sling over his shoulder and looking forward to hosing me down at the first opportunity. But now I had two advantages: it was dark, and I knew where I was going. I reckoned I'd have an hour at the Bolthole before he caught up with me.

I tabbed rapidly towards the gully, the gorse scratching against my gaiters. The ankle wasn't in peak physical condition after my tumble, but the pain was nothing to shout about. The snow was deeper now that it wasn't being blown straight off the hill, but easy enough to walk through. I had to exercise a bit of caution about the terrain beneath it. I wouldn't worry about leaving a trail until after I'd prepared my killing area.

There were no straight lines here, so I left the NVGs in my daysack for now, and didn't waste time and energy looking back over my shoulder. If he'd made distance and closed up enough to take a shot, I'd soon know about it.

The ambient temperature was a few precious degrees warmer in the lee of the ridge, and the further I went, the more my plan came together in my head.

The top of the gully was funnel-shaped, and led to a group of bare rocks the size of standing stones, but more haphazardly arranged. The one on the right was at least twice my height, and stood proud of the hill. The two to its left leaned against each other, as if they were on the way home from a great night out and hoping to bump into a kebab shop. These were the legs of our elephant.

Though it wasn't visible right now — since snow had drifted across it — the entrance to Trev's cave lay between them.

13

I unslung my daysack. The white stuff was pretty fresh, so my first task was to make it more compact. I pulled out the shovel, unfolded its handle and shaft and gave the whole area around the base of the stones a good smacking with the blade.

When it was a bit more solid, I dug a nice hole, as low as I could because heat rises, packing the sides as I went, until I no longer felt any resistance. I slid in feet first, dragging the rest of my kit behind me.

I didn't want to draw attention to my hideaway yet, but fucking about in the dark was going to waste too much time. I shut my dominant eye to avoid completely destroying my night vision, powered up the torch app on my iPhone without looking at it directly with my open eye, and had a scout around.

Nothing much had changed — but, then, I hardly expected the local council to have called the decorators in. There were a few empty Red Bull cans, some discarded food packaging and a pile of slightly charred kindling.

I emptied the daysack and bulked it out with the packaging, cans and some of the sticks. I put the stove and mess tin on the ground, laid out six hexy blocks on each, then piled their waxed cardboard boxes and every bit of kindling I could find on top of them. Hexamine was toxic when it burned, so it wasn't designed for use in confined spaces, but I wasn't planning to stay.

I got some more water down my neck along with a power bar to boost my blood-sugar level. Then I put a match to my little hexy bonfires. Once they'd caught, I put my iPhone back in my pocket and brought out the G3. Satisfied that it still had a strong enough signal, I selected its loudest and most irritating ring-tone and left it on top of my daysack, a couple of feet inside the entrance to the cave.

I strapped the NVGs to my forehead but didn't lower the eye-cups. Like most military kit, the PVS-7 was designed to perform in extreme environments, so a cold night out in the wilds of Welsh Wales wasn't going to throw it into a spin.

I fastened the crampons to the soles of my Timberlands, grabbed the ice axe and the shovel and crawled back through my tunnel. I opened my dominant eye as soon as I was outside and moved immediately to my left. I didn't want to be silhouetted against the glow from the snow-hole for any longer than I had to be.

When I'd reached the far side of the tallest of the stones, using what was left of my night vision to smooth over my tracks as I went, I climbed straight up the hill and tucked myself behind it, to prepare for what I hoped might happen next.

14

I put the shovel aside and stamped the snow flat behind the rock until I had a firm platform from which to operate, then pulled down the NVGs, switched them onto infrared and adjusted the focus and intensity of the image.

AN/PVS-7s were standard issue for US land forces, and it didn't take long to see why. With little ambient light but a dramatic contrast between the snow-covered ground and the shadow of the rocks and trees, it was as if my immediate surroundings had been transformed into a vivid black-and-white movie that someone had washed with green.

Back in the day, the principal problem with these things, apart from their weight, was that any bright flash would trigger a complete whiteout on your retinas. Now anything less than a mega candlepower spotlight would just look like a budget-size UFO. And I didn't expect Sniper One to be carrying a mega candlepower spotlight as well as a big fuck-off weapon.

I eased the monocle around the inside flank of the rock, until I had as clear a view of the gully as possible without emerging from cover. A roe deer materialized thirty metres away and stood stock still. For a moment, as the flakes danced around her, it was as if she was posing at the centre of her very own snow globe. Then she pricked up her ears, glanced rapidly left and right, and took off towards the ridge. She'd caught either my scent or somebody else's.

I ducked back out of sight and gripped the shaft of the ice axe with both hands, testing for weight and balance before putting it down within easy reach.

The next time I looked, my pursuer had emerged from behind the flank of the hill. I didn't have time to take in every detail of his waterproof clothing and equipment, but I didn't need to. All that mattered was the weapon he carried.

The largest arms manufacturer in the former Soviet Republic was an outfit called OSJC 'IZHMASH', founded by Tsar Alexander I in 1807. Their plant at Izhevsk had turned out more than eleven million rifles and carbines during the Second World War. It was still the proud producer of the Kalashnikov AK-47 and the Warsaw Pact sniper's favourite, the Dragunov SVD.

These things weren't as well engineered as the Winchester or the Remington and didn't guarantee their pinpoint accuracy, but in the right hands they could do some serious damage. I had the feeling that this one — an SVDS with folding stock extended — was in the right hands now.

15

He spotted the glow from the Bolthole immediately, and got the butt in his shoulder as he advanced.

I stepped back, removed my left glove and powered up the iPhone again, shielding its glow in my right palm. I pressed 'A' once, then the stop bar the moment I heard the G3 ring.

A nanosecond later I heard nine rounds being pumped into the mouth of the cave, followed by the distinctive metallic clicks of a mag being removed and replaced while he still had a round in the chamber. Good skills. This lad wasn't fucking about.

The silence returned.

Even the wind seemed to stop and wait for his next move.

Then footsteps crunched towards me through the snow.

Going into slow-mo, I slid the NVGs carefully off my head and put them down beside the shovel, pocketed the iPhone and pulled on my glove. Taking a deep breath to oxygenate myself for the drama ahead, I retrieved the ice axe and rose to my feet.

The crunch rate slowed and began to sound more cautious, but Sniper One kept on coming.

I heard his waterproofs rustle as he moved.

He'd keep his SVD in the aim — no way would that butt be taken out of the shoulder now. Finger pad on the trigger. Safety lever down and off. Eyes flicking left and right as he advanced towards his target.

He'd kick my beautifully sculpted snow tunnel apart with his boot. Then he'd have to stoop down to look inside. That was the moment I wanted to be on top of him. Give him no time to react. No room to move.

It wouldn't take him long to discover that he'd emptied his magazine into my daysack. But by then his night vision should be well and truly nailed by the hexamine blaze. Even if it wasn't, I'd have to crack on and take him, to render his rifle a whole lot less effective than it had been when Trev's eyebrows were at the centre of the optic.

The crunches came to a halt.

I flexed my finger muscles, closed both hands over the grip of my ice axe and bent my knees. As soon as he leaned down to inspect what lay behind the entrance, he was mine.

I could hear him breathe.

He was at the mouth of the cave.

I stepped out, axe raised above my head, eyes focused on the space between his shoulder-blades as he crouched below me.

The almost subliminal clink of crampon on rock and the sixth sense shared by every hunter in the universe made him look up before my feet had left the ledge.

He threw himself sideways and tried to roll away before I could swing the pick down — tried to get out of my range, heave his barrel up and get a round into me. But it wasn't working.

My crampons dug into the snow. I zeroed in on his centre mass and cannoned into him. I wasn't aiming my weapon with any precision. All I wanted to do was drive four or five inches of sharpened metal into him as far as I could and take it from there.

I managed to make contact. With all the movement going on beneath me, I couldn't immediately tell where the pointy bit had connected, but I felt it tear into flesh and muscle and the shaft juddered as I raked it up his spine. He grunted or cursed and twisted away, wrenching himself clear of my ice axe and putting some space between us. Blood glistened around a big tear in his waterproof top.

I raised the pick above my head for a repeat performance as he turned towards me again. The pain must have been outrageous, but it didn't seem to register. He kept on coming, filling the air with the stench of garlic, sour cabbage, untipped cigarettes and unbrushed teeth with every tortured breath.

His neck muscles tautened as he strained to bring up the Dragunov's muzzle so he could blast a hole in my chest, and I suddenly knew beyond any doubt that he was going to do it before I could bring my weapon down again.

I let go of the grip with my left hand and kicked out. I missed the barrel but connected strongly enough with his arm to shunt the muzzle off at an angle.

I felt the round before I heard it. It kicked off millimetres away from my right cheek, smashed the ice axe out of my hand and sent shock waves along my arm. The impact propelled me backwards but I somehow managed to stay upright. I knew that if I went down now, it was over.

I was fresh out of options as he brought the weapon back up. All I could do now was take one step forward and launch myself at him, feet first.

My right crampon caught him in the gut. I felt its claws rip into him, but he just took the pain. My left crampon clattered against gunmetal. Without any purchase, I lost my balance and had to jerk back and plant it in the snow again to stop myself falling.

Its claws were too short to puncture an organ, so I raised my right foot and stamped on his face instead. I channelled my entire bodyweight through that one leg and kept it there. He finally let go of the Dragunov and grabbed my ankle, but instead of dislodging my boot he forced its metal sole to grate against his jawbone. His flesh fell away like raw meat spilling from a mincer.

He bucked and heaved and flailed his arms, fingers scrabbling to reclaim his rifle. I kept my right foot in place and skewered his neck with the left. For a moment I didn't think that was going to stop him either.

His lips peeled back in a ferocious snarl, but blood gushed from his mouth instead of sound. He arched his back and shuddered, like he'd chewed on a power cable, then lay very still.

16

I fetched the Dragunov and pushed up the safety lever on its right-hand side, then removed my gloves and went through Sniper One's pockets. I didn't expect to find anything, and I wasn't wrong. Apart from a half-empty packet of dextrose tablets and two hundred and fifty quid or so in well-used notes poking out of a money clip, they were empty.

I kept the cash and powered up the torch app on my iPhone so I could take a closer look at him. You're never at your best when your face has been rearranged by a set of crampons, but even on a good day this guy wouldn't have turned heads on the catwalk. If he had done, he'd have had to choose a different line of work. Snipers and surveillance operators aren't supposed to stand out in a crowd. With his closely cropped hair, broken nose and cold grey eyes this lad was every bit as forgettable as I was. And we pretty much shared the same tailor.

I unzipped his waterproof top and wrenched open the layers of fleece and thermal kit beneath it. There were no coal-dust tattoos telling the story of his life — just the sculpted pecs of a man who took his fitness seriously.

Then I caught sight of something on his neck. At first glance I assumed the crimson splash was blood or possibly a birthmark. When I turned his head and ran the beam beneath his shattered jaw

I realized it was neither.

This was quality ink work, somewhere between a starburst and a multi-leaf clover. It reminded me of the so-called roses that decorated the roads and pavements of Sarajevo when the locals had filled the Serb mortar scars with red resin to honour their dead.

Well, I wasn't in the mood to honour this fucker. I put my gloves back on, grabbed him by the legs and dragged his body into the Bolthole, leaving a trail of dark red deoxygenated blood on the snow. I sat him against the rock wall and reunited him with his Dragunov in the flickering light of my hexy bonfire.

As soon as the weather cleared and the ramblers got back into their anoraks, this area would turn into a major crime scene. I needed to make distance.

17

I legged it back to St Ellyw's as quickly as possible after picking up what was left of my kit.

The daysack had been well ventilated, but it would live to fight another day. The Samsung G3 had been terminated with extreme prejudice, along with the chicken casserole MRE pack. The manufacturers insisted these things could survive a 380-metre drop, but a blast of 7.62 was more than it could handle. The hotpot was miraculously unscathed.

I picked up the Defender of the Faith way after midnight, as another wave of snow began its assault. All sign would have been covered on the hill by now.

I headed west past Brecon until I found a couple of artics parked up in a layby and joined them. I left the engine on and the heater running while I warmed Trev's hotpot in its FRH (flameless ration heater) pouch. MREs weren't everybody's favourite snack — as squaddies we'd called them Meals Refusing to Exit — but after freezing my arse off in the Black Mountains it ticked all the boxes. It also gave me something to munch as I thought about my next move.

If Trev was right about the Head Shed killing their own, I had to ID who was loading the rounds. So the first step was to try to find out why. And since none of us knew who we could trust, I had to be more careful than he had been about the questions I needed to ask — and about selecting the people I could look to for answers.

Harry's boy was clearly off limits, so I had to go a few different routes. And I didn't have much time. I hadn't broadcast my presence back in the UK, but I reckoned it wouldn't be long before whoever had wanted Trev dead managed to put two and two together and come after me.

When I'd finished eating, I unfurled my Gore-Tex hood, put on my gloves and got my head down in the driver's seat. That way I could stay as close as I could to what little warmth was leaking out of the heating vent.

It wasn't the Ritz, but it beat the shit out of lying in a snowdrift with my brains dripping off a nearby tree.

PART THREE

PART THREE

1

St Francis Xavier's Roman Catholic Church, Powys

Thursday, 26 January
08.13 hrs

I'd always steered clear of confession.

I could see the attraction of wiping the slate clean with a few Hail Marys, but I'd done some things over the years that I wasn't proud of, and had never felt comfortable with the idea of spilling the details. The secret of keeping things secret was never, ever, to share them with anyone else.

I didn't care about people standing in judgement against me, I just preferred not to give them any extra sticks to beat me with. Whoever said, 'Knowledge is power,' knew what they were talking about.

I'd given Anna the edited version of my life, of course, but she hadn't bought it. She'd seen me in the shit a good few times, and with her journo hat on she was brilliant at uncovering stuff people wanted to hide. From the moment I met her, I'd had the slightly scary feeling that she understood me a whole lot better than I understood myself. Slightly scary because I discovered that it was one of the many things I really, really liked about being with her.

The only other person I'd allowed anywhere near the truth was Father Mart. I trusted him completely — which was why I was now sitting in a little wooden box in the corner of a church about fifty Ks north of his cottage. I needed to bring him up to speed on the events of the last twenty-four hours, and find out if he could fill any of the gaps.

The bench groaned as I shifted from one buttock to the other to try to make myself comfortable. Some hope. These places weren't built for comfort. They were built for penance. But also for anonymity, which suited me fine right now.

I couldn't help wondering about the kind of exchanges that must have taken place through the perforated screen that separated the sinner from the priest. And if the magic ever worked.

I ran a fingertip across a bit of graffiti some choirboy had scrawled in felt-tip while waiting to admit what he'd really done with the Communion wine: *Beware! Sudden prayers make God jump!* I didn't know if Father Mart ever checked out this side of the booth, but I thought he'd probably like that.

The throaty growl of the 911 and the echoing clank of the heavy oak door told me he was on his way in. I kept eyes on the entrance through the gap in the velvet curtain.

Father Mart ducked his head towards the altar and made the sign of the cross before turning in my direction. His trainers squeaked on the quarry-tiled floor and the curtain rings on his side of the booth rattled as he stepped inside.

There was a moment's silence. '*In nomine patris, et filii, et spiritus sancti* ... Do you repent of your sins, my son?'

I couldn't see much through the screen, but I swear there was a gleam in his eye. 'How long have you got?'

'Good point, Nicholas. That might be a conversation for another time ... '

' 'Fraid so, Father.' I paused. 'You were right to be worried. Trev's dead. A professional hit.'

I heard a deep sigh.

'Who?'

'No idea. He won't be doing it again.'

Father Mart knew better than to ask for details.

I asked him if he knew about the claymore in Trev's front hall.

He didn't.

2

Father Mart's bench creaked as he shifted position. 'I've asked around, Nicholas, and got nothing.'

'Well, now's a good time to stop asking. There's some high-level shit going on out there, and for the time being, no matter how long you've been on His firm, I don't think we can rely on the Good Lord's protection.'

'Perhaps I should pay a visit to Barford . . . '

'We should both steer clear of Barford right now. I think Trev had a pretty good idea who might be behind this, and he was dead set against going.

'Maybe there's another route to the truth about Harry's boy. You know any of his mates?'

'He kept his emotional cards pretty close to his chest. But, then, don't you all?' Father Mart went quiet for a moment. 'I can't think of any, apart from Guy Chastain and Scott Braxton. The three of them were almost inseparable.'

'Where can I find Scott?'

'On the post-mortem slab, I'm sorry to say. He was the boy they're saying Sam Callard killed in the CQB Rooms.'

It was starting to sound like this lad's friendships lasted about as long as mine did. 'No one else?'

'Well, there's Ella, of course. His girlfriend. But Trevor took the precaution of hiding her before he hid himself.' He took a couple of deep breaths. 'I've got to admit that I thought he was overreacting when he told me.'

'I don't suppose he mentioned where?'

That made him chuckle. 'It was on a need-to-know basis. And he didn't think I needed to know.'

'Tell me about her. And maybe you could tell me about Sam too. I didn't watch out for the boy like Trev did . . . '

I didn't say that the few times I'd been with Sam Callard when he was a kid I hadn't been able to shake the image of his dad's face out of my head. I didn't need to. Father Mart had done his best to deal with all that shit years ago.

'She's a great girl. A GP. They've been together for a couple of years. He had a pretty tough time during his last tour in Afghan. She picked up the pieces.'

'I thought that was your job.'

'As you well know, Nicholas, I need all the help I can get.'

'What happened to him?'

'He refused to talk about it, even to Trevor, and Trevor was like a father to him.'

I gave a wry smile in the shadows of the confessional. Being like a father, as far as I was concerned, meant staying as far away from my son as possible.

'But I know it haunted him. You could see it in his eyes. He's not alone in that, of course . . . ' His voice tailed off.

Father Mart had seen more than his fair share of the wreckage of men from the war zone. Some

99

could wear it lightly. Some couldn't. In the silence that followed I found myself thinking about the lads I'd known who'd carried it around with them like a sack of shit until they could no longer take the smell, and Harry's face loomed large again.

This wasn't healthy. I cut away.

'What's the timetable for the court martial?'

'I get the feeling they're fast-tracking it, but I'm not certain. They like to bury these things as quickly as possible, don't they? And they'll do it behind closed doors. In the National Interest.'

'Could you find out who's in charge of the Article 32 investigation?' The accused had the right to a thorough and impartial investigation into the incident before any general court-martial proceedings.

'I'll try.'

'And the name of Sam's lawyer?' I warned him again not to rattle any bars on any more cages. Then I asked him the next most important question of the morning. 'How's the 911 in the snow?'

'For once, I have to say I'd rather be in the Defender.'

3

Before leaving, I told Father Mart also to watch out for Postman Pat. We needed to catapult him into twenty-first-century comms so we could make contact from time to time when we needed to, and he could pass on any int he came by.

In the meantime, he gave me Ella's home address and the name and location of her practice in Gloucestershire. Thank fuck it wasn't in Hereford. Trev had been rattled enough by the MRUD to leg it out of town, and with good reason, so even the old haunts were no longer safe havens for me. Even if the connection between the Credenhill blackout and the Black Mountains sniper wasn't clear, the threat level was.

We swapped car keys and I threw my kit under the bonnet of the 911. I was going to miss the Defender of the Faith, but a priest in a Porsche — especially *my* Porsche — would stick out like the balls on a bulldog, and I didn't want Father Mart drawing unnecessary attention to himself. He had links with Trev too.

There would probably come a time when I'd have to ditch my boy-racer wagon, but where I was going next it would fit right in.

He gripped my hand. 'Look after yourself, Nicholas.'

'You too, Obi-Wan.'

His brow furrowed for a moment before he

tuned in. 'Indeed. We must both beware of the Dark Side.'

* * *

Without getting stupid about it, I'd decided to give H as wide a berth as possible, so headed north-east for Ludlow. I stopped at a service station, filled the tank and grabbed a fistful of clear polythene gloves.

By the time I had dropped down to Evesham and spent some time in an internet café, the snow on the windscreen and tarmac had been replaced by drizzle. Their pig roll wasn't as good as the one I'd had in Brynmawr, but it was enough to keep me going as I Googled Dr Eleanor Mathieson and her surgery.

I then pointed the 911 towards a part of the planet that seemed to be entirely populated by Range Rover Evoques, royal tree-huggers and signposts to villages with names like Upton Snodsbury.

As I drove, I wished I'd been able to hide Father Mart as well as Trev had hidden Ella, but he was never going to change his style for anyone. I hoped that his God would keep an eye on him — or at least remind the bad guys that, however much you could brush aside pondweed like me and Trev, the death of a Catholic priest who was also a local legend wouldn't go unnoticed.

* * *

When I was growing up on our South London estate, I'd thought villages like Chipping Campden only existed on railway posters, and as I parked up within reach of the high street, I still felt like I'd entered a fairy-tale world of home baking, scented-candle shops and honey-coloured stone.

I saw the medical practice almost immediately — a handsome double-fronted building with cream-painted rendering. Dr Eleanor Mathieson and Dr Grace Nichol were two of the names on the brass plate beside its entrance, but all except one of the 'Doctors Parking Only' bays were empty. I walked straight past. I had a home visit to make before I started to quiz her friends.

I ducked into the first dry cleaner's I came across. They were very happy to give me a wire coat hanger in return for a couple of quid in their Help for Heroes collection tub. As I moved on, I bent the wire back and forth until it snapped into two six-inch lengths. I curved their tips and slid them into my pocket. You could get lock-picking sets from Amazon, these days, but my homemade versions worked pretty well, and didn't have 'Burglary in Progress' written all over them.

4

Oak Leaves was the last cottage in the lane, at the edge of a stretch of woodland that must have given it its very cosy name. I didn't approach it directly: I had no idea if whoever owned Sniper One would have eyes on the place, but since it was one of a small handful of known locations linked to Harry's boy, I had to assume they did.

I went back into rambler mode, vaulted the first stile I came across on the opposite side of the road and strode along a right-of-way that sloped gently upwards at the edge of a field, taking me further away from her front door. The grass was slippery underfoot, not crisp, and the ambient temperature was mild. Shafts of sunlight cut through the scudding clouds.

Five or six gates further on, and now sheltered by the rolling hill from the houses on the lane, I turned left along a hedgerow and followed it to the far side of the wood. A small herd of cows raised their heads as I passed, then lost interest when they realized I wasn't bringing food.

There wasn't another human being in sight, but that didn't mean I could relax. I approached the wood with caution, but I also had to look as though I belonged there. These small rural communities kept an eye out for strangers, particularly when the neighbours were away. This wasn't the home of the folding-stock Dragunov, but a hand-tooled Holland & Holland over-and-under could do plenty of damage in the wrong hands.

I needn't have worried. The treeline offered some cover, but the growth was manicured, not wild. It was perfect for a kids' game of hide and seek; it wasn't Rambo territory.

Ella's side door wasn't overlooked, and was sheltered behind a five-foot stone wall. I emerged from the wood and swung myself up and over it, landed softly on the path, stopped and listened. When I was satisfied that the rest of the world didn't care what I was up to, I stepped into the kind of porch where you'd be able to slip off your green wellies before popping in for tea and crumpets.

I took out my bits of coat hanger and slipped on my polythene service-station gloves, then reached for the very shiny brass handle and turned it. You felt like a complete dickhead if you got busy with your lock-picking kit, only to discover that it was already open.

They never were, of course.

But this one was.

There were three possible reasons why.

One: Ella's mum was looking after the place.

Two: Ella had been in too much of a rush to lock up when Trev told her it was time to leave.

Three: her security was spot on, but someone had made entry after she'd gone, either in pursuit of her or because they'd wanted to turn the place over.

I looked at the mechanism. It was often easier to open these things than close them down.

I decided not to waste time trying to work out which it could be. I'd find out soon enough.

5

I eased the door back on its well-oiled hinges and stayed on the threshold, slack-jawed, listening for movement. The house was small enough and old enough for me to register a mouse moving upstairs.

There was no need to clear the whole house before I nosed around. After five minutes I was satisfied that there wasn't a fully primed MRUD sitting there with my name on it, and that, apart from the heating system, nothing and no one was still interfering with the air molecules inside the cottage. I stepped into the lobby and closed up behind me.

Leaving my wet Timberlands on the mat, I moved past a rack of Barbour and Driza-Bone waterproofed coats, hats and scarves into a neatly organized kitchen. The Aga was on, but throttled back. I crossed burglary off the list. Everything seemed to be in its proper place.

The Rolodex beside the phone was filled with names, addresses and phone numbers in immaculate copperplate. That told me not all doctors had shit handwriting, and Ella took a lot of care with her surroundings.

I couldn't tell whether any of the cards had been removed, but there were no obvious gaps. I keyed Grace Nichol's mobile number into my iPhone, in case she wasn't at the surgery when I got back there.

A wood-burning stove stood in the living-room fireplace, freshly laid, ready for the end of the day. The shelves either side of it were lined with hardcovers and paperbacks — everything from chick lit to the classics and a bunch of military memoirs — a state-of-the-art sound system and family photographs in silver and leather frames.

Sam obviously avoided the camera as energetically as I did, but there were two shots of other men in uniform. Google had told me that she had a brother and a father in the Green Army, so I assumed this was what they looked like. I wondered how they'd feel about having a court-martial defendant in the family. Ella and her mother shared the apparently effortless good looks that seemed to bless the county set. Harry would have been proud.

One frame was empty. I figured it must have been a snap of Ella, and that it had been taken. The second sign of slack drills — or maybe the intruder didn't care? Either way, it was a problem. I liked players who were in control of what they were doing. That way I knew what I was up against.

I checked out the contents of a small roll-top desk without much hope of discovering anything as helpful as a forwarding address, but you never knew what might trigger a connection or a memory, and sometimes what you didn't find turned out to be as useful as what you did.

I uncovered a red slip file containing a print-out of Guy Chastain's VC citation and a replica of the medal, which looked like they were ready for framing. Tucked in behind them was a handwritten note from someone called Stephen thanking Ella for her kind letter of condolence and doing his best to convince himself that at least Chris had died doing what he loved. I'd read a lot of letters like that, and some of them were true.

The two bedrooms upstairs were so snug I half expected to see Goldilocks in a big double bed catching up on her beauty sleep. The wardrobes weren't full, but the rails and shelves were still well stocked with man stuff and girl stuff.

The bathroom had a tub you could do lengths in, gleaming taps, designer candles and big fluffy towels. The medicine cabinet was almost empty, apart from a bag of cotton-wool pads, some sterile dressings, a roll of Elastoplast, a couple of crêpe bandages, a bottle of Armani aftershave and half a packet of sertraline.

I'd never taken happy pills myself, though I knew one or two lads who couldn't get through the day without them — and I didn't think they were there to treat Ella's OCD. I pocketed the dressings, and one of the bandages.

I scanned the immediate area through the first-floor windows: a row of quite spacious, carefully managed gardens, each with a selection of oiled teak chairs and tables. At the far end of Ella's was a sage green designer shepherd's hut with cast-iron wheels, a wriggly tin roof and a chimney.

No one was in sight, but I wasn't going to risk crossing sixty feet of open ground and poking around in full view of the next-door neighbours.

They wouldn't call out the Specialist Firearms Unit, but a chat with the Gloucestershire Constabulary was the last thing I needed. I wanted to keep below the radar for as long as I possibly could.

The digital clock on the bedside table told me it was 2:45. I'd come back and take a look outside some time after last light.

6

I went back downstairs, pulled on my Timberlands and exited. I turned left instead of right on
the far side of the wood and paralleled the
treeline in the opposite direction to the way I'd
approached.

I stopped alongside the first fence I came to,
grabbed one of the barbed-wire strands and
drew it across my calf, tearing a hole in my jeans
and enough of the flesh beneath to make the
blood flow without doing any serious damage.
Then I fastened one of the dressings over the
wound with the bandage, clumsily enough to
make it seem like I was in need of professional
help.

★   ★   ★

The receptionist at the clinic glanced up from
her computer screen as I came through the door
and gave me one of those looks that said I was
extremely welcome, but shouldn't make the
mistake of thinking I'd be attended to
immediately.

Was I new to the area?

I explained that I was only there on a walking
holiday and, embarrassed, showed her my hastily
strapped calf. Barbed wire. Incredibly stupid. I
asked if I could see Dr Mathieson. As luck would
have it, she was a friend of a friend.

The receptionist pursed her lips regretfully and told me Dr Mathieson was on leave, but if I was happy to wait, perhaps the doctor on duty could see me. I told her I didn't want to waste their precious time, obviously, but maybe they could dress the wound properly and give me a tetanus jab.

She handed me an NHS form to fill in and motioned me to a seat in the waiting area beside a woman with a sprained wrist and an old boy who should never have developed a taste for Capstan Full Strength. Half an hour later she announced that Dr Nichol was ready to see me.

A fraction the other side of forty, Grace Nichol obviously wouldn't take shit from anyone, but the laughter lines around her eyes told me that she could still see the funny side of things. She invited me to take off my Timberlands and 'pop up' on her examination couch.

As she folded back my freshly torn Levi's and unpeeled the bandage I asked after Ella, and got the raised eyebrow in return. I sensed her body stiffen too, but I might have imagined that.

'She's a friend of a friend. Well, a friend of the son of a friend. A friend who's dead now . . . '

Instead of responding, she started to give my calf much more attention than it really deserved.

I didn't want to put her on Red Alert, so I kept my tone light and waffly. 'I guess you'll know Sam. Haven't seen him for quite a while, but I served with his dad, back in the day.' I gave her a cheesy grin. 'Don't panic, I'm not going to pull up a sandbag and bore you with old war stories . . . '

111

She peeled back the dressing and tutted — the kind of tut that made it clear I'd been a very silly boy. When she looked up, her expression was softer. 'They've gone away. They needed a break.'

'Not surprised. I heard he had a rough time in Afghan, and that means everybody suffers. Me and Harry spent most of our time messing around in Catterick, but these lads have been right at the sharp end . . . '

Her look said, 'Pull the other one,' and I liked her even more for that. It also gave me the feeling she knew very well that Sam was in the Regiment, and that Harry and I had been too.

She cleaned the wound and applied a fresh dressing, then told me she would give me a tetanus injection, to be on the safe side.

'So if you'd like to take off your jacket and roll up your sleeve . . . '

I did as she asked and got a needle in the arm.

She deposited the wrapping and the used syringe in the sharps bin and sat down behind her desk while I sorted myself out. As I pulled on my bomber I became aware that I was being scrutinized quite closely. I met her gaze. It made me feel like I had when I was caught cheating at school. Not that I'd gone to school much.

'Why are you *really* here, Mr . . . ' she glanced at my freshly scribbled NHS form ' . . . Jones?'

I gave her my best puzzled expression and pointed at my leg. 'World's biggest idiot . . . I was enjoying a day out when I tripped over a fallen fencepost . . . '

I got the eyebrow treatment again. 'So they

don't have much barbed wire in . . . now, where was it? *Catterick*?' She gave each syllable of 'Catterick' equal weight, in case I hadn't yet realized that she didn't believe a word I'd said.

I kept eye to eye for long enough to know that I wasn't going to get any help unless I made some attempt to level with her. 'Cards on the table?'

She nodded.

'Another very old mate of ours told me Sam's in trouble, and could use some help. I figured that Ella might be able to shed some light on things . . . '

She put her elbows on her desk, linked her hands and rested her chin on her knuckles. 'A very old *military* mate?' She did that trick with the syllables again.

My turn to nod.

She sighed. 'At the risk of stating the obvious, that's where my problems begin.'

She paused, like she'd reached a fork in the road and couldn't make up her mind which direction to take.

'Don't get me wrong, Mr *Jones*, I'm sure the army is positively bursting with champions of justice and truth, prepared to give their lives in defence of the realm, but it appears there are also those with a rather different agenda. And how can one tell the difference between them?'

I'd reached that fork in the road as well. 'It's not only your problem. It's mine too. I've been in the game for far too long, in one way or another, and even I don't know who I can trust.'

For the first time since I'd come into the room

113

I saw a look of real distress cross her face.

'Ella and Sam had been going through difficult times since the moment he got back. I didn't realize how difficult. You know how it is. We work extremely closely, but try not to invade each other's personal space. I tried to get her to tell me what was wrong, but she wouldn't say. She couldn't even talk to her father or brother about it.'

'How long will they be away?'

She shrugged. 'As long as it takes. Whatever that means.'

'I guess you don't have a contact number?'

She shook her head. 'Whenever anyone calls for her, our receptionist takes a message or gives them Ella's mobile. Not everyone takes 'no' for an answer, of course. Her uncle got in a bit of a strop about it the other day. Said he'd called her a dozen times without getting any kind of response. The poor girl didn't have the heart to tell him that's because Ella's BlackBerry is permanently switched off.'

'Does she have it with her?'

'No.'

She reached into her top drawer and held up a small black slab of plastic in a worn leather holster. 'All she said when she handed it to me was that they had to drop off the grid. Completely.'

7

The light was fading as I crossed the road to the Red Lion. Grace had told me they used to pop in for a glass of something at the end of the day when Sam was away.

I followed the signs to the Gents, took a piss, then filled a basin with warm water and freshened up for the first time since I'd left Father Mart's. I didn't normally worry about stuff like that but there was something about the Cotswolds that demanded my best behaviour.

It was too early for the evening trade to have really kicked off, so I had the front room pretty much to myself. An old guy with rosy cheeks, big sideburns and the kind of eyebrows you usually only see in cartoons was busy with landlord stuff behind the bar. He gave the thumbs-up to the Olde Trip, so I ordered a pint and a home-baked pork pie and dragged up a stool.

The mouth-watering smell of the pie made me realize I'd hardly eaten that day. I demolished it in about ten seconds along with half the pickle jar and ordered another. When my host saw I was in the mood for company he came over and polished some glasses while we talked about the ale, the weather and the walking.

I put on my sheepish look and told him about my barbed-wire adventure. He showed me a scar on his forehead where he'd recently been attacked by a lamp post, and told me in hilarious detail how he'd once been chased by a bull. We were the best of mates in no time.

'Sounds as if you spend even more time at the doctor's than I do . . . '

He beamed. 'I nip in there every chance I get. Gorgeous girls, bless them! Spoken for, I know — but a fellow can dream, can't he?'

Dreams were close to the top of my list of things to avoid wherever possible, along with bullet-headed men waving sniper rifles, but I grinned and wondered aloud whether he knew when Dr Mathieson was due back. 'She's a friend of a friend. And I have a feeling I used to know her uncle . . . '

'Norman? Lovely bloke. No airs and graces, even though his brother was a general. Used to drop in here regular, before he got poorly.'

'He's still around, then?'

'Only in a manner of speaking, I'm afraid.' His brow furrowed. 'Up in the churchyard. He passed away three . . . no, four years ago. Some sort of cancer, I think.'

I figured that Norman wouldn't be calling the practice from beyond the grave, but wasn't going to ask whether he had any other brothers. I didn't want to ring the sort of alarm bells that I had with Grace. I looked suitably mournful. 'I'll have to go and pay my respects.'

8

We waffled on for another twenty minutes or so and then the bar filled up enough for him to be diverted and me to pay my bill and give him a cheery farewell.

I picked up the 911 and pointed it back in the direction of Oak Leaves. I wasn't in the mood to stumble around in the long grass and bracken now that it was dark. It was well past the rambling hour and, in any case, I didn't want to make a night of it.

I drove a couple of hundred metres past Ella's cottage, pulled up off the road beside a five-bar gate and doubled back. I dipped into the wood at a point far enough from the house to take advantage of the cover but close enough not to have to crash around through too much undergrowth.

I followed the wall until I was behind the shepherd's hut, then stopped and listened to the sounds carried on the night wind. An owl called from somewhere to my half-right, trees rustled and a fox shrieked further away. I'd always hated that sound. Now these bad boys were turning their backs on country life and heading into the 'burbs, you heard it all the time. I never knew whether it meant they were having sex or fighting over the remains of a KFC Boneless Banquet. Maybe they couldn't tell the difference either.

One or two lamps glimmered from behind the

next-door neighbour's curtains, but the cold would persuade most people to stay inside. Although the sky was clearer than it had been earlier, the moon wasn't bright enough to mark me out.

I gave my ears a quick rub to take the chill off them, then hauled myself over the wall and sheltered in the gap between the stonework and the side of the hut. I dipped into my coat for the polythene gloves and waited for my night vision to improve.

Close up, it was obvious that this bit of kit had never been near a sheep, unless one had lost its way and wandered into the garden by mistake. The paint was showroom fresh. Maybe it had been Sam's welcome-home present. I was getting the impression that the Mathiesons weren't short of cash.

There was no window on this elevation, so I had to ease myself around the corner and up the steps before taking a look inside. The three-lever mortice lock on the stable door took me about ten seconds to pick. I closed it quietly behind me.

I found myself inside a designer bothy on wheels. I'd been in five-star hotel rooms that weren't this luxurious. There was a bed with a blue-and-white-striped duvet, two matching chairs, a powder-white chest of drawers, a table with a couple of chunky Scandinavian glass candle-holders and yet another wood-burning stove.

The chest was full of man stuff — casual kit, mostly — and another half empty pack of

118

sertraline, which gave me the impression that though the hut might have been the venue for romantic dinners it sometimes doubled as Sam's hide when he needed the world to go away. I rummaged through anything that had a pocket but found nothing more than a few squares of man-size Kleenex.

The stove had been used recently, but not cleaned or fully reloaded. I opened its door. A fistful of kindling, a fresh firelighter and four or five crumpled envelopes lay on the ash. Inside one of them, postmarked Monday, 9 January, was a hastily scrawled note: *Mate, sorry about last night. Pissed again. Story of my life, these days. Not good. I can't promise not to repeat, but I'll do my best. It's a fucker, isn't it? Ever, Scott.*

I re-crumpled and replaced it, and swung the door closed.

Outside, I was just about to climb back over the wall when something made me hesitate. I knelt down, slid beneath the hut and rolled onto my back. There was two feet or so of clearance between the ground and the underside of the structure.

The woodwork was as neat and symmetrical here as it had been up above. The access hatch at the end furthest from the steps was so carefully dovetailed into the main frame that, if I hadn't spotted the finger-hole that triggered its bolt mechanism, I wouldn't have noticed it.

I slithered across the damp grass, using my elbows, heels and shoulder-blades, and released it. At first, all I could feel was some electrical wiring, an insulation membrane and, between the joists, that fluffy stuff you find in the loft when your cold-water tank springs a leak. But when I shoved my arm as far as I could into the space below the floorboards, I touched something that hadn't been part of the manufacturer's spec.

I managed to get enough purchase on the chamois-leather package to extract it. Inside was a Browning Hi Power 9mm pistol with a loaded thirteen-round mag and a spare.

There were some people who believed that if you were in the Regiment you never went anywhere without one of these lumps of metal tucked under your bomber jacket, even in your spare time. But they could dream on. It looked like I'd uncovered Sam's second court-martial offence.

Luckily I wasn't in the army any more. I was about to put the spare mag in my pocket when I felt a vicelike grip on both my ankles, and my arse began to slide back into the open.

9

I firmed up my grip on the Browning, flicked off the safety catch and racked back its topslide. The metallic movement didn't eject a chambered round before picking up the top one from the mag. I felt the burr hammer move back against the web of skin between my thumb and forefinger as the rest of me emerged from the underside of the hut.

I grasped my right wrist with my left hand and raised the muzzle.

'What the *fu* — ?'

Being on the wrong end of a weapon was usually enough to stop anyone who wasn't used to it in mid-sentence, even a big lad in wellies and a boiler-suit.

I kept my voice low and in control. It was blindingly obvious that a combine harvester was more likely to be his weapon of choice than an MRUD, but he still didn't look pleased. 'Hands *up*. Come on, let me see them . . . '

He let go of my legs, almost in slow motion, and did as he was told.

I gestured for him to step back and got to my feet, keeping eyes and weapon on him throughout, in case he suddenly felt he had to do something stupid.

He didn't need further encouragement. He looked like a power-lifter who'd forgotten his weights.

'You can put 'em down now, but keep your distance.'

He lowered his arms. His fingers were like prize marrows. For a moment, he seemed not to know what to do with them. Then he hooked his thumbs in his thick leather belt.

'You a mate of Sam and Ella?'

He nodded so hard I was worried he might do something bad to his neck. 'I'm Gerry . . . from the top farm. I was just . . . I look after the grass . . . you know, the garden . . . I keep an eye — '

'All good.' I didn't need his full CV. 'Look, mate, I'm a friend of theirs. Not here to nick the family silver.' I put the safety back on and shoved the weapon into the waistband of my jeans. 'I'm — '

'Military?' He'd managed to get his head back on an even keel.

My turn to nod. 'Yup.' I tapped the weapon. 'Sorry about that. You got me worried.'

He was so relieved I thought he might try to reach out and hug me. 'You got me worried too. You're not the first person I've seen snooping around here since they left. Some were your mates in uniform, obviously. I can always tell them a mile off. But the others weren't.'

'Others? When? Did you ID them? Maybe see a vehicle? Do the police know?'

He went quiet for a while. Maybe five questions at once were a bit much for him.

'A couple of nights ago. I didn't see 'em close up, but there were two of them. And no sign of a car. I don't bloody bother with the law any more. We've had a load of machinery nicked these last

122

few months, and they're never around when you need them . . . '

I let him drone on about diggers and cutters and balers going missing. Then he started harking back to a golden era when everybody around here left their doors unlocked and there were more bobbies on the beat, and I decided enough was enough.

'Look, mate, I've got to go now. Report back. But when Sam and Ella reappear can you let them know Tony called in? Tell them hello from me?'

He said he would.

'But carry on keeping an eye out, eh?'

Gerry nodded again, slowly this time, as Middle England's deep-seated trust of authority kicked in and began to make his world a nicer place.

He shifted slightly awkwardly from one foot to the other and I thought for a moment that he was going to tug his forelock. Instead he turned and trudged back the way he must have come.

I only stayed long enough to replace the hatch cover beneath the hut.

PART FOUR

PART FOUR

1

Salisbury, Wiltshire

Friday, 27 January
11.21 hrs

Ken Marabula had been my first sergeant in Malaysia. His favourite gag was to warn us young troopers not to turn our backs on him at mealtimes. He told us that in Fiji in his grandfather's day they'd often marinate a guest or two in coconut milk and add them to the menu. 'Nothing personal, man. They just loved the taste of Long Pig.' He'd lick his lips like Hannibal Lecter and give us the kind of leering grin that made us sleep with one eye open.

In his quieter moments he used to admit that cannibalism is not actually as popular, these days, as it once was, particularly in the UK. I found that quite reassuring, especially when we got pissed together on a big night out, but I still kept my distance from the earth oven. They'd dig a big hole in the back garden, then cook chicken and fish and stuff on a bed of charcoal embers covered with leaves.

Ken and his fellow islanders followed in the footsteps of local legends, like Laba and Tak, the boys who'd held off at least two hundred and fifty Communist insurgents at Mirbat in 'seventy-two with a twenty-five pounder, an

127

assault rifle and — because Tak had been shot in the shoulder — only three arms between them.

Laba had taken a round in the jaw early on, then one in the throat after fuck knows how many hours, which left Tak holding the fort. Neither of them got VCs because the Head Shed didn't want to go public on the Regiment being there, but Laba was still the only member of the Special Air Service to have had a statue dedicated to his memory.

Ken had enlisted in Nandi with a few of his mates and got the first plane to Heathrow. He'd kicked off his basic comms training near Salisbury, fallen for a local girl and still called it home forty-odd years later.

He had been to some places and done some things in the meantime, first with the Regiment and then on the Circuit. The Iranian Embassy balcony in 1980 was the most crowded piece of real-estate on earth, if you believed even half the people who claimed to have been on the team. Ken really had gone in through the front window, though he would never boast about it. He never boasted about anything else either, which was one of the reasons his and Jill's place was my next port of call. Another was that his and his nephew's names were on the list me and Trev had agreed by the dam.

I'd overnighted at the Hunter's Lodge on the outskirts of Wincanton, in return for a handful of Sniper One's notes. They'd given me a warm welcome in the bar, and apologized that the kitchen was closed. That wasn't a problem for me. I'd already stopped for a burger and Coke outside Chippenham and only needed a shit, shower and shave, followed by a good night's sleep.

★ ★ ★

The cathedral spire was better than satnav when you needed to find your way to Salisbury. At 123 metres it was the tallest in Britain, and had been for more than seven hundred and fifty years. I'd first seen it when I'd spent a few weeks at Larkhill Camp, up by Stonehenge, during my early days with the Green Army.

I followed the ring road and took the turning to the Culver Street multi-storey car park. I didn't want to leave the 911 anywhere near Ken and Jill's. I didn't think I'd been followed from Gloucestershire, but Salisbury was the next best thing to a garrison city, and if Trev was right about the CQB shit going all the way to the top, I didn't want to tempt Fate.

I swapped my Gore-Tex for my bomber jacket, made sure I was out of sight of the CCTV cameras, then slid the Browning into my belt and the spare mag into my left pocket. Another old habit: the weight of the mag made it easier to flick back that side of the jacket if you had to draw down — not that it would make much difference with a case of beer and a bouquet of flowers under my arm.

★ ★ ★

Ken claimed that Fiji wasn't as close to Paradise as the fantasy travel ads would have you think,

129

but every time I'd been to their neat terraced house on the south-eastern edge of the city I couldn't help wondering whether the old boy really didn't hanker for the white beaches and clear blue water of his birthplace. Whatever, as soon as you walked through Ken and Jill's front porch you knew this was home.

I'd called from the Hunter's Lodge so they were expecting me. I'd told Ken to fire up the earth oven and stand by for fresh supplies of beer — but to go easy on the kava. They came over a bit sensitive when you refused to get their ceremonial drink down your neck, but I'd explained that something was up, and I couldn't afford to shift onto Fiji time. I didn't add that I'd always hated the stuff, that it made my cheeks go numb and tasted like washing-up water.

Ken hadn't changed a bit. He still had a face like a bag of walnuts. He gave me the world's biggest man-hug before I'd even stepped into their hall. It reminded me that rugby football was as much their national sport as cannibalism, and that you sometimes couldn't tell between them.

Jill stood behind him, as trim and blonde as she'd always been. When I'd got my breath back I held out the Cobra to him and the flowers — tulips that were so deep a purple they were almost black — I'd brought with me from Wincanton to her. I presented them with an exaggerated bow. 'Your favourites, Mrs M. The same colour as your husband.'

That earned me a smile and a pantomime curtsy from Jill, and a thump on the back from

Ken that rearranged most of my internal organs. We moved through to the garden room, from where I could see that the man of the house had already got busy with a fork and spade.

I turned to him as we took our seats. 'I was joking about the earth oven.'

'Good. I was doing the border.' His weather-beaten face creased into a grin. 'I'm not going out there after dark in this weather, man. We'd freeze our coconuts off, eh? But we'll treat you to some quality Fijian MRE this evening, that's for sure. It's been a while . . .'

2

I spent the afternoon swapping war stories and banter with Ken, over biscuits and a brew, followed by another brew. And another.

We also touched on the news from the camp — or, rather, the fact that there wasn't any. Rumour control was rife with speculation, but there still seemed to be a lockdown on any reliable detail. DSF was having a serious sense-of-humour failure.

I didn't bring up the subject. He did.

When I made a stab at looking blank he rolled his eyes and grabbed my arm with his paw. 'Get real, man. I wasn't born yesterday, eh? You've been off the grid for God knows how long — in Moscow, the last I heard — and suddenly you're on our doorstep, minutes after some serious shit has happened behind the wire in H, involving Harry's boy . . . '

He let his words hang in the air between us.

'Also, we know you're not here for the *kava*, and you've got a pistol in your waistband . . . '

It was my turn to look embarrassed. 'Sorry, Ken. I didn't mean to treat you like an idiot. I'm just not sure who I can quiz about this.'

'No apology necessary, man.' He sat back and smiled his Zen smile. It reminded me why I'd always liked him, and why I was there. 'I'm flattered that you want to talk to me, eh? It means you still trust me, and trust is a big thing for people like us, especially at a time like this. It's a pity this new DSF doesn't seem to understand that.'

He took a long swig of his brew before continuing.

'But I also know it means you can't risk contacting any of your old mates on the inside, especially not the Head Shed, or your not-so-friendly friends at the Firm, because they stopped sending you Christmas cards way back. So that leaves us black fellas, eh?'

It wasn't really a question, but I answered it anyway. 'The white fellas are taking the piss big-time right now. This won't be the official version, but one of them took off Trev's head with a Dragunov in the Black Mountains two days ago, then tried to do the same to me.'

'Did he succeed?'

'Funny.' I knew Ken was as keen not to think about what had happened to Trev's head as I was. 'He got close. But he won't be sending any more Christmas cards either.'

His eyes narrowed and he nodded slowly. 'Like I said, man, none of us believes in coincidences.' He paused. 'And what I'm going to tell you isn't one either. Fred's in town. We've asked him to join us, eh?'

Ken may have looked like a giant teddy bear, but he was still switched on. Fred was his nephew, currently at Credenhill, and a key member of what the lads now called Fiji.com. He was also high on the list of people I needed to speak to.

3

Fred Marabula arrived in time for the first beer of the evening. He was a smoother, more aerodynamic version of his uncle, with a finely tuned engine and go-faster stripes. His hair was slicked back and shiny, and his jawline was sharply chiselled, but there was also something charmingly old-fashioned about him. He even called me 'sir' a few times, though I told him not to.

Fred was content to swap small-talk for as long as we were in the mood, while one Fijian delicacy after another arrived at the table for dinner. I'd never met him before, but his reputation travelled before him, and not only because Ken was his number-one fan.

From the moment he'd arrived in the UK, Fred seemed destined for great things. Before we could blink, he'd got himself a degree in politics, philosophy and economics and played fly-half for the Scots Guards. He passed Selection the same year as Sam. They'd both spent six months in Afghan with B Squadron last year.

I asked him how well they knew each other.

He didn't answer immediately. 'As you don't need me to tell you, sir, we depend on each other completely in the battle space. But the truth is we're not that close. Sam spent most of his time with Scott Braxton and the boss, Guy Chastain, especially after Kajaki. We used to call them the Three Amigos.'

At first glance, Fred seemed to have been less affected by the Afghan experience than Harry's boy. As the evening drew on, though, I began to realize that was only skin deep. He didn't turn into a rug-chewing maniac, but once we'd dispensed with the usual Camp Bastion banter and I asked him what had rattled Sam so badly, a haunted look came into his eyes.

'Kajaki?'

He nodded. 'You know how important that installation is. The livelihood of the surrounding area depends on it.'

'What happened?'

'It started as a pretty routine night op. The engineering crew were due in before first light to complete maintenance work on one of the dam turbines.

'The Taliban were well aware that it had to be fixed at some point, and we'd heard they were aiming to take the repair team on once it was in place. Two Rifles were tasked to secure the high ground before the boiler suits arrived with a platoon-strength escort to get to grips with the hardware.

'Then Intelligence got wind of a couple of big Taliban players planning to be there to co-ordinate the attack. It was a golden opportunity for us to cut off two of the serpent's heads with one blow, so we were tasked to be at the dam six hours ahead of the infantry. The plan was to be there in plenty of time before the players appeared, then ID and lift them.'

'How many of you?'

'One eight-man patrol. Guy was in charge.'

135

'Sam and Scott were on the team?'

'Sure.' His expression clouded. 'And Chris Matlock.'

Chris, who had died doing what he loved . . .

I was suddenly aware that Ken and Fred were both looking at me slightly strangely. I must have spoken aloud. 'What went wrong?'

There was a long silence.

'Everything.'

4

'The Chinook dropped us ten Ks away from our target and we tabbed in at last light. You know what it's like up there. Whoever has control of the high ground is king, especially around the mouth of the dam, and we wanted to be dug in well before the players showed up.'

I could tell from Fred's body language that a part of him was already back there.

'Some hope. The Taliban were already waiting, precisely where we wanted to be. God knows how many of them. We started taking fire seconds after we got in the zone.

'We knew we wouldn't get anywhere near the players without top cover, so we took cover beneath an outcrop, Guy got onto the task commander back at Bastion, and he sent in the Apaches. Then we split into two groups, to work our way around each flank in time to cut off their escape.'

He leaned back and massaged his right knee.

'It was never going to be easy fighting our way uphill.'

I nodded. It never is.

'It was almost vertical in places. We should have brought belaying ropes and crampons. We were in our regular kit, hanging on with our toecaps and our fingernails. But by then we were committed.

'My group managed to stay together. Guy's . . .' Fred concentrated hard on ripping the lid off another bottle of Cobra. He wasn't thirsty. He just needed to buy himself some time. 'Guy's team weren't so lucky.'

He gripped the beer bottle but rotated it on its base instead of raising it to his lips. 'They found their way into a gully. Like a lift shaft, in cover, all the way to the top. They piled up it, thinking all their Christmases had come at once.

'When we heard the Apaches, we thought we were back in the driving seat. They started to hose down the high ground and the Taliban scattered. The four of us had skirted around the back of their position, as we'd planned, and were laying down some fire . . . ' He closed his fingers around the neck of his bottle like he was trying to throttle it. 'Then we heard Chris lose his footing over the PRR . . . '

Chris Matlock had been bringing up the rear. Maybe he got careless. They heard him say, 'Fuck,' then a scrabbling sound, then nothing. They reckoned that either his headset had become disconnected or his radio had been shunted off his body armour as he bounced back down the mountain.

'He must have fallen thirty metres, Nick, maybe more. The Amigos couldn't call down to him without giving away their position, and he couldn't call up.'

'Sam went after him. But he wasn't quick enough. The Taliban got there first. At least a dozen of them, Sam told us. All over Chris, like maggots. And they carried him off. He didn't even fire a round. He must have damaged himself or got separated from his weapon on the way down as well.'

138

Fred went silent again, staring right through me. Ken moved in closer to him and clapped a party-size arm around his shoulders. After a moment, he continued.

'The Taliban kicked off two or three RPGs at the Apaches and they lifted away. The helis with the bayonets weren't due to show up for another couple of hours. Everything went quiet.'

They could see movement below them through their NVGs, but couldn't be certain where they'd taken him. The ground dropped away in a series of terraces. They headed back downhill, away from the reservoir. But the main enemy force had dug themselves in a couple of hundred or so further on, and had no intention of letting Fred's lot get any closer.

They knew that the Taliban were up to something, but every time they raised their heads, they got brassed up. The Three Amigos were in a similar position, five hundred further along the bank of the reservoir.

Then the screaming began.

First it carried to our guys through the night. Then Chris's captors got his PRR working again and fed it straight into their heads.

Fred swallowed hard. 'I've never heard a sound like it. I hope I never will again. His cries drilled into my soul. But his whimpers were almost worse. His cries were filled with pain, but also defiance. The whimpers were filled with desperation, then despair.

'About fifteen minutes in he was pleading with them to end it.'

The distress on Ken's face was something I'd

never seen before. He was hurting more for Fred than he ever would have done for himself.

'We finally hooked up with the Amigos at first light, when the Two Rifles helis arrived. The screams had stopped well before then, and the enemy melted away.'

They made their way down, keeping eyes on the ground for booby-traps and on the hill for snipers. There was a massive overhang at the bottom of the escarpment. Beneath it, they found Chris's body nailed to a wooden cross. Not a Jesus-type cross — a diagonal cross, so his arms and legs were splayed.

Fred sucked a lungful of air through his nose, trying to keep the memory at bay. Then he focused on me again. 'You know the colour of that terrain, Nick? The deepest rusty red, the colour of blood. It was like every drop of Chris's blood had been soaked up by the Helmand dust. His flesh was like raw chicken meat . . . '

I knew what was coming.

'Those fuckers had skinned him alive.'

Ken tightened his grip on the boy as his shoulders started to heave. Fred chewed on his upper lip and started to shake his head, as if he could shake away the images that had been seared into his mind.

It wasn't working.

'Jesus Christ, Nick . . . Those bastards had even peeled off his eyelids.'

5

I got up and went outside. He needed some space. They both did.

My breath billowed in the cold night air and the frosted grass crunched beneath my feet.

I watched Ken and Fred through the window. They weren't talking much. There wasn't much to say. Jill came through with a big pot of coffee and gave her nephew a hug. I left them alone for another quarter of an hour or so before going back to my seat.

'Sorry, Nick . . .' For the first time since he'd arrived, Fred couldn't quite meet my eye.

I waved it aside. It was time to bin the emotional shit. 'I've only really kept track of Sam's career through Trev, who never claimed to be the world's most objective judge . . .'

Fred smiled, relieved to have escaped Kajaki. 'Sam thought the world of you.'

I frowned. 'We hardly knew each other, mate . . .'

Ken sparked up: 'But you have history, man. Harry passed away when Sam was only a kid, but he used to talk about you all the time, eh? Said he wouldn't have made it through Iraq without you.'

Fred chipped in again: 'Sam takes you people very seriously, you must know that. But it's not all good. You cast a long shadow. A lot to live up to. Guy felt the same way. His dad set the bar

141

really high. He never stopped beating himself up about it.'

I could imagine that. The colonel never asked anyone to do something he wasn't prepared to do himself, but being his son couldn't have been easy. 'You served with him, didn't you, Ken?'

'Sure I did. Sierra Leone, Iraq, Bosnia, you name it. Top man.'

I'd first bumped into Chastain in Northern Ireland. We were never going to be best mates, but that was one of the things I liked about him. Being everybody's friend wasn't a CO's job. Standing by his men was, and he never let us down. It didn't matter where — under fire, undercover, back at base, in a hospital bed: whenever the shit hit the fan, he was there for us. And he didn't mind who he pissed off in Whitehall, which must have been the reason he never climbed any further up the greasy pole.

He also knew more about classic and asymmetrical strategy than anyone else I've met. And it didn't matter which theatre you picked, from the Battle of Hastings onwards, it turned out to be Chastain's special subject on *Mastermind*. I guessed that must have made things even more difficult for Guy. He didn't just have the shadow of his father's achievements hanging over him but a thousand years of military history as well.

It seemed like a good moment to pay a visit to the CQB Rooms. I fixed Fred in my sights. 'Mate, is it possible Scott's death had anything to do with what happened at Kajaki? I mean, did Sam take his eye off the ball? I'm getting the impression that he was a bit of a mess . . . '

Fred ran his fingers through his very shiny hair. 'The truth is we were all pretty shaken. I still hear Chris's cries in the night. I try and block my ears, but it makes no difference. I guess Sam and the Amigos felt that to the power of ten. It doesn't matter what you tell yourself, if you're that close, the same questions keep rattling around in your head. Could I have saved my friend? What if I'd reacted quicker? Maybe got to him before the Taliban did?

'But if you're asking me if Sam had lost the plot so badly that he shot one of his best mates during training, the answer is absolutely not. They were so close they were almost telepathic.

'And, by the way, Sam never had negligent discharge in his life.'

'Were you in the room when it happened?'

'No.' His jaw clenched. 'But I'm pretty sure Sam wasn't either.'

6

Fred was i/c Red Team, rehearsing a heli insertion — four of them fast roping from a Eurocopter above the CQB Rooms. Sam was Blue Team's commander, coming in via the rear. Scott was part of the crew already inside; some were playing the hostage role, some were kidnappers.

The whole of B Squadron were completely mystified about what happened next. Even the squadron sergeant major running the exercise couldn't make any sense of it. The only thing they knew for certain was that Scott had taken a round in the back of the head.

'Where did they find his body?'

'Nobody seems to know that either. But one of the rumours is that he was tied to a chair.'

'What did the SSM say?'

'Jack Grant? I know he was gutted. But apparently no wiser than anyone else.'

I'd never met Jack, but I knew he was old school. The word was that he'd keep flying the flag long after the flagpole had been blown to matchwood.

'Do you think he'd fill in some of the gaps, if he was asked the right questions? Or is he keeping his mouth zipped now, like everyone else?'

Fred lifted his hands, palms upwards. 'He's one of DSF's blue-eyed boys, so I wouldn't count on it. And, anyway, he's back in Afghan.'

'Was that always the plan?'

'No. He's on the same rotation as the rest of us. Something came up.'

I bet it did. 'Bastion?'

'Nobody knows.'

'Have Sam's defence team done the rounds yet?'

Fred shook his head. 'You know how long these things take.'

I did. Especially when no one at the top of the shit heap really wanted to hear the answers to some pretty basic questions. And the ones who knew the answers were prepared to go to any lengths to stop those questions being asked.

Before leaving, I asked him if he'd been present at the action for which Guy Chastain was awarded his VC. He hadn't. He'd taken a round in the leg a couple of days after the Kajaki incident. It had become badly infected, and he'd been casevaced back to the UK. He rubbed it again now. It still gave him shit when the atmospheric pressure changed.

Ken saw me to the front door and gave me another man-hug.

I waved a hand back in the direction of the garden room. 'He's a good lad, Fred is. No wonder you're proud.'

'The best, eh?'

'Seeing you together makes me wonder why you guys never had any kids of your own . . . ' As soon as I'd said it, I wished that I hadn't.

His walnut face crinkled into that familiar grin. 'Who says I didn't, eh? You know us Fijian

145

boys . . . ' Then a faraway look came into his eyes. 'I'd have loved a whole rugby team, man. But I loved Jill more. And . . . well, sometimes these things don't work out the way you planned, eh?'

We stood on the threshold, slightly awkwardly, for a moment longer.

'How about you, Nick?'

I shrugged. 'Like you said, Ken, sometimes these things don't work out the way you planned.'

7

Fleet Services, Hampshire

Saturday, 28 January
13.03 hrs

I thought that taking the scenic route out of Salisbury would probably be an error, even before pointing the 911 north up the A360, but sometimes you just had to put these things to the test. And I wanted to check out the lie of the land around Larkhill and Barford. Time spent on reconnaissance was seldom wasted.

I first noticed the gunmetal-grey Mondeo, one up, when I turned onto the A338 at Shipton Bellinger. I couldn't get a clear picture of the driver, but got a glimpse of Boris Johnson hair. He kept his distance, three or four vehicles behind me, but made the mistake of doing so with unnatural consistency. I kept at a steady sixty along the Thruxton stretch, which must have pissed off everyone except Eddie Stobart's boys, then put my foot down by the Andover turning.

I kept a careful lookout for unmarked police cars to begin with, then just sat back and enjoyed the power of the machine, the growl of the engine, the fact that it did everything I told it to without arguing about it.

When the Mondeo was still in sight at Popham

147

I was pretty sure it was no coincidence. I hung a left past the Basingstoke crematorium and mooched around for a while in the Festival Place shopping centre. I wanted to carry on travelling light, so I bought myself a daysack without holes in it and a change of shirt, socks and boxers.

Back in the driving seat, I slid the Browning from my waistband and wedged it under my right thigh, grip outwards. The Mondeo popped into my rear-view again at Junction 5 on the M3. I was now absolutely certain he wasn't simply a fellow traveller on his way to London for dinner and a show.

When I pulled off the motorway at Fleet Services, I knew it was time to return the Porsche to Father Gerard until this shit was over. I was going to miss it, but I didn't think he'd mind: it was still ten weeks until the end of the National Hunt Season.

The Mondeo found a space on the far side of the parking area. The driver didn't get out. I waited five minutes before heading inside to the Gents. When I emerged via Waitrose after a decent interval with a bunch of bananas and a bottle of designer water, his wagon was empty.

I wandered across to the nearest refuse bin, got the water down my neck, then threw away the bottle and the bag. Keeping eyes on the entrance to the shops, I peeled three bananas and ate one. No one seemed to be taking a special interest in me, but I didn't expect my new best mate to be standing in the doorway with a set of binoculars.

On my way back to the 911, I bent down and

rammed the other two bananas as far as I could up the Mondeo's exhaust. It had been our favourite party trick since a bunch of us had seen *Beverly Hills Cop* during our early days in the Regiment, and it still cracked me up all these years later. Unless he was a big Eddie Murphy fan, it would take him a while to work out why the Ford's ignition system was suddenly letting him down.

8

I made it to the Farnborough exit without my shadow reappearing, and took off cross-country, steering clear of the military choke-points clustered around Aldershot.

I took far too long to get to the Church of the Most Holy Redeemer, but I wanted to try to avoid leaving Father Gerard with any unwanted visitors. I also needed to find a choggy shop in a backstreet in Kingston.

I dipped into the first one I came to. The lads who ran it were big fans of flickering neon and sold everything from dodgy DVDs to Elvis costumes and previously enjoyed satnavs. I spent the rest of Sniper One's hard-earned cash and some of my own on four second-hand unlocked Nokias.

Three were for me and one was the late Christmas present I'd promised Father Mart. I bunged fifty quid on each of the Lebara pay-as-you-go SIM cards.

The software at GCHQ had been designed to track who was contacting whom rather than the content of their messages, first off, so text traffic on these gizmos would have a good chance of staying under the radar as long as we didn't communicate anything that set their alarm bells ringing.

9

Father G was en route from Lingfield to Saturday-evening mass, but still managed to give me the impression he had all the time in the world.

He got even more cheerful when I suggested that he swapped the 911 for his Skoda instead of hiding it away in his lock-up, and threw open the boot of his wagon so I could transfer my kit. I asked if he wanted to remove the rosary beads hanging from his rear-view. He shook his head. He had a feeling I could use the Good Lord's help and, anyway, he had a spare.

Before we said our goodbyes I gave him one of the Nokias and asked him to get it to Father Mart ASAP. In return, he gave me the name and address of a friendly B-and-B.

On the way there I made a rare sighting of a public phone box. I didn't want to use and bin one of my spare mobiles, so I filled the slot with coins and called Cyprus. An old mate of mine who'd retired from the Green Army had managed to swing a civvy admin job for himself at RAF Akrotiri. It was Bob's way of living the dream.

'Beats a wet Saturday night in Salisbury, Nick, I kid you not,' he'd told me, the last time we'd shared a brew. 'Sure, I'm chained to a keyboard or buried in a filing cabinet from nine to five every weekday, but the rest of the time it's sun, sea and quite a lot of . . . ' He'd licked his lips. 'If you take my meaning. You know the island's patron is Aphrodite, the Greek goddess of love and beauty?'

He'd obviously read the brochures. And since he looked like a greyer, more spiky-haired version of Barry Manilow, I reckoned he'd be like a pig in shit there.

Bob picked up on the third ring, so I guessed it was still too early in the tourist season for his escort duties to have kicked in big-time.

Troops returning from Afghan stopped by the base for four days' decompression. Regiment lads didn't stay as long as the rest, but I thought it might be worth asking Bob to keep an eye out for Jack Grant. I told him I'd connect from time to time and asked him to keep his mouth shut.

He knew me well enough not to ask why.

PART FIVE

1

During two separate ambushes in Al-Amarah in 2004, Private Johnson Beharry saved the lives of at least thirty comrades while being hosed down by a blizzard of incoming AK-47 rounds and RPGs, one of which detonated on the hatch cover of his Warrior, seven inches from the front of his head.

When he was awarded the Victoria Cross for 'extreme gallantry and unquestioned valour' the following year, he didn't have a clue what it meant. Mind you, he had an excuse. He'd spent most of his life up a hill with his nan in the far north of Grenada. Bermondsey was only a stone's throw from the Imperial War Museum, and when I was busy nicking trainers off the back of other people's barrows down there, I'd never heard of the VC either.

Maybe it was because I hadn't seen *Zulu* as a kid. It wasn't until much later that I soaked up the story of how eleven were won during the course of one engagement at Rorke's Drift. Maybe it was because they've only handed out a few more than that in total since the Second World War — Beharry was the first living recipient in nearly forty years. Whatever, although I quite fancied the idea of being saluted by the chief of the General Staff if I passed him on the square, I'd never fantasized about winning one myself.

155

Most other soldiers I knew felt the same way. And the few times we came across someone with VCs in their eyes, we tried to stay out of their way. Self-sacrifice is one of the boxes you have to tick, and that's not always healthy. You don't even get on the shortlist, these days, unless you've had at least a 97 per cent chance of not surviving the action, and some commentators believed that it should only be awarded posthumously.

It wasn't always like that. When they first started awarding them during the Crimean War, Queen Vic wouldn't pin one on your chest unless you were still around to tell the story.

The VC and GC Association looked after the interests of the winners, past and present. They nurtured the handful of survivors, making sure the old ones got to their reunions and the young ones didn't end up folding themselves inside bits of cardboard in doorways off the Strand. They also protected the memories of the dead.

The Association didn't always see eye to eye with the MoD, but its HQ overlooked the Horse Guards Parade ground on one side and Whitehall on the other — which was why I wasn't about to swing by their offices on Monday morning. I never felt completely comfortable in the corridors of power at the best of times, and this wasn't the best of times.

Besides, I thought I might have another way of finding out some stuff I needed to know.

2

I'd first worked with Maggie in Derry in the late eighties. I'd been press-ganged into 14th Intelligence Company — which we called the Det — and she'd been seconded from the Firm (MI5). It hadn't been a career choice for either of us, but we both seemed to thrive in an environment where we had to be switched on 24/7.

I used to call her Moneypenny because she was a bit starchy on the outside but kind of sexy too — not that any of us lads with overly long sideburns and five days' stubble got to put that to the test. She christened me Bag O'Shite. It wasn't until we had a PIRA active-service unit under surveillance past dark o'clock one night that I got to see her in action.

We'd pinged a bomb factory in a dilapidated house not too far away from the Holy Child Primary School. The players had been mixing low-explosive cocktails in an industrial coffee grinder and had an arms cache in the back garden. Our job wasn't to pile in and turn the place over: it was to keep an eye on things until we could put away as many of them as possible.

We were walking up an alleyway that ran along the back of two rows of terraces between Bogside and the Creggan with a pocketful of miniature transmitters. The plan was to secrete the devices inside the PIRA weapons and see where they ended up. Our lords and masters put ops like this under the heading of 'technical attacks'; we called it jarking. The opposition were wising up to it, but we still got a good few results.

The rain hung in the air around us and the alleyway stank of piss. Only one street lamp in five seemed to work, but that was enough to make the garbage bags glisten and pick out the rats crawling over them. It was also enough for the shadows of the four hooded figures that suddenly appeared behind us to dance along the slimy breezeblock walls that hemmed us in. The players were checking us out.

Maggie and I both had 9mm shorts tucked into our waistbands, but that didn't give us an edge; if we drew down, we were compromised big-time.

I ran through our options. There weren't many, and run like fuck was shaping up to be my favourite. Maggie had other ideas. She grabbed my arm with her right hand and gripped the very greasy hair at the back of my neck with her left. She pushed herself against me.

Leaving my right arm free to draw down if her diversion didn't work, she raised her lips to mine and kissed me long and hard.

I stopped in my tracks. Our shadows did too.

Then she turned back towards them and unleashed an Ulster-accented fusillade that can't have been on the syllabus at Cheltenham Ladies College. 'What the fock are youse pervs looking at? Can't a girl have a moment to herself in this focking town?'

They spun on their heels and slouched back

the way they'd come. One of them kicked a can along the path in front of him so we knew he had more important things than shagging on his mind.

I breathed out slowly and grinned. 'So, where were we, Moneypenny?'

She brushed my arm aside and gave me a bollock-shrivelling glare. 'Don't get any ideas, dickhead. That was for their benefit, not yours.'

Nothing ever happened between us, either then or in the years that followed, but later the same evening she gave me the kind of smile that made me think it might still be on the cards. 'You know what 'Creggan' means, Bag O'Shite? It means 'stony place'. Isn't that fun?'

3

South London

Sunday, 29 January
12.00 hrs

Maggie binned the security services at the end of our Derry tour and joined an NGO — Save the Children or Oxfam or something like that. Then a handful of years ago she'd got a job with the secretary of the VC and GC Association. She told me she wanted to spend some time in the world as it should be: she'd got a bit tired of the way it actually was.

'A world full of dead medal winners?'

She gave me an old-fashioned look. 'You're smarter than that, Bag O'Shite. I mean a world in which people confronted by the most testing of circumstances teach the rest of us how to behave, a world where generosity of spirit is the keynote.'

I wasn't as smart as she seemed to think I was, but I liked her take on courage. I didn't really believe it, but I liked it.

That exchange ran through my mind as I sat in the Skoda not far from Denmark Hill, with eyes on the small but perfectly formed semi she shared with two Persian cats. The house had been empty when I arrived, but I'd seen breakfast stuff on the table by the window in her

160

kitchen/diner and her bicycle was missing, so I reckoned she hadn't disappeared for a weekend in the country. And if she had, so what? I'd just wait out.

Cornell's Professor James Maas coined the term 'power nap' in the nineties, but every squaddie since the dawn of time has known that getting your head down for anywhere between six and thirty minutes gives you optimum battery recharge without the disadvantage of sleep inertia. The trick is not to get caught doing it on stag.

I wasn't sure whether the sudden shift in the air molecules inside the car had woken me, or the coldness of the muzzle against the soft skin below my ear. Either way, I needed to sharpen up my act. I'd messed around with my body clock a fair amount in the last week or so, but that was no excuse: it was the story of my life.

I stole a glance in the rear-view, but whoever was behind me had taken care to stay in the blind spot. I eased my right palm in the direction of the pistol grip.

'Raise both hands very slowly and place them on top of your steering wheel. Do not make any attempt to reach for the Browning beneath your thigh.'

The voice was low, but crisp and authoritative. I did exactly what it told me to.

4

'I know you can't teach old dogs new tricks, Bag O'Shite, but when you can't even get the old tricks right any more, I'd say it's time to start looking for alternative employment.'

Maggie removed the mouth of her Coke bottle from my neck.

'Let's do us both a favour and get you off the streets. Fancy a brew? You look as though you could use a shot or two of caffeine. Unless you'd prefer to stay out here and say a few Hail Marys instead.' She gestured at the rosary beads swinging gently from the rear-view.

I replaced the Browning in my waistband and exited Father Gerard's wagon. 'I thought you'd never ask, Moneypenny. As long as it's proper builders' tea. I don't want any of that fruit-flavoured shit you posh birds go for.'

Maggie had a hint of grey around the temples but looked as good as she had in Derry. She squeezed my arm as she steered me across the street. 'Don't worry, Stone. Your secret's safe with me.'

We went a couple of paces further.

'Nice car, by the way . . . ' She could no longer stop herself snorting with laughter.

★   ★   ★

The cats weren't in any hurry to make me feel at home. Maybe they'd seen me asleep at the wheel

162

as well. The expression in their cool green eyes made it clear that, as far as they were concerned, my stay was very, very temporary.

Maggie's place was filled with fascinating stuff. Leather-bound books spilled off her shelves. Her walls were covered with antique prints of mosques and deserts and men who looked like Lawrence of Arabia. A curved Omani ceremonial dagger with a jewelled silver hilt hung beside a framed service sheet from the ceremony at Westminster Abbey commemorating the 150th anniversary of the Victoria Cross. When I leaned in closer I saw that the surviving recipients had signed it for her.

She flicked on the kettle and dug around in the fridge. 'I'm afraid I can't stretch to spicy chicken kebabs without a bit of warning, but a club sandwich wouldn't be out of the question.'

I helped her clear the breakfast things from the table I'd pinged earlier and sat down.

She ate with the precision she brought to everything else I'd seen her do. I wolfed my plateful of food, got some of the brew down my neck and spent a minute or two fiddling with the handle of my mug.

When I looked up, Maggie was giving me the same eyebrow treatment that Grace Nichol had when I was trying to convince her that my visit to Ella's surgery was a complete coincidence.

She wiped her mouth with a linen napkin. 'So what's up, Stone? Social calls never used to be your thing, did they? Unless you were looking for a shag or a boys' night out.'

I guessed I'd always been pretty transparent to

163

clever women, and perhaps not so clever ones as well. The thought occurred to me that Anna would have liked Maggie as much as I did, and it was one of the things that made me smile.

I gave her a boiled-down version of my quest. It wasn't quite the truth, but it wasn't packed with outright lies either. And I didn't feel the need to tell her what had happened to me and Trev over the border.

Maggie remembered Harry from one of those boys' nights out in H, but hadn't made the connection between him and Sam. I kicked off by admitting that I hadn't kept as much of an eye on the boy as I should have done, for Harry's sake, and was doing my best to make up for that now.

'I know the PTSD label is being slapped on every veteran these days, but the more I hear about what these three kids went through on that last tour of Afghan, the more it seems like that's what we're talking about here. You know about Chris Matlock?'

She nodded sadly. 'They're not spreading it about, obviously, but Mickey Chastain told me.'

'Sounds like the Kajaki scars ran deeper than anyone realized. I can't help wondering whether Guy's death tipped Sam and Scott right over the edge. I've read the citation, but those things only ever give us the headlines . . . '

She recharged the teapot and spent a moment or two deciding where to begin.

'An int source on the ground told them that there was a humongous subterranean arms cache in a fortified Taliban position north of Koshtay.

164

RPGs, SAM-7s, IEDs, anti-tank rounds, the lot. As you know, they'd stop at nothing to take out an Apache or a Chinook, and there was enough there to decimate an entire squadron.

'The ordnance was too deep for a surgical strike from the air, so Guy Chastain was tasked with locating and destroying it, with a 40 Commando platoon in support. He selected two other boys in black to go with him.'

'Sam Callard and Scott Braxton . . . '

Maggie dipped her head. 'The target was an old frontier post . . . ' She told me the plan had been to approach it from the river, with an Apache two-ship from 656 Squadron providing top cover. A two-hundred-metre stretch of open ground on a fairly sharp incline separated the first line of defence — a metre-thick mud and stone wall — from the water. The Apaches' first task was to blow a hole in it, then give the fort itself the same treatment.

The good news was that the helis' scanning equipment had picked up the heat-signatures of a fairly tight defending force — twenty or twenty-five bodies max. The bad news came later. The network of tunnels beneath the Taliban position didn't only contain arms and ammunition. There were another hundred or more insurgents down there too, waiting for our people to land in their laps.

5

The initial insertion took far longer than anyone had bargained for, and shortly after they'd given each of the walls a dose of Hellfire, the helis had had to lift off back to Bastion with some kind of malfunction. The invading force were without top cover for no more than twenty minutes, but twenty minutes is time enough for the Mother of all Clusterfucks.

Sam and Scott were first through the inner breach, which meant that they had a ringside seat as the Taliban they hadn't known about began to emerge from their wormholes. They called in a contact report to the marines behind them. All well and good, but it meant that our lads were on their own in there, counting the nanoseconds before they'd need to call on Father Mart to administer Last Rites.

Guy wasn't going to let that happen. He led a 40 Commando detachment through the first wall and told them to spread out left and right, hosing down the enemy as they went. Then he extracted his mates under covering fire.

Maggie needed a breather at this point too. I wasn't surprised. She described the action like she was there. She stood up and took a turn around the workbench. I took another swig of my brew and waited for her to continue.

Eventually she came back and sat down beside me.

I gave her a gentle nudge. 'It's what happened next that I'm not at all clear about.'

She gave a deep sigh and looked away. When she turned back I could see tears in her eyes. 'Guy didn't just save their lives. He remained determined to complete the mission. And he did.'

I shut up now. She really didn't need me on her case.

'The drone footage tells us it was five metres or so from the inner wall to the entrance that led to the cache, through a building that looked like a small bunker, and down a thirty-foot shaft. After they'd discovered the scale of the enemy defence, there was only going to be one way to destroy it. And that was the way Guy chose.'

It must have been a bit like the shell from the *Bismarck* that had sunk HMS *Hood* in 1941: straight down the funnel and into the magazine, with only three survivors. Except it wasn't a shell, it was an SAS captain taking a nosedive with an HE grenade in each hand.

Fuck knows how he made it to the cover of the bunker. Maggie said the drone footage became pretty surreal after he'd got Sam and Scott off the hook, and looked more like a Schwarzenegger movie than real-life.

The silence in her kitchen was so thick at that point you could have cut it with a knife. Even the cats had caught the vibe and stopped complaining about my invasion of their personal space.

I had the feeling that the same thought was crossing both our minds: that the line dividing a truly selfless, heroic sacrifice and the last desperate act of a man who can't live with the legacy of a previous mission was sometimes incredibly thin.

6

It took a while for Maggie to sort herself out.

She disappeared to the bathroom to blow her nose and, by the sound of it, to splash her face. She looked like shit when she came back, but her eyes had stopped leaking by the time she'd pulled a bottle of wine from the fridge.

We waffled on about the Det and which joints used to do the best pizzas and kebabs in Derry. I asked her why we hadn't ever quite got it together — whether she had a rule about not shagging guys she was working with. She laughed and told me, no, she had a rule about not shagging guys whose sideburns were bigger than their IQ. Fair one. I knew I'd been pushing my luck.

She told me about a few of her NGO experiences in Sudan, Sierra Leone and Palestine, and some VC stuff I hadn't heard.

Eric Wilson's story was one of her favourites. He had been awarded the medal posthumously in 1940 for defending a hill in Somaliland for forty-eight hours after failing to hear the signal to withdraw. When the Italians finally overran his position all they found was a pile of dead bodies — a handful of soldiers from the local Camel Corps, their British officer and his pet terrier. Then one of them discovered that the officer was still breathing. Two months later, after a spell at an enemy field hospital, Captain Wilson was

169

spotted in a PoW camp in Eritrea, and lived on very happily for a further sixty-eight years.

I refilled both our glasses, even though I hadn't attacked mine as hard as she'd attacked hers.

'You mentioned Mickey Chastain . . . ' We'd never been on first-name terms, so it came out sounding a bit bone. 'How's he coping?'

'He's devastated, of course. Guy was their only child. But incredibly proud too, and I guess that's what keeps him going when he's not being the world's policeman. I've spent quite a bit of time with him on this statue business.'

I paused. 'I'm not sure about the statue. But maybe that's because I'd spend every minute of every day tracking down the men who killed my son, rather than trying to turn him into a museum exhibit.'

'I completely understand why he's so deter-mined to push it through, despite getting so much stick from the old guard.' She frowned. 'But I've got to admit, I'm in two minds too. The VCs *are* a special breed. I'm in no doubt about that. And yet, as Queen Victoria said, 'All my soldiers are brave.''

I'd always thought that was a very nice thing to say, even though it was complete bollocks. Some soldiers are brave. Some aren't. And some are complete shitheads. Just like everyone else on the planet.

We both looked down into our glasses. I mentioned the CQB mess, and wondered how far she thought DSF and his crew would be prepared to go to keep it under wraps.

She didn't have to give it much thought. 'Their default position is to keep secret things secret, needless to say, now more than ever, as far as the new regime is concerned. And as the different elements of the security services find themselves in competition with each other for a share of the dwindling defence budget, every visible sign of weakness is a really big issue.'

'So?'

'So I'd say that they'd do whatever it takes.'

I didn't ask whether she thought that might include sending a gun for hire across the Black Mountains to drop an ex-member of the Regiment.

I stayed long enough to watch her finish the wine, then the cats got their wish.

She gave me a quick kiss on my cheek before I opened the front door. 'So . . . what next, Bag O'Shite?'

'I reckon I need to get your mate Mickey onside. Harry's boy could use some help from the grown-ups.'

'I think you'll find he's gone to sort out Syria. So good luck there . . . '

PART SIX

PART SIX

1

Tower Bridge, London

Monday, 30 January
09.00 hrs

Astra had only been in business for a little over a decade, but it was already up there with the big boys. With shiny glass and steel offices in the City of London, Washington, Hong Kong, Dubai, San Francisco, Mexico City, Sydney and probably Beijing, for all I knew, they covered every part of the waterfront, from BGing to cyber security, and boasted a list of government contracts that must have really pissed off the competition.

When Chastain had finally binned the military, mostly as a protest against the MoD's failure to give due care to the physically and psychologically wounded members of his regiment — but more than likely with a helping hand between his shoulder-blades — he'd hooked up with a mate from the State Department. The maverick tendencies that had hampered his progress on the inside became a positive advantage at a 'safe' distance, and there wasn't a door the two of them couldn't open in the Anglo-American Military-Industrial Complex.

Risk mitigation was the name of their game, and raw courage their stock in trade, so I guessed that Guy's VC wasn't going to do them any harm at all. Even if it was only half a step away from a kamikaze mission, it would supply Astra with all the right kind of headlines for years to come.

I called their London office on the first of my new Nokias from a concrete bench overlooking the Thames by Tower Bridge, and asked to be put through to the colonel. Maggie hadn't been wrong: an alarmingly crisp and efficient executive assistant told me that he was currently away on business, but expected back towards the end of the week. Could I leave my name and number? I told her it wasn't urgent, and I'd get back to him later.

I sparked up the other one, my hotline to Father Mart, and the message icon flashed almost immediately. It was clearly going to take him a bit of time to master the art of predictive text, but he'd managed to send two sets of contact details: the major in charge of the Article 32 investigation, and Sam's defence counsel.

I decided to give the major a miss. There was no way the court-martial staffers would invite me in for a cosy chat. But I needed to connect with Sam's barrister. I swapped Nokias again, rang his number and told the clerk who picked up that my name was Nick Jones, and Father Martyn had encouraged me to call. We fixed an appointment at his Inner Temple chambers for later in the afternoon, 'after Mr Blackwood has concluded his day in court'.

I wandered over to the parapet and watched the froth riding on the dark currents as they swirled beneath me. HMS *Belfast* sat at anchor to my half-left, and the Tower of London stood to attention straight ahead, surrounded by cranes tasked with filling every spare inch of space around it with riverside apartments for offshore investors who didn't care about the view.

I wasn't far from the point where the headless torso of a Nigerian kid had been spotted floating in the water shortly after the 9/11 attacks in 2001. The police had never nailed his killers, even though they found out exactly where the little boy had come from, and the route he'd taken from Benin City, via Hamburg, to London. They also knew he'd been sliced up in Lewisham as a sacrificial offering to a Yoruban river god, whose protection was needed for a monster people — and drug-trafficking opera-tion.

They'd released the photos of the victim — bright eyes, bemused smile — quite recently. Since becoming a dad myself I'd found that kind of image increasingly difficult to delete from the data base inside my head.

I'd got a room at the back of the Premier Inn on Tower Bridge Road. It had a car park of its own, but I liked to keep my options open, so left the Skoda in the underground complex at Butler's Wharf.

This part of Bermondsey had been my adventure playground as a kid. I'd lived in a council block thrown up after the war on the Tabard Estate, about ten minutes west of Tower Bridge Road, between Guy's Hospital and the Elephant and Castle.

Demolition was the Luftwaffe's favourite job, so there had been plenty of vacant sites around there when I was growing up, and it was still a maze of newly restored, half-built and terminally dilapidated buildings. It was a pig's breakfast of a place, and I loved every inch of it.

I went to a primary school near the chocolate factory. I hadn't been a big reader in those days, so had no idea about Willy Wonka and Charlie Bucket and the Golden Ticket. Maybe that was why lotteries had never been my thing — as far back as I can remember I'd always tried to improve the odds on a good result.

That didn't stop me fucking up big-time on a regular basis, of course. It always took me a while to learn from my mistakes and, after one scrape or another, I was a regular visitor to Guy's Hospital or Southwark nick.

But I always looked on the bright side.

Whether I'd lacerated my hands on the broken glass along the top of the Kirby Road sweet-shop wall, or had my collar felt for any one of a hundred different reasons during my time as the world's youngest South London criminal mastermind, at least I'd got the day off school.

2

The mixed bag of tourists and punters doing business from out of town didn't seem to mind that the Premier Inn wasn't as shiny, these days, as it probably once had been, and neither did I. I only needed somewhere to leave my daysack and get my head down, and if it was good enough for Lenny Henry, it was definitely good enough for me.

I had some time to kill, so instead of going back to my room I wandered east along the river to the freshly polished wharves and warehouses that used to conceal Fagin's hideout, and where Bill Sikes ended up hanging himself.

Oliver Twist hadn't been on Anna's reading list, but way before I'd ever tried to read a novel I'd nicked one or two of Dickens's from a dusty old bookshop in Greenwich. They smelt of leather and had great pictures, so I'd guessed they were worth a bob or two.

The bookseller used to crouch over a high table at the back of his store, as old and dog-eared as his books, mumbling to himself as he turned the pages. His mad white hair looked like an explosion in a feather-pillow factory and at first I couldn't tell whether he was covered with dust or dandruff, so I'd made the same mistake I had with the Doodlebug expert and dismissed him as a sad old nutter.

The first couple of times I'd lifted his gear he

hadn't seemed to notice. The third time I slid one under my shirt, he suddenly appeared behind me. His gnarled hand shot out and gripped my wrist.

I thought I was fucked. I couldn't move an inch, and could almost hear the police siren on its way towards me. But all he did was put it back on the shelf and hand me another instead. '*Great Expectations* is a work of genius,' he said. 'But you should start with *Oliver Twist*.' Then he asked me if I wanted to join him for a brew.

I nodded, speechless, then managed to summon up the courage to ask if he had any biscuits.

When the kettle had boiled he handed me a steaming mug of tea and some custard creams and fixed me with the kind of beady-eyed stare big old birds give you at the zoo. 'You bunking off? Dodging school?'

When I told him that was what I did most days, he pointed at the book and said he was going to call me Dodger. I must have looked severely puzzled, because he then told me the story of *Oliver*.

After that, he'd invite me in for a chat every time I passed. 'Dodger,' he'd say. 'Consider yourself at home.' It was only later, when I saw the musical on TV, that I realized this was another of his little jokes, but after a while, I did. He'd entertain me with the most amazing tales of Dickens's London. I stopped nicking his stuff and started calling him Fagin.

He died years ago, surrounded by his treasures, but I heard his voice in my ear again as

180

I wandered through the labyrinth of passageways that surrounded St Saviour's Dock.

I had a feeling that if I did decide to buy a place of my own, it would be an apartment somewhere near here. I didn't fancy a designer barge, however seductive the estate agent's bollocks tried to be. I'd developed a liking for multiple exits over the years, and though I enjoyed the water, I hated being marooned in it. Back in the eighteenth century, according to Fagin, the river was so busy that incoming cargoes were often stranded long enough for pirates to attack them at their moorings. I reckoned there was a lesson there for all of us.

There seemed to be a dry cleaner's on every block, but the further you got from the river, the more haphazard this stretch of the city became. Duplex penthouses for baby fat-cats fought for space among dilapidated tenements. Upmarket artisans' cottages stood alongside chunks of waste ground overrun by brambles and strewn with rusting supermarket trolleys.

In one of them I saw a Russian T34, barrel sweeping across Page's Walk, which someone had painted sky blue with big white spots. When they'd first got hammered by it in 1941, the legendary German generals Guderian and von Kleist called it the deadliest tank in the world. Every home should have one.

My stomach suddenly reminded me that I hadn't had anything to eat since Maggie's club sandwich, so I headed down to the Café Reality on the New Kent Road. I'd been there a couple of times before — they served up a great full

181

English and didn't piss around with their brews. And, besides, I loved its name.

After getting some more calories down my neck, I bimbled back towards the river by the scenic route. I used the Shard as my cathedral spire. It hadn't yet opened its doors, but was already the tallest inhabitable building in the European Union and towered over my old manor, like a giant CGI space rocket.

Funded by a big slice of Qatari cash, London's newest landmark was bang next door to the outpatients department that used to be my second home. Its highly polished hoardings were keen to share the excitement about the imminent opening of the Shangri-La Hotel at its base. I'd had a couple of beers at the one in Hong Kong when I was a young squaddie pretending to be James Bond, so I knew the chain had got its name from a novel about a lost valley whose inhabitants never grew old. Maybe that was because they all had corporate expense accounts and never even had to look at their own bills, let alone pay them.

I still couldn't get my head around the distance that existed between the haves and the have-nots in this part of town. The shiny steel and glass world rubbed shoulders physically with the minging one I was passing through now, but in every other sense they were a million miles apart.

I skirted a derelict community centre that had once housed a karate club and a gospel assembly room. A torn plastic banner proclaimed, 'Jesus Christ is the same yesterday, today and for ever!'

but He seemed to have abandoned this place a while back to the dossers and graffiti artists.

I saw movement behind one of the splintered sheets of plywood that cloaked its covered walkway and became the target of a hostile glare from deep inside a random collection of nylon sleeping bags, plastic bags and mouldy old bits of carpet.

Further along the street a sign on a ramshackle church building with a barbed-wire crown and bars on every window invited passers-by to come inside and enjoy their Christmas Fayre. As well as Santa's grotto and tombola, Irish coffee was on offer. I was gutted to have missed it.

3

The Tabard Estate had been rebranded as the Tabard *Gardens* Estate, which meant that the grass was mown and the patch where the dogs used to shit was now called the Nature Area.

Scaffolding was the business to be in around here, and the lads who owned Sky's the Limit obviously took their holidays in the Bahamas. Although there wasn't a hi-vis jacket or a hard hat in sight, their pipework seemed to be propping up every building, and there was a tower at the corner of the block where my best mate Gaz used to live.

His flat was boarded up, but the building had been treated to a spray with a power-washer and a new coat of paint since I was last here. The railings and fire-escape ladders on every walkway gleamed in the winter sunshine, and so did a silver three-litre Audi convertible in a nearby parking space. That made me smile. In the good old days a wagon like that would have been up on bricks as soon as the driver's back was turned, and everything removable flogged out of a van ten minutes after that.

One summer, after bunking off school in the mornings, the two of us wasted a good few afternoons on the roof above his third-floor flat. Gaz's mum helped out on a fruit and veg stall in Borough Market, so we'd wait for her to go down there, then nick a pack of his dad's condoms and fill some with mustard, some with ketchup and some with water. We'd sling them in a Co-op carrier-bag and climb over the railing by their front door and onto the fire escape.

Since fire escapes are designed to go south rather than north, there was a gap between the top rung of the ladder and the guttering. We had to haul ourselves over it with the help of a slightly dodgy cast-iron waste stack. We broke a lot of tiles in the process, but once we were on the ridge, we felt like we ruled the world.

In the main we'd sit up there and swap man talk. Sometimes we'd flick through our *Victor* and *Commando* mags and make the kinds of noises kids do when they're imitating a main battle tank or a GPMG. And sometimes we'd set up our fire position, select an enemy target, calculate range and angle of elevation, and let the Squareheads and the Nips have it down in the square. Political correctness hadn't been invented then.

Mostly we'd just leave a trail of red and yellow splodges on the Tabard Road, and if we were really lucky, on the bonnet of an armoured troop carrier disguised as a VW camper. The only time we scored a direct hit on an enemy soldier it turned out to be one of Gaz's mum's mates and we were in a world of pain.

She never got the stain out of her dress, but that wasn't what made the two of them go ballistic. '*You stupid little fuckers!*' they yelled when they finally caught up with us. '*What the fuck do you think would have happened if you'd fallen off that roof?*'

Me and Gaz looked at each other like we'd each grown a giant light bulb on the top of our head. We hadn't thought of that.

We never went up there again. I often wondered whether our cache of war mags and spare ammo was still under the ridge cap we'd loosened on our first mission.

4

Arriving at Hare Court after dark was like walking into a different century. This world still seemed as if it were lit by gas lamps and candles, and populated by men in tailcoats busying themselves with quills and ledgers.

The space between the red-and brown-brick buildings was part-paved, part-gravelled, with a scattering of evergreen shrubs and wooden benches that looked like they'd never been sat on. It wasn't that kind of place. Everything here was designed to send one message: Stand up straight and pay attention, because nobody has bigger brains or bigger bollocks than the Law.

I didn't yet know about his bollocks, but the size of Geoff Blackwood QC's brain was not in doubt. I was surprised that his wig was big enough to keep it warm. He tossed it onto a nearby pile of documents and waved me towards the kind of leather wing chair you didn't see much outside old-school gentlemen's clubs.

Once he'd extracted himself from his gown he started to look almost human — mid-forties, maybe, blond hair swept back over the ears, the kind of complexion that you probably only get when you spend your weekends at a shoot or in a friend's chalet in Verbier.

He sat down at his burgundy-topped mahogany desk and unfolded a pair of extremely expensive rimless reading glasses. He placed them very precisely on the end of his nose, beneath a pair of clear hazel eyes, which gave the impression that he wasn't just looking at you, he was staring into the depths of your soul. He hadn't said a word yet, and I was already pleased that he was on Sam's side.

'So . . . Mr, er, Jones . . . Father Martyn believes you may have something to contribute to the Callard case.'

I knew his clock was ticking, so I briefed him swiftly about serving with Harry, and told him I had a witness who was present at the exercise in the CQB Rooms who might be prepared to testify that Sam was nowhere near Scott Braxton when the fatal shot was fired.

Blackwood wrapped his left hand around his right fist like one was paper and the other was stone. 'You won't be surprised to hear that I'm not permitted to share any privileged information that may have a bearing on the outcome to these proceedings, but I can tell you that we have a problem. Sergeant Callard has admitted to a negligent discharge. He has also refused to provide us with any helpful information of the kind to which you claim to have access.'

'Has anyone managed to track down the SSM?'

He leaned forward. 'I'm told that Squadron Sergeant Major Grant is currently overseas on a clandestine operation. I imagine he will miraculously reappear on the courtroom steps, leaving us no time whatsoever to question him in any detail.'

'Could you enter a plea of mitigation, if push

188

comes to shove? Unsound mind, or whatever you guys call it? The deaths of two of his mates in Afghan seem to have really messed him up. One was particularly brutal.' It wouldn't save Sam's career in the Regiment, but I figured that being RTUed (returned to unit) was a whole lot better than a manslaughter rap and a dishonourable discharge.

Blackwood removed his glasses and placed them carefully alongside his wig. 'I can only achieve as much as my client permits me to. But I believe him to be innocent of the charge, and can assure you that I will do everything possible to leave the court in no doubt of that.'

'How long have we got?'

'The trial date has not been set, but I'm sure you know how these things work. The opposition can bugger around for ever with their Article 32 investigation, if it suits them, then catapult us into court with less than two weeks' warning. Even the least explosive of these proceedings needs to be swept under the carpet, as far as the top brass are concerned. And a fatality behind the wire at Hereford is far from that.'

He unfolded the glasses again and replaced them on the end of his nose. It was clearly a ritual that had become so instinctive he no longer realized he was doing it.

'I think we can safely say that the event that led to Sergeant Callard's court martial is top of the list of stories the director of Special Forces doesn't want to see breaking out of Barford, let alone being given a starring role on *News at Ten*. And he'll go to considerable lengths to ensure that neither of those things happens.

'They'll take a leaf out of your old reference manual, Mr Jones. Speed, aggression and surprise will be their strategy.' His eyes glinted. 'Suffice it to say that I will prepare our position with all the energy and commitment Samuel Callard has the right to expect.'

5

I hailed a black cab on the Embankment and paid off the driver by the wobbly pedestrian bridge that led from St Paul's Cathedral to Tate Modern. It showed the city at its sparkling best on a clear night, and I needed some time to think. I also needed to check whether anyone was taking an unhealthy interest in my movements. I'd just left another known location, and that would be the first port of call for any trigger.

The bridge was a great place to start scanning for a follow. It was the only way to get across the Thames at this point, unless you walked on water or were prepared to tab some distance up or down stream. I stopped on the South Bank and swapped banter with a couple of smiley Rastafarians playing Bob Marley songs under a street lamp, not too far away from a sign that said *No Buskers*.

They treated me to 'Three Little Birds', competing for a moment or two with the beat of a passing heli's rotor blades. I lobbed a pound coin into their guitar case and turned back towards the Globe Theatre. The leather jacket, jeans and trainers that had trailed me from the St Paul's side was still on the bridge, taking a great deal of interest in the view east. You'd come a long way to see the *Belfast*, the Tower of London and Tower Bridge under floodlights, but the wind had sparked up again and it was too cold for sightseeing.

It was definitely time for a warming brew. The Costa joint beside the *Golden Hinde* would be the perfect place. It served big frothy coffees, and was situated at a chokepoint in the riverside walk, which gave me eyes-on in both directions. But I wasn't going to go there straight away.

I might have been wrong about the jacket. It was like a uniform out there: every self-respecting heavy had to wear one. During my time in Moscow and Moldova I'd been chased around and shouldered aside by so many of these guys I'd started to dream about them. So, at some point in the next hour, I needed to know for sure whether I'd been pinged or he was merely a third party.

Before I went the barista route, I paid a flying visit to the Anchor. It always amused me to be having a drink at the spot where Samuel Pepys had watched the Great Fire of London, and where the locals had once enjoyed a bit of bull-and bear-baiting instead of Grand Theft Auto on the PlayStation, but maybe that just meant I was another mug punter who'd fallen for the olde-worlde PR pitch that yelled at us from every leaflet and beer mat.

Behind the pillar-box-red-painted woodwork was a warren of dark panelled and oak-beamed bars and function rooms. It was also on a corner site, with three or four exits onto the street, one of which faced the archway on Clink Street that ran beneath Southwark Bridge, which made it perfect for what I had in mind.

Glasses chinked and after-work waffle spilled

onto the pavement as I pulled open the door closest to Shakespeare's favourite theatre. The evening crowd were already getting well stuck in. I eased my way through to the nearest bar and ordered a pint of their 1730 Pale Ale, then struck up a conversation with the guy who was best positioned to allow me to keep eyes-on the entrance I'd just walked through.

The fact that he looked like he'd got back from Afghan the week before was a bonus. He wasn't wearing combats and didn't have a Bergen at his feet, but there was something in his eyes and the way he carried himself that said he'd recently been teleported from a different planet. A planet where discipline was everything and dropping your guard could have fatal consequences. If you knew the signs, you could always tell.

Sure enough, he'd been with 1 Yorks, bouncing between FOBs in the Nahr-e Saraj district of Helmand with the Danish Battle Group. I wondered whether he'd bumped into my old mate Jack Grant along the way — highly unlikely, but you had to ask. The only Grant he'd come across was an illegal bottle of Scotch. He laughed. Tasted like shit. Give him a Jägerbomb any time.

Someone behind me started boring his girlfriend shitless about the clash of cruelty and high comedy in *Twelfth Night*. Me and Yorkie both rolled our eyeballs, but I didn't turn and tell the dick-head that clashes like that were an everyday thing in the battle space, because Mr Leatherman chose that moment to poke his head through the door.

6

Yorkie was also drinking the 1730. I asked him if he fancied the other half, keeping Leatherman at the periphery of my vision. I wanted to take a good look at him, but if I was under surveillance, I didn't want him to know I was aware.

As the barman pulled the pint, the guy in the doorway couldn't seem to make up his mind whether to join the party or look for somewhere quiet for dinner. He eventually headed back outside, having given me long enough to clock that he hadn't just been to the same tailor as my Moldovan pursuers, he'd been to the same gym and barber as well, and his skin was as grey as a sunny day in Transnistria.

Yorkie and I carried on waffling about soldier shit as the guy behind me moved on to the Problem Plays, whatever the fuck they were. I glanced around the room and caught sight of the girlfriend's expression in the process. That one look told me it was the Shakespeare expert who had the problem: he definitely wasn't on a result.

I gave it another half-hour before downing the last of my beer, shook Yorkie warmly by the hand and went through to the Southwark Bridge exit. A small crowd had gathered by the Clink Street arch to take photographs of an old boy in a top hat playing 'Ain't We Got Fun?' on a giant flaming tuba. Not many of his admirers seemed to be throwing coins into his collection box.

I joined them for a minute or two, then moved on in the same direction. The posters outside the Clink itself proudly claimed that it was 'the prison that gave its name to all others!' It was past closing time, so I was too late to join in 'the rodent hunt for kids'. Not that I needed to: I had one all of my own.

I stayed at Costa long enough to get a brew down my neck and catch up on the newspaper reports of David Cameron's recent meeting with President Karzai at Chequers, 'where they signed an enduring strategic partnership between the UK and Afghanistan', which must have given both of them a nice warm glow.

Leatherman seemed to have melted away. But then again, he didn't need to walk past the big plate-glass windows I was stationed beside. He knew which pipe his rat had gone down. Maybe he was just waiting to zap me at the other end of it.

You didn't have to try too hard to switch into holidaymaker mode along here — this part of Bankside always did it for me. I eased myself to the front of the throng oohing and aahing at the *Golden Hinde*. No one could pass it without being gobsmacked by how Francis Drake and his crew had sailed around the world, nicking doubloons from Spaniards, in a hunk of timber not much bigger than a stretch limo. And that gave me plenty of opportunity to check for the presence of men in leather jackets from three different approaches.

I took a right immediately after a line of Boris Bikes and a sign that invited me to become part of the London Bridge Experience — London's Scariest Attraction! There was no sign of a shadow as I walked through the station towards Guy's Hospital and the Shard, using the construction-site stuff as cover. By the time I emerged on the other side of the medical students' hall of residence, I had two.

My mate from the wobbly bridge was behind me again, and his cousin was about fifty to my right and closing. He could have been heading for the Leather Exchange on Weston Street — this part of town was Tannery Central — but I doubted it. He was working so hard to ignore me that my internal alarm bells started ringing big-time.

I heard the heli rotors again as I ducked into Southall Place, and glanced up at the blinking light five hundred feet above me. I lengthened my stride, then jinked half-right onto the edge of an estate that was still in the queue for the Tabard Gardens facelift and hadn't yet tuned into the concept of the motion sensor.

There were no straight lines here, and no security lights to let the Leathermen monitor my progress from the ground. I sprinted down a stretch of pitted tarmac between a row of garages and balconies hung with washing. Satellite dishes sprouted from the brickwork like fungi and TV sets glowed and flickered behind the net curtains.

This was my turf. I'd take them through a series of bottlenecks and see how they liked it. Then, if I couldn't split them up and take them one by one, I'd disappear.

7

A monster wheelie bin had spewed garbage across the mouth of the alleyway that zigzagged left and right at the end of the row of garages. I took the corner at speed and nearly lost it as my Timberlands hit something slimy that I hoped wasn't dog shit. I had enough on my plate without the stench of that stuff following me around for the rest of the night.

I bounced off a wall and a stretch of wriggly tin hoarding before I levelled out again, and jarred my right shoulder. It sent my central nervous system an immediate message of complaint and I told it to go fuck itself. These boys weren't going to wait for me to call for a masseur and a tube of ibuprofen gel. I gave it a quick rub and carried on. I couldn't hear footsteps behind me, but the wriggly tin had clanged like a gong and I needed to make distance.

I turned right and looped through Empire Square, staying within the shadow of the trees, past the Marlin Apartments, an upmarket development for business and leisure guests, who'd scratch their heads if you mentioned the words 'Premier' and 'Inn' in the same sentence.

The good news was that if it had been dog shit on the sole of my boot, it wasn't there any more. The bad news was that the Leathermen were still together, and sticking to me like a cheap suit.

The heli had lifted away, but as I left the west side of the development they appeared three hundred behind me, shoulder to shoulder, the far side of the trees.

I legged it across Tabard Street and worked my way around the back of Tabard Gardens, slaloming through a bunch of pub-goers as I went. When I reached the block where me and my mate Gaz had spent what the psychopath-detector shrink would call our formative years, I reckoned I had about a five-hundred-metre lead. I hoped it would be enough.

I hung a left past the refuse bunker by the Audi convertible's parking space and up the main stairwell, triggering a chain of motion sensors as I went. Too bad. Maybe they'd be on a short time lapse to help save the planet. No such luck. The lights were still blazing away as I belted towards the neat plywood boarding that encased Gaz's flat while the developers worked their magic, but by then I'd realized they could operate in my favour. If I was stranded on the walkway when the Leathermen turned the corner, I was in the shit. If I'd managed to get up the fire escape, I'd be back in deep shadow.

There was going to be a big difference between a skinny eight-year-old scrambling that final length of cast-iron pipework on a summer afternoon and his older, chunkier self trying to pull the same stunt on a cold winter night, but I didn't have a choice.

Somewhere nearby I heard a yell, followed by what sounded like a plate smashing. At first I thought it might be some drama on the TV but

198

then a door burst open on the walkway immediately below me and a male voice said the dinner was shit anyway and he was going down the Oak. A female one told him not to bother coming back any time soon.

I couldn't have asked for a better diversion. I moved Sam's Browning from my waistband into the right pocket of my bomber jacket, zipped it tight, swung my leg over the rail and started to climb.

8

The metal rungs of the ladder chilled my fingers to the bone. They were also slippery as fuck. When I reached the top one the security lights were still going strong and the Leathermen were either keeping to the shadows beyond them, or hadn't been putting in enough hours on the treadmill.

Keeping a tight hold on the fire escape I grabbed the far side of the waste stack with my right hand and wedged my right boot on the bracket that strapped it to the wall. I reminded myself that Jesus Christ was here yesterday, today and for ever, and brought my left hand and boot across to join them.

The guttering was cast-iron too, and mounted on the rafter tail fascia eighteen inches above my head. Me and Gaz hadn't thought twice about swinging from it when we were kids, but the waste stack was the only route I could take now. The thing had put up with sixty-odd years of shit and was still there to tell the tale.

I slid all my fingers behind the pipe and pre-pared to shimmy up it, a bit like Ken Marabula and his Fijian mates would have climbed a coco-nut palm when they were kids. The trick was to go hand over hand and place even pressure on the mortared recess above each course of bricks with every upward toehold. If I just scrabbled around and hoped for the best, I'd end up wrench-ing the whole thing off its anchors.

The pipe left the wall at a 45-degree angle then straightened again once it had cleared the eaves. My shoulder ached and my calf muscles started to burn as I hauled myself past the overhang. I pushed the sole of my right Timberland against the final strap and felt the top of the stink pipe bend even further outwards. The bracket shifted and one of its screws popped out of its fixing.

Flying blind, my left foot managed to find enough purchase on the junction for me to be able to launch first my torso and then my right knee over the edge of the roof. I lay there for a moment, face down, going nowhere, with my left leg and some of my arse hanging into space.

The pantiles were textured, so their surface friction stopped me sliding straight off them, and because they were constructed from interlocking ridges and valleys, I was able to grip them firmly enough to pull my whole body out of sight of the parking area.

When I'd put some space between my feet and the gutter, I slowed my breathing, opened my mouth and listened. A couple of dogs started a barking competition somewhere near the Nature Area. All they needed was for a couple of urban foxes to join the party. Behind me, a police siren whooped its way along the Old Kent Road. In the silence that followed, the cold and damp started to eat through my jeans and bomber jacket and into my flesh.

I couldn't resist reaching out and testing whether our ridge cap was still loose. It was. But I'd probably never know whether our cache had been disturbed because I couldn't risk taking a look. I didn't want to present a silhouette above the crest.

I flattened myself against the pantiles and hoped that the heli I'd spotted earlier hadn't been in the business of spotting me. A warm body on a cold roof would have glowed big-time on its infrared scanner screen.

The pub crowd started to spill out onto distant pavements. One bunch of mates laughed much more loudly than you'd expect on a Monday night. Car doors slammed and engines fired up. A girl in high heels click-clacked along Tabard Street, shrieking into her mobile. By the time she was out of earshot, her bestie knew more than anyone needed to know about her day, and so did I.

Everything went quiet again. TV sets were switched off and lights dimmed below me. My shoulder throbbed and I felt a twinge of cramp in my right foot. I wasn't going to sit up and take my Timberland off, so all I could do was flex my toes as much as I could and try to ignore it.

I was about to ease myself across the ridge and down towards the scaffolding tower on the garden elevation when I heard footsteps by the stairwell. Whoever was down there was keeping to the far side of the refuse bunker, because the motion sensors weren't getting excited. Maybe the lad who hadn't liked his dinner was about to settle down for a night among the bin bags.

Then the security LEDs flashed on and someone not too light on his feet did his best to tiptoe along the walkway towards Gaz's boarded-up front door.

9

I told myself that there were any number of reasons why you might want to hang around outside an uninhabited third-floor flat after midnight with the temperature uncomfortably close to freezing.

But I knew that wasn't true.

He was so close I could hear him breathing.

I visualized Leatherman Two on stag behind the bins while Leatherman One tried to look like he belonged on the walkway ten feet beneath me. Maybe he was wearing the same expression he'd used when he was admiring the view from the wobbly bridge. Maybe he was checking out the top of the waste stack and thinking, Fuck that for a game of soldiers. It's one screw head away from falling off the wall . . .

He gave himself five, coughed up a mouthful of phlegm and gobbed it over the railing. Then he swung himself out onto the fire escape and began to climb towards me.

Beyond filling my lungs with oxygen, I didn't move a muscle. There was still a chance he'd lose his bottle when he saw the stink-pipe bracket close up. Either way, he'd keep his closely cropped head below the parapet for as long as he possibly could in case I was waiting to kick it off his shoulders.

Five more minutes ticked by and the lights cut out.

Ten minutes after that he still hadn't shifted.

That meant he was coming on up. He just needed to wipe the glare of the LEDs from his retinas and build his night vision first.

I patted the Browning through the outer skin of my bomber jacket, though I knew I could never use it. If I was right in thinking they were mates of Sniper One, a round between the eyes was probably what these lads deserved, but it would take a lot of explaining. Which was going to leave me with a bit of a challenge if the first thing to appear above the guttering was the suppressor of a CZ-99 short.

I heard movement, and the waste stack gave a wobble. I braced myself, still not wanting to raise my head and present a bigger target. The top of the stink pipe leaned further away from the parapet, first by a few inches, then by a foot or more. As Leatherman's fist appeared, followed swiftly by his face, the second screw popped out of its fixing.

Without an anchor, the segment of the stack that jutted out beneath the overhang headed further south. Whatever his previous plans had been, he was fast running out of choices. He clung to the pipe with his right hand and groped for the guttering with his left.

He might have ended up taking a nosedive into the tarmac without any help from me, but I wasn't going to leave that to chance. I grabbed the loose ridge cap with both hands, twisted round onto my arse, flexed my knees, arched my back and launched it at him like a missile.

When four kilos of prime Old English

terracotta catches you on the nut, it can really spoil your day. Leatherman's grip didn't slacken immediately, but I could see his motor functions were well scrambled. He shook his head and flexed his closely knit and increasingly bloody eyebrows, then raised the fingers of his left hand to the wound, gave a low, caveman growl and plummeted into the darkness.

10

I didn't stick around long enough to see where Leatherman One landed, but it didn't sound good. I'd never forget the splat a ketchup-filled condom made when it hit the pavement, and this lad's skull did much the same.

As his mate ran over to say his goodbyes I hotfooted it to the scaffolding and half slid, half clambered down to Tabard Street, vaulted the park railing and ran for the cover of the landscaped mound and the trees beyond. Leatherman Two wasn't going to wait for the paramedics to arrive, and I didn't fancy giving him the opportunity to take up where his cousin had left off.

I took the turning to Eastwell House, the block I'd lived in when I wasn't mortaring the square with Gaz. I thought about lying up behind the dosser's hoarding for a while, but when the sirens sparked up behind me, I decided to go straight back to the Premier Inn, pick up my gear and get out of there.

The first part of that plan went as smooth as silk: I slid my access-card into the slot by the back entrance and strapped my daysack onto my back. The second didn't. I crossed Tower Bridge Road and ducked back into Tanner Street. As I followed it round in the direction of Butler's Wharf I was nearly sideswiped by a black Passat, one up, travelling at speed.

I veered right past the coffee company at the

entrance to Rope Walk and the wagon disappeared into the tunnel beneath the railway line. I knew it wouldn't take the driver much time to reverse up or complete the Tower Bridge Road circuit. The gates into Rope Walk were barred and locked, so I sprinted down Maltby Street and took the next left underneath the arches. If I couldn't make it straight back to the Skoda without a tail I'd aim for the maze of alleyways between here and the river.

The sirens were still going strong on the other side of the tracks. I couldn't help wondering what the boys in blue would make of Leatherman's strange decision to climb a waste stack after dark, and how long it would take the forensic crew to connect the traumatic injury he'd sustained from the ridge cap with the fall that killed him. I also wondered whether they'd find a rose-coloured tattoo beneath his collar.

I crossed the road that ran along the north side of the railway and nipped into the Arnold Estate. You'd have to be a genius to navigate through this warren in a wagon, and if you stopped for more than five minutes, day or night, the local lads would have it on a low-loader, heading south, with a For Sale sign on the windscreen. Most of the time they lifted bikes, laptops and smartphones, which they fenced in Brick Lane — if they could be bothered to go over the river. It was the kind of place I needed right now.

I'd zigzagged through a couple of archways and around a play area and got most of the way to the rat run through to Jamaica Road before I heard footsteps in pursuit. I didn't bother looking over my shoulder. It wasn't going to be good news.

I switched direction towards a group of teenagers with hoodies and jeans hanging off their arses. They were clustered under a street lamp, next to a beat-up metallic orange Subaru Impreza with the world's biggest rear spoiler and red flames stencilled above the wheel arches. Their cigarette tips glowed extra brightly as I approached.

The footsteps slowed behind me, then stopped. I gave the boys my most cheerful grin. 'Lads, how would you like to earn yourselves fifty quid?'

There was a glimmer of interest, but their expressions told me that these were hard men here, and I shouldn't forget it. The one with the most zits slid off the Subaru's bonnet and came over to invade my personal space.

'How would *you* like to eat shit?'

He was close enough for whatever he'd eaten for dinner to make my eyes water.

I kept the grin in place. 'I drank shit once. But that was for a bet.'

Even the meanest and ugliest of them was immediately onside.

'Fuck *off*! You're kidding, right?'

I shook my head and dug five ten-quid notes out of my jeans. 'I don't do kidding.'

'What's the catch, wanker?'

'No catch. See that guy in the leather jacket behind me?' I flicked a thumb back over my shoulder. 'He's really getting on my tits. All I need is for you lot to go and fuck him up a bit.'

'Easy.' Zitface took the money, counted it, and put it in his parka. 'But it'll cost you a ton.'

I sucked my upper lip to demonstrate that I was no pushover, then fished out another thirty. 'Here. That makes a tenner each.'

His eyes narrowed. 'Why don't we beat the shit out of you instead, and help ourselves to the rest of your money?'

'I'll tell you why.' I took his hand, pressed the other three notes into the palm and closed it for him, firmly and not very gently. Then I took half a pace towards him, so our noses were almost touching, and patted the chunk of metal in the side of my bomber. I wasn't enjoying the smell of his breath, but I wanted him and his mates to get the message. 'Because that's a gun in my pocket. I'm not just pleased to see you.'

To give the kid credit, he stood his ground. 'Did you really drink shit?'

'Sure. A turd in a pint glass. And for a whole lot less than you're getting on this job.'

He gave this some thought. I could almost hear the cogs engage.

He took a drag on his cigarette and let the smoke leak from his mouth and nose. 'What's the secret?'

'The secret?'

He nodded, keen to know.

'You've got to chug, not chew.'

He winced, and screwed up his face almost as much as I must have done when I was in the process of winning the bet. Then he took a couple of steps back, gathered his crew around

209

him, and gave them a note each as he mumbled his battle plan.

They straightened up and brushed me aside as they swaggered past, on their way to the Gunfight at the OK Corral. It was great to watch. When they were five paces away from Leatherman Two, they stopped, flicked back their parkas and loosened their imaginary Colt .45s in their imaginary holsters.

The astonished look on his face was worth every penny. Which was just as well, because fifteen seconds later they pissed off in all directions without laying a finger on him.

Fair one.

At their age, I'd have done exactly the same.

11

At least I'd bought myself a little bit of distance and some time to catch my breath. As my new best mates scattered across the estate, I turned and bolted for the more upmarket labyrinth of designer workspaces and apartment buildings around St Saviour's Wharf.

When I'd got halfway down Mill Street the footsteps echoed behind me once more. This time I did look round. I couldn't see him, which made me reasonably sure he couldn't see me. I clambered over a gate to my left and darted down a passage between two converted warehouses that led to the Devil's Neckinger.

The Neckinger was one of London's many underground rivers, and marked the border between Bermondsey and Southwark. It flowed from somewhere near the Imperial War Museum, beneath Elephant and Castle, and joined the Thames at St Saviour's Dock.

From the moment Fagin had told me about it, I'd always loved the name. It came from the Devil's Neckerchief, which is what they called the executioner's noose back in the days when they hanged convicted pirates from the gibbet at the inlet's mouth and left their corpses on display downstream.

The gibbet no longer took pride of place there, but the yuppies still had the use of a Victorian derrick every fifty metres or so along the shored-up bank of the tributary, in case they needed to hoist their very expensive furniture through the gable windows. The hooks and chains were silhouetted against the night sky to my right, above a walkway I now realized I couldn't reach via dry land.

When the gate at the entrance to my passageway started to rattle, I knew there was no going back. It was low tide right now. I'd have to take my chances in the mud.

I grabbed a mooring rope and abseiled down the very slimy stonework between two of the oak pillars that lined the bank. As I went, I remembered Fagin saying that this place used to be Cholera Central, and not just because of the pirates' bloated corpses. Untreated sewage, festering sheep, rotting fish, the eye-watering fluid from the tanning factories — it all used to flow down here. But fuck it: this wasn't the first time I'd been up Shit Creek without a paddle.

My plan had been to move as soundlessly as possible down the riverbed, keeping as close to the shadow of the oak pillars as possible, until I reached the first of the ladders that would take me up onto the walkway. As the silt gripped my Timberlands and crept up beyond my knees, I knew I had no choice but to stay exactly where I was. The distance between high and low tide was about five metres at this time of year. Maybe I'd be able to wait an hour or three and swim for it.

I raised my hood for a bit of extra warmth and cover, and slowed my breathing.

I heard the scrape of a boot somewhere above me, then a throat being cleared. A gob of phlegm the size of a jellyfish landed in the mud a metre away from me and glistened in the ambient light. I didn't look up; just leaned in closer to the woodwork and hoped the next wouldn't land on my head.

12

I watched the river creep up the inlet towards me. I didn't have much choice. For the last hour Leatherman Two had been sitting on the edge of the dock, swinging his feet above me and smoking an endless chain of foul-smelling cigarettes. I was coated with mud and slime from mid-thigh down, and it was doing its best to infiltrate beneath my jeans and squeeze itself into my boots.

The only good news was that the position of Leatherman Two's knees seemed to be stopping him pinging me. Or maybe he knew exactly where I was and had decided to prolong the agony. Either way, I'd have to move as soon as the water reached me. I couldn't stay there and let it freeze my bollocks off. I couldn't reach his boots and pull him in without climbing the rope, and that was looped around the top of the pillar right next to him. But if I left my current hiding place I'd present him with a clear and very slow-moving target — and that always gave me a really bad feeling between the shoulder-blades.

The water had reached bollock height when I heard an indignant shout followed by a muffled grunt. Seconds later a body flew over the parapet and disappeared head first into the creek about three metres away from me.

The mooring line twitched alongside me, like a dancing snake. 'Wake up, wanker. You can't stay there all night.'

I looked up. I couldn't see the zits under the shadow of the hoodie, but I recognized the voice. Two or three more figures appeared alongside him as I gripped my end of the rope. They all seized their end, like they were finalists in a tug of war, until Zitface raised his hand and the thing went slack again.

'Just one more thing, before we pull you out of that shit. It's gonna cost you another fifty.'

I nodded like a mad person. As Leatherman Two fought his way upright and finally broke the surface with a look of undiluted hatred on his face, fifty quid sounded like the deal of the century.

13

The Arnold Estate dudes heaved me out of St Saviour's Dock, then cut the rope so Leatherman Two couldn't join us in too much of a hurry. The last I saw of him he was still flailing about in the water and yelling very unfriendly things in my direction. I hadn't picked up much of the ragtag collection of Balkan languages during my trips to Bosnia, but I knew what *kurvin sine* meant. It was Serbian for 'son of a whore'.

Another fifty quid changed hands and I was enjoying a shower in Zitface's mum's flat. I managed to hose off the Timberlands, but even in a world heaving with dry cleaners, I decided it was easier to bin the jeans. As luck would have it, his stepdad had a spare pair pretty much my size. Zitface held them up for me to admire like I'd just dropped into a Giorgio Armani store for a browse. 'Yours for a bargain price . . . '

Maybe that was because the not completely genuine eagle logo had been riveted onto the arse pocket upside down.

'Don't tell me, let me guess. Fifty quid?'

'Sixty.'

'Won't your stepdad miss them?'

His normally impassive face broke into a smile. 'Who gives a shit? He fucked off six months ago.'

I guessed he hadn't left a forwarding address.

I handed over another bunch of notes and we shook. At that point it struck me that I didn't even know his name.

'Before I give you every penny I've got, maybe we should introduce ourselves? I'm Nick.'

'Dave.' He hesitated. 'But it wasn't always Dave.'

'Don't tell me . . . When you arrived from the Planet Krypton, it used to be Clark Kent.'

He frowned and shook his head. He didn't know what the fuck I was talking about.

'Nah. I never met my dad, but they say he came from the Yemen. He called me Osama. But my mum changed it about ten years ago. Fuck knows why. I was just a kid.'

My dad hadn't come from the Yemen, but we clearly had a lot in common. I told him a few stupid stories about me and Gaz and growing up on the Tabard while he rooted around in the fridge and conjured up a five-star full English, eggs, bacon, sausages, beans, the lot.

I watched in admiration. 'Mate, you should be on *Master Chef* . . .

He started to waffle a bit more freely as we ate. He told me a bit about his crew, and the day to day shit they got up to. As I wiped the fried bread around my nearly empty plate I felt a big stupid grin take over my face. Some things never changed.

As I turned to go he asked me if I needed him to look after the weapon. I told him I was happy doing that myself, but he should keep an eye out for angry Serbs in leather jackets.

He nodded. 'Specially if they've been down

217

the ink slinger.' He rubbed his neck. 'What's that fucking thing all about?'

'I'll get back to you on that.'

He whistled up the lads who'd hauled me out of the creek for one final mission — escorting me to the Butler's Wharf car park. As they drifted away I realized I'd had more fun with Dave and his mates in the last few hours than I'd had pretty much since I'd binned the military. I was going to miss them.

★ ★ ★

I should have chucked the Nokia I'd used to call Blackwood's chambers and the Astra HQ in the river before taking off on my Bermondsey sightseeing trip. Instead I put it in a Jiffy-bag in a Hounslow all-night store, covered it with stamps and mailed it to an estate agent's address in Newcastle that I'd plucked off a random website. Better late than never — and if it was being tracked, maybe it would be a waste of someone else's time, not just mine.

I stuffed my bomber jacket into the daysack with my Russian tank commander's hat and pulled on the Gore-Tex. I left the Skoda in the long-term car park at Heathrow with Sam's Browning and second mag tucked into the spare tyre, then tubed it to West Brompton and caught the train to East Croydon. After doing some of the kind of anti-surveillance shit that I'd done on Bankside the previous evening, I headed for Gatwick and took the first flight I could get to Vienna.

If the Leathermen were going to make a habit of chasing me around, I needed to find out who the fuck they were, and who was pulling their strings.

PART SEVEN

PART SEVEN

1

Rasskazovska, Moscow

Wednesday, 1 February
10.05 hrs

I'd lost count of the number of movies I'd seen that featured a lone figure standing on the wrong side of a railing, gazing at the life he could no longer share, but I'd never thought I'd be in that man's shoes.

Now here I was in Anna's gated enclave, watching her hold our son in the saddle of a little wooden dinosaur on a spring while the older kids ran around, leaping on and off the roundabouts and swings. It was six degrees below outside, but some genius had erected one of those inflatable plastic domes over the playground for the winter months and pumped it full of warm air.

She seemed happier than I'd seen her in a while, and even more beautiful. And our boy was loving every minute of it. His chuckle was completely infectious, and bounced across the play area. I couldn't wait to show him what fun you could have with a condom full of ketchup.

The midnight Aeroflot connection to Domodedovo had been full of men in leather jackets, but none of them seemed particularly interested in me, or not enough to join me for my second

223

breakfast of the day. I'd called in at Shokolad-nitsa after we landed and got a ham and cheese pancake and a mug of their world-famous hot chocolate down my neck while I checked out the surrounding area. Then I'd mooched out to the yellow cab rank and, after a short negotiation involving both dollars and roubles, took one to Moscow's eastern margins.

2

The truth is I wasn't sure what kind of welcome I was going to get from Anna. I hadn't called ahead, in case she was having a bad-hair day and wanted me to keep my distance.

When she finally caught sight of me, she screwed up her face like I was someone she'd bumped into in another life, and she could no longer remember my name. But then she swept our little soldier off the dinosaur, both of them giggling like lunatics, and brought him over to the gate.

She held him up to me. 'Darling Nicholayevich, this is your papa. You have his eyes. Hopefully you won't decide to follow his choice of career . . . '

Her expression was still guarded. No surprises there: she'd thought she'd cleared me out of her life a week ago. But he wriggled with delight.

I reached out and took him, as carefully as I possibly could.

She finally gave me a smile. 'He's a little boy, Nicholas. He's not made of glass!'

As I drew him to me, he clutched my nose between his thumb and forefinger, gave it an experimental twist, then settled his head on my chest, under my chin. He smelt of warm milk and fruit purée and everything good. For about the first time in my life, I wished I'd bothered to shave.

I held him close and shut my eyes. Which was

a mistake. A big mistake. I suddenly pictured myself at the edge of the Grwyne Fawr Dam, my little boy in my arms. Heard the crack of a high-powered rifle. Watched helplessly as the 7.62mm round lifted off the top of his head, just above the eyeballs, like a soft-boiled egg . . .

'Nicholas . . . What's the matter?' I felt Anna's hand on my arm.

I blinked, momentarily disoriented. 'Nothing.' I held our son more tightly. 'All good.'

Our place — Anna's place — was a two-storey, three-bedroom villa with all the trimmings in a brand new community not far from the Borovskoe Highway. It had cost two million plus of the dollars I'd lifted from a Narcopulco-based drug baron, who'd threatened my family last year, and it had been money well spent.

The developers had taken some stick from the tree-huggers for bulldozing this stretch of woodland, but they'd left enough silver birches to shelter each property from the next when the leaves were out, while not giving the inhabitants a sense of total isolation. Knight Frankski had really come up with the goods. It was just what she'd wanted: an even better place to bring up your kid than the Tabard Gardens Estate.

I carried Nicholai inside and strapped him into his very shiny baby bouncer. I put it on the table where he could have a good look around while I reached for my daysack.

I peeled back my cuffs to show I had nothing hidden up my sleeves, then, as if by magic, I whipped out a couple of parcels I'd had gift-wrapped at Gatwick: a teddy bear in a Tower of London Beefeater uniform for him, and perfume for her.

The girl at the duty free didn't need me to tell her I was out of my depth. She'd guided me gently to the Chanel counter when I'd explained what I was looking for and plucked a bottle of Coco Mademoiselle from the display. Apparently it had top notes of Tunisian Curaçao and was just the thing for pretty girls on motorbikes.

Anna gave me that look again — like I was someone she didn't completely recognize — but this time it was immediately filled with warmth. 'Nicholas . . . You've never done that before . . . '

I shrugged. I might even have blushed. I didn't think I'd ever done that before either.

Whatever, they both seemed to work OK. Nicholai started chewing the teddy bear's ear, and Anna gave me the biggest smile I'd seen from her for as long as I could remember.

When she'd fixed us a couple of George Clooney specials from the coffee machine, she finally asked the question that had been on her mind since the moment I appeared. 'So, Nicholas . . . Are you planning weekly visits?'

I told her not to panic. 'Only when I really need your help.'

I gave her the watered-down version of my recent Serbian experience, and made a rather bad attempt at drawing Sniper One's tattoo on her notepad. 'I thought it was a birthmark at first, but close up, it's quite intricate. It reminded me of those mortar scars in the pavement that the Sarajevo locals used to fill with resin during the siege.'

'The Roses?'

I nodded. 'But maybe it's just a coincidence.'

She gave me her version of the eyebrow treatment. 'You don't believe in coincidences, remember?'

'When I was in Bosnia with the Firm in 'ninety-four, there was a rumour about a Serbian brotherhood, a kind of secret society, forged among the killers on the hills surrounding Sarajevo, or maybe even before that. They don't seem to advertise themselves on the net. I couldn't find a single thing about them when I pressed the Google button in the Gatwick departure lounge.'

'Most secret societies try to stay away from Facebook.' I could see that her mind was whirring. I always loved it when that happened. Except when I was at the sharp end of any conclusions she came to. 'I need to talk to Pasha . . . '

I liked the sound of that. Pavel Korovin was a good guy. He had been Anna's editor at *Russia Today*, and they'd spent quite a bit of time saving the world together when we'd first met.

'My guess is you needed to know this yesterday?'

I grinned. 'Early last week would have been even better.'

She gathered her coat — the one that looked like a giant duvet — fur hat and gloves, kissed Nicholai on the top of his still not very hairy head, and made for the door. 'Look after him, will you? I'll try not to be too long. There's plenty of stuff in the fridge . . . '

3

Not too long ended up being about two hours. When she whizzed back through the door the newshound in her couldn't conceal its excitement, and the mother couldn't hide her concern.

'Where's Nicholai?'

'In his cot.'

'You managed to make him go to sleep?'

I shrugged. 'He was a bit knackered after we finished the obstacle course and the judo session.'

She gave me an old-fashioned look. 'Judo?'

'Yup. Karate too.' I threw some exaggerated martial-arts shapes. 'The whole black belt, Seventh Dan thing.'

'Very funny.'

'Actually, we just had a man-to-man in the hot tub. Then he asked if he could have a bite to eat and get his head down. All that dinosaur riding takes it out of a guy.'

She gave me a glimmer of a smile, but I could see she'd switched into business mode.

She threw her coat, hat and gloves onto the settee and sparked up the Clooney machine again. With a couple of frothy cappuccinos on the go, we sat at the table and she took a dozen printed sheets of A4 out of her satchel. She shook her head when I reached for them. 'Unless your Russian is a lot more fluent than it was a week ago, you'll have to settle for the pictures.'

229

She fished a page full of images out of the pack and handed it across to me. They were an odd bunch, ranging from pre-revolutionary political cartoons of dastardly men with Rasputin hair, fizzing bombs and Cyrillic captions to more contemporary photographs of the kinds of guys you didn't want pointing guns at you in the Black Mountains. And among them were two close-ups of someone's neck freshly inked with the rose-coloured tattoo.

'These are not good people, Nicholas.'

I looked up. 'I was definitely catching that vibe.'

'I'm being very serious. Do you know about the Black Hand?'

'Sure. People used to whisper about them in Sarajevo. Pretty much kicked off the First World War by assassinating the Archduke Franz Ferdinand. But I thought they'd all been rounded up and put in front of the firing squad the year before the Armistice.'

She sipped her coffee and flicked through the pages. 'That's certainly the official story. But they have very long memories in the Balkans, especially when there are scores to settle. And you don't start a global conflict one minute, then disappear in a puff of smoke the next.

'They were formed in 1901 — the usual cocktail of high idealism and low conspiracy, zealous altruism and criminal self-interest. After the 1917 trials they went to earth. The White Hand replaced them, apparently in opposition, but cut from similar cloth. They disappeared from sight too, many among the Allies, some time after arranging the 1941 Yugoslavian coup.'

She responded to my quizzical look by telling me a bit about the White Hand's plot to stop Yugoslavia joining forces with Germany, Italy and Japan by accelerating seventeen-year-old Peter II's accession to the throne. The Brits were also in it up to their eyeballs. Peter's godfather was King George V, and he'd been to school in Wiltshire. It sounded like these guys had a finger in every pie.

'There were splinter groups too, of course, guilty of varying degrees of extremism. One particular band was responsible for many of the endless mortar and sniper attacks on the people of Sarajevo and the other cities under siege during the war in Bosnia. Its members distinguished themselves by their brutality, and their badge of so-called courage.'

She picked up my crap drawing and coloured it in with a red felt-tip. 'Red is the colour of power and energy in Serbian culture. These people go by the name of Crvena Davo — the Red Devils. And you were right: the tattoo is a representation of the Sarajevo Rose.'

When she'd finished, she gave me some serious eye to eye. 'These people aren't going to visit us here, are they?'

'I'd be able to answer that more reliably if I knew what they wanted with me. But I didn't come here in a straight line, and don't worry, I'm not staying.'

Before feeding Nicholai she made us sandwiches. As we munched our way through them she threw me the question that I'd been grappling with since the Bolthole. 'What possible connection

231

could exist between a Serbian brotherhood and an accident at SAS HQ?'

'I guess it's still possible that there isn't one, that they have their own agenda. But I think these guys are guns for hire, brought in by someone — or some people — pretty high in the chain of command to prevent whatever really happened there going public. Either way, I'm hoping I might find some answers in Belgrade.'

'Pasha says he would be happy to help. He went to Bosnia when he was a student. With the convoys. Taking food and medical supplies in, and Muslim children out. He still has nightmares about it.'

'He's not the only one.' I'd come across a few paramedics and UNHCR guys who'd done the same run, and they'd come away with PTSD big-time. There were about sixty thousand people in Goražde, including refugees — far too many to supply from the air.

'He also made good friends. He's got some names. One was the leader of a Muslim resistance group, but Pasha fears he and his family might have died when their village was overrun. Another is a translator. And there's also an imam, I think.'

That made me chuckle. There had to be a priest somewhere in the mixture. They were starting to behave like London buses.

'It's good to hear you laugh, Nicholas. I was worried about you earlier, when you first held our son. What was going on out there? You looked like someone had trodden across your grave . . . '

It was worse than that. Much worse. I'd watched someone tread across his. But telling that to Anna would only freak her out. I shook my head. 'Sometimes I'm just blown away by how important you guys are to me.'

Her hand briefly touched mine. 'And that makes you sad?'

'No. What makes me sad is knowing that you were right when you told me the best way of keeping you both safe is for me to stay away.'

I didn't add that I was a little bit sorry that she was so much nicer to be with now I wasn't fully in her life than she had been when I was.

4

Arbat Ulitsa was one of the oldest streets in Moscow. The tourist blurb claimed that it dated from 1493, but didn't mention that Ivan the Terrible's execution squads, the Oprichnina, had had their HQ there. Anna had told me that when she was busy educating me in life and literature. Tolstoy mentioned the Arbat in *War and Peace* as a key location; Napoleon torched it in 1812 during the Battle for Moscow. If you wanted to fuck over the Kremlin, this was your best route in.

In the middle of the nineteenth century it became popular with writers and artists. I wasn't sure whether they'd have wanted to gather at the Starbucks. It was in the same block as a pharmacy and a clothes store, on the ground floor of a rather severe precinct about a K to the west of Red Square. I arrived there half an hour early, via the Arbatskaya.

When we'd lived in the centre of town, I'd dropped by the Metro whenever I got the chance. It was an amazing place — a red-painted, concave-fronted blend of theatre, blockhouse and gun emplacement above ground, and a chandelier-decked cathedral beneath. I'd never forget my first trip to Grand Central Station in New York, but this place, with its epic moulded arches, marble floors and pillars, was something else again.

I headed for the Starbucks counter and got something big and frothy on the go. I told the barista my name was Nicholayevich. She just smiled and wrote *Nic* in the box on the side of the cup.

Pasha poked his head through the door as I ordered a refill. He was compact and intense, with bright, inquisitive eyes behind gold-rimmed glasses. His tight, curly black hair was threaded with grey. If Hollywood had been looking for a sensitive but dedicated Bolshevik revolutionary for a remake of *Doctor Zhivago*, or maybe one of those mega-smart academics grappling with the mysteries of the mathematical universe, he'd have been perfect casting.

His English was a whole lot better than my Russian. It was a whole lot better than my English, come to that.

He ordered a double shot of espresso, shrugged off his coat and pulled up a chair. We exchanged small-talk, mostly about Anna and our boy, but he knew time was short. 'So, Nicholai, she tells me you are . . . researching . . . the Crvena Davo?' He wanted me to be in no doubt that there were other words he could have used instead of 'researching'.

I told him that a friend of mine had come into contact with one of the brotherhood, and the experience hadn't been good. So, yes, I did need to know more about them.

He'd been to Bosnia several times in the early nineties, and managed to get inside Goražde twice. 'I was just a kid, really, and wanted to make the world a better place. As you may know from the name Korovin, or perhaps Anna has told you, I'm from a Muslim family, so eastern Bosnia seemed like a good place to start.'

There were a number of NGOs operating under the UNHCR umbrella, and he had joined a group of French, British and German volunteers dedicated to the task of taking food and medicine into the cities under siege. They didn't make it if the Serb checkpoints weren't in the mood, but they never stopped trying.

'Of course there were many moments when we felt like we were banging our heads against a very big and very unforgiving brick wall, and we all knew the shelling would begin again as soon as we left, but most of us felt that if we managed to save one life, it was all worthwhile.

'I'll never forget the reception we had from the people of Goražde the first time we made it through. They clapped and cheered and embraced us. Old men with tears in their eyes. Women and children weeping with happiness.'

I remembered Trev telling me similar stuff. He'd set up an observation post on the roof of the Hotel Gradina when he'd been there in 'ninety-four. There was no electricity to spark up the lift system, and the stairwell was filled with people — live ones sheltering from the snipers and dead ones who either hadn't managed to or had just run out of road.

'They greeted us with flowers. I have no idea where they'd managed to grow them — the whole city was a wasteland, a mass of twisted metal and fractured concrete.'

Pasha paused, lost in the memory, then turned

236

the intensity switch up another notch. 'That was when I realized we weren't only bringing them supplies. We were bringing them hope.

'I never felt that when I was in Bosnia at the end of 'ninety-four. I was buried under cam-net on a series of hillsides, guiding in Paveway bombs with a laser target designator. I was what they used to call 'the man in the loop'. It meant that I was on the ground, breathing their oxygen, while a nice girl in a bunker in Nevada pressed whatever buttons needed pressing. And if they decided that the target should live to fight another day, there was nothing I could do about it.

'We took out a couple of their ethnic-cleansing supremos, but when it came to saving or improving the lives of the poor fuckers at the sharp end, I couldn't lift a finger, just watched helplessly as women and children were raped and slaughtered in the streets. I had a ringside seat at the world's ugliest circus.'

He gave me a sad smile. 'Ah . . . the agony of men with guns who may not squeeze the trigger . . . '

'Fair one. But you must have suffered the agony of men who have no guns.'

He didn't need to think too hard about that. 'Of course. Every minute of every day I was in the Balkans, and many since. But at no time, perhaps, as badly as when I first encountered the work of the Crvena Davo.'

5

Pasha's eight-vehicle convoy had made it through the Serb cordon that surrounded Goražde for the second time in mid-June 1993. The UN had declared it a Safe Haven a couple of weeks earlier.

'Those Safe Havens really were magic, weren't they?'

There were six of them in the care of UNPROFOR, the United Nations Protection Force, authorized by the Security Council to defend their citizens by 'all necessary means, including the use of force; Sarajevo, Srebrenica, Tuzla, Žepa and Bihać were the other five. Goražde was the only one not to fall, but it clung to its so-called freedom by little more than its fingernails.

The UN didn't cover themselves in glory in the nineties. They stood by and watched the genocide in Rwanda and, despite the sabre-rattling, did much the same in Bosnia. Ten thousand people died in Sarajevo during its four-year siege. More than eight thousand men and boys were massacred in Srebrenica in less than seventy-two hours in July 1995, right under the noses of their blue-bereted guardians. When the Canadian and Australian troops began to take down the snipers on the hillsides, they were withdrawn.

Pasha took a couple of deep breaths, but I

could see that all these years later he was still vibrating with rage.

'We arrived in Goražde a handful of days after more than fifty of the city's inhabitants had been killed in a Serb artillery attack on a first-aid clinic. As we unloaded the trucks a woman stumbled towards me, carrying what looked like a bundle of rags. When she came closer, I saw of course it wasn't rags. It was the body of a child. A little girl, she can't have been more than four or five.

'She had been hit by shrapnel from a mortar blast before we entered the city. She was bleeding from wounds in her cheeks, legs and chest, but alive. I think her mother confused me with someone who could perform miracles. We had brought food and bedding through the blockade, so of course we could mend her daughter.

'I tried to explain I wasn't a doctor, but either she couldn't understand or she didn't want to. Our translator, Aleksa, took charge immediately. She was only nineteen, even younger than me, but you know how such conflicts can bring out the best in a human being as well as the worst. She told me the first-aid centre was out of action, because of the shelling, so we must take the little girl to the hospital across the river.

'I expressed some concern about the snipers in the surrounding hills. She said the child would die without proper medical attention, and we still had fifteen minutes left of our two-hour ceasefire. We didn't have time to finish unloading and then drive, but we could probably make it on foot.'

Pasha's jaw clenched and he lowered his eyes to examine what was left of his espresso.

'I wrapped the child in one of the blankets we'd just brought in. I'll never forget the look she gave me as I took her into my arms. A look of absolute trust. Everything would be all right now.

'Her mother told us her name was Amina. In Arabic, Amina means 'faithful'. Did you know that, Nick? It also means 'protected'.'

He stopped again, and swirled the coffee dregs in his cup.

'Aleksa, Amina, her mother and I arrived at the bridge across the Drina with about five minutes to go before the end of the ceasefire. It was about a hundred metres wide, a steel frame on two concrete supports, beneath which they had suspended a wooden walkway to protect pedestrians from snipers. I went first. I looked down at her and smiled, hoping that I appeared more confident than I felt.

'Once we'd moved away from the bustle around the convoy, it was completely, eerily quiet. The little girl must have been in great pain, but she didn't even whimper. The birds had stopped singing — maybe they'd forgotten how. All I could hear was the sound of our footsteps on the planks. And then, as we emerged on the far side of it, a single shot.'

6

Pasha pulled back the left sleeve of his fleece and then of the shirt beneath. There was a raised three-inch scar on the outside of his biceps, halfway between his shoulder and his elbow. 'This is the path the bullet took after it went through Amina's head . . . '

Try as hard as he might to put some distance between himself and that single traumatic event nearly two decades ago, I could see he was still struggling. It was written in every muscle of his face and upper body.

'Anna said you still have nightmares.'

'I have some good days. And, of course, Anna and I have witnessed and reported upon many other episodes of extreme brutality and corruption. But that's the one which keeps coming back. The look of trust in that little girl's eyes. The blood blossoming on her forehead as she lay in my arms at the end of that awful bridge. The touch of her mother's hand on my cheek, so gentle, even though she knew her daughter was dead.'

'It wasn't your — '

He held up his hand. 'Don't, Nick. Don't tell me it wasn't my fault. Of course, deep down, I know that. In my head I know it's not about blame. I know it shouldn't be about guilt either. It's about being in a world of shit and trying not to sink too deep. Yet in my heart I can't stop

241

wondering why the sniper in the hills chose to take her instead of me. And it's her eyes I see when I close mine.'

He wrapped his fist around his cup like he was trying to squeeze the life out of it, then left its crumpled remains on the table between us.

I'd hardly touched mine.

He looked at it, then at me. 'I don't know about you, Nicholai, but I could use a real drink.'

He knew a place nearby that served at least thirty different kinds of vodka. I told him I didn't have time to try them all.

He guided me north of the Arbat, then fractionally east towards the Lubyanka. His bar was in a basement, and even darker than the Moscow afternoon. He ordered a couple of shots of Stolichnaya Gold for each of us and got embarrassed when I insisted on paying.

Pasha raised his glass and toasted Nicholai, but I knew he was still thinking about the little girl on the bridge. After we'd both taken a sip he continued his story.

He had carried Amina back along the walkway. Aleksa went to find the imam, who supervised the washing of Amina's body in scented water. They didn't wrap her in a shroud. She was a martyr: she had to be buried in the clothes she was wearing when she died. Pasha had accompanied her body to the gravesite, and watched as she was buried on her right side, facing Mecca.

Muslims, like Catholics, believe that a better life beckons for the departed. I'd never really bought into that, but took some consolation from the fact that Amina's agonies in this one had been cut short. She hadn't shared the fate of another kid called Zina, who'd died of multiple gunshot wounds a few feet in front of me when I'd had Ratko Mladić in my sights. She'd tried to escape from a bunch of his thugs who were busy gang-raping her mates. She was fifteen years old and dreamed of being Kate Moss, and I couldn't lift a finger to help.

I also thought about the women I'd seen hanging from trees along my route, and the ones I'd heard about who'd thrown themselves and their babies into a lake rather than endure the brutality of their advancing enemy. Sometimes suicide beat the shit out of survival. And when the Bosnian Serb leader was put on trial for war crimes in The Hague last year, it wasn't a moment too soon.

Pasha did his best to savour the vodka, but he looked like he'd rather drown himself in it. 'The imam told me who had done this terrible thing. I'd heard rumours about the Crvena Davo, of course, but never had first-hand experience of them. I tell myself that I have lived to fight other battles, in other ways, but the truth is this: if I had possessed a gun at that moment, and known how to use it, I might well have gone in search of vengeance.'

I knew that feeling, big-time. And I found myself wondering if vengeance was on the Leathermen's agenda. Had Trev crossed them during his Hotel Gradina stint? Were they aware of my LTD tasks? Did they know I'd once tried to put a two-thousand-pound bomb up Mladić's arse a hundred Ks or so north of Sarajevo? We knew these lads didn't forgive and forget.

'The imam counselled me wisely. Like Martin Luther King, he believed that an eye for an eye leaves the whole world blind, and that while there could be no possible justification for Amina's murder, these conflicts are never straightforward.

'Yes, the Serbs were determined to starve the Muslim enclaves into submission. But the Muslims themselves were not averse to using convoys like ours as shields, and siting their gun batteries behind hospitals like the one we were trying to reach.

'When a tank stalled on the outskirts of Goražde, they tore the Serb crew limb from limb, literally, with their bare hands. So it's not difficult to understand how their compatriots were brainwashed by the propaganda about the atrocities committed by the advancing Islamic hordes.'

He wasn't wrong. The Bosnians might have looked like Worzel Gummidge, with full yokel gear and string tied round their trousers, but they also had some very unlovable moments. And there hadn't been only one war in the Balkans, there had been hundreds.

'And look at Srebrenica. Sure, Mladić and his Scorpions were responsible. But they did what they did with the help of Greek and Russian volunteers — so I and my fellow countrymen must for ever share that shame.'

I didn't turn down the offer of a second vodka

when it came. I wasn't going to use it to celebrate the imam's eye for an eye theory, though. Sure, you had to break the cycle at some point — anyone who'd been on the sharp end of a Balkan thousand-year vendetta didn't need that message to be spelled out — but there was a time and a place for everything, and after hearing what Pasha had told me, I was even more pleased that I'd helped one of those fuckers take a nosedive off a Bermondsey roof.

It wouldn't bring any of the Aminas and Zinas back, but it would go some way towards evening the score, and help stop me barking at the moon.

7

Pasha gave me contact details for Aleksa and the imam, and promised to set up meetings with both of them.

I took a cab back to Anna's villa and asked if I could borrow her Range Rover for a couple of hours. We'd traded in the Touran after Nicholai was born. Anna liked the idea of keeping him as safe as possible on the road, and so did I. The place I was about to head for was full of the things. It would fit right in.

I set the satnav for a *dacha* the size of the Kremlin about forty-five minutes to the north-west. It was owned by a Ukrainian oligarch called Frank Timis. You wouldn't want Frank as an enemy, which was one of the reasons he was a good man to have onside. We weren't best mates or anything, but I'd rescued his son from al-Shabab, Somalia's answer to the Taliban, and he'd become my private banker after last year's Mexican trip.

We'd lifted twelve million dollars of cartel drug money from an *estancia* outside Narco-pulco, and Frank was still busy filtering it into the real world for us. He wasn't doing it entirely for sentimental reasons: he'd end up trousering 25 per cent.

Frank's village was a throwback to the time of the tsar. This was where the serious money came to get away from the stresses and strains of the big city. Three- and four-storey timber-built palaces with high walls and sweeping driveways stood among huge trees.

I let Frank's people know I was approaching when I reached the outskirts, and his vast wooden gates slid back as I arrived. I drove past his snow-covered pool and playground, and a sprinkling of shadowy figures patrolling the grounds beyond them, then parked up alongside his fleet of shiny black wagons. They all had red diplomatic plates to help beat the Moscow jams.

It was even colder here than it had been in Anna's enclave. The chill wind made our Black Mountains bolthole seem almost tropical by comparison. The short journey across Frank's veranda to his enormous kitchen felt like a polar trek.

The triple-glazed, aluminium-framed door and the original hand-carved monster behind it opened into a world of gleaming marble and stainless steel.

'Niiiiiiiiick . . . '

As I shook the snow off my boots a small person rocketed across the polished stone floor and wrapped his arms around my legs.

Frank was sitting in his favourite spot, behind a white marble table at the centre of the room. He was a compact, neatly groomed man with a very big presence. He smiled quietly as his little boy clutched my knees, then after a couple of beats decided that was enough affection for one day. 'Stefan . . . '

The boy stepped back and looked up at me. He had wide, smiling eyes and dimples in his cheeks. I ruffled his hair, then rotated him back towards his homework.

Frank waved me in the direction of a coffee machine the size of a nuclear reactor. This was only my third time here, but it already seemed like a bit of a tradition. I fired up a double espresso and took a seat opposite him.

'So, Nick. Mexico again?'

I shook my head. 'Serbia.'

At some unseen signal a soft and cuddly version of a large, brightly painted Russian doll suddenly appeared. She dipped her head respectfully at us and wiped her hands on her apron, then swept Stefan up in her arms and carried him out of earshot.

I showed Frank Anna's Crvena Davo print-out and told him they'd taken out a friend of mine. 'I need to find out more about them. I need to find out who has let them loose.'

He examined the photographs, giving particular attention to the ones of the tattoo, and nodded slowly. 'Sarajevo?'

'And Goražde. But all that shit was nearly twenty years ago.'

He fixed me with his ice-cold eyes. 'What is twenty years in a war that has been waged for a thousand?' He ran a hand across his perfectly shaved chin. 'I have heard a little about them, but they have never interfered with my business, so I regret to say that I cannot help as much as I would like. I can only tell you what you know already. These are bad people, Nick. Garbage.'

The eyes glanced down at the pictures again before returning to meet mine. 'And you remember what I told you about garbage?'

How could I forget? In the last twelve months we'd followed the refuse trail to Somalia and South America. 'If you want to find garbage, you must go to the garbage dump.'

He nodded like a benevolent teacher, then stood up. As always, his jeans were so carefully ironed you could have cut yourself on the crease.

I asked him for one more favour before I left. He had sent his boys round to look after Anna and Nicholai while I was in Mexico. Anna's enclave was *über*-secure, but I needed him to keep an eye on them now.

I dropped the Range Rover back there forty-five minutes later. She suggested that I stay the night, but couldn't disguise her relief when I stuck to my guns.

PART EIGHT

PART EIGHT

1

Ulica Pariska, Belgrade

Thursday, 2 February
09.55 hrs

I caught the late Turkish Airlines flight from
Vnukovo to Aerodrom Nikola Tesla. The
eight-hour stopover in Istanbul suited me fine: it
gave me plenty of time to switch back to my
bomber jacket. It was also a fraction of the price
of the Lufthansa non-stop, and only a nutter
would take it. Or someone who didn't want to be
followed.

I sat next to a Serb in his thirties on the final
leg of the journey. He was beanpole thin and
dressed in black. He'd gone for the Russell
Brand look — long dark hair and a wispy beard
— rather than the jarhead and leather-jacket
combo, so he clearly had a big sense of humour.
Seconds after take-off he pointed at the
emergency exit alongside us and told me he'd be
very happy to open the door if I wanted to leave
early.

I thanked him, but said I was planning on
going all the way to Belgrade because I'd never
been there before. He didn't need any further
encouragement. For the rest of the flight he told
me what I had to see (the fortress, the St Sava
Temple, the NATO bomb damage), and what I

253

had to eat and drink (*ćevapčići*, which sounded like the Serbian version of a lamb kebab; *karadordeva*, rolled veal coated with breadcrumbs and stuffed with cheese; *slivovitz*, their plum-flavoured rocket fuel, and a bucket or two of Lav beer). He even pointed me in the direction of a nice little hotel halfway along Vajara Djoke Jovanovica, on the southern edge of town.

I thought for a moment that he was going to offer to escort me there, but he left with a smile and a handshake at Passport Control and I headed for the hire-car counters beside the arrivals hall.

2

Pasha had managed to fix me a meeting with Aleksa at her home on the Morava River in the early afternoon, and with the imam by the Belgrade Fortress after Maghrib, the sunset prayers.

The Audi A3's satnav told me that the drive to Aleksa's place would take two and a half hours, so I programmed it with the evening's RV point first. I wasn't going for the full Russell Brand tour, but I didn't want to meet anyone, however friendly, in this neck of the woods after dark without recceing the surrounding area in advance.

The Belgrade Arena was already looking forward to hosting Il Divo and Jennifer Lopez later in the autumn as I passed through New Belgrade, where gleaming space-age office and residential developments did battle with bog-standard Communist-era monstrosities in uniform shades of brown and grey. The traffic ground to a halt under a motorway bridge long enough for me to admire a few samples of Belgrade's finest spray-paint artwork, and a portable toilet that seemed to be so full of shit its door could no longer close.

I found a parking space on one of the side-streets leading off Ulica Pariska. Thumbing through the guidebook I'd bought at the airport, I looped back onto Kneza Mihaila, the pedestrian street that ran through the centre of the old town and led to Kalemegdan Park and the fortress.

The pavement cafés were already humming with locals and the odd tourist. I wasn't sure whether they were doing their best to smoke themselves to death or just trying to avoid eye contact with the bootleg DVD vendors and wizened old ladies flogging long-stem crimson roses for a handful of dinars. Along with the rest of the world, they all seemed more interested in whoever was at the other end of their mobile phones than the person sitting opposite.

I dodged a couple of crowded trams on my way across the main and walked down an avenue lined with trees and market stalls piled high with Serbian infantry helmets and Red Star Belgrade football scarves. It wasn't cold enough for Russian tank commanders' furry hats.

I passed the Monument of Gratitude to France and scanned the benches to its left, spaced around a bronze fountain whose centre-piece was a fisherman strangling a snake. Pasha had told me this statue was known as *The Struggle*, and it was where the imam would meet me at the end of the day.

Two teenage girls rocketed past me on their rollerblades, following the promenade that fringed the western battlements. The citadel itself dominated the skyline ahead of me, a haphazard collection of weathered red brick and crenellated stone fortifications commanding the high ground above the point at which the Danube and Sava rivers met.

I turned right towards a white clock tower and skirted the first of a series of moats, which now housed a tennis club, and another with a floodlit basketball court. I followed a bunch of lads in running kit and headphones through two heavily defended archways then went right again, dropping down into a third defensive trench.

This one was filled with a ramshackle assortment of First and Second World War howitzers and armoured fighting vehicles that were fighting a losing battle against hordes of advancing dandelions. A Yugoslav Heavy Tank, based on the Soviet T34, stood on a concrete stand, turret closed and barrel threatening a nearby tree. It had a drab green paint job, and didn't look as though it was having nearly as much fun as its cousin in Bermondsey.

The display led up to Marshal Tito's mausoleum in the House of Flowers. Tito was quite a guy. He awarded himself the Order of the People's Hero three times over. He probably deserved it. He managed to hold Yugoslavia together for forty years.

Something made me glance back up at the parapet above the arch behind me, where a uniformed figure, weapon at the hip, was silhouetted against the winter sky.

3

The trench curved to my left, between bulging stone battlements and a huge red-brick wall punctuated at regular intervals by barred windows and arched metal gates. The display of weaponry ran out after about a hundred metres, at an ancient motor patrol boat filled with plastic carrier-bags and discarded Coke bottles. Veins of rust crisscrossed its dull grey paintwork, like spiders' webs.

The crazy paving petered out and a rough gravel path snaked through the weeds and clumps of coarse grass towards two massive stone towers that stood guard at the north-east corner of the complex. When I reached the archway at their base, the running team had disappeared.

I tabbed past a deserted café and down a set of steps to the two small garrison chapels. In one — the Rose Church, dedicated to the Blessed Virgin — a bearded Orthodox priest presided over a baptism, surrounded by ranks of burning candles, gold-framed religious icons and a tight-knit group of warm, friendly participants and onlookers. This was the first place I'd been in Belgrade, apart from the airport, where only the wicks were smoking.

The hillside beneath the churches dropped a hundred metres or so to the Danube. I turned back and took the walkway into that corner of the fortress. I made my way towards the exit beneath the clock tower, then circled back to the Audi. It was time to hit the road south.

The very polite satnav voice sounded like a Harry Enfield impression of a wartime BBC radio announcer as he invited me to prepare myself for every twist and turn through the centre of the city. He didn't warn me about the tramlines, though, and made no mention of the bomb damage.

I'd heard a lot about the NATO strikes against Milošević during the Kosovo crisis in 1999, but this was the first time I'd seen what had happened at the sharp end. The Ministry of Defence and General Staff HQ on Kneza Miloša Street had taken direct hits, and the scars still showed. No light shone from the interior of the building, and a tangle of rusting steel rods and crumbled concrete hung out of a gaping hole in its side, like guts oozing from a shrapnel wound.

Satnav guided me onto the main to Čačak via Lazarevac and Ljig and a few other seriously unpronounceable places and got quite worried when I turned and doubled back a few times then went down a one-way street in the wrong direction to see if I'd picked up a tail. Once I'd cleared the suburbs I was pretty sure I hadn't.

The odd brightly painted show home stood out among the skeletal ruins that now gathered from time to time at the edge of the potholed tarmac. Some of the half-built structures looked like they were preparing for a brighter future; others had just given up hope, and one or two were so heavily coated in graffiti they could barely stand up.

These places weren't teeming metropolises. They seemed to be inhabited mostly by old men playing cards and drinking Lav, a few younger men in tracksuits or hi-vis jackets standing by big holes at the side of the road, skinny girls in stone-washed jeans, and bold women with dyed crimson hair who kept everything going.

I realized I'd half expected Serbia to be entirely populated by unfriendly fuckers with tattooed necks and Dragunov rifles. I'd got some hard-eyed stares, but what I'd seen so far was a slightly sad country inhabited by people who were trying to make a go of things, and seemed happy to share what little they had after two decades or more of serious shit.

A father and son were turning a pig on a spit in their front yard while their next-door neighbour did his best to breathe some extra mileage into an ancient tractor with a welding torch. Most of the advertising hoardings seemed to be celebrating local beers and politicians up for re-election. A few featured sultry women inviting us to enjoy a night out at Belgrade's Grand Casino, or to invest in skimpy Italian underwear. Fuck knew where you were supposed to buy it out here, though: most of the shops only sold fruit and veg, motor mowers or plastic chairs.

Rubbish spewed from every wheelie bin, but the polished marble roadside shrines shone in the sunlight and were covered with fresh flowers. Dogs appeared to roam at will, but they were well fed and didn't look like they'd been bred to sink their teeth into the legs of passers-by or spread killer diseases. If Nicholai had been born in Serbia I'd have advised him to go into the headstone business or become a vet.

I couldn't read most of the graffiti any more easily than the Cyrillic street signs, but as I drove on I noticed one slogan being regularly repeated. At first I saw 'HH', alongside a crude graphic of a sniper sight. Then 'HEAD HUNTERS', written in English. I had no idea who these lads were, but I was pretty sure they weren't in the corporate recruitment game.

4

As I moved further south and west into the hills I got the sense that my surroundings were becoming more prosperous. There was the same random arrangement of fresh paint, collapsing roof beams and rust-eaten wriggly tin, but the more ragged smallholdings were now rubbing shoulders with huge plum orchards and vineyards. And the weather-beaten Ladas and Yugos and Zastavas shared parking space with one or two very shiny 4WD Mercs and BMWs.

The slopes steepened and the lush greenery gave way to sheer rock faces that soared upwards from each side of the road. I'd Googled this neck of the woods during my downtime at Istanbul airport, so I knew it had provided a refuge from the conflicts that had raged across the Balkans for at least the last seven hundred years. Catalan mercenaries, Ottoman Turks, you name it: if they were on your tail, one of the three hundred monasteries that once filled the Ovčar-Kablar Gorge was the safest place to be.

I drove beneath an iron bridge, which carried the rail line from one tunnel to the next. This was the point at which the Morava River carved its way most dramatically between the two neighbouring mountains — the Ovčar and the Kablar — and Aleksa had told Pasha that she'd pick me up from a waterside café just beyond the hydro-electric dam.

The Restoran Santa Maria was tethered to a jetty, with an off-road parking area above it. I got there about twenty-five minutes early, ordered a beer and a plate of homemade sausages, then sat and watched the ducks and herons doing the things that ducks and herons do when they're a safe distance away from men with shotguns.

The very smiley waiter poured me a glass of Lav and reappeared with enough sausages and chips to feed a medium-size family. It was no hardship getting them down my neck: they were freshly grilled and tasted great. 'Beautiful, eh?' He beamed and spread his hands. I nodded enthusiastically. I wasn't sure whether he was talking about the food or the view, but he was right about both.

A small boat with an outboard motor chugged across the river towards me with a woman at the tiller and a couple of mop-haired boys in the bow. It wasn't until she'd tied up close by and the kids had piled out onto the pontoon that I realized this was my two o'clock appointment.

Aleksa was in her late thirties and had the slightly careworn look I'd come to expect in a country where everyone had a complicated past and nobody's future was secure. Her light brown hair was drawn back in a loose plait and she wore no makeup. She shepherded her kids through the door and smiled as I got up to greet her.

'Nick, you are so very welcome here.' She gestured towards the boat. 'I hope you don't get seasick. Our home is just around the bend, on the other side of the river. I thought it would be

263

easier to take you there in the boat. And the boys are very excited about having a British visitor.'

The boys looked a lot more excited about rocketing around the café like heat-seeking missiles, but I took her word for it. Close up, I could tell that many things haunted her, even in this picturepostcard setting, but she had a still centre. I had no difficulty seeing what the nineteen-year-old Pasha had found so inspiring about her.

I scoffed my last sausage, handed the waiter fifteen euros and told him to keep the change. He couldn't believe his luck. In the nineties there were times when you'd have needed a wheelbarrow full of dinars to pay even the smallest bill here. The local currency was stronger now, but you knew where you were with a pocketful of Western notes.

The boys calmed down for long enough to introduce themselves. The six-year-old was Goran and his younger brother was Novak. I asked Aleksa if they got tennis gear for every birthday. She smiled and shook her head. 'Mladen — my husband — plays whenever he gets the chance, but they couldn't care less about tennis, I'm afraid. Only football. They're mad keen Manchester United fans.'

We stepped into the boat and Aleksa sparked up the outboard. A heron left his perch at the far end of the pontoon and took off across the river with a slow beat of its massive wings. A group of wood- and stone-built houses clung to the far shore but, apart from one old boy busy doing boaty things, I couldn't see any sign of life.

264

Aleksa steered us expertly across the murky but mirror-still water, following the river as it zigzagged left and right. The boys asked in halting English if Wayne Rooney was a friend of mine. I told them I'd seen a few Millwall games, but didn't know much about football. They watched me with saucer eyes and wondered what kind of lunatic didn't want to share the Man U magic.

Maybe half a K later we pulled up alongside a dark-stained wooden jetty. I climbed out and tied up, then hoisted the boys onto dry land.

The four of us walked up a path that led between two strips of lawn to a small white-painted, terracotta-roofed family house. Aleksa threw open the door and apologized for the fact that her husband would not be able to join us. Mladen was on a trip north, to Novi Sad. 'He's an engineer. He and his team rebuilt the Liberty Bridge after the bombing, and he goes up there from time to time to make sure it's not falling down again.'

She got a brew on and offered me some more homemade sausages. The boys were definitely up for it, but I was already stuffed.

When I'd exhausted my Man U knowledge, which pretty much began and ended with a couple of stupid stories about George Best and Eric Cantona, Aleksa suggested that they went to their room and played. I said I'd catch up with them later.

We took the brews into a sun room that looked out over the river, and I heard myself giving her a much clearer account of my difficulties with the Leathermen than I'd intended. After Pasha's emotional account of their Goražde experience, I thought it would be insulting not to. I didn't mention Sam Callard or the CQB link, but gave her the basics about Trev and my Bermondsey adventures.

Aleksa warmed her hands on her steaming mug of tea and thought about where to begin.

'The most important thing for you to bear in mind is that the Crvena Davo are a little bit like your Provisional IRA. They began as an offshoot of a politically motivated, revolutionary movement, but swiftly became criminals. Now they are more interested in profit than ideology.'

'And in vengeance?'

'Of course. They dress it up as a matter of honour, but there is no dignity in it. And, like many people in this . . . complicated part of the world, they have long memories.'

I asked her if she minded me asking her some really bone questions. She smiled and told me I should go straight ahead, and be sure that she'd tell me if she wasn't in the mood to answer.

For starters, I wanted to get my head around how she now fitted into this landscape. 'You're a Bosnian Catholic, am I right?'

She nodded. 'Though I don't go to church much, these days. My faith has been quite severely tested over the past few years.'

'And yet you live a hundred Ks *this* side of the border, and just a hundred and fifty from Goražde. That can't be easy. Pasha told me about the little Muslim girl on the bridge . . . '

'Where do *you* live, Nick?'

I'd been asking myself that for longer than I could remember, but I gave her the simple answer. 'London, mostly. South London.'

'So, only a few miles from where your fellow countrymen killed their king a little over three hundred and fifty years ago, and where four of your own extremists murdered fifty-two people in 2005.'

Fair one. Shit happened everywhere. No one was immune.

'I do have a simpler answer, though. Mladen is a Serb. I first met him when he was constructing water wheels along the Drina. They only generated enough power to run a radio and one forty-watt bulb, but we should never underestimate the importance of a friendly voice and a single beam of light in a world of darkness. His family come from here. And you can see how beautiful it is.'

She took a sip of her brew, hesitated, then put the mug down on the table beside her and got up. 'But if you really want to try to understand this place, you must come with me.'

5

The hill rose sharply behind the house. The first seventy metres or so had been terraced — by some of Mladen's mates and a JCB, I guessed — and each level had a specific purpose.

The first contained the kind of veggie garden I'd only ever seen in magazines. The next one up had a set of mini goalposts at each end and the skid- and stud-marks said it had seen some serious footie action. Another was paved in old stone and brick; a table and chairs and a couple of teak sun-loungers were arranged around a barbecue that had been an oil barrel in a previous life.

She guided me up to the final tier, just below the treeline. In pride of place stood a couple of very shiny black marble headstones beneath a cherry tree, surrounded by a white picket fence. An image of the dead had been etched at the centre of each.

The one on the left was a memorial to Adrijana Vlašić, a striking woman with fire in her eyes and severe but immaculate hair. She was born on 12 August 1947 and died on 3 April 1999. Dragan, her husband, had had the world's biggest moustache, but I guessed his wife had worn the trousers. He'd survived her by about six months. Fresh flowers decorated their graves.

Aleksa dropped briefly onto one knee and crossed herself.

'Your mum and dad?'

She shook her head. 'Mladen's.'

I looked again at the dates. 'The NATO bombing?'

She nodded slowly. 'Adrijana went to visit her sister in Novi Sad. They were going to do some shopping. She might have lived if the missiles hadn't cut off the power to the hospital.' She reached out and traced the etchings with her fingertips. 'Dragan died of a broken heart.'

'I'm sorry . . .'

Her eyes were shining when she turned to me. 'It wasn't your fault, Nick. Though I imagine in other circumstances it might have been.'

She gave me a glance that was penetrating enough to make me wonder what else Pasha had told her about me. 'And that's not why I brought you up here. I'm still trying to work my way through this. I was an interpreter during the war, as you know, based mostly in Sarajevo and Goražde, first for the NGOs, then later for your military.

'I saw terrible things, of course. The assassination of Amina at the bridge across the Drina was among the worst, but there were others. And I knew that no one side was exclusively to blame.

'I also saw the so-called peacekeepers in action — which meant not only failing to keep the peace, but standing by as the atrocities unfolded. You know that Edmund Burke quote, Nick? 'All that is required for evil to triumph is that good men do nothing'?'

I did, actually. It was one of Anna's favourites.

'But I still believed that you and the

269

Americans had our best interests at heart.' She sighed. 'Then Kosovo exploded and NATO bombed our cities for seventy-nine days to teach Milošević, a genocidal lunatic, a lesson. Cluster bombs in residential areas, for Christ's sake. Missiles with depleted-uranium warheads. And yet the Belgrade cab drivers now treat the wreckage on Vardarska Street as if it is as big a tourist attraction as the fortress and St Sava's Temple.

'Many, many civilians were killed. It was an ecological disaster too. Fifty thousand tons of crude oil went up in flames at Novi Sad refinery. Fifty *thousand*! Sure, Serbia's major cities weren't emission-free zones in the first place, but think of all the toxins floating around in the atmosphere when something like that happens.'

She turned back to the headstones. 'I guess what I'm trying to say is that, though I know Adrijana's death is nothing compared to the massacres Milošević was responsible for, these small, private tragedies are often the ones that affect us most. And this one taught me, once and for all, that the guys in the white hats aren't always on the side of justice and truth, and that Edmund Burke was right. Each of us, as individuals, must stand up for what we believe in.'

She waved in the direction of the boys. They'd changed into their Man U strip and were demonstrating some serious moves around the goalmouth below us. 'If we don't, what kind of world will we pass on to them?'

I'd never kidded myself I could change the world. I just hoped I could protect Anna and Nicholai's bit of it. I'd always known that the guys in the white hats were the ones you really had to watch: they had a nasty habit of stabbing you in the back when you least expected it. But I was moved by her passion, and her distress. And I'd begun to understand her intense desire to save her boys from going through the shit that she'd been through.

We walked back into the sun room and she sparked up a new set of brews.

'Do you have kids, Nick?'

Once again, I found her question difficult to avoid. I told her about Anna and Nicholai and coming to the conclusion that they were both safer if my world didn't come knocking at their door. And for all her determination to be there for Goran and Novak, she was the first to really understand.

Her expression softened. 'Anna sounds quite wonderful. I'm also sure that Nicholai will have your strength. I hope he will come to understand, as she does, that there are some battles that have to be fought on one's own . . .'

I couldn't quite meet her gaze. 'I just hope he won't grow up thinking I'm a complete prick who did a runner at the first available opportunity, and never did anything useful, like build a bridge or help one bunch of people understand what the other bunch is really saying.'

'I'm sure he will forgive you for that.' She reached across and touched my arm. I looked up and saw that her eyes had begun to sparkle. 'But I'm not so sure he'll be so understanding when he finds out that you're not a close personal friend of Wayne Rooney.'

271

6

I managed to steer the conversation away from me, and back to the Crvena Davo. Aleksa's careworn face returned. Like Pasha, she still found it difficult to cut away.

'I heard many things about them, and we were never far from the things they did, particularly in Sarajevo. At one point during the siege they transported some of the wealthier and more twisted inhabitants of Belgrade — at a price, of course — to the hillsides around the city for a weekend's hunting. Only it wasn't bears and boars and game they shot. It was human beings — women, and children like Amina.'

I'd heard that rumour too. But this was the first time I'd heard that the Leathermen were behind it.

'It was only later that I saw them up close. I was the interpreter for one of the UN legations during the run-up to the Dayton Accords in late 'ninety-five. It meant spending an unhealthy amount of time making peace with people I'd have preferred to stake out in the dust and watch being eaten by soldier ants. But we kept telling ourselves it was for the Greater Good.'

'It's one of the reasons I never fancied wearing the blue beret. Where did you go to meet them?'

'They don't have an HQ, sadly — or your NATO friends could have sent them a missile from the Adriatic. We met them in the hills, a different place each time.'

'Who was in charge?'

'There was probably a hierarchy at the beginning, but one of the challenges of coming to any kind of agreement with them was that they operated like a loose federation rather than a single entity. I always thought of them as a series of roughly connected snake pits — it didn't matter how many you killed, there were always enough left over to keep spreading their poison. I don't know whether that was intentional — to make them less easy to identify and undermine — or accidental.'

It wasn't a big surprise. I hadn't expected them to be under the supreme command of an Osama bin Laden figure whom I could locate, interrogate and kill. But it didn't make my mission any easier.

'Who was on the UN team?'

'Oh, a mixed bag of American and British military and so-called strategic experts. I worked most closely with an English colonel, very smart, very courteous. Special Forces, I think, though of course he never said. He wanted to stake them out in the dust as well, and didn't mind them knowing that. They really respected him.'

I wasn't sure I wanted to hear the answer to my next question, but I had to ask it. 'Can you remember the colonel's name?'

She looked at me like I was a dickhead schoolteacher and she was the smartest kid in the class. 'Of course! I saw him again a couple of weeks ago. The Crvena Davo called him Hladno Oružje. It used to make them laugh.'

I had to admit that my Serbian had never been as good as her faultless English.

She smiled again. 'Sorry, Nick. Hladno Oružje means 'cold steel'. The colonel's name was Steele.'

I did my best not to react. 'A couple of weeks ago? I hadn't realized you were still on the translating circuit.'

She laughed. 'I'm not really. But I like to keep my hand in. I love all this . . . ' she motioned towards the hillside and the water ' . . . but I do need to escape it from time to time. The meeting with Steele — Major General Steele now, did you know? — wasn't entirely professional, though.

'During the war, one of your navy pilots was shot down and rescued by a Muslim resistance group, then sheltered by some of your military friends in Goražde. In the mood for reconciliation, the diplomatic community thought it would be a good idea to reunite the various participants at a reception there. It's always nice to have something to celebrate . . . '

'I don't suppose . . . '

'No, Nick. I said it was a celebration. Representatives of the Crvena Davo were definitely not invited.'

7

I talked with Aleksa until mid-afternoon. I knew I'd never overcome her boys' disappointment about me and Wayne Rooney, but I got them quite excited when I demonstrated a couple of judo routines before they bundled me into the boat.

We chugged past the herons to my hire car. One or two lights started to spark up across the lake as we said our goodbyes. Goran went into shy mode but Novak reached up and gave me a quick hug. Aleksa apologized for going into rant mode and not being much use to me. I told her she had nothing to be sorry about, and that she'd been a whole lot more helpful than she knew.

She asked me to come back one day with Anna and Nicholai, and meet Mladen. She thought we'd like each other *very* much — though he could be a bit boring about bridges. I smiled but said I couldn't make any promises.

I clambered up to the parking area and asked satnav to return me to the capital via Požega, through the other side of the gorge. I didn't want to cover the same ground I had on my trip out.

On the way up the river I passed a layby where a blond guy in a black parka, combats and trainers was standing, head bowed, beside a small marble shrine. I couldn't see the dates, but the picture on the plaque showed a young lad, early twenties at most, with a gold cross on one side and a BMW logo on the other.

I drove on, past a gypsy camp, a whole load of monasteries and a quarry with its own railway station. It was well past last light when I got back to Belgrade, and the fortress was floodlit. I parked outside the zoo and skirted the first set of battlements. There was a chill in the air, but the locals were out in force, wandering back and forth between the cafés in the pedestrian street and the promenades that wove through the citadel.

I checked out the area surrounding the snake statue fountain and took a seat some distance away from the nearest street lamp, facing the direct route from the city's only remaining mosque.

The imam showed up a few minutes before eight. He was wearing a white *kufi* prayer cap and a shiny quilted jacket over his ayatollah kit. His neatly trimmed beard was streaked with silver, and he didn't have a metal claw or mad, staring eyes. He struck me as something special even before he opened his mouth, an Islamic version of Father Mart.

I stood as he approached and he shook my hand warmly. He apologized for being a fraction late. 'Reports differ, Nick, but some claim that there were once as many as two hundred and seventy-three mosques in Belgrade. Now Bajrakli is the only one, so my days are full.'

I told him I was grateful for any time he could spare me, and that Aleksa had asked to be remembered to him.

A smile lit up his face. 'The young translator? How wonderful. A remarkable girl. There were very few happy moments in Goražde back then, but spending time with people like Aleksa and our friend Pasha was always a privilege.'

'Do you have more happy moments now, Imam?'

'There are no truly safe havens in our world, Nick, as I think you know. But Allah is merciful, and my work is needed here.' His smile broadened. 'Which brings us back to Pasha. He said you could use some help — though not necessarily of a spiritual nature . . . '

I knew he was my kind of priest. I told him that a friend of mine had become a target for a gang I thought might be the Crvena Davo, and I needed to discover more about them. He nodded slowly as I described the rose-coloured tattoo.

'On the neck?' He pointed to the patch of skin between his collar and his right ear.

'Yes.'

'I think I may be able to put you in contact with someone who will be able to give you useful information.' He paused and gave me some serious eye to eye. 'But I must ask you to give me your assurance that this is not about revenge. God asks us to fight evil but, more importantly, to forgive. And in a world such as ours, the vengeance trail, once begun, is never-ending.'

'It's about fighting evil, Imam.' He didn't need to know that I'd already killed the fucker who'd killed Trev.

He nodded, satisfied. 'I have spoken today to a man who comes to the Bajrakli to pray. His name is Wenceslas.' He raised the tips of his fingers to his neck again. 'He has such a tattoo. But he has turned away from the Davo. He has studied the Qur'ān for these many months, and converted to Islam. If you wish it, he is prepared to give you any advice you might need in dealing with this threat. However, like me, he will not put lives in jeopardy.'

I asked when and where we could do a debrief.

'How well do you know our city, Nick?'

I told him about the handful of locations I'd passed in the wagon, and my circuit of the fortress that morning.

'Then you may have seen the covered area beside the St Petka Chapel, on the far side of the battlements that surround what they call the Upper Town.' He looked at his watch. 'My new friend is waiting for you there.' He raised his right hand. 'Go in peace, Nick. And may Allah deliver a pleasing resolution to your mission.'

8

I waited for the imam to disappear beneath the trees that lined the first part of his route back to the mosque, then got up and headed around the statue of the lad grappling with the snake.

I glanced down to my right as I crossed the pedestrian bridge for the first archway. Floodlights glared across the clay court at the corner of the moat. A couple of lads were whacking tennis balls across the net at each other. Every time their racquets connected, the impact echoed off the walls like gunshots.

I veered left through the fortified gate beneath the clock tower, leaving the First and Second World War armaments display stretching down the trench on either side of me. This way I'd cut the corner I'd wandered around this morning.

The covered courtyard outside St Petka's was at the bottom of a small flight of stone steps that led from the Rose Church. I stayed in the shadows of the arch beneath the twin towers, opened my mouth and listened. The murmur of conversation floated towards me from the direction I'd just come, but I couldn't pick up any sound of movement or voices ahead or below.

As I was about to move on, I heard a muttered oath and footsteps moving away from me. Maybe my mates with the headphones were still up and running. Maybe someone was having a late-night argument with God.

Then again, maybe not.

I had a bad feeling about this.

I emerged from the shadows into empty space. A couple of candles flickered in the rack outside the Rose Church, but whoever had sparked them up was long gone.

I stopped and listened again at the top of the steps.

A dog barked further down the slope, somewhere in the dead ground between the trees and the river. I might have heard a groan or a sigh closer in, but I wasn't sure. It could have been the rustle of leaves and creak of branches in the night breeze.

Treading carefully on the tips of my Timberlands, I made my way to the walled courtyard below. The chapel door to my half-right was shut, but there was a glimmer of light from the wall lamp beside the arch framing the startlingly blue portrait of St Petka. There was a gated exit to a paved pathway ahead, and benches to my left under a tiled shelter.

I could see no sign of the imam's most recent convert, yet I sensed that something had recently disturbed the quiet serenity of the place. I swung open the gate and looked up and down the pathway that ran along the side of the chapel. There was no hint of activity, innocent or hostile.

I moved back into the centre of the yard. To the right of the lamp, in deep shadow, was the mouth of an alley that led to yet another set of steps, at the top of which I could just make out the silhouette of yet another corner tower.

Halfway up them, hugging the chapel wall, was some kind of obstacle.

As I moved towards it, and my eyes adjusted to the layers of darkness, I could see that it was a body.

9

The lad sprawled beside the chapel wall wore a white *kufi* prayer cap, like the imam's, and a tufty beard. His body was still warm but he had no pulse.

I couldn't see his neck clearly enough to tell whether he had a rose-coloured tattoo, and I didn't want to move him, but his eyes were wide and his tongue protruded from his mouth, like an eel, so I suspected that he'd been garrotted. Unless he'd just bumped into a particularly brutal mugger, Wenceslas had paid the price for turning his back on the Crvena Davo.

Which meant that I needed to get the fuck out of there.

Since the footsteps I'd heard were going downhill, I figured that heading back up would be my best call. I'd had a good day out: I didn't want to spoil it by being jumped on and given the piano-wire treatment somewhere in the trees.

I retraced my route up the steps to the Rose Church, only pausing long enough to notice that the candles had gone out. I stayed close to the wall as I looped back to the arch beneath the twin towers. I moved through it and left up the path that would take me across the walkway and into the old citadel.

I was halfway there when two lads in beanie hats and matching black Adidas tracksuits with white diagonal go-faster stripes below the knee

282

emerged from the fortifications ahead of me. They weren't there to take the air. I pivoted round and aimed myself back downhill. As I reached the bottom another two in matching kit appeared in the archway I'd just come through from the church.

I swerved immediately left towards the armaments display. That part of the trench wasn't floodlit, but the sky was clear and the moon was strong enough to cast its own pattern of shadows. I stayed close to the brick wall on my left flank, to try to avoid presenting a silhouette to my pursuers. I reckoned that if I could get back to the floodlit archway that linked the clock tower to the tennis club, the Adidas team would have to think twice about initiating a contact.

I glanced over my shoulder. Two of them were following me along the trench; the other two had stayed on the walkway. When I turned my head back another two figures had materialized at the corner that led to the rusting patrol boat. I couldn't tell whether they were in matching tracksuits, or carrying weapons, but I was pretty sure they weren't just here for the beer.

None of the judo routines I'd shown the kids that afternoon would keep four switched-on attackers at bay, and there was no way I could climb either of the walls — I'd checked them out during my morning circuit — so I knew I was in the shit. I needed to keep them guessing for as long as possible, so I kept on walking and scanned the ground in front of me for anything I could use as a weapon. If I was going the same route as Wenceslas, I'd do my best to take one or two of them with me.

I passed two of the gateways in the brickwork on my left, both chained and padlocked. The lads coming towards me were now no more than fifty feet away. The ones behind were closing fast.

As I passed the third arch the gate swung open and two big boys in parkas and combats grabbed me and pulled me inside. One of them had Boris Johnson hair. He pointed a rock-steady Glock 16, complete with suppressor, at my forehead and raised an index finger to his lips. His mate held me from behind, the palm of his left hand pressed against my mouth. I didn't know what they were up to, but I got the message.

Our hidey-hole smelt dank and mouldy, not the nice aroma of freshly dug earth, but of somewhere sad and unloved. It was the kind of place only the fungi came to party when the lights were low. The scent of my captor's freshly soaped hand was almost a relief. He kept it firmly in place beneath my nostrils as four sets of footsteps converged on the path immediately outside. I didn't know why. I wasn't about to cry for help.

There was a muttered exchange among the Adidas team. Then I saw a shadow fall across the gate and a bunch of fingers the size of Serbian homemade sausages grip the centre bar. I was tempted to give them a good kick, just for the hell of it. It could hardly make things any worse.

Boris's blond hair flicked back as he swivelled and aimed the muzzle of the Glock's suppressor at them instead of me. He pushed back the gate and moved out into the trench. There was no arguing about the size of this boy's bollocks.

His mate strengthened his grip. I guessed he wanted me to know that our job right now was to stay exactly where we were.

10

The silence was electric. The bad guys were obviously as impressed with Boris's bollocks as I was. For a moment, you could have heard a pin drop. Then I heard more approaching footsteps. I couldn't see who they belonged to, but the Adidas team's body language told me the new arrivals weren't fully paid-up members of the Davo fan club.

Boris let them have it with a barrelful of high-voltage Serbian. I could only make out about one word in ten, but it was impossible not to catch his drift. The Davo raised their hands and backed off. By the time my captor indicated that the two of us should step outside to join his mate, everyone else had melted away. The entire stretch between the twin towers and the corner by the armaments display was deserted.

My guy released me, but let me have a good look at the blade he had strapped to his left wrist. Boris waved me on with his Glock, then tucked it under his parka and down the front of his combats. I was surprised there was room in there. They escorted me up the trench, one of them at each shoulder. I wasn't sure whether they were making sure I didn't do a runner, or on BG duty.

We tabbed along the row of weaponry and through the archway beside the basketball court. I got a closer look at my new best mates now that we were surrounded by floodlights. I didn't know where Boris had sprung from, but if he wasn't the guy I'd spotted in the Mondeo near Barford and then again in the layby above the Morava River, he had an identical twin. His sidekick remained invisible, even when you could see him.

They frogmarched me past the Monument of Gratitude to France and the bronze lad throttling the snake in the middle of the fountain. I found myself thinking about the imam and his determination to stay off the vengeance trail. I wondered if he'd feel the same way when he buried Wenceslas tomorrow.

I made to go straight on to the souvenir stalls by the main, but Boris and the Invisible Man funnelled me left towards the zoo. I didn't ask how they knew where I'd parked the Audi. Warp-speed Serbian was way beyond me and, anyway, they didn't seem in the mood to chat.

A couple of deep, feral roars came through the railing that surrounded the big-cat enclosure about eighty metres ahead of us. Maybe I was wrong about the wagon. Maybe they were just going to feed me to the lions and be done with it.

The zoo closed at five during the winter, but they steered me straight towards the entrance. Then, sharing a grin, they grabbed me by the biceps and dragged me to my wagon. Grey forced me to spread my legs and put the palms of my hands flat on the roof, and Boris fished around in the pocket of my bomber jacket and extracted the fob.

He pulled open the driver's door and they bundled me inside, doing that thing the police do with your head when they want you to look like a prick but not damage yourself on the frame.

I made myself comfortable, and gave a bit of thought to what might make a deadlier weapon than the satnav in the Audi's glove box. Then I realized that neither of the boys was coming along for the ride, and Boris was holding out the fob, letting it dangle on its shiny ring in front of me.

I reached up to take it, but for a moment he held it firm, and leaned in towards me. His stubble had a hint of red and his eyes were killer blue. They didn't blink even a little bit as, in clear Estuary English, he wished me a pleasant flight home. Just not in those words. What he actually said was 'Now fuck off back to Heathrow. And save us all some grief.'

11

Under his close scrutiny I pressed the panel for Aerodrom Nikola Tesla on the satnav's Recent Destinations screen.

I didn't know how the two of them fitted into all this, but as I pulled away from the animal kingdom, neither seemed too sad to see me go. I kept eyes on them in my rear-view. They made no move to follow. Maybe they already had some of their mates primed and in place.

The Air Serbia flight I was aiming for checked in shortly after eight in the morning, so I wasn't going to bother with a hotel. I'd pull in wherever the truck drivers hung out between here and the terminal, and get my head down in the wagon.

PART NINE

PART NINE

1

Allerdale, Cumbria

Saturday, 4 February
08.35 hrs

I'd been to the Chastain ancestral home only a couple of times, when the team had gathered to fine-tune the Swedish op. We never said the word 'deniable' out loud, but we all knew there wasn't a snowball's chance in hell of it being officially sanctioned, so it made sense to hold the briefing sessions a comfortable distance from Stirling Lines. It didn't necessarily mean I had a standing invitation to go back there, but I was pretty sure the colonel wouldn't tell me to clear off if I dropped by on my way north.

Ravenhill had been in his family for ever, and not having Guy around to take over the place was going to add another fistful of salt to his father's wound. Continuity and inheritance had never been big issues for the Stone clan, but every nook and cranny of this place felt differently. From the moment you pulled in through the main gates, and wove through landscaped woodland that must have been planted up six generations earlier, you knew that the Chastain roots ran deep.

The main house was a whole lot grander than anything I'd been used to. It was tucked into a crescent of oak, hornbeam and Scots pine, with a sweeping view across the greenest of rolling green fields to the eastern shore of Bassenthwaite Lake.

We weren't talking Downton Abbey here, but we'd stayed over in the converted stable block during the planning phase, and could have had a couple of bedroom suites each.

Yet more stone outbuildings and what now looked like an oak-framed boathouse completed the fairy-tale set-up. Harry, Trev and I had run around the estate for an hour every morning before our full English, and never reached the boundary wall.

I parked the Skoda alongside a Range Rover and a very shiny Maserati, and told it not to be embarrassed. I probably needn't have bothered. It had spent its whole life doing God's work.

I didn't expect an immediate answer when I lifted and dropped the gleaming brass knocker on the Chastains' front door. It would take them a while to tab all the way to the hall. I gave them ten and was about to repeat the process when I heard footsteps on the gravel from the direction of the lake.

The colonel and his wife appeared in the kind of well-used country kit that had seen some proper action on the peaks and fells, not just in the Regent Street boutique window. Their immaculately sculpted hair was greyer than when I'd last seen them, and it was impossible to miss the sadness in their eyes, but they were still Mr and Mrs Charisma.

I kicked straight into apology mode but

Chastain held up a hand before I'd got halfway. 'Sergeant Stone, a pleasure to see you as always. My assistant said you'd called. What a pity you couldn't join us for breakfast.'

They ushered me into their well-upholstered world of gilt-framed military portraits, Afghan rugs and antique clocks. A regimental snare drum, which had been converted into a table, perched next to a wing chair beside an open fire. A bronze cast of a giant hand, dulled by age, index finger outstretched, stood in one corner of the living room.

Chastain followed my eyeline. 'It was chopped off one of Saddam's statues. Or so the guy claimed when I picked it up in Basra *souk*.' He came as close to smiling as I guessed he could manage, these days. 'I suspect he had a team of people knocking them out by the dozen in a sweat shop round the corner.'

Mrs Chastain laughed dutifully, then escaped to the kitchen. She reappeared briefly with a teapot, cups, saucers, milk and homemade flapjacks on a tray that matched the drum. 'I'll leave you gentlemen to chat. The chores won't look after themselves, alas.' She hovered for a moment. 'How very nice of you to visit, Nick. Guy would have appreciated it enormously. And we do too.'

She was in the kind of pain I guessed even sertraline couldn't soothe, so there was something desperately touching about her attempts to fortify herself behind a wall of politeness.

When she'd gone, Chastain busied himself with the brew. 'I'm afraid Guy's death has rather

295

ripped the heart out of her.' He waved a hand around the room. 'And out of this old place too. He and I were hardly ever here for more than five minutes at a time, of course, but, my God, it's empty without him.'

'I read the citation. He was incredibly . . . ' I searched for the right word, and didn't necessarily find it. 'Brave.'

'Yes, Nick. He was.' He stopped messing around with the crockery and fixed me with some serious eye to eye. 'But that won't stop me missing him.'

I didn't have a clue how to deal with this. When Chastain had been my OC, death in action had been part of the deal. We'd met it with dignity or black humour, depending on the circumstances and on who was in the room. He'd never been short of the right things to say when the occasion demanded, and his presence alone reassured those around him that, though we might be in the shit, he was the man to dig us out. Now his defences were down, and he was just a grieving dad.

I knew this was the point I should have waffled on about heroism and selflessness, then maybe gone on to fill some more silence by talking about the statue. I probably would have done if Mrs Chastain had stuck around. But the colonel knew the form, and I'd always found it easier to fight on for live people rather than dead ones.

He handed over my brew and offered me a flapjack. I gave it a munch, mostly so I could leave a decent interval before I spoke again.

'I dropped in to pay my respects, but also to

296

see if you had any int about the fuck-up in the CQB Rooms. I'm trying to find a way of digging Sam Callard out of the shit.'

I hoped he might seize the opportunity of shifting back into OC mode, and he did.

'A dreadful mess. I don't know all the details, I'm afraid, but I'm sure that damn fool Steele is devoting a disproportionate amount of time and energy to keeping whatever happened under wraps instead of taking the bull by the horns and doing something useful.'

He clearly wasn't Steele's number-one fan, but that was probably because the general had achieved both the rank and the job that Chastain would have killed for. Whatever, I decided not to share my suspicions about DSF's recent activities.

'I was hoping you might have some . . . insights . . . Perhaps even be able to help get the lad off the hook. Couldn't we get a shrink involved? I think those two were far more deeply affected by Chris's death, then Guy's, than they were able to admit.'

The fire had come back into Chastain's eyes. 'I couldn't agree more. Steele and the stiff-upper-lip brigade don't buy into combat stress. They seem intent on returning us all to the Dark Ages. I half expect them to start shooting troopers at dawn again, or dispatching them down the mines with LMF labels round their necks.'

LMF might have stood for 'Lazy Mother Fucker' now, but back in the Second World War it had meant 'Lack of Moral Fibre'. I never got too exercised about that. The attitude he'd described was always going to be a part of the

297

establishment mind-set.

He sat forward in his chair. 'Have you got a minute? There's something I'd like to show you.'

2

The boathouse was a stone-based, oak-framed building. It was no longer the glorified garden shed that I remembered from the days of the Sweden briefing, where a bloke could escape for the afternoon with a tin of varnish, some sand-paper and a couple of paint brushes. It had been converted into the kind of quality accommodation you'd be looking for from a five-star holiday let.

Wide wooden steps led down to a sundeck and a jetty, which ran about ten metres into the lake and ended with something that looked like a small mandarin temple on stilts.

Not for the first time, Chastain read my mind. 'It was Guy's idea. When he was about fourteen he told us he needed somewhere his parents wouldn't be able to breathe down his neck twenty-four/seven.' He allowed the sadness to flicker across his face in a way that I guessed he tried not to when he was being the strong one. 'The trials and tribulations of being a much-loved only child . . . '

He steered me round to the lakeside entrance and brought out a nice big bunch of keys.

The interior was part boy-heaven and part shrine to this boy's over-achievement. A homemade catapult sat on a shelf alongside a bowl of conkers and four or five gleaming silver cups. A Scalextric set the size of Brands Hatch ran along one wall. Posters of Michelle Pfeiffer and Buffy the Vampire Slayer were pinned to a corkboard. Dark blue painted oars with gold lettering were suspended above a pair of shiny blue caps with the kind of tassels I'd only ever seen on pole dancers in a Hong Kong nightclub.

A framed reproduction of Kipling's poem 'For All We Have and Are' took pride of place beside Guy's citation and medal. I remembered the Kipling. Chastain had screwed it to the wall of his office at the Lines, and tried to make us memorize it. He'd quoted it in his team talk before we infiltrated Iraq, like he was auditioning for a part in a Shakespeare epic.

'*What stands if Freedom fall?*
Who dies if England live?'

I reckoned most of us agreed with the first bit, but had a bit of a question mark over the next. The colonel had been chuffed to fuck when he delivered the final couplet, nodding in my direction across the mess:

'*There is nothing left today*
But steel and fire and stone.'

He'd ended his speech with a big, beaming grin, and 'But I'm sure you gentlemen will agree that if the Stone bit turns out to be the case, we're in worse trouble than we thought . . .'

I took a closer look at the citation, and the medal above it. 'Shit . . . That's not the real one, is it?'

Chastain nodded. 'Damn fool spot to keep it, given its value. We'll hand it over to the Imperial War Museum at some point, of course, depending on what happens about the statue. But Marcia wanted it to be here for a while, since we have no body to bury, no ashes to spread. Some days she just sits with it, gazing out across the lake, remembering the times we now realize we rather took for granted.'

I reckoned she was so far into the happy pills that she couldn't tell which way was up, but I didn't tell him that. I gave him a rueful smile instead. 'I'm sure my mum would have done the same. Just without the conkers and the boathouse. We didn't have much call for that sort of thing on *our* estate.'

He seized the chance to retreat behind half-witted banter. 'I thought Bermondsey was heaving with places like this. Where else did all those pirates live?'

'Mostly down the market or the betting shop.' I scanned the shelves and walls and comfortable furniture. 'But none of us would have turned up our noses at somewhere like this. It must have been like growing up in the world's nicest toy shop.'

He disappeared for a moment into his own personal time-warp. 'I often wonder whether he might have preferred having a dad around, instead of an impatient stranger who was too busy imposing his idea of justice and truth on Johnny Foreigner to play hide and seek or throw a rugby ball around.'

'You were there when it counted.'

'Kind of you to say that.' He paused. 'You never had kids, did you, Nick?'

It was on the tip of my tongue to tell him about Anna and Nicholai, and to share one or two of the things I'd had on my mind recently, but I shook my head. 'I guess I might have done if I'd had a boathouse like this.'

He lifted the VC display off the wall and polished the glass with his sleeve. As if he needed to. 'We all used to take the piss out of tea and medals, didn't we, back in the day? Now I find that this little piece of Chinese bronze and its crimson ribbon mean a great deal to me. A very great deal indeed. But I'm afraid it doesn't buy me any favours in the corridors of power.'

He fixed me with those cool blue eyes.

'So, short of taking the law into one's own hands, we have little choice other than to watch the court-martial machinery grinding its way to some no doubt undignified and clandestine conclusion.'

I met his level gaze, and tried to work out whether he'd just said what I thought he'd just said. 'You always used to tell us that a little choice is better than no choice at all . . . '

For a split second his expression reminded me of the one Koureh had used in the Baghdad interrogation centre when he brought out a new set of pliers. 'That has certainly been my mantra.'

He put back the medal and attempted to recapture his old maverick charm. 'But on this occasion you'll understand why I couldn't possibly comment.'

He switched his attention to a point beyond the temple, where a strengthening breeze had begun to interfere with the mirrored surface of the water. I wanted to ask him about the Crvena Davo and Boris and the Invisible Man, but I knew the conversation was over.

I asked him to thank Mrs C for the brew and told him I'd see myself out.

3

Rannoch Moor, Glencoe

Saturday, 4 February
15.00 hrs

By the time they'd chucked me my sand-coloured beret, Al Gillespie was already a legend in the Regiment. Not only did he have the world's biggest moustache, but he'd somehow managed to get his hands on a Stinger in the Falklands, almost before anyone else knew they'd been invented, and took out an Argentine Pucará operating from a makeshift grass strip at Goose Green.

He'd started his own security outfit — mostly BGing and keeping an eye on North Sea oil rigs — when he left Hereford, and invited me to join him. There had been quite a few times over the years that followed when I wished I had. He was the most modest man I knew, and one of the smartest. He might have looked like a walrus on happy pills, but he had a mind like a steel trap.

Alasdair Gillespie Security was now known as AGS. We called it SAG and took the piss out of him mercilessly for it, but I was pretty sure he'd have the last laugh. AGS didn't operate on anywhere near the same scale as Kroll or Astra, but its portfolio included a number of specialist services including hostile-environment training

304

for the international news media and testing the security of a whole heap of government installations.

He hadn't yet realized his dream of becoming Monarch of the Glen, but he did have a nice little place at the foot of a hill just south of Mallaig, with a magic view of the Isle of Skye. And as he dragged visitors across the heather, pointing his thumb-stick at a mountain stream sparkling in the sunlight one minute, then at a storm front darkening the Cuillin Ridge the next, he'd bellow, 'Who could ask for more?' He'd mean it too.

To get there I took the road through Glencoe.

I wasn't easily spooked, but this place did it to me every time.

It wasn't simply the starkness of the winter landscape, the feeling of isolation, or the way the mist advanced up the valley that got to me — I knew plenty of places like that.

The sound of the wind was sadder than a piper's lament, and even before I'd stumbled on the memorial and got interested in its history, I knew that something really bad had happened here.

On 2 February 1692, during the aftermath of the Jacobite Rebellion, a hundred and twenty men under the command of Captain Robert Campbell arrived on the doorstep of Alasdair Maclain, the Twelfth Chief of Glencoe. The Campbells already had a big reputation for slotting their rivals and nicking their lands, but the Maclains offered them food, drink, lodgings and the best Highland hospitality for the next ten days.

On the order of the king, the killing began at oh five hundred on the eleventh. The chief was shot as he got out of bed. His wife was stripped and abused and died of exposure the following day. Houses were torched. Thirty-eight men, women and children were murdered. Of those who tried to escape across the mountains, at least forty more didn't make it.

The government went into cover-up mode. No one was ever brought to trial. But worse still, as far as the locals were concerned, the massacre was 'murder under trust'. The Highland Jocks got as pissed off as the Arabs did if they were hosed down by people they'd invited round for dinner.

The Gillespies belonged to Clan Campbell, whose motto was 'Never forget'. We liked to remind Al of that from time to time. But you had to choose the right moment. He didn't always see the funny side of it.

4

The snow-capped peaks of the Three Sisters scraped the sky to my left. I hung a right as I approached Loch Leven and drove uphill, towards the outward-bound centre Al often used when his lads were taking men and women in suits on leadership courses, or teaching Swedish TV journalists how to avoid being slotted by rocket-propelled grenades.

I parked the Skoda next to an AGS minibus and went into the reception area of a building that looked like it had been carved out of a chunk of granite, then lined with tartan. A girl with red hair and a beaming smile told me I was in luck. Today's team-building exercise was taking place at the boulder garden, not too far upriver.

Half an hour's tab took me to a campsite beside a stretch of swirling rapids, randomly sprinkled with rocks, where two groups of seven in stern-rigged inflatables were paddling like crazy to stop themselves being tossed into the icy melt-water. The side of the valley rose behind them, vividly striped with green and rusty red, then topped with white.

While his sidekicks ran around on the bank in matching orange Helly Hansen gear, Big Al stood on a medium-size meteorite in an olive green parka and a kilt, waving his thumb-stick at them, like he was conducting the Last Night of the Proms. His 'tache had expanded into the kind of beard that any polar explorer would have killed for.

After ten minutes of this, I began a slow handclap.

Al turned, IDed his audience and roared, 'Who invited you, Stoner? Didn't you read the sign? It said 'No Fucking Sassenachs'!'

I moved over to the bank. 'There was another sign right next to it saying 'No Fucking Campbells', so it looks like we're both in the shit.'

The rafters reached a strainer — a narrow rock corridor where the stream flowed faster and dropped four or five feet before cascading across the boulder garden. The paddle captains yelled urgent commands as they battled with the surging currents.

'Dig! Dig! *Dig!*'

Both crews did their best to jump to it, but I could see that some of them were starting to wish they'd stayed behind their desks, within easy reach of the coffee machine.

Al leaped off his granite podium and came over to thump me in between the shoulder-blades. 'Great to see you, Nick. We heard a nasty rumour you'd defected.'

I thumped him right back, but before I could say anything, the second raft cartwheeled against a stone pillar on the far side of the staircase, then broached. It bucked and reared and banged an anxious dark-haired girl into the froth. She flailed around for a moment and then disappeared. Her helmet bobbed back into view almost immediately, but she didn't.

I threw off my Gore-Tex armour and dived in after her.

Fuck, it was cold.

I managed to remember which way was up, thrust my head out of the white water and attempted to carve through it with a chaotic combo of breaststroke and crawl. I felt like I'd been caught in a monster washing-machine drum with a couple of overexcited inflatable hippos for company.

I closed in on where I'd last seen the girl and spotted a spiral of what might have been weed and might have been hair below me, then a flicker of blue beneath it.

I kicked hard, arced down towards her and scrabbled around until I'd managed to hook my frozen fingers around the strap of her life jacket. Lungs bursting, I yanked her upwards, but lost my grip when I broke the surface and a rogue paddle smacked me behind the ear.

I went under again, arms and legs flapping around big-time, and now I really didn't know which direction to turn. Highland-spring water could really mess you up when it was forced into your mouth and eyes and up your nose under pressure, at the same time as bowling you over and over and over until you didn't care how the story ended.

The outside of my head collided with a lump of granite and the inside of it made a horrible echoing sound and then went black.

5

People talked a lot of bollocks about near-death experiences. Top of the list was seeing a man in a big white beard beckon you down a long corridor into a world of blinding light, or watching your whole life unfold in front of you, like a DVD in fast forward.

I'd been in plenty of contacts where every extra breath I took was a bonus, but I'd never been in a situation like this. Maybe I saw Anna smile her sad Abba smile, maybe I saw my boy reaching out to me. I couldn't say for sure. But the next thing I knew was that a Jock in a big red beard was yelling at me from across the world's most enormous parade ground.

It took me a while to stop shivering and start making sense of what he was saying.

First off, I thought he was ordering me to give him fifty more push-ups and threatening to put me on a charge if I didn't do it double time.

Next I got the weird idea that he was awarding me the Victoria Cross, then taking it away again because (a) I was an idiot and (b) I wasn't dead enough.

After I didn't know how long, I realized I was managing to hang on to what Al was saying instead of just lying there helplessly as his words dribbled out through the cracks in my brain.

I was in the recovery position, wrapped in a foil blanket, sucking in air like an industrial

310

bellows. My head pounded and my throat and chest burned as I did so, but I couldn't get enough of the stuff.

I twisted onto my back and glimpsed another foil-wrapped figure stretched out a few feet away from me. A shock of dark hair fanned out across the heather around her head and an anxious medic knelt by her side. Gobs of bile-streaked vomit clung to the strip of coarse grass between us.

The chill air stung the bare skin below my hairline and above my right ear. I ran my fingertips over a ragged tear and they came away bloody.

'Don't worry about that,' a voice said. 'We'll give you a couple of stitches as soon as we get you back to the centre.'

Team Orange had formed a close circle to provide us with shelter from the wind. When it came to raising the hypothermia-sufferer's core temperature, every little helped.

Al began to swim into focus. He was standing over me with a tartan blanket round his shoulders, water dripping off his hair, his beard, at least three layers of fleece, and a very sodden kilt. His sporran was nowhere to be seen.

The veins pulsed at his temples as he scraped back his mop, and his face was like thunder. I guess I must have been dreaming about the medal. He was absolutely ballistic.

'What the *fuck* was that about? This place is crawling with very, *very* experienced people whose job it is to make sure everything works, and that includes the health and safety piece.

And you think it's a great idea to drop in off the street and play lifeguard?' He waved at the girl. 'She might have died as a result of you blundering around in there. You might have died . . .'

He drew a deep, ragged breath. 'And who's going to pay for my fucking kilt?'

I looked up at him and tried to get a grip on my breathing. 'Aren't you supposed to give me the kiss of life or something? Maybe shine a torch in my eyes and ask me to count backwards from a hundred?'

One or two of Al's lads had to turn away to keep their smiles under control, but the boss wasn't amused. 'I'm serious, Nick. That wee act of heroism might have been completely instinctive, but it was totally out of order.'

I sat up and shook the last of the river out of my ears. After a couple of goes the girl managed to do the same. She looked about twelve. Her skin was ghostly, but her eyes were bright. She spoke so softly that it took me a moment to register what she'd said.

'You risked your life for me. Thank you.'

I smiled and patted her wrist, as you do when you're old enough to be someone's dad. Then I realized something was missing. I still had the spare mag in my left pocket but no longer had a chunk of metal digging into my small intestine. Shit. I must have lost the Browning during my close encounter with God's washing-machine.

Team Orange took a couple of paces back as a Defender emblazoned with the AGS logo — one of the stretch jobs with a bench seat on each side

312

running front to back — bounced off the road towards us.

I held out a hand so Al could haul me up. 'I don't know about you Jocks, but I reckon the swimming team could do with a brew.'

6

I'd never minded sleeping in ditches or wearing the same kit and smelling of shit and cam paint and feeling my toes stick together in my boots for weeks on end, but I couldn't remember a shower that had felt as good as this one.

Al's lads had bundled us into the Defender and taken us back to the centre, stitched and dressed the wound on the side of my head and handed us mugs of hot chocolate and shampoo and gel and fluffy towels.

I'd piled my spare kit on a chair, turned on the water and stepped into the cubicle. The trick was not to crank up the heat too fast, but to give yourself the chance to ease into recovery mode. I must have let the jets play on my neck, shoulders, chest and back for nearly half an hour, and by the end of it I felt like I'd had a full body massage as well as a wash.

Al looked like a new man too. I found him in the bar beside a roaring log fire with a slug of single malt at his elbow. Someone had found him another jumbo-size kilt and the freshly groomed walrus look was back in place. But there was a sadness about him too. Maybe the Glencoe thing seeped into your bones if you stayed too long.

He waved me towards a much-loved leather armchair and leaned in close as I sat down. 'Sorry, Nick. I was a bit of a pillock back there.'

I'd been right about his mood. Light-hearted

314

banter wasn't called for right now. 'No, mate. I'm the one who should be apologizing. It was your show. And a dickhead in walking kit should never try to hoick someone in a life-jacket and wetsuit out of an ice-cold river.'

One of Al's assistants brought me another hot chocolate. I was drowning in it, but she was obviously taking the 'no alcohol or caffeine' instruction seriously. They both acted as vasodilators, accelerating blood flow to the surface of the skin when it should have been focusing hard on your vital organs.

We both gazed into the dancing flames.

I was the first to break the silence. I tapped the dressing above my temple. 'I must be going soft in the head. I used to be able to make a pretty cold-blooded risk and reward assessment at times like that, but now, if a kid's involved, I just leap in with both feet.'

He sipped his Scotch and rolled it across his taste-buds. Then he tilted his great hairy head. 'Me too. Especially since Catriona got sick.'

'Catriona? Al, I had no idea . . . '

'You've not been around. And we haven't broadcast it. Partly because it's private . . . ' He hesitated. 'And partly, to be honest, because I just don't want to believe it . . . Cancer. She was diagnosed four months ago.' He kept his eyes on the fire. 'I must be losing it. Spend my whole life meeting every incoming round head on, now this happens and I'm running for cover.'

'The girls?' Mel and Elspeth were late teens, early twenties.

'In pieces, obviously. Not that they'd let you

315

see it. They're a whole lot better at dealing with it than I am. You know how it is with women. They do useful shit and tell you what's on their mind. I'm just a big fat inarticulate jelly.'

He finally turned back to me. 'D'you fancy coming up to Arisaig for tonight? I could use the company. Cat's halfway through her chemo at the Beatson, so she's staying in Glasgow.' He paused. 'And I guess you've not come all the way to the Highlands simply to take a wee dip in our legendary spring water.'

7

We piled into the Skoda and headed north to Fort William, then west along the road that would take us to the sea.

Al was in the mood to talk, so I let him. My very old Jock mate needed to say some things out loud and listen to how they sounded. He didn't need my input.

I wasn't surprised that Catriona's illness had rocked his world. They'd been together since the dawn of time, and family was everything to them. I'd always envied him the stuff I'd never had, but now I found myself being quite relieved that I hadn't completely lost the ability to cut away when everything went to rat shit.

The sun began to dip below the hills as we skirted Loch Ailort, turning the ridges black and highlighting the ribbon of sky beneath the cloud with red and gold. For a moment I thought I understood why you might want to tell the rest of the planet to fuck off, and disappear to a place like this. And the loneliness you might feel if the woman you'd always counted on sharing it with might no longer be there to enjoy the view.

Fort Gillespie was a traditional white pebble-dashed house with a steeply raked slate roof, sheltered by the hill but high enough up it to look out over the beach to the islands beyond. You couldn't get much further west than this on the UK mainland, and it felt wild and elemental,

317

close to the edge of the world.

Inside it felt like the kind of place you'd never want to leave on a winter's night, especially if you fancied antlers hanging on your walls, sheepskin draped across your chairs, and everything else in sight to match your kilt. Even the photo frames were tartan.

Al must have pointed a camera at his daughters every five minutes for their entire lives, but the stand-out shot was of Catriona, the spitting image of the girl Mel Gibson went to war for in *Braveheart*.

Al looked a bit sheepish when I came into the kitchen and spotted a sink overflowing with unwashed dishes. I got busy with hot water and Fairy Liquid while he dived into his fridge and produced a haggis the size of an RPG, left over from Burns Night. He brought out pots and pans and busied himself at the range. I peeled some potatoes, then made myself useful with the log stack and sparked up a fire. He unearthed a couple of candles and an unopened bottle of whisky.

We sat down in front of bowls of steaming mashed potato and some orange shit that tasted a whole lot better than it looked. I poked my haggis with a fork. 'Remind me. What's in this stuff?'

I knew he was watching me.

'Food of the gods, my friend.' He attacked his with relish. 'Nothing better on a cold winter's night, apart from a sixteen-year-old Lagavulin.'

He reached for the Scotch and popped the cork.

We raised our glasses.

The first toast was to Catriona and his girls. The second was to Trev.

I frowned for a couple of beats. 'Trev?'

He looked startled. 'You don't know?'

'Don't tell me, let me guess. All those Swedish words he learned have suddenly come in useful. He's bouncing around in Stockholm with some gorgeous blue-eyed blonde instead of taking my calls.'

His face fell. 'Trev's dead, Nick . . . '

My surprise might have been manufactured, but my distress was still closer to the surface than I'd bargained for. 'How? When?'

'I don't know chapter and verse, but the medics reckon he had a massive heart attack.'

This time the disbelief was easy. I'd like to have had a one to one with the doc who'd seen what a polymer-tipped 7.62 round can do to a man's head, then diagnosed his problem as a dodgy ticker. 'Heart attack? Trev? He might have abused himself over the years, but he was fit as a butcher's dog.'

'Perhaps it was triggered by the whole Sam Callard mess. Sam was like a son to Trev. That must have hit him really hard.' He put down his knife and fork. 'Jesus, Nick . . . I'm sorry you had to hear it from me. I know you lads were close.'

'It was Sam I wanted to talk to Trev about. And I need your take on the whole gangfuck in the CQB Rooms too.'

I told him I'd heard some quite confusing rumours about the live firing exercise and the bullet in Scott Braxton's head, and the events that had led to Sam being banged up at Barford on a manslaughter charge. And I wondered why Jack Grant had been hidden away in Afghan at warp speed.

He didn't know anything about Jack Grant, but he'd heard the rumours too — and that was all they were, as far as he was concerned, rumours. 'Not much of this kind of shit gets piped north of the border, these days, and to tell you the truth, I don't go in search of it. Our Whitehall briefs tend to depend on us keeping our heads down and our mouths shut.'

Fair one. Al was a big lad, and I knew he'd have to tread gently through those minefields if he wanted to keep the government contracts coming.

I asked him if he was still having fun breaking into nuclear reactors to test the alarm systems. I'd done one or two freelance jobs for him on sensitive installations in the early days.

'Not so much. But they like us to keep them on their toes.'

'I don't suppose you could lay your hands on the security spec for a Green Army set-up, could you?'

He didn't answer immediately. The haggis and the Lagavulin suddenly demanded his full attention. After a bit of clinking of cutlery and refuelling of our glasses he gave me eye to eye again. 'Who's asking?'

'Well, it's not the Russians, is it, mate? It's me. It's probably an even worse idea than leaping into that river of yours, but Sam Callard needs

320

somebody's help, and now Trev isn't here to give it, I reckon I'm the next in line. And what with the lockdown, I won't get anywhere fast if I submit an application form for a prison visit.'

It was my turn to reach for the single malt. Pinpricks of light glinted off the Gillespie family crystal as I raised the tumbler to my lips.

'So that means I might have to lift him.'

8

If Al was surprised, he did a good job of hiding it. He sat there like a bearded sphinx and let me waffle on.

'I mean, not right now or tomorrow, but if all else fails I'll need to get into Barford before the trial kicks off. The Ruperts are closing ranks, and you don't need me to tell you how loaded these things can be. Sam must know what really happened in the CQB Rooms, and what led up to it. I need to hear it from him.'

I'd spent time at Barford as a Green Jacket. Back then it was just like any other bog-standard military camp — barracks, prefabs, a mess or three, rows of red-brick family quarters, squash courts, a fair amount of open space, maybe even a cricket pitch. You could wander in and out whenever you felt like it. But that was years before they'd built the shiny new Military Court Centre — and before Osama bin Laden and his disciples put pretty much every base on amber or red alert. If I was going to pay Harry's boy a visit now, I'd need all the help I could get.

'Have you talked to Chastain? Maybe he could shed some light on it. Flex some muscle, even. The great thing about the colonel is that he's both old school and a maverick. He's on first-name terms with the Big Dogs, but still happy to throw away the rule-book when he needs to.'

I told him I'd dropped by the Chastain country seat, but he'd not been optimistic about outflanking the process.

Al hauled himself up from his chair and disappeared outside to the woodpile. There were plenty of logs beside the grate, so I guessed he needed some more thinking time. He came back ten minutes later with another armful of tree trunks and tossed a couple onto the fire.

When he sat down again he had his serious face on. 'I don't have the blueprints in my bottom drawer, if that's what you mean, but I'll see what I can do.'

After we'd won the Battle of the Haggis he reached for the bottle again with all the determination a Jock can muster when there's a world to put to rights, and a fearsome amount of whisky drinking to be done.

Back in the day he'd have insisted on me matching him dram for dram, then brought out the bagpipes in case I'd forgotten which road we were taking to the bonnie, bonnie banks o' Loch Lomond. Now he didn't seem to mind that I wasn't pouring Lagavulin down my neck as speedily as he was, and the pipes stayed on the chair in the hall.

I wasn't about to swing into tree-hugging mode or get dewy-eyed about my true love and the moon coming out in the gloaming, but this seemed like the right moment to let him know that a whole lot of us owed him big-time, and that we wouldn't forget it in a hurry. I even heard myself thanking him for dredging me out of the boulder garden earlier in the afternoon, and risking his clan tartan in the process.

He didn't know where to look, so he just got more Scottish. 'Och . . . think nothing of it, laddie . . . I wouldnae be here if you hadnae hauled me out of a fair few scrapes . . .'

He probably wasn't wrong, but these things had a habit of evening out in the end; we all knew that. We'd fought alongside each other in two or three actions that had hit the headlines, and plenty more that would never see the light of day, and we didn't need to remind ourselves of them now.

Except for one.

'Well, there was that contact outside the chippie in Bolton. You definitely wouldnae be here if I hadnae paid the bill. Those Turkish lads were about to have a major sense-of-humour failure.'

Trev had been there too, and that triggered another round of war stories. Though we'd never really been the Three Amigos, we had a lot of shared history. But, try as hard as we might to lose ourselves in it that night, it became painfully obvious to us both that our exchanges of banter were barely skin deep. The coincidence of Trev's death with Catriona's illness had really messed Al up.

I had no idea what time we finally turned in, but not long after I'd settled beneath a couple of tartan rugs and another pile of sheepskins I heard a muffled roar of pain.

I slid out of bed and went back downstairs.

A crumpled figure sat beside the log pile. The light cast by the glowing embers of the fire was enough to show me that he was clutching the frame of the *Braveheart* photograph to his chest.

9

We were both up shortly after first light.

Al had a vat of porridge bubbling away on the range. There was no sign of the Lagavulin bottle, or of the raw emotions it had helped to bring to the table. He pulled back the curtains to give us a better view of the mist that blanketed the Cuillin and the gunmetal-grey waters of the sea loch. That was when I noticed the neatly wrapped package beside my table mat.

'I thought you might be missing that. You don't survive long up here without the right weaponry.' He whipped one of those stupid Jock knives with a polished antler handle and a very shiny blade out of the top of his sock and sliced a banana into two bowls, then drowned it in porridge.

'I've always wondered what those things were for.'

I unwrapped the oil-cloth and replaced the Browning in my waistband.

His expression was impossible to read. 'That was the other reason I didn't want to risk anyone else pulling you out of that river.'

He handed me my bowl and a pot of honey and fixed us both a brew.

As we munched our way through it, he told me he'd decided to give team-building a miss today: there were plenty of lads in orange to keep the flag flying while he spent some time with

326

Catriona. I suggested he hitch a lift to Glasgow in the Skoda — if he could still use the company. I promised to give the Campbell gags a rest on the road through the glen.

★ ★ ★

The Beatson was a state-of-the-art complex on the Great Western Road, north of Clydebank. I didn't see Catriona, but Mel came down to say hi, and to shepherd her dad inside. He was clearly in good hands.

I scribbled my iPhone number on his wrist with a felt-tip and told him to give me a call whenever he had a spare five minutes. Then I gave him some of that awkward waffle you hear yourself reaching for when you're trying to bridge a gap that you know can't be bridged. He nodded silently and gripped my hand. He seemed to have shrunk during the journey down.

Something made me ask the Detective Columbo question as I was getting back into the Skoda. 'Oh, one more thing. Do you know anything about a bunch of psycho Serbs with odd tattoos on their necks? They used to fuck people over from the hillsides above Sarajevo and Goražde . . . '

His brow creased and something like recognition glimmered briefly in his eyes. 'Maybe.' Then he pursed his lips and shook his head. 'No. I heard rumours, but I never came across them personally.'

I turned Father Gerard's wagon south again, stopping for fuel and a shot of caffeine when I'd made some distance. I wasn't going to sit around and wait for Al to come up with the goods on the Barford front. He had a lot of other shit on his mind. And I had no idea whether my old mate at Akrotiri would be able to get me within reach of Jack Grant. Which meant that Ella Mathieson remained my prime target. I texted Father Mart. It was time for a visit to H.

It's never a great idea to stick your head in the lion's mouth, but I'd made a bit of a habit of it over the years, and there were some things that just had to be done.

10

St Francis Xavier's Roman Catholic Church, Powys

**Sunday, 5 February
19.15 hrs**

The church was even colder after dark than it had been first thing in the morning. A handful of candles flickered in a tiered rack beneath a small metal cross alongside the confessional booth. Apart from the shadowy figure behind the screen, the place was empty. Maybe that was why I lit one for Catriona.

Father Mart gave a wry chuckle as I closed the curtain and sat down. 'We'll make a believer of you yet, Nicholas.'

'I'll put the flying pigs on red alert, Father.'

He chuckled again. 'I'll let Father Gerard know. We'll certainly be needing them at Cheltenham.'

There was a moment's silence. 'What happened to your head?'

'Long story, but no real drama. I took a dip in a mountain stream and had a close encounter with a rock.'

I told him I was planning a visit to Trev's, and asked if I was going to get any nasty surprises. He thought not. The house was all locked up, waiting for probate. 'I think he had a sister somewhere, Australia or New Zealand, but I fully expect to hear that he's left the bulk of his estate to Harold's boy.'

'What's happened to the dog?'

'Icarus? He's my new house guest. Only temporarily, of course, but I must say I'm enjoying his company. And he can smell a rat at fifty paces.'

'That could come in very useful right now.' I didn't tell him that Icarus could also smell an MRUD from about the same range.

'Is the key still where Trev used to leave it?' He'd never liked carrying it around with him, particularly when he was out on the piss, so he hid it by his side door, under a little concrete Buddha.

'No. It's in the pocket of my cassock. I'm keeping half an eye on the place.'

'Al thinks he died of a heart attack.'

'I suspect the powers that be decided a heart attack might be more palatable than announcing that he'd been assassinated by a sniper in an area of outstanding natural beauty.'

'Have the powers that be made any other announcements I should know about?'

'They're still devoting all their energies to keeping this thing under the radar. And the trial is definitely going to be held behind closed doors. Mr Blackwood called with the date, by the way: a week this Wednesday.'

'Does that mean Jack Grant is due back from Afghan?'

'The squadron sergeant major of myth and legend? Well, if he is, DSF and his chums certainly aren't shouting about it.'

I don't know why, but I'd been expecting Icarus to be some kind of super-toned Labrador or Collie or something. The bright-eyed creature that yapped at me from the Defender's passenger seat as we left was a wire-haired Dachshund with legs that were barely long enough to keep his dick off the ground.

Father Mart knew exactly what was going through my mind. 'I like to think that Trevor would enjoy the fact that his sense of humour lives on. And, of course, we must all take encouragement from his belief that, if we put our mind to it, even the most vertically challenged among us can fly too close to the sun.'

11

I reckoned Trev's place had to be the starting point of my search for Dr Eleanor Mathieson. I wouldn't be the first person to have had that idea, and there was no way Trev would have left any obvious clues, but I needed to get back inside his head. His semi on the northern edge of Hereford was my best route there.

I parked the Skoda three streets away from Holmer Road and tucked the Browning under my bomber jacket. I gripped Trev's keys in my right hand, pointy bits outwards between my fingers, handles resting against my palm.

His tidy red-brick stood on a corner plot, behind a hedge that could have done with a short back and sides. I approached from the right, on the opposite pavement, and walked past, keeping it in my peripheral vision. Fifteen minutes later, I completed a circuit that brought me back along the side of the property, parallel to the path that flanked the house and led to the garage and back garden.

I couldn't see movement beyond the frosted glass in the front door, or the darkened ground and first-floor windows. The house wasn't just still, it was completely devoid of life.

I pulled on my last pair of polythene service-station gloves. I wasn't breaking in, but I still didn't want to leave my prints. I turned the keys in the mortice and Yale locks and the door

332

swung open on well-oiled hinges. I stepped into the hall and closed it softly behind me, took off my Timberlands and waited for my vision to adjust to the ambient light from the street. Everything seemed to be in its proper place, but every fibre of the interior told the same story: Trev wasn't here any more, and neither was Icarus, so why should it give a shit?

I quickly scanned the living room, study/office and downstairs toilet, then the two bedrooms, bathroom and junk room on the floor above, and ended up in the kitchen, which filled the rear extension. The fridge was empty and switched off, but the kettle still sparked up. I found a box of Yorkshire Tea and a can of condensed milk in a nearby cupboard, so the trip was already a success.

I sat at Trev's table, watching the steam spiral off the surface of the brew, and started to get in the zone. Part of my training with the Det had been about cutting through other people's homes like a scalpel, either to identify and uncover their most carefully concealed secrets, or to find the most perfect place to leave something that would compromise them later, and allow us to fuck them over pretty much any way we wanted.

To begin with I'd thought that after growing up in Bermondsey I had nothing left to learn, but 14th Intelligence Company took me to a whole new level. We honed our covert entry skills until they were so sharp we could cut ourselves on them, and combining speed and precision became second nature. It wasn't just about infiltrating somebody's house: it was about burrowing into the fabric of their life.

Trev had been through the programme as well. It didn't guarantee that I'd find something here, but it did mean that if I came away empty-handed, it wouldn't be because I'd messed up.

Trev didn't like surprises . . . But he loved puzzles . . . The words repeated themselves in my head like a mantra as I went through his place again, from top to bottom, with a fine-tooth comb. He made mistakes, sure. We all did. But he didn't do anything by accident.

I kicked off by hoisting myself into the roof space through a hatch above the top landing. There was nothing folded into the insulation strips or nestling in the cold-water tank. I lifted a couple of loose floorboards under Trev's bed. There was nothing taped underneath them, and there were no false linings to the cupboards. Someone else had already given every mattress a seeing-to, including Icarus's — clinically, with a razorblade or a Stanley knife, not like a berserker — but I was pretty sure they'd been wasting their time.

No, not just pretty sure.

I knew it, beyond any doubt.

Trev would need me to find my way to Ella if he couldn't make it, but no one else. Which meant that every known location, from a favourite rented villa to an apartment belonging to a distant cousin — even somewhere you might spot in the background of a holiday snap — was too high risk.

I went through his desk and his filing cabinet anyway, scanning every document and every random scribble on every scrap of crumpled notepaper, looking for any hint of a signal that was meant only for me.

There was an amazing amount of shit to sort through. Trev's enthusiasm for languages — which basically boiled down to an enthusiasm for shagging the girls who spoke them — had taken him all over. Sweden was still high on his list of favourites, but so were France, Germany, Italy, Portugal, even Russia — though he'd kept very quiet about that.

The shelves in his work area were heaving with dictionaries, phrasebooks, maps, guides, military and cultural histories, language-course CDs. *The Dangerous Book for Boys* leaned against a copy of *Brainteasers for Kids*, in case I hadn't yet got the message. I gathered a selection, fixed myself another brew and flicked through them at the kitchen table.

Some had the corners of their pages turned over to mark an entry that had triggered his interest. Some didn't. Some were circled in red. Some weren't. I couldn't see any logic to it, any pattern. And I began to understand that that was the whole point of the exercise.

Speed. Precision. Speed. Precision. And no random surprises.

It had taken a while, but I was suddenly in Trev's space. All this stuff added up to one big tease: *Looking for Ella? She could be anywhere.* I could hear his voice in my ear. And I knew he would have been as amused by the idea of her pursuers rushing around on a series of wild-goose chases as he must have been when he named Icarus.

I started seeking out the gaps, and that was when my antennae started to go into overtime.

Why would Trev risk leaving me a message written in plain sight, on the off chance that I might be passing by, when he was going to take the trouble to meet and tell me what he needed me to know?

There was a crash about ten feet away from me, followed by the splintering of wood. I whipped the Browning out of my waistband and hit the deck. In the silence that followed I heard the creak of rusting hinges, then another crash.

I moved to the window by Trev's side entrance and saw his garage door flapping around in the wind. I washed up my mug, put it back in the cupboard and reclaimed my Timberlands. Then I found a padlock in the top drawer of a nearby utility chest and fastened the thing shut on my way out.

The little concrete Buddha by the step just kept on smiling.

12

I swung the Skoda in alongside Defender of the Faith and stood on the anchors. A nanosecond later I hammered on Father Mart's door. When he pulled it open, I piled straight past him. 'Where's Icarus?'

He followed me to the kitchen and gestured towards a newly installed fleece-covered beanbag in front of the range. 'Where else?'

Icarus was stretched out on top of it, on his back, like he'd been spatchcocked. He opened one eye, gave me a look of extreme displeasure, and closed it again.

Father Mart tilted his head.

'Trev said something by the dam. It's only just clicked. 'When your own semi becomes the battle space, what's the world coming to? You, Father Mart and the dog are the only people I can trust.''

I undid Icarus's collar. A small brass disc hung from its buckle; the kind that carried your phone number or the contact details of the local vet in case your dog did a runner. It had a smiley face embossed on one side and a six-digit sequence scratched on the other. 121492. It sounded like a grid reference but, without the right map, it meant nothing to me.

Father Mart picked up on my disappointment and held out his hand. 'Well, you've done your bit, and Icarus has too. So I guess that means it's my turn.'

He sat by the table and I pulled up the chair opposite him. He gave the surface of the disc a rub with his thumb. 'One, two, one, four, nine, two . . . He won't just have left us with part of a telephone number, so what else could it be? A licence number? A car registration?'

He turned it over and over.

'A date, perhaps? There aren't fourteen months in the year, so maybe there's some American angle. The fourteenth of December 1992?' He looked up at me. 'Does that mean anything to you? Were you with Trevor in December 'ninety-two? Somewhere in particular?'

I shook my head. 'We were in Sweden that May, then I got sent to try to talk some sense to the FBI during the Mount Carmel siege the following spring, but Trev wasn't part of the team.'

'Mount Carmel?'

'Waco, Texas. David Koresh. You remember. A bunch of religious nutters bent on self-destruction . . . ' I gave him my naughty-schoolboy smile.

He wasn't listening.

'Perhaps it's nothing to do with you two. What if he's trying to draw our attention somewhere else? The second of January 1492. A Columbus connection? Maybe. But Columbus discovered the New World later . . . '

He sprang up and went next door, where I could hear him riffling through his desk and bookshelves. He returned with an A5 Jiffy-bag and a battered volume from the *Encyclopaedia Britannica*. 'Just been doing what you might call some joined-up thinking . . . '

He slid a small and very beautiful book of photographs of the Alhambra from the bag. 'This arrived for me after you left for London. A gift from Trevor.' He handed me the card that had been attached to the jacket with a paperclip. I'd recognize Trev's scrawl anywhere. It was even worse than mine. *You'll like this, Father*, it read. *Your team won.* The caption beneath his message told me that the picture on the other side had been taken from the Comares Tower.

I scratched my head. 'Now I'm feeling really stupid . . .'

Father Mart was firing on all cylinders. He could barely keep the lid on his excitement as he flicked through the *Britannica*. 'Here we are. Abu 'Abd Allah Muhammad XI, last Nasrid Sultan of Granada, Spain . . . They called him Boabdil. Ferdinand and Isabella captured his stronghold on the second of January . . .'

' . . . 1492.' I was getting the hang of this. 'A famous victory for the left-footers.'

'I've always felt a bit sorry for Boabdil. He had the mother from hell. She turned him against everyone, including his father, and the poor lad lost everything. Even then she wouldn't let up. As he turned to catch his last glimpse of the Alhambra from the pass through the Sierra Nevada, he got a bit emotional. She just sneered at him and said, 'Don't weep like a woman for that which you failed to defend like a man.''

I grinned. 'Some of my mates on the estate had mums like that.'

I asked him if he had a good-sized map of southern Spain.

The thing he brought back had seen some action in its time. Much folded and dog-eared, it looked like a veteran of several Sierra Nevada missions. We spread it out on the table between us, and Father Mart ran his index finger down the route that Boabdil would have taken from the city he lost to the Catholic invader. I pictured his mum giving him regular clips around the ear as they went.

'Here's the Alhambra. And here's the Puerto del Suspiro del Moro. Their path must have followed what's now the main road to Motril.'

I asked him to repeat the Moro bit.

'Puerto del Suspiro del Moro.' He beamed. 'The setting for my favourite part of the story. It means the Gate of the Moor's Sigh. Needless to say, it's become a bit of a tourist attraction.'

I scanned the area around it. Padul. Otura. It didn't seem too densely populated, probably because of the mountains, until you got to the city of Granada, about eleven Ks to the north.

It was time for me to brush up on my flamenco.

PART TEN

PART TEN

1

Plaza de la Marina, Málaga

**Monday, 6 February
18.09 hrs**

The Air France flight from Charles de Gaulle was heaving with retired couples, elbows out, dripping with bling, en route to the Costa del Sol. They seemed to have sprayed each other a uniform shade of orange to help get themselves in the mood.

This time I'd taken a parking spot in the long stay at Gatwick and doubled back to St Pancras via Victoria. I exited the Eurostar at the Gare du Nord and messed around with the usual anti-surveillance drills before catching the RER B train to CDG. If Father Mart had read Trev's signal right, I didn't want to lead the opposition straight to Ella's hidey-hole.

After freezing my bollocks off in Glencoe, the Black Mountains, Moscow and Belgrade, the south coast of Spain provided a very welcome dose of Vitamin D. I began to see why the Old and the Gold were so determined to be first onto the transfer bus. Fifteen degrees wasn't exactly sweltering, but it was a whole lot better than Eskimo weather.

I hired a Seat Leon with a bit of extra welly under the bonnet and pointed it onto the main.

The sky was a blinding blue and the signposts told me I was a hundred Ks east of Gibraltar. I hadn't been down there since 1988, and that was no holiday either. The Det weren't legally authorized to operate outside the Province, but when you were in pursuit of an IRA active-service unit with a wagonload of high explosive, you had to bend the rules. We'd followed them onto the Rock and taken out all three before they'd had the chance to initiate the device.

I could still reach Granada in time to find a hotel and have a mooch around before dark o'clock, but only if I went direct and didn't check the rear-view on a regular basis. I bought the most detailed map of Andalucía I could find and took the scenic route instead, first to Málaga harbour, then into the maze of high-rises and historic ruins at its centre, where Moorish castles, Roman ruins and the huge Baroque cathedral rubbed up against formal gardens, upscale boutiques, Michelin-starred restaurants and bustling *tapas* bars.

Then I drove west through the urban sprawl and along the coast to Marbella as the sun began to dip below the peaks of the Sierra Blanca, floodlights bathed the gin palaces in the marinas and the shadows cast by the palm trees lengthened across the beaches.

Throughout the process I concentrated hard on getting lost and doubling back as often as you would when you're a Brit tourist who didn't know what he was doing on the right-hand side of the road and hadn't paid the extra euros for a satnav. Once I was satisfied that nobody in the queue of traffic behind me was performing the same tricks, I worked my way north towards Córdoba, then looped back through an endless succession of olive groves to the city Boabdil had surrendered just over five hundred and twenty years before.

2

The Hotel Villa Oniria was a newly restored nineteenth-century residence that marked the third point of a triangle linking the Alhambra and the Plaza Bib-Rambla, a square near the cathedral that seemed to be the place to go if you were in the mood for a drink and a bite to eat. I'd never been to Granada before, so it seemed as good a place as any to start my quest. It was also small, quiet and friendly, had its own parking garage, a floodlit fountain in the atrium as well as in the garden, and several exits.

The receptionist was very pleased to see the colour of my money, and didn't seem too alarmed by the purple bruise that had started to make its escape from beneath the dressing above my temple. I was shown to a room on the third floor.

I left the dressing in place but had a shit, shower and shave, then sat and studied the map to get my bearings. I wasn't going to get on Trev's Boabdil trail until first thing in the morning, but I hated not knowing which way was up.

The first thing I noticed as I hit the streets was that although the city was not stuffed with holidaymakers and the locals were obviously suffering from the economic downturn they were incredibly welcoming — and didn't take the piss at the first sniff of a cash transaction.

I found a *tapas* bar on a corner of the Plaza Pescadería, with high stools, tables on the pavement and gas heaters that looked like flaming dustbin lids on poles. The waitress looked like she'd been to a few bull fights in her time and immediately took charge. A plate of ham and beans, a bowl of squid and another of fried peppers said I hadn't been wrong to let her. I even decided to dust off my Spanish. I'd never be able to hold a candle to Trev on the language front, but she didn't seem to mind.

Out came the map and a fingernail the colour of blood traced my best routes around town, into and out of the Albaicín and up to Boabdil's fortress.

Halfway through, she pointed the same fingernail at my head and asked me if I'd had an argument with *mi esposa*. I laughed and told her that I'd been climbing at the weekend and had an argument with a rock.

When she'd finished my virtual guided tour I ordered a black coffee and watched the locals wander past. A bunch of teenagers smoked themselves to death on the other side of the promenade and a guitarist tugged on our heartstrings with his version of the theme tune to *The Deer Hunter*.

I walked back to the hotel via a circuit of the cathedral and a stretch of the Cuesta de Gomérez, one of the routes up to the Alhambra, whose floodlit ramparts glowed red and gold against the night sky above the city.

3

Alhambra, Granada

Tuesday, 7 February
08.00 hrs

The citadel was a twenty-minute tab from my breakfast table. I got to the ticket office shortly after it opened at eight. It was already humming with tourists and school trips and the odd serious-looking academic, but the scary queues that every website threatened in the height of the season were nowhere in sight.

I wandered through the Generalife Gardens, which gave me the chance to check out the fortified heart of the complex from the east, as well as the city beyond. It was no accident that this place was called the Hill of the Sun. I wasn't sure what I was looking for. I just knew that Trev hadn't presented us with the coordinates of the journey by accident, and if I followed his route, either I'd find Ella or she'd find me.

Until I'd hooked up with Anna, I'd never really given stuff like formal gardens a second glance. I'd enjoyed the view from the roof of Gaz's block in the Tabard, but only with a ketchup-filled condom in hand and as a potential battle space. Later, foliage of any kind was a source of cover, not of decoration or reflection. As with so many things, *mi esposa* had put me right on that.

I reached the Nasrid Palace half an hour later. Anyone who reckoned that Islam was about exploding rucksacks and rabble-rousing ayatollahs should have hung out there for half a day. Allah's PR department was really missing a trick. The lads who had designed the Alhambra aimed to create an earthly paradise, and that beat the fuck out of blowing up whoever didn't get your vote.

I followed a family of Canadians into the Palace of the Lions and sat at the edge of a courtyard watching the parents and the kids ooh and aah as they circled the twelve stone beasts that spouted water into the fountain at its centre.

I walked across the white marble paving of the Court of the Myrtles, stopping for a moment to admire the reflection of the Comares Tower in a formal pond my guidebook told me was thirty-four metres long and seven metres wide. Again, there was a stillness to the place which spoke to me in ways that I couldn't remember being spoken to before.

The guidebook also mentioned that an inscription in the Southern Gallery read: *May our Master, Emir of the Muslims, receive God's help and protection as well as a glorious victory.* Abu 'Abd Allah was Boabdil, so the magic hadn't worked for him.

My next stop was the Comares Tower itself, where Boabdil and his council had taken the decision to surrender. Legend had it that when his mum heard the news, she gave him another severe bollocking from one of the tower's balconies. She waved her arm across the

349

opposite hillside and the city beneath it and yelled, 'Look at what you surrender, and remember that all your forebears died as kings of Granada, but now the kingdom dies in you . . .' Trev hadn't chosen Father Mart's postcard by accident. I wanted to take a closer look at that view.

I wasn't disappointed when I got there. Framed by the arched window ahead of me, the Albaicín rose from the Darro River at the foot of the citadel and spread across the hillside, a tightly knit jumble of whitewashed walls, terracotta roofs and canvas awnings, punctuated by cypress trees and cascades of bougainvillaea. Two churches with angular, box-shaped towers dominated the skyline, one faded red-brick and one crisp white.

I scanned my map, and pictured the pleasure Trev would have taken as he assembled his next set of clues. The red-brick was the Iglesia del Salvador; the white — which the guidebook claimed had the best views of the Alhambra — was San Nicolás.

4

The Mirador de San Nicolás was a cobbled terrace beside the church, with a stone cross at its centre and seven or eight trees. Sunlight filtered through their bare branches, warming the small groups of shirt-sleeved tourists who'd found their way through the maze of alleyways that led up from the river.

Some clustered around a hairy flamenco guitarist and bongo-drummer duo giving its all to everybody's favourite bits from *Carmen*; some were being hypnotized by a jewellery seller; most just hung out on the retaining wall or the chunky stone benches and soaked up the scenery. A couple of donkeys wandered past, looking severely unimpressed.

I continued to go with the flow. It wasn't difficult. The Alhambra palaces were every bit as amazing from this side of the valley as the guidebook promised. I ordered a coffee and a sticky bun at a nearby café and kept eyes on the comings and goings in the plaza. The jewellery seller was doing a roaring trade.

Before heading back to the hotel to pick up my hire car, I dipped inside the church. A priest in a cassock was busy straightening prayer books and wiping specks of dust off the kind of pews that were designed to keep you awake during the sermon. He smiled and nodded as I lit a candle. It wasn't becoming a habit: I needed to look like

I had a reason for being there.

On the way through the centre of town I bought a pay-as-you-go mobile and two local network SIM cards, then got some *tapas* down my neck for luck.

5

I cleared the light-industrial wasteland that spread across the southern fringe of the city and pointed the Seat down the Autovía de Sierra Nevada towards the mountains.

I wasn't about to spend quality time at every one of the endless stream of venues along the route claiming some connection with the Moor's journey to temporary retirement, but I reckoned the Hotel Restaurante Boabdil and the Suspiro del Moro campsite were well worth a visit. Both were within gobbing distance of the pass, which the sign told me was 865 metres above sea level.

I didn't go there directly. I drove past a team of cyclists taking their high-tech Lycra kit and crash helmets for a ride, and hung the first available left to Otura. I bimbled around the town for a while, admiring the churches, the rental villas, the brand new terraces, the weird mixture of smart construction sites and tangled scrubland.

I parked up alongside a sports centre where they were holding some kind of martial-arts contest. Then I moved on to the Santa Cristina Golf Club, and watched a group of lads in brightly coloured, diamond-patterned V-necks and shiny trousers bounce their buggies around brilliant green fairways and sparkling water features, against the backdrop of snow-capped mountains.

When I was satisfied that no one cared what I was doing or where I was going, I drove back to the roundabout that crossed the *autovía*. As soon as the Hotel Restaurante Boabdil came into view, I knew it wasn't the place I was looking for: too close to the main; too overlooked; anybody staying there for more than forty-eight hours would draw attention to themselves too easily.

But the campsite was something else again. I pulled in between a white van and a line of firs in the car park and walked through the front entrance. The two- or three-acre corner plot was surrounded by thickly planted evergreens, and each of the mobile-home spaces had its own tree-lined shelter.

There was a shower and toilet block, but the bungalows were all self-contained. It was a bit like a caravan park in Southend we used to go to when I was a kid, but with sunshine and great-smelling food. You could lose yourself in there quite happily for a month or two.

The sign under the clock hanging outside the reception area said I was welcome, but the guy behind the desk didn't seem so sure. He had a Shakin' Stevens quiff and matching black shirt but had binned the pink jacket and warm smile.

He thawed a little when I told him I was looking for somewhere to stay for a few weeks later in the spring — bring the family, play some golf, go to the beach some days, I'd heard it was only thirty-five minutes away. But the shutters came down again when I asked if I could take a look around.

'I very much regret, Señor . . . ' He pointed to

a sign on the wall — an icon of a human being in a circle with a red diagonal slash across his bollocks — that gave a clear answer to my question. 'Our regular guests value their privacy. I could escort you, of course, maybe show you inside one of the vacant bungalows . . .'

I said that would do nicely, told him my name was Nick Jones, and that his place had been recommended by a good friend of mine in the UK. There was a flicker of interest when I mentioned Trev's name, but perhaps he was just being polite.

We skirted a small and well-shaded playground where a couple of kids were firing imaginary AK-47s at each other from behind the cover of the seesaw and slides. He guided me towards an avenue about a third filled with camper vans, then right, past a drinking fountain, to a row of reasonably secluded wooden bungalows on stone plinths, each with its own veranda.

A couple of lads in Hawaiian board shorts and US college hoodies wandered across to the table footie as Shaky steered me up the nearest set of steps. I glimpsed a curtain being drawn across a window three bungalows down. I didn't see a face, but I saw a smiley emoticon on a white T-shirt stretched across the kind of pectorals you only got from regular trips to the weight machine.

Shaky's show home slept two — or four, if they were feeling intimate — and had its own kitchen, bathroom and sitting room. I told him it was perfect for what I had in mind, and he got very cheerful indeed when I suggested a cash deposit. That bought me the deluxe tour, which allowed me to scan the full layout of the complex, including the swimming pools and restaurant block. I kept half an eye out for the smiley T-shirt as we went, but it was a no-show.

Back at the reception desk Nick Jones filled in a booking form for some imaginary dates in April and May, and wrote down one of his new mobile numbers where it asked for contact details.

As I left, the Lycra lads sped past on their racing bikes, legs pumping like their lives depended on it.

6

Mirador San Nicolás, Granada

Wednesday, 8 February
10.37 hrs

I was up at first light the following morning, showered, then swapped my dressing for a skin-coloured plaster. The stitches were working their magic and the bruising had retreated. I now looked like I'd had a minor disagreement with a door frame rather than a major one with a slab of Scottish granite.

I had the Spanish version of a full English just up the street from the hotel and stopped by the payphone at the main post office on my way up to the citadel. Bob didn't answer as quickly as he had the last time I'd called, but he had some news for me. Jack Grant's name was a last-minute addition to the flight manifest for an incoming C17 Starlifter from Camp Bastion, due into Akrotiri tomorrow afternoon.

I began my second Alhambra circuit as soon as the main gates opened, taking my time at the key locations I reckoned Trev had been pointing me towards. When no one tapped me on the shoulder I retraced my route to the Mirador San Nicolás.

I'd put the Seat back under cover at the Villa Oniria when I'd returned from the campsite and

357

headed out for my second helping of ham and beans and another side order of peppers. I never used to care much what I got down my neck, particularly when I was on an op, but this stuff tasted a whole lot better than a ready meal, and my own personal tour guide was keen to know how my day had been.

I took the same table at the café by the San Nicolás church and tucked into the same coffee and sticky pastry. The flamenco and bongo combo were touring elsewhere, but the jewellery seller was still sending customer after customer away with shiny stuff they'd suddenly realized they couldn't live without.

My bill arrived on a small metal saucer. The waiter hung around long enough to pick up my handful of euros and to say that my friend would be in the church at eleven thirty. My iPhone told me I didn't have long to wait.

I went inside and chose a pew at the back, away from the spots and candles that surrounded the altar. The priest gave me his usual smile of welcome. I picked up a service sheet and thought beautiful thoughts, keeping the main entrance in my peripheral vision.

Tourists came and went. Then a figure blocked out the sunlight pouring through the doorway. All I could see to start with was a monster silhouette. This lad had a torso like a wrecking ball. I hoped I was right in thinking he was on our side. As he stepped out of the shadows I got a clearer picture: a younger — mid to late thirties, maybe — blonder version of Trev. I spotted the image on the T-shirt beneath his partly zipped jacket. A smiley emoticon. Either this was the world's greatest coincidence, or I'd been reading Trev's signals right.

He wandered around the body of the church, then found himself in need of a moment of reflection alongside me. He asked if I minded. His English had the combination of fluidity and precision that all Scandinavians seem to bring to it. Less musical than the Norwegians, but not as flat as the Danes, I guessed he must be Swedish.

He glanced at the freshly applied plaster on my head and raised a questioning eyebrow.

'I've been bashing my head against a brick wall.'

He smiled. 'I know that feeling.'

He didn't rush it. It wasn't that kind of place. We both tuned into the whole meditative vibe. We didn't look at each other, but kept an eye out for hostiles. Eventually he spoke again.

'I've been coming here every couple of days since our friend passed away. He wasn't a religious man, but I know that's what he would have wanted.'

'I'm sorry I kept you waiting. It took me a while to get the message.'

He chuckled quietly to himself. 'He didn't have a lot to laugh about after he found the MRUD, but he was very amused by the method he chose to pass it on to you. He said that you haven't always been the world's greatest dog lover.'

'He's not wrong.' Without making it too obvious, I peeled back my right sleeve so he could see the pattern of canine tooth-marks on my forearm. 'But it's the big ones I have a problem with, not the ankle-biters.'

He nodded to himself. 'How is Icarus?'

'Still smiling.'

'Excellent. I'll be glad to stop wearing this T-shirt. It's not really my style.' He turned towards me and held out his hand. 'Good to meet you, Mr Jones. I just wish it had been under different circumstances. My name is Jesper.'

'Ex-SSG?'

The Särskilda Skyddsgruppen was effectively Sweden's version of the Regiment. These boys were good news. Their special operator training took more than a year, and included HAHO and HALO parachuting, explosives, sniper and special weapons, and VIP protection. Trev's babysitter wasn't going to fuck about if everything went to rat shit.

'And ex-Arctic Rangers.' Jesper grinned. 'But I first met Trevor a long way from the snow, in what we used to call Zaïre.'

'Bet he couldn't wait to show off his Swedish.'

'It was very impressive, actually. But really designed for people he wanted to sleep with. We were both extremely pleased to discover that I wasn't one of them.'

'Lucky you were available at such short notice.'

'Trev didn't believe in luck, as you well know. He had me on standby before Christmas.'

We turned like a couple of synchronized swimmers as another bunch of people came through the entrance. I recognized the Canadian family I'd followed into the Palace of the Lions. But I was paying less attention to potential observers than I was to Trev's timeline. I'd made the mistake of assuming that the shit hadn't hit the fan big-time until the gangfuck in the CQB Rooms, but that hadn't been until 11 January. I now knew that Trev and Sam had prepared the groundwork for Ella's disappearance three or four weeks earlier.

'So what happens next?'

He interlaced his surprisingly delicate fingers and cracked his knuckles. 'What would you like to happen?'

That was an easy one to answer. 'I'd like to find a way of getting my young friend out of the shit, and I don't have a whole lot of time. I was hoping his girlfriend might be able to help.'

'Come to the Generalife Gardens at five o'clock this evening. The path at the back, among the trees, leading away from the palace.'

He eased himself out of the pew, nodded to the priest and left.

7

I got back to the Alhambra complex at four and bimbled around the Patio de la Acequia and the palace colonnade with the other sightseers before finding a sheltered bench with its back against the east wall and a drop-dead view through the trees to the citadel and the city and the Sierra Nevada.

Jesper appeared at the end of the path to my left, at the southern corner of the garden. He'd changed his T-shirt. The new one featured Mick Jagger's freshly detonated lips and celebrated the Rolling Stones' A Bigger Bang tour. I wondered if it was another of Trev's jokes.

The girl beside him was in jeans and a plain crimson Puffa jacket. I didn't recognize her immediately, even though I'd studied the Mathieson family photographs. Her hair was short, spiky and black as a raven's wing. She wore no makeup, and the lack of Vitamin D and the strain of the last few weeks were etched on her face.

Jesper stayed on stag at the corner and motioned Ella towards me.

'Dr Mathieson.' I stood up and gripped her hand.

'Hello, Nick.'

Her voice was melodic and slightly husky.

We sat down and did our best to look like we were doing nothing more than watching the sun dip towards the Comares Tower. I waited for her

362

to start talking. I didn't want to crowd her. And it wasn't long before she did.

'You knew Sam's dad, didn't you?'

'We did a lot of stuff together, I guess me and Trev and Harry were best mates when we were younger.' I didn't tell her I was probably responsible for Harry's death.

'Trev has been killed, hasn't he? Jesper is trying to shield me from how bad things have got, but I knew even before you appeared.' She gave a soft smile. 'Bless him, he's just like Sam. They both forget that GPs sometimes have to be grown-ups too.'

I nodded.

'Were you there?'

I nodded again.

She gripped her denim-covered knees. 'Was it horrible?'

'It wasn't good. But it was quick.'

She shifted for a moment into doctor mode and reached up to touch the plaster beneath my hairline.

I gave her a wry grin. 'We can save that story for another time.' I paused. 'I met your friend Grace. You'll be pleased to hear she was no help at all.'

'Have you seen Sam?'

I told her I hadn't. 'Trev thought it might do more harm than good. I've made contact with the lawyer, though. A guy called Blackwood. Serious player. But he seems to be getting some quite strange signals from your boy. I wondered if you could shed any light on that.'

She frowned. 'What sort of strange?'

'He doesn't seem to want to help his legal people — or anyone else — get him off the hook.'

She gave a deep sigh. 'This may sound like an odd thing to say about one of you Special Forces heroes, but Sam was really, really scared. Scared for both of us — scared enough to ask Trevor to arrange for me to disappear. I don't know why. But given what's happened to Trevor, I guess he was right to be . . . '

I asked her to tell me when things had started falling apart. 'It was before the CQB mess, wasn't it?'

The pain sprang into her eyes like I'd flicked a switch. 'Oh, way before . . . Chris and Guy died in Afghanistan, but in one way or another that last tour went a long way towards destroying them all.'

Her jaw clenched. I told her to take her time.

'Sam had nightmares from the moment he came back. He refused to tell me any of the details, said it wasn't my problem. But of course it was, wasn't it? You can't be in love with someone and stand back and watch as they shrivel up in front of you without it becoming your problem too.'

She gazed out through the trees, but she wasn't even noticing the view. 'Have you ever had the night sweats, Nick?'

She didn't need an answer.

'We've got this lovely place in our garden back home, a kind of Ralph Lauren version of a shepherd's hut, with a chimney and steps and wheels so you can tow it around. I hoped it might be somewhere Sam could find some peace and quiet.

'It seemed to work, some days. Other days he'd draw down the shutters and lock himself away in there to grapple with his demons. Sometimes I'd manage to persuade him to stay with me, or I'd sit by his bed and watch over him, the way some parents watch their new-born babies to make sure they're still breathing.

'When he got the sweats, he'd repeat one word, over and over, like a mantra. A name. It sounded like an Afghan name. To start with, I couldn't hear it clearly — I assumed it was the place Guy had won his Victoria Cross. But it wasn't.'

'Kajaki, maybe?'

'No.' She lowered her head. 'I know about Kajaki. Well, I know as much as Sam and Scott were prepared to tell me. I could never work out whether they were trying to protect me from the most disturbing details or couldn't bear to revisit the experience. But it was somewhere else. Sounded like Cushty, except that it definitely wasn't. Koshty, maybe?'

'Koshtay.'

'Is that a place?'

'Yup. And you're right. It isn't where Guy won his VC. But it's not too far away from it.'

8

I was still grappling with the timeline.

'Ella, Jesper told me he was on standby before Christmas. I knew things had gone pear-shaped at Kajaki, but I didn't know that Trev and Sam felt under serious external threat even before the CQB incident.'

She raised her hands helplessly. 'I had no idea either. Not *really*. As far as I was concerned, when Sam wasn't battling with his own nightmares, he was trying his best to stop his friend unravelling.

'The Chastains very sweetly invited the three of us to Guy's medal ceremony in November. They're so determined to build something positive from it. Admirable, really, but it seemed to tip Scott right over the edge.

'He was in a really bad place during the run-up to Christmas. You know how emotional that time of year can be. His girlfriend left him quite soon after they got back from Helmand and his mum was completely out of her depth.

'That whole period was utterly miserable. But it wasn't until the weekend after Twelfth Night that Trev and Sam sent me away.'

'They didn't tell you why?'

She shook her head. 'I asked, of course. They said it was safer if they didn't go into any detail. 'Need to know' — isn't that the phrase you all use? And though I was worried about Sam's equilibrium, I'd spent enough time with Trev to take his advice very seriously indeed.

'Something happened on that Saturday night, Nick. Sam and Scott went out on the town together. The Spreadeagle, the Barrels, the Vaults — you know, the usual places. They ended up at the Green Dragon. I don't know what happened along the way, but it was serious enough for them to put me on a ferry to Esbjerg with Jesper the following afternoon. We took a week to get down here on his motorbike. They thought it would be best to take the scenic route.'

'I take that one all the time.'

So she'd left before Scott's note arrived. *Mate, sorry about last night. Pissed again. Story of my life, these days. Not good. I can't promise not to repeat, but I'll do my best. It's a fucker, isn't it?* It would have come through Sam's door on the Tuesday, and twenty-four hours later his best mate got a round through the back of the head.

I swivelled towards her. 'Do you mind me asking some more questions?'

She told me to go ahead. A smile flickered across her lips. 'My schedule's pretty clear today . . .'

'Why didn't Sam come with you?'

'He asked for leave, but they refused it. He didn't want to risk going absent without leave. And he reckoned that Scott needed his help more than I did. How ironic is that?'

'Do your parents know where you are?'

Her smile broadened. 'You wouldn't ask that if you knew them. How can I put this? My father is a high-ranking cavalry officer. He doesn't do

367

naked emotion, even at the Cenotaph. He's a lovely man, but the last time I confided in him was when I got chucked out of prep school — and that was only because I knew there was a letter on the way to them from the headmistress. So when Trev and Sam said it would be better not to, I didn't have a problem with that.'

I didn't either. It made no sense to set up a hide, then broadcast its co-ordinates over pink gins at the Cavalry Club.

'Did you spend much time with Scott?'

'As much as we could manage. His dad's dead, his mum's got Alzheimer's, so when Sophie — his girlfriend — left, he was more dependent on us than ever. He was a really great guy, but what happened to Chris completely ripped him apart. They should have put him in the psych ward for some proper counselling and pastoral care, not sent him to the Killing House.'

A young couple appeared on the path to our right. They looked for a moment as if they were aiming for the bench alongside ours, then realized that me and Ella were in a full-on conversation, not trying to decide where we might go for dinner. They gave us a friendly wave and walked on by.

I knew there was no diplomatic way of asking the next question, so when their footsteps had receded I just dived in. 'Ella, is there any possibility at all that Sam could have fired that round? I mean, accidentally. He was obviously pretty strung out too . . . ' I didn't mention the fact that I'd poked around in her medicine cabinet and his drawers and found the sertraline.

368

She raised her eyes to mine. 'Sam isn't in great shape, Nick, but he's dealing with it. Everyone, apart from Trev and me, still thinks he's Superman. He's not chewing the carpet. He hasn't lost his marbles or forgotten how to work a safety catch.

'He called me after the live firing exercise . . .' She caught the expression on my face. 'Don't worry. We were in Salzburg on a pay-as-you-go. Jesper took it apart immediately afterwards and threw all the bits into the Salzach River.

'Anyway, we talked. He was gutted about Scott, obviously, but he was very, very lucid. Sam doesn't know what happened in that room, and for one very good reason. He wasn't there.'

'So why is he facing a potential manslaughter charge, and why isn't he levelling with Blackwood?'

She turned away from me again and tried to focus on the sunset. I looked over her shoulder at Jesper. He was cool, but tapped his watch. I nodded.

'I don't know why Sam hasn't confided in Blackwood, Nick. I'm not *au fait* with how these proceedings work. But I'm *absolutely* certain he didn't kill Scott. He only told DSF or whoever that he'd been responsible for a negligent discharge because he figured that the detention facility at the Military Court Centre, under lock and key, was the safest place he could be right now.'

9

I watched Jesper and Ella join the queue of punters filtering out of the main gate, hanging back so that I could keep an eye out for interested observers, and to minimize the chances of us being connected in plain sight.

They crossed the main and made their way to the Alhambra Palace Hotel car park, where Jesper took a couple of helmets out of the side boxes of a black BMW R1200GS Adventure. Good choice. It was one of my favourite machines, and not just because Ewan McGregor and the Hairy Bikers gave it their vote. The double overhead camshaft the Berlin boffins had introduced on the 2010 model had given it some extra kick and increased its redline limit to 8500 r.p.m. It had a top speed of around 130 m.p.h. and wasn't shy of going off-road.

Jesper threw his leg over the saddle and Ella climbed on behind him. They disappeared downhill with a low growl and a flash of tail lights. I threaded back to the Cuesta de Gomérez, the tree-lined walkway that led towards the city centre, as the street lamps sparked up.

Granada Cathedral was a giant brown baroque wedding cake. If it didn't have a hunchback in its bell tower, it should have done. The three grand arches at the front were floodlit — I could see their glow as I approached them from the side, down an alley that was in the middle of a facelift. It was lined with sheets of wriggly tin suspended at head height on metal poles, beneath which were either locked, graffiti-covered roller shutters, or open souvenir shops that weren't yet doing a roaring trade.

A crumpled figure sat hunched at the corner, in the shadow of the hoarding. Taking refuge behind a grubby black ninja *niqab*, she could have been anywhere between eighteen and eighty. As I approached her, all I could hear was the echo of my footsteps and her low moaning, punctuated by the occasional rattle of a few coins in the bottom of a paper cup.

I thrust my hand into my jeans pocket for a couple of euros. She struggled to her feet as I moved forward to add them to her collection and muttered something I couldn't quite make out. I leaned in closer and cocked my ear. I still couldn't understand what she was saying, but by then I didn't need to.

She peeled her equally grubby cloak far enough back to let me see what she was carrying in her right hand. I got the message. From now on her fully cocked and silenced Llama Mini-Max .45 sub-compact was going to do most of the talking. These things were small enough to put in a clutch bag, but they had a ten-round, double-stack magazine, which was more than enough to turn this into a very bad day out.

Now we were breathing each other's oxygen, I also couldn't help noticing that she had three days' stubble beneath her *niqab*, and a very steady aim. I thought about asking whether a five-euro note would settle it, but the glint in the eyes told me not to.

The cup disappeared, and the Llama said I should follow its owner as he reversed into the darkened passageway that I could now see over his shoulder. I followed its instructions.

I was on full alert, hopefully better late than never. I could hear a bunch of kids playing football in the square I'd been aiming for. I could hear the click-clack of stiletto heels about ten metres behind Niqab. And the heavy-breathing presence at my back.

I glanced down at the matt black lump of metal pointed at my centre mass. The Mini-Max wasn't a hundred per cent reliable: it had a tendency to catapult its ejected cases into the user's forehead, and a reputation for jamming. But I wasn't about to depend on that. I wondered whether I could interfere with the topslide.

The click-clack came nearer. That wasn't necessarily good news. If my mate in the *niqab* got trigger-happy, he wouldn't only take me out, but anyone else within reach. I couldn't just hear the breathing behind me: I could feel it on my neck. In a perfect world, I'd throw myself right or left and let them slot each other.

The click-clack came to a halt.

'Señor?'

Niqab stopped dead but didn't turn towards the newcomer.

I recognized the voice. I was pretty sure I'd recognize the fingernails too.

'*Señor . . . Are you . . . OK?*'

I opened my mouth to respond but Niqab's head shook and his eyes left me in no doubt that an answer wasn't called for.

I felt a blinding pain as Heavy Breather hit me just behind my right ear. Pinpricks of light danced across my retinas and my knees turned to liquid.

10

'Señor . . . *Señor?*'

Her tone was urgent.

The ground was rock hard beneath my shoulder-blades but her fingertips were cool on my brow.

I could hear the blood pounding through my head. I hoped it wasn't in a hurry to escape onto the paving stones. I reached up and slid my hand to the spot where Heavy Breather had connected. There was a lump the size of a golf ball, but the skin wasn't broken. He must have been carrying a cosh — leather, probably, filled with lead shot.

I opened my eyes.

The waitress from the tapas bar was kneeling over me, her very worried face inches from mine. 'Are you all right? Should I call the police, maybe?' She straightened and fished around in her handbag for her mobile.

I took a couple of deep breaths and was about to tell her not to bother when she held out a half-litre bottle of mineral water instead.

I raised myself on my elbows. She flipped back the lid and put it to my lips. It tasted magic. After three or four gulps I managed to crank myself into a sitting position.

Her eyes were wide. 'Who were those people?'

'Never seen them in my life. Where did they go?'

'Back towards the cathedral, I think. Did they rob you?'

I tapped my pockets and shook my head, then wished I hadn't.

She helped me to my feet. 'You should see a doctor, maybe.'

I thanked her and told her I'd be fine.

I left her at the corner and unscrambled my brain cells as I headed back to the hotel. It was good to discover that they were still capable of firing up, but not at all good to hear what they were saying to me. Niqab and Heavy Breather hadn't just been there to nick my holiday money, which could only mean one thing right now. They hadn't just pinged me. They'd pinged Ella and Jesper as well.

11

The receptionist at the Villa Oniria conjured up my Seat at the double and I went direct to the *autovía*. I kept half an eye on the rear-view, but I already had a bad feeling about this, and figured that speed was more important than camouflage right now.

The evening traffic was fairly light, so it didn't take long to get to the Suspiro del Moro turnoff. If Jesper and Ella had come straight back, I reckoned I'd be forty-five minutes to an hour behind them. Less if they'd zigzagged. I hoped they'd zigzagged.

The campsite forecourt wasn't awash with light, but I wouldn't have cared if it had been. The fact was we'd been compromised, and our number-one priority was to get out of there, and worry about reinstating our cover later. I exited the Seat and pressed the padlock button on the fob.

There were three other hire cars parked up, but Jesper's GS was nowhere in sight. I allowed myself a sliver of hope that they were tucking into paella somewhere along the way, and I'd got there first.

Shaky appeared at my elbow as I steamed past the reception area. He didn't point at the *Prohibido* notice this time, just looked worried. He didn't need to ask where I was going, which was another bad sign. I reckoned the privacy of his regular guests had already been invaded big-time.

The lamp above the veranda was on, but the interior of the bungalow was dark and the curtains drawn. The GS glinted on its stand beneath the side window. I'd have given good money for a 9mm Browning in my waistband as I approached, keeping to the cover of the trees. Even a Mini-Max would have been better than nothing.

I glanced to my right and saw that Shaky was having similar thoughts. He slid a hand inside his jacket and brought out a knife.

I shook my head and indicated that he should let me take care of it. Unless this boy suddenly turned into Zorro, he was going to do himself more harm than good with that thing. I'd seen plenty of lads who didn't know any better finish a night out on the receiving end of their own blade.

He didn't go all macho on me, just passed it across with barely disguised relief. I motioned to him to stay at ground level, hugging the stone plinth, and held his weapon in my right hand as I mounted the steps.

The tin roof extended over the decking in front of me. The door was partly glazed, with a window to the right, a plastic table and chairs to the left. There was no cover to speak of — a round would have blasted through the lightly timbered walls of this place with energy to spare — but I ducked towards the table anyway. At least I'd be out of plain sight.

Shaky crouched motionless behind me,

precisely where I'd left him. I moved as close as possible to the entrance, opened my mouth and listened. I could now see the flicker of a TV screen and hear staccato voices and canned laughter. There was also some kind of scrabbling and a low groan.

It didn't sound like a fight.

And fuck it — I wasn't here for the sightseeing.

I gripped Shaky's blade, threw open the door and dived left, keeping low.

12

The place looked like it had been hit by a tornado. The TV set, fixed to the wall on a metal arm, looked like the only piece of kit to have been left unscathed.

Jesper lay beneath it, surrounded by broken and splintered furniture. Blood leaked from a gash in the side of his forehead, which pretty much matched the one I'd picked up at Glencoe. His wrists had been plasticuffed together behind his back. His ankles were plasticuffed too. He'd brought his knees up to his chest, and was trying to roll onto them and lever himself up.

The shattered remains of a glass vase and half-open daffodils were strewn among the wreckage in the centre of the room. A photograph of Ella, which I was pretty sure had once sat in a frame at the house she shared with Sam, lay in a pool of water alongside them. I stepped over it and helped him to his feet.

I sliced through the plasticuffs as I quizzed him. He wouldn't have expected me to play Florence Nightingale and, besides, we both knew I didn't have the time.

'How many?'

Jesper showed me three fingers, then raised them to the wound beneath his hairline. They came away smeared with crimson.

'Do they have her?'

He managed to do words this time. 'Don't

379

think so . . . She ran . . . '

'When?'

'Fifteen minutes . . . Twenty, maybe . . . '

'Where?' Jesper wouldn't have spent the last three weeks flower-arranging and watching *Spain's Got Talent*. He'd have recced the immediate area and planned escape routes and actions for Ella in case everything went to rat shit.

His chest was still heaving, but he was starting to grip himself. 'The restaurant . . . plenty of people . . . through the trees . . . the other side of the pool . . . Then across the roundabout to Otura . . . '

'Nick . . . ' He stopped me as I reached the door.

I turned back in time to catch his bike keys.

'Take it. Quicker.'

I fished out the Seat fob and chucked it to him. 'It's out front. We'll RV at the golf club.'

Shaky stepped aside to let me pass. A look of pain seized his face as he checked out the damage. I unclipped the GS's side boxes and left them by the steps. I didn't know what kind of terrain I might end up cutting through, and that lessened the chances of getting tangled in the foliage. I'd do without the skid-lid, for the time being at least. I needed eyes and ears on max strength.

I saddled up, kicked the bike off its stand and fired the engine. The rear wheel skidded round behind me as I pulled a tight U-turn, spraying dust and gravel shrapnel across the side of the bungalow.

The restaurant had a viewing tower from which you could share Boabdil's last glimpse of his surrendered kingdom, but I didn't expect that to be top of Ella's list of priorities. I parked the GS, ran up the red stone steps and veered right to the eatery. It was busier than I'd expected. There was a buzz of conversation and the clink of cutlery. I spotted four or five possibles: girls with short dark hair and their backs to me. I wandered through the place as you do when you're meeting up with friends, but she wasn't one of them.

I politely declined the restaurant manager's offer of a table and looped back to the car park. I flicked the GS out of neutral again, followed the curve of the building, mounted the pavement and found a gap in the wall of cypresses that opened into the olive grove. I really liked this machine. It pretty much did what you told it to, and responded with a soft purr at low revs rather than a boy racer's shriek.

Away from the ambient light of the campsite and restaurant complex my vision took a hammering, but the sky was clear, and though the moon wasn't full, I reckoned it was plenty good enough to see where I was going, and not so bright that I'd become the world's easiest target. Short of giving it a sharp tap with a hammer, I couldn't kill the low-beam headlamp, but I'd try to avoid squeezing the brake unless I really had to.

The olives were twelve or fifteen feet high and thickly leaved. They'd been planted with geometric precision on a grid designed to facilitate machine harvesting. I rode five or six trees in, then hung a left and throttled back, so I was moving slowly enough to be able to check along the aisle between each row, a bit like you do when you've lost your mum in the supermarket. I didn't expect Ella to stand out in the open and wave and yell, 'Over here!' but I thought she might hear the bike and head towards it, hoping it wasn't hostile.

The west side of the grove bordered a huge expanse of flat, open ground. I stopped inside the treeline and scanned it for any sign of activity or disturbance. There was none. I pulled another U, headed back to the centre and hung a left. My plan was to crisscross the plantation at thirty-metre intervals until I reached the far side or found Ella.

Either way, I'd then head across the main to Otura.

13

I'd covered a lot of acres by the time I got to the northern boundary. I didn't bump into any Leathermen or Llama-toting transvestites on the way, but I didn't find Ella either.

This side was marked by a berm, about a metre high and a couple of hundred long. I slowed the GS to a halt and switched off. For the next five minutes, I sat there in the darkness and listened to the soft tick of the cooling engine and the gentle breeze through the trees.

Then I pulled the GS onto its stand again and scrambled up the berm. It dropped away to a dried-out irrigation ditch, which the locals had used as a garbage dump. A wire-link fence stood on the far side of it, then the shadows of a more densely planted stretch of evergreen woodland. I couldn't see any way through.

I was about to turn back and saddle up when I heard another sound, somewhere below me and to my right. I stood stock still for a couple of beats and heard it again.

An owl.

No.

A not very good impression of an owl.

And, though I didn't know much about the private life of birds, I was pretty sure they preferred trees to ditches.

I slid down the bank and moved carefully along the bed, doing my best to avoid disrupting loose rocks and scrub.

I'd gone about ten metres when my path was partly blocked by a couple of lacerated bin bags, a pile of empty cans and a discarded mattress. I sensed rather than saw a figure pressed against the earth behind it. It didn't move as I eased myself around the pile of crap.

'*Nick* . . .'

She didn't know that the sound of a whisper often carried further than a murmur. She hadn't had much practice at this sort of shit.

As she stepped towards me I could see that her Puffa had a tear and her jeans were ripped across the knee — not too bad for someone who'd spent the last couple of hours evading hostiles and legging it across unfamiliar territory.

'Let's move.'

I wasn't about to stop for a chat. We could play catch-up later.

14

I didn't thrash it until I'd stitched a line along the base of the berm and we'd hit tarmac. The GS's stability was legendary, but I'd rolled one or two on loose terrain in my time, and it was no fun for whoever was riding pillion. And there was a gate at the corner by the road, so I didn't have to do the Steve McQueen trick with the barbed-wire barrier.

I didn't go straight to the Santa Cristina either. I jinked the GS around the backstreets of Otura first, to make sure we didn't have an escort from the Crvena Davo or their mates.

Ella was the perfect passenger: she didn't try to squeeze the life out of me when I throttled up, despite the shit she'd just been through. If she hadn't done this stuff before, her trans-European marathon with Jesper had been the best kind of training.

The construction cranes reached silently for the sky and the karate kids had shut up shop for the night, but the golf clubhouse was awash with light. There was still business to be done at the nineteenth hole. A few Seats were scattered around the place, but none of them was mine.

I pulled up on the far side of the parking area, beside a clump of cypresses and firs that edged the fairway. I cut the engine and the headlamp but we didn't dismount. I wanted to be able to take off immediately if there was a drama before the Arctic Ranger showed up.

She loosened her grip around my waist but her face and shoulder muscles were taut as bowstrings. 'Jesper?'

She was dreading the answer.

'He's good. Should be on his way here now.'

She heaved a sigh of relief.

'Ella, what happened back there?'

'Two of them were waiting for us in the bungalow. With guns. A third followed us in from a car outside. Needless to say, Jesper didn't go quietly. While they were trying to deal with him, I ran for it — that's what he'd told me to do — before they had time to get organized. I didn't think I'd get a second chance.'

'He wasn't wrong.' I half turned towards her, still keeping eyes on the entrance and scanning for other observation points. 'What made you decide on the owl thing?'

She managed a smile. Some of the tension of the last few hours was starting to leak out of her. 'Jesper took me through a whole range of possible scenarios. He told me we needed a signal that only we would recognize. I remembered something Sam had told me about his dad's favourite party tricks.'

I smiled too. 'Harry's owl impression was even worse than yours.'

'Sam says he did pigs and cows and dogs and sheep as well.'

'Yeah. They were all shit.'

'Of course they were. One of your most important jobs as a dad is to embarrass your kids, isn't it?'

I thought about that for a moment. 'I guess. My stepdad pretty much left me to embarrass myself. I didn't let him down.'

We listened to the night sounds and the occasional burst of laughter from the clubhouse. The party was hitting its stride.

She gestured towards the warm glow from the windows. 'Does it ever feel weird doing the things that you have to do — things like this — while the rest of the world carries on regardless?'

'I never wish I could spend more time with people in very loud diamond-patterned pullovers, if that's what you mean.'

She didn't do the eyebrow trick, but came close. 'You know very well that's not what I meant . . .'

She went quiet for a moment, but I could see she needed to fill the silence.

'Sam says he can't remember Harry talking much about the Regiment. And Trev didn't either. He thinks maybe they were hoping he'd try something else.'

'Well, that worked a treat, didn't it?'

'He says they both talked about you, though.'

'Shouldn't you have taken that as a warning?'

She shook her head. 'Does everything have to be a joke with you guys?'

Anna used to ask me much the same question. I gave Ella much the same answer. 'It's what keeps you going when things can't get any worse. You know that.'

She nodded slowly. 'So what happens now?'

There were at least a dozen responses on my

list. I went with the simplest. 'We both shut the fuck up and wait for Jesper. We'll give him another half-hour.'

388

15

We didn't have to wait that long.

The Seat turned in through the main gates, drew to a halt about ten metres away from us and flashed its main beams. Jesper emerged from the driver's door and raised a hand. He went round to the rear hatch for the side boxes as Ella and I got off the bike.

She leaned in to me as we moved forward. 'Is he really OK, Nick? He seems ... '

The words died on her lips as we got close enough to see two other figures in the wagon.

Shaky was rigid, eyes wide, facing forwards in the passenger seat. He had a pistol stuck in the back of his head. I couldn't see much of the guy holding it, but I could tell he wasn't fucking about.

A third figure stepped out of the hatch, and he wasn't fucking about either. He pointed the muzzle of his suppressed weapon at Jesper's centre mass. I'd been wondering about the complete absence of hostiles in the olive grove. Now I knew the reason why.

Jesper walked back towards me, his hands linked behind his neck, obscuring the second hostile. His head wound was still leaking and blood dripped from another couple of gashes in his cheek onto his shirt. They'd obviously tried to persuade him to talk, but the glance he gave Shaky told me which of them had given away the RV.

I sensed Ella tensing herself, preparing for her

389

second runner of the evening. Surrender wasn't on her agenda.

A heavily accented Middle European voice came from behind Jesper's left shoulder. 'Tell the girl that if she tries to escape again, we will shoot you and both of your friends.'

Ella didn't need Jesper to pass on the message. It was already loud and clear.

Jesper's captor instructed him to lie face down beside the wagon, hands behind his back. That was when I got my first really good look at him. I'd never seen him without his *niqab*, but I'd have recognized those ugly little boot-button eyes anywhere. I guessed his mate in the wagon was Heavy Breather.

He told Ella to sit down and put her hands on her head, then threw a couple of plasticuffs onto Jesper's back and motioned me towards them with the muzzle of his Llama. 'Wrists. Tight.'

I knelt over Jesper and messed around with the ties for a moment, hoping Niqab would make the mistake of coming within reach. He didn't. He'd underestimated the opposition once tonight. He wasn't going to do it again.

'Tighter.'

When the cuff had begun to bite into Jesper's flesh I was told to lie alongside him. The tarmac was still warm from the day's sun, but it could have been cold enough to freeze my bollocks off for all I cared.

Shaky was hauled out of the Seat by Heavy Breather and put on plasticuff duty. The boy was shitting himself. Even in the shadow of the wagon I could see rings of sweat beneath his armpits as he stood over Ella. He was trembling so badly it took him two or three attempts to engage the plastic tongue into the teeth of her clasp and draw it through.

When her wrists were secure, it was my turn.

Shaky was a bit quicker with the cuff this time. Niqab kept an eagle eye on the process, but never came close enough for me to have a crack at him.

Heavy Breather manhandled Ella into the passenger seat and got back in behind her. I got the strong impression that he had a score to settle. She'd made him look like a dickhead a couple of hours ago, and any chance he got to hurt her from now on, he'd take.

16

Once both doors had banged shut, Niqab told me and Jesper to get to our feet and walk towards the clump of trees behind the GS. We were directed to a bare trunk a metre inside the treeline and ordered to stand either side of it. Shaky looped another plasticuff around our ankles, then Niqab lobbed a roll of gaffer tape at him and told him to wrap us in it, back to back, starting with our mouths.

As he peeled off the first six inches and raised it to my cheek, Shaky gave me an agonized look. I knew he wasn't just thinking about the two of us: he was flapping big-time about how the rest of his day was going to pan out.

Shaky circled the tree, binding the two of us in a spiral of tape. Niqab motioned for him to step back when he reached our waists. He finally came so close to me I could smell his last couple of meals, and turned up the wattage in those shiny boot-button eyes. Then he punched me hard in the gut and kneed me in the bollocks.

I couldn't bend an inch, either to protect myself from further attack or bring up my knees to stop him doing it again. I tried to suck as much air as I could through my nostrils, and did my best to ignore the pain that kicked off precisely where he'd connected and then spread fiercely, down my legs and up to my throat. A stream of hot bile threatened to invade my nose and mouth, but I somehow managed to force it back.

Shaky carried on with the job. By the time he'd reached our ankles he'd used most of the roll and we weren't going anywhere fast. But at least we could breathe, and I was pretty sure they weren't going to go to this much trouble, then put a round into us.

I could no longer focus on Niqab, but sensed that he was now well pleased with his evening's work. And as my nerve endings gradually settled back into position, I consoled myself with the thought that, if he and Heavy Breather were close mates of the Leathermen and Sniper One, I'd got off very lightly.

Shaky's final task was to whip the GS's keys out of the ignition and destroy the valves on both tyres. When he'd finished, Niqab escorted him to the Seat, gave him the plasticuff treatment and bundled him into the boot.

Two more doors slammed and seconds later the wagon pulled a U and headed back towards the main.

Jesper gave a grunt and we both tried to twist and wrench our way out of our gaffer-tape cocoon. But Shaky had done his job far too well. It looked like we were going to have to rely on the lads in the diamond-patterned pullovers to get us out of the shit. I hoped they weren't settling in for the night.

17

Santa Cristina, Otura

Thursday, 9 February
01.30 hrs

The golfers at the Santa Cristina finally stumbled out of the bar at one thirty in the morning. Finding a Brit and a Swede tied to a tree at the edge of their car park was a bit of a bonus.

The lads were still pissing themselves with laughter after they'd unpeeled us, and we joined in the hilarity. They assumed we were the hapless victims of a stag-party stunt, and we played right along with it. We all agreed that, when you're in the right mood, there's nothing funnier than having your mates bind you from head to foot in gaffer tape and let the air out of your tyres.

As soon as the golfing team had gone I called the hire car company to report the theft of the Leon. They were pretty relaxed. The local police had already found it abandoned on the main to Jaén.

We left the Santa Cristina and hot-wired the first wagon we came to without an immobilizer. Jesper drove me back to the campsite. We agreed that he'd head for Jaén and try to pick up Ella's trail. Wherever they were taking her, we reckoned that it would probably be by road. Getting onto a plane or a train without her raising the alarm would be impossible. She'd already shown them what she was made of.

A roll-on roll-off ferry would work, if they drugged and hid her, but we both reckoned they'd go overland. Niqab and Heavy Breather weren't going to garrotte her and dump her body, or they would have done it by now. I was pretty sure she was more valuable as a hostage. Whoever had her could stop Sam telling the truth about the CQB Rooms.

I didn't have time for a wild-goose chase across southern Spain. My best chance of getting Ella and Sam off the hook was to ambush Jack Grant while he was still in Cyprus — which meant taking the first plane I could out of Málaga.

Jesper asked me a couple more questions before he made for the *autovía*. 'How many times have these Serbs got close to you?'

'Six.'

I knew what was coming.

'So why have they not taken the opportunity to kill you?'

'The first two times, I killed them instead. The next three they were interrupted. Then they decided to tape me to a Swede. Maybe they thought that was enough punishment.'

A cab pulled up at the front entrance to the campsite at pretty much the same time Jesper left. The passenger door burst open and Shaky stumbled across the gravel. He didn't know whether to be in deep mourning for our friend or just plain relieved that he wasn't lying in a ditch with a bullet in his head.

He jabbered away in a mixture of Spanish and English. From what I could make out, the Madre de Dios had smiled upon him in her infinite kindness and Niqab and Heavy Breather had dumped him by the roadside on the northern edge of Granada, cut the plasticuff off his ankles but not off his wrists, then left him to it.

I didn't hold out much hope that the Madre de Dios would be as kind to Ella. She'd have been transferred to some kind of van with room to keep her out of sight every time her captors needed to cross a frontier.

Shaky drove me to the Villa Oniria to pick up my kit, then back down to Málaga. He probably thought it was the only way he could be sure of getting rid of me. He denied it big-time, but before dropping me off in the outskirts he said he wouldn't mind if we didn't come back to the campsite later in the spring.

I told him not to worry about the deposit. He could use it to buy some new furniture.

Then I took a cab to the airport and caught the next Lufthansa flight to Larnaca, with a brief stopover at Frankfurt.

PART ELEVEN

1

Larnaca, Cyprus

Friday, 10 February
02.40 hrs

The posters promised that the Cyprus Girl Guides Association and the Limassol Majorettes would be rehearsing hard for their parade on Sunday week, and the Limassol Antique Cars Club would be preparing to drive around the city 'in carnival mood', but right now the Larnaca airport arrivals hall wasn't exactly a thrill a minute.

It was well before first light and the lads at Passport Control were in zombie mode. The only action around there came from the baggage carousel and the mop squad.

The tourist invasion for next week's Limassol Carnival was still about thirty-six hours away, but the world's biggest supply of cab drivers was already milling around outside the Customs gate and keen to have my business. I responded with a smile and a shake of the head. I needed the flexibility of a hire car.

My Spanish experience didn't set the alarm bells ringing at the desk, so I was on the main to Limassol in an underpowered Suzuki jeep by three fifteen. One of the things I liked about this place was that they still drove on the left. And it

399

was a good time to make the journey: there wasn't a lobster-coloured Brit on a quad bike in sight.

This stretch of coastline ran for about a hundred and fifty Ks, from Larnaca Bay to Paphos. It had worked hard to become a tourist Mecca since the Turks invaded in 1974, but Cyprus remained a broken land. The skeletal remains of whole villages were still caught in the UN-controlled buffer zone that separated north from south. You didn't need to get up close to the Green Line to see the scars, though. They ran through every Cypriot's heart.

Their island's long and volatile history of invasion and annexation stemmed mostly from its location at the eastern end of the Mediterranean, forty-three miles from the Turkish coast, which made it the perfect jumping-off point for any major power in the mood for further expansion.

The Assyrians had had a crack at it, and so had the Egyptians, the Persians, the Romans and the Ottomans. And though the 'seventy-four gangfuck was always cast as a little local difficulty between two tribes who'd been enemies since the dawn of time, it had had much more to do with the American determination to fill a vacuum before the Russians filled it first.

And the Brits hadn't covered themselves with glory at that point either. They'd sat and watched from the security of their coastal bases as the place had gone up in flames. Greek Cypriots from the north were evicted from homes their families had lived in for ever, and Turkish Cypriots from the south suffered a similar fate.

There were still two thousand officially on the missing list nearly forty years later.

RAF Akrotiri was a couple of hundred miles closer to Bastion than it was to Brize Norton, so it wasn't just the Club 18–30 beaches and 340 days of sunshine per year that made it the ideal R&R point for returning troops.

As well as providing one end of the air bridge to and from Afghan, it was also a major Mediterranean search-and-rescue centre, operating 24/7, with nearly a thousand permanent staff. I'd spent some time there on my way back from Gulf War One, and despite the friction of partition, I could think of worse places to keep an ex-soldier away from the dole queue.

The closer you got to Limassol, the more you felt like you were wandering into a Mediterranean version of Miami. The place was huge, and the seafront was lined with high-rises — hotels, offices and apartment blocks — busily elbowing aside the more colourful relics of its rich and complex past. As I drove in towards the marina, I could see the McDonald's Golden Arch and the red and white TGI Friday's strip lighting up the skyline.

This might have been the clubbing capital of the eastern Med, but Bob had told me that for him it was strictly weekends only. The rest of the time he was tucked up in bed with a cup of cocoa by ten thirty so, no, he wouldn't be around to welcome me.

He had given me the name of a taverna that opened early enough for us to hook up for a brew before he went to work. I turned right, away from the palm-tree-lined avenue that ran alongside the beach, past the Agia Napa cathedral, and into the maze of one-way streets that surrounded the Old Town. I parked up at the edge of a deserted square, wound the seat back and got my head down for the couple of hours or so that remained until first light.

2

It wasn't long after sun-up, but the covered fruit and vegetable market was already bustling with activity. It reminded me a bit of the old East End markets that I used to wander past as a kid when I'd bunked off school, but with the outrageous rainbow-coloured produce you could only ever grow in a land of perpetual sunshine.

The artisans' stores were starting to open too: clothes were being hung out on rails and tables loaded with the kind of souvenirs you'd wonder why you'd bought when you got home.

I found my way to the pedestrian street that led to Bob's taverna, a bunch of freshly scrubbed wooden tables and cream parasols gathered by a faded blue door. The buildings were mostly no more than two or three storeys high here, some bare stone, some rendered, with delicate wrought-iron balconies jutting out over the pavement.

I was ushered to a seat by a waiter with the kind of moustache I'd only ever seen in the Go Compare commercials. I ordered a big frothy coffee. I quite liked the local concoction, but you had to be in the mood for a cup of something that was half sugar and half something that looked like the stuff I'd had swirling around my bollocks in the Devil's Neckinger, and I wanted a brew I could linger over.

Bob appeared from around a corner a

403

hundred down and raised a hand as he walked towards me. I hadn't seen him for half a decade, but he hadn't changed much. Having traded in his uniform for a Hawaiian shirt, he looked even more like Barry Manilow than Barry Manilow did, these days. We'd always called him Mandy when we were young squaddies, but now wasn't the time to remind him of that.

He took the chair opposite me. The waiter greeted him like an old friend and he ordered himself the usual, which turned out to be a mug of builders' tea and a fried-egg sandwich. I got the feeling this was his local canteen. I refuelled my brew and asked for a pig roll and we waffled on in catch-up mode.

Bob looked at his watch. I noticed a slight clenching of his jaw muscles. Either he was going to burst into song, or he wasn't a totally happy bunny.

'I don't know what this is all about, Nick, but I'd say Grant is on a very high wire and trying not to look down. He talks the talk, but it's not difficult to spot that there's a whole lot of bad shit going on in his head.'

'Afghan can do that to a guy.'

He gave me a look that said he didn't have time for any more fucking about.

I put down my brew. 'Bob, I don't know him. And I don't know exactly what he's got to hide. That's why I'm here. That's what I need to find out. I've got one dead mate on my hands and two live ones I owe big-time, and I'm pretty sure Jack Grant holds the key to the mess they're in.'

He nodded. 'OK. So I caught up with him as

soon as he came out of the Starlifter. He didn't want to stay on the base for a nanosecond longer than he had to. I told him he could have the spare room in my apartment for a couple of nights. He almost bit my hand off.'

He unclipped a biro from his shirt pocket, wrote an address on a serviette and slid it across the table. 'It's on the first floor. I'm not entertaining much at the moment, and I thought we might need to keep an eye on him. Upwards of a hundred and fifty thousand people live in this slice of Paradise, and that doesn't include the tourists — so there are plenty of places you can lose yourself if you want to.'

'Does anyone else know he's there?'

'Sure. I put out an all-stations alert.' Bob looked at me like I was a complete lunatic. 'What do you think?'

'Sorry. How many entrances and exits?'

'Just the one, if you don't count the upstairs balcony.' He hesitated for a moment. 'I don't have another spare set of keys, I'm afraid. You'll have to use the legendary Stone charm to talk your way in. He won't be expecting you.' He gave me a Manilow-size grin. 'Try not to destroy the door. It's an old one, painted red, and I've got to like it. Also, it would really piss off the landlord.'

He stood up and reached for his wallet.

I waved it away, and thanked him for playing a blinder.

3

We agreed that we'd connect later, when he'd finished at the base. I told him I'd be sure to pay for any damage. His expression said he wasn't sure if I was kidding. I wasn't sure myself.

I finished my brew as I watched him walk away.

Bob's apartment was half a K to the north of the taverna, and a few streets to the west. I left my bomber jacket in the boot of the Suzuki, bought a straw hat, a white linen shirt and a pair of sun-gigs from a nearby shop, then wandered up there.

The rendering on the front of Bob's building was a faded mustard yellow and in need of some running repairs, but his balcony was immaculate: a metal table and two canvas director's chairs stood between a couple of terracotta pots that trailed bougainvillaea through the wrought-iron railing.

His front entrance was flanked by two sets of awnings that had seen better days. A clothes store took up the ground floor and all sorts of local gear hung from its frames and rippled gently in the breeze.

It was after eight now, but I couldn't see any sign of movement as I passed by on the other side of the road. The paint job on the window shutters matched the door, and they were still closed.

I busied myself with the kind of shit tourists do on a Friday morning, trying stuff on and wondering whether my auntie would prefer a Limassol ashtray or a pot of local honey, but keeping eyes on the red door and shutters.

I latched onto a group that were admiring the icon stall outside a small, stone-built church. There was a very shiny one of St Nicholas that I'd have liked to buy for Father Mart.

Shortly before nine the shutters folded back and a figure stepped out onto Bob's balcony. I picked up the icon and held it in the sunlight. That way I looked like I had a reason for being there, at the same time as keeping Grant in my peripheral vision.

He was dressed a bit like me, but without the hat and shades. His hair was closely shaven and his skin was weathered. I wasn't near enough to see the whites of his eyes, but his body language said he wasn't going to swing into fully relaxed holiday mode any time soon.

After five minutes' taking in the view he disappeared back inside. Ten minutes after that, the red door opened and he headed south, in the direction of the water. He'd found a baseball cap and some wraparound Ray-Bans somewhere inside. The tension continued to radiate outwards from his shoulder muscles, but he didn't seem to be target aware. There was no ducking in and out of shop fronts, pausing to tie his shoelaces or walking around three sides of a square.

He headed straight for the pedestrian zone and stopped at the first secluded taverna he came across. I went and bought a newspaper. By the time I'd mooched over and taken a seat four tables away from him, Grant was tucking into a plate of ham, egg and chips. He was safely in the shadow of a stripy awning, back against the wall, the cap and gigs firmly in place.

I ordered up my third frothy coffee of the day and got stuck into yesterday's news. Karzai had survived his Chequers experience, but the enduring strategic partnership didn't seem to have made any difference to the number of lads killed or maimed by Afghan roadside bombs since I'd read about the visit in the Costa by the *Golden Hinde*.

I moved on to the crossword page and wished Trev was there to help out. Maybe he'd have been able to tell me what I should be doing next. And maybe he could have got in the way if my target decided to do a runner.

SSM Grant didn't look keen for a chat, and I was 99 per cent sure that wasn't about to change, but I thought he might be in a better mood if I let him finish his breakfast before I invaded his personal space.

There wasn't going to be an easy way of doing this. He was clearly in no hurry to get back to Brize and prepare for his court appearance, and not looking for company now, so I wasn't going to bounce over and pretend I'd mistaken him for an old mate, or cheerily ask him what his plans were for the carnival. I decided my only option was Immediate Action: go straight in there, seize his full attention, then try to keep it for as long as possible.

4

I waited until he'd taken his final mouthful of ham and eggs, then folded my newspaper, picked up my brew and moved over to his table.

'SSM Grant?'

I still couldn't see his eyes, but every muscle in his face told me I wasn't even a tiny bit welcome.

I took off my hat and sun-gigs. He didn't follow suit, but he did stay where he was.

'You're a bit of a legend in the Regiment, Jack. Everyone I talk to says so, and we both know that kind of respect isn't easy to come by in H. So I was hoping you'd be good enough to help shed some light on one or two dark places for me.' I thrust a hand towards him. 'My name's —'

'I know who you are. And I know why you're here.' The lips moved, but the rest of him didn't. He ignored my outstretched hand.

'Then you'll also know that Trev's dead. Head job.'

I tried and failed to read the expression that lay behind his Ray-Bans, but saw him go absolutely still, apart from the pulse throbbing at his temple. 'No . . . ' He swallowed hard. 'Not Trev . . . '

I nodded.

'Who dropped him?'

'Some people we should have taken down way back in Sarajevo.'

I let the silence stretch between us.

'What really happened in the CQB Rooms, Jack?'

He did peel off his Ray-Bans now. I could see the very real distress in his eyes, and the white lines chiselled in the deeply tanned skin around them. 'You've got to believe this, Nick. It was to protect something very, very precious. It wasn't meant to be the first shot in a war.'

Grant leaned forward, put his elbows on the table and massaged his face with his hands. I remembered Bob's line about the high-wire act. When he managed to compose himself, he raised his head again and met my gaze.

'This isn't the place.' He glanced left and right. 'You know where I'm staying . . .'

I nodded.

'Meet me there in an hour. I've got one or two things I need to sort.'

He read my expression. 'I'll be there.' He paused. 'Really.'

I waited for a couple of beats before nodding again.

He called for his bill and chucked a ten-euro note on the table when it arrived. Then he did hold out his hand, and we shook. His palm was cool and his grip was firm.

When he began to retrace his route, he did so head high. He was a man with a mission.

5

I got up as soon as Jack had turned the corner. I left the rest of my brew and binned the newspaper too. I'd never been any good at crosswords.

The sun was higher in the sky, and the digital temperature display outside the *pharmakeia* on the other side of the street told me it was sixteen degrees and counting.

I stayed fifty behind him as he made his way towards the seafront. He crossed the main and found a seat overlooking the water. I took cover beneath an awning outside a book store at the corner. A group of kids clambered over a bunch of stone eggs on a raised platform to Jack's left, pissing themselves with laughter. He didn't give them a glance, just stayed where he was, stock still, staring at a huge blue tanker moored in Akrotiri Bay. I couldn't work out if he was waiting for somebody, or grappling with the mysteries of the universe.

The beautiful people sat and sipped iced Frappuccinos at a café a hundred or so further along the beach to his right. In another life I could have been plastered with factor-30 on a day like this, enjoying the view. I thought about that sometimes. I wasn't haunted by it, just thought about it.

I remembered what Aleksa had said about good men doing nothing. I was pretty sure doing

411

nothing hadn't been Jack Grant's problem. He didn't strike me as that kind of guy. I suspected that he'd done something bad for the best of motives, and then found that he couldn't square it away. I hoped I might be about to find out what that was.

Nobody showed. After about fifteen minutes he got up and walked towards the café, then turned and headed back into the Old Town.

The mid-morning sunlight was bouncing off the walls and the shiny roofs and windscreens of the parked cars that now lined Bob's street. Following Jack still wasn't difficult. He didn't look left or right. He made straight for the red door, whipped out a key and went in. I stopped about twenty away and waited.

The shutters stayed closed. The building didn't have air-con, so I guessed that was the best way to keep it as cool as possible, even this early in the year.

I scanned the area each side of me. All I could see was the usual smattering of holidaymakers checking out the souvenir stalls and clothing stores.

I wandered back up to the church and paid some close attention to the display of saints and martyrs again. I put a euro in the collection box, lit another candle and kept eyes on Bob's place as the flame guttered in the breeze.

6

I sparked up my iPhone. The time display told me we'd left the taverna three-quarters of an hour ago. The text-message icon blinked on. Al Gillespie wanted me to call him, soon as. I slipped it back into the pocket of my jeans and went and knocked on the red door.

There was no response. Not a creak or a groan or the sound of a footstep inside.

I knocked again.

Still nothing.

I pictured Jack's sudden calm at the taverna, and his unnatural stillness at the seafront. I had a bad feeling about this.

I pushed the panels immediately above and below the keyhole.

They both gave inwards with minimal pressure. The door hadn't been bolted, top or bottom.

I stepped back, glanced up and down the street, trusted in the cover of the parked wagons and the hanging clothes, leaned forward and shoulder-charged Bob's landlord's precious piece of woodwork beside the handle. There was a splintering noise as the deadlock said goodbye to its housing and the thing swung open.

I stepped inside and pushed the door closed behind me. Bob was going to have to devote an hour or so of his evening to a bit of DIY on the frame, but I didn't think it would spoil his weekend. I was less sure about what I was about to find on the floors above.

The shutters front and back must have been louvred, because there was still a fair amount of ambient light. Everything I could see was as well cared for as the balcony. The staircase ahead of me was a combo of spotless tiled treads and a polished hardwood rail that ran up a bare stone wall.

I called Jack's name and still got no answer.

An intricately worked Turkish copper coffee pot, with a spout curved like a dagger, stood on Bob's hall table, beside a carved wooden bowl full of stuff he didn't want to carry around with him. I grabbed it by the handle and headed up the steps.

Bob's apartment was on two levels: a lounge with kitchen/diner, which opened onto the front balcony, and, as far as I could tell, two bedrooms and a bathroom on the top floor.

The main living space — desk, table, chairs, sofa, flat-screen TV and hand-woven rugs and cushions — was empty and undisturbed. The back bedroom wasn't. As I reached the landing a familiar metallic odour caught in my throat.

I eased my back against the wall, tightened my grip on the coffee pot and stepped inside.

7

Bob's spare room was decked out with local weaves and joinery, as neatly arranged as they were in the rest of the apartment. The big difference was that almost everything within reach of Jack Grant's shattered head — the Limassol Carnival poster hanging behind him, the wall, the ceiling, the bedcover, the night table — was covered with blood.

Some leaked out of his mouth and down his chin. Some dripped off the fingertips of his right hand to feed the glistening pool that had gathered around the SIG Sauer P226 on the floor beside his chair. The rest seemed to be running in rivulets down his back and across the bare boards towards me.

His body was completely still, face up, eyes wide open, like he'd just spotted something really interesting on the freshly stripped but recently stained roof beam.

Jack was indeed old school. He needed to do the decent thing. He'd been trapped in a burning building for the last four weeks, and finally spotted an exit.

There were no signs of a struggle. I was in no doubt that he'd welcomed the 9mm round that had removed the top of his skull and taken away his pain.

8

I reversed out of the room and moved back downstairs. I wiped my prints off the coffee pot with my shirt-tail and replaced it on the table.

I took a box of Swan Vestas out of Bob's man bowl and pulled the door shut, holding the handle with my sleeve and wedging it against the frame with a couple of matchsticks. It wasn't foolproof, but I didn't have time to fuck about.

Finding a body in his apartment wasn't going to brighten up Bob's evening, but the police wouldn't need Inspector Poirot to tell them it was a suicide. He wouldn't need to mention my name. I'd just have to take some flak from him later.

I turned the first corner I came to and binned the hat and sun-gigs, then headed for a nearby store and bought a baseball cap, a pair of fake Oakleys and a blue shirt. I bundled my white one under the seat in the changing cubicle. There were smiles all round as euro notes found their way out of my jeans pocket and into the till.

The rest of the world were tucking into their first kebabs of the day as I legged it back to the Suzuki.

At the edge of town I drove past a group of lads who were busy building a bonfire in a field. They'd stuffed an old pair of jeans, a shirt and a shopping bag with straw, and one of them was painting it with eyes, nose and mouth. It looked like the kind of monstrosity we used to perch outside Elephant & Castle tube when we were kids, trying to strong-arm commuters into filling our plastic beakers with coppers for 5 November.

They'd never heard of Guy Fawkes here, of course. You couldn't tell by looking at him, but this was an effigy of Judas Iscariot. The Cypriots torched him every Easter as a punishment for betraying Jesus.

PART TWELVE

1

St Francis Xavier's Roman
Catholic Church, Powys

Saturday, 11 February
08.00 hrs

I'd called Al from the payphone in the Larnaca departure lounge before leaving on the next flight to Heathrow.

He was trying not to get too carried away by the news that Catriona seemed to be responding to her treatment at the Beatson. And he wanted me to know that he'd dug up a contact that, given a bit of warning, could get me inside the Military Court Centre at Barford without broadcasting it to the Head Shed. I told him Sunday or Monday after dark o'clock would be good for me.

Four and a half hours in the air gave me a chance to sort a few things out in my mind and put together a plan of action for the next couple of days.

Ella had been convinced that something had happened on the night of 8 January which had severely rattled Sam. Scott had done or said something stupid enough to prompt the letter of apology I'd read in the shepherd's hut. Jack Grant hadn't topped himself in Limassol for no reason. I was pretty sure he'd decided Scott was a loose cannon, and triggered the CQB gangfuck.

My first stop was going to be Father Mart's HQ. I texted him on the coach transfer to Gatwick.

I pulled the Skoda out of the long-term car park about fifteen minutes short of one. I filled the tank at Leigh Delamere services on the M4, tucked Sam's Browning under my right thigh and got my head down under the Gore-Tex for a few hours. I woke myself up with a brew and an egg sandwich before moving on.

Frost dusted the fields and verges on the final run-in to my favourite confessional. It was crisp and cold and a bit of a shock to the system after Cyprus and southern Spain, but at least I was driving away from the snow that, the radio told me, was bringing things to a standstill on the eastern side of the country.

Father Mart was already in place by the time I arrived at the church. I stepped into the booth, closed the curtain and gave him the boiled-down version of my pilgrimage to the Puerto del Suspiro del Moro and my trip to Limassol, but didn't hold back about Jack Grant's death or Ella's kidnapping. I needed to level with him, and he needed to know the truth.

When I'd finished, there was a silence the other side of the screen.

'Nicholas, I had a visit while you were away. At the house. Someone from DSF's office. He wanted to make contact with you . . . '

This wasn't good, but at least Father Mart's visitor hadn't had a leather jacket and a rose-coloured tattoo. 'What did you tell him?' I wondered whether it was OK with God for him to be a bit economical with the truth.

'I told him . . . ' I saw that gleam in his eye again as he leaned forward. 'I told him that you and I had spent some time together, but I didn't share the Lord's knowledge of your precise whereabouts.'

I smiled. 'Would the Lord mind if you helped me access Hereford without putting my head above the parapet?'

I explained what I needed to do, and he told me he believed that the Lord would be as accommodating as possible.

2

When I emerged from the church, Father Mart had already pulled open the rear door of his Defender. I folded myself into the boot and he threw a stripy woollen blanket over me, which smelt vaguely of Icarus.

He fed some monk music into the CD player and sparked up the ignition, floored the gas pedal and slalomed through the lanes and then onto a straighter road, which meant that I no longer had to protect my head from constant collision with the Land Rover's fuselage. I figured we were now on the main into Hereford.

There was a bit more slaloming, but like you do in town when you're taking a series of rapid lefts and rights, and doing your best not to smack into the wagon in front or someone crossing the road.

Finally he rammed on the brakes, wrenched the gearstick into reverse, did a quarter of a doughnut, threw it into neutral and switched off the engine. I took a couple of deep, Icarus-scented breaths and eased my bruised flesh away from the lumps of metal that anchored the vehicle's rear seats to the floor.

The driver's door opened and closed, and I lay there and waited. Either he'd decided to deliver me, battered and bleeding, to DSF after all, or we were sitting in the car park behind the Green Dragon. I'd soon find out.

About ten minutes later, the rear door opened and I felt a blast of cold air as the edge of the blanket lifted. One very sparkly eye, half a bushy white beard and a couple of inches of dog collar came into view.

'A nice man called Ted is happy to see you. He's new here, but I told him you've been a regular customer since the Dark Ages. I've given him a rough heads-up, as we agreed, and he's going to do his best to help us.'

The blanket descended for a moment, then rose again. 'Oh, and you're about ten feet away from a rear entrance, with not a soul in sight.'

I pushed the rest of my camouflage sheet back, swung my legs out over the tailgate and sat up. Father Mart proved to be a master of the close target recce. The sight that greeted me was precisely as he'd described.

On the basis of what Ella had told me, I'd decided to start where Sam and Scott's evening ended, then work my way back through the Vault, the Barrels and the Spreadeagle until I could establish the connection between them beyond any doubt.

I managed to lever myself onto firm ground and allowed him to escort me through a small warren of passages and into a back office with flowery wallpaper and a swirly carpet. There was hardly enough room for me, him, a desktop computer that looked like it was powered by steam, and a lad with gold-rimmed Japanese-businessman's glasses, freshly waxed hair and a pocketful of biros.

He thrust out his hand, then drew it back and

left it hanging, worried that he'd already overstepped the mark.

'You must be Ted.'

He nodded at me with barely controlled excitement.

'Has the father explained why we're here?'

The nodding went into overdrive, then suddenly stopped. 'A bit, yes . . . He says you need to find someone for a friend.'

'Yup. A girl we know was in your bar about a week after New Year's Eve. She rather fancied a guy she spent some time with, but she didn't get his name.' I gave him my best embarrassed look. 'From her description, we reckon it might be a mate of ours called Jack Grant.'

Ted nodded. 'Jack's a regular. He's got an account.'

'He's abroad right now, but is there any way you could check if he was here that night? Her birthday's coming up, and if we're right, a bunch of us thought we might try and get them together again.'

'Which night?'

'Eighth of January. A Saturday.'

'I was off. But I could ask around . . . '

'That would be great, Ted. Thank you.'

As he made to slide out from behind his monitor I held up my hand. 'But, hey, we don't want to put you to any trouble. Why don't you just check out your receipts? That would tell us for sure, wouldn't it, unless he paid cash for some reason?'

Ted ran a fistful of fingers anxiously through his hair. 'I . . . I don't think I'm supposed to do that . . . That information is quite private . . . '

426

Father Mart gave him the sort of look that he must have handed out immediately after a five-star confession. 'Only the level of expenditure would be private, my son, and we aren't asking for that . . . '

That was good enough for Ted. He reached into the drawer below his keyboard and brought out a wad of receipts bound together with a bulldog clip. He started to leaf through them. When he'd got to the last slip he shook his head apologetically. 'They should be in alphabetical order but . . . well . . . you know.'

He brought out another. Same result. 'I'm really sorry . . . '

His disappointment was genuine.

I didn't hide mine.

Then I had an idea.

'What time did you close?'

'Well, it's the hotel bar, so it's a bit flexible . . . '

'Maybe he stayed late. If he paid after midnight, would that register as a ninth of January transaction?'

He fished out another wad. Halfway through, his expression brightened. 'Good news. Jack H. Grant. He signed his bill at twelve forty-seven.'

We grinned and punched the air, like we'd just found the winning lottery ticket. I'd never seen Father Mart do that before. But, then, I'd never been to the races with him and Father Gerard.

'Thank you, Ted. I have a feeling that you'll have one very happy lady on your hands.' I clapped him on the shoulder. 'But I guess you're no stranger to that, eh?'

427

3

When I responded to Al's text, he said that his man at Barford could get me in to the Military Court Centre detention facility tomorrow evening, when the place wasn't crawling with people. He told me where to park up. Sergeant Mackenzie was from 4 Rifles. He'd pull up alongside my wagon in a standard-issue Land Rover Wolf 90 at 18.30 precisely, flash his main beams twice, and ferry me through the barrier.

I'd need my Nick Jones ID: my cover story was that I was part of Geoff Blackwood's defence team. I could tell he was trying hard to stop himself laughing. 'So the Inner Temple dress-down Sunday look is the one to go for. Your bomber, Levi's and Timberlands will have to take a rest, mate. It's high time you bunged them in the incinerator anyway. They were minging when we drove down to Glasgow, and that was ages ago.

'Oh, and get yourself one of those yellow legal notepads — and some kind of Gucci slipcase too. You'll need the guys on site to take you seriously.'

I drove into Bristol and joined the crowd of Saturday-afternoon shoppers at Cabot Circus.

★ ★ ★

Two hours later even my mum wouldn't have recognized me. If I still had one. I'd had my hair

428

trimmed and my stubble shaved. Gant and Hugo Boss had kitted me out with a smart overcoat, a blue blazer, button-down shirt and sand-coloured chinos that had cost me two trips to the ATM. I'd stuck with the Timberlands, though — just replaced the boots with very preppy deck shoes.

If he'd pinged me standing in front of the changing-cubicle mirror in this outfit, Al would have pissed himself, no question — which would have been right out of order for a Jock who spent his whole life in a tartan skirt. But I reckoned the Premier Inn at Andover was going to be very pleased to see me.

I shoved all the new gear into a couple of big paper bags and went in search of a stationery shop. Mission completed, I got back to the Skoda and texted Jesper on my final unused Nokia. He texted back almost immediately to say he was still checking out the French border crossings, without any joy.

It wasn't a big surprise. Wherever she'd been taken, Ella would have made the journey wrapped in gaffer tape, and well out of sight.

4

Salisbury Plain, Wiltshire

Sunday, 12 February
18.03 hrs

The lion's share of the territory to the immediate north of Barford Camp was MoD property: mud, undergrowth, trees and tank tracks, and a succession of firing ranges. The warning signs that surrounded it weren't emblazoned with skulls and crossbones, but their red lettering left you in no doubt that you entered this space at your peril. If a Challenger didn't get you, a lump of unexploded ordnance probably would.

I switched off my headlamps a couple of hundred before I turned off the road and parked up beside Range Number 2. Street lamps were dotted along the edge of the camp, but the nearest one was at least half a K away. It was almost completely dark there. I pressed the button that cut the Skoda's interior lights. I didn't want them to spring on when I opened the door.

I slid the Browning out from under my right thigh, thumbed on the safety and wrapped it in a supermarket carrier-bag, along with the spare mag. I hadn't followed Al's advice about my bomber, Levi's and Timberlands. I'd bunged them in my daysack with my other kit and left

430

them at the Premier Inn.

I didn't mind hiding stuff in the wagon on neutral ground, but Barford was top of the list of known locations: I didn't fancy leaving anything that could be too obviously traced to me while it was here. And if I ended up lifting Sam, I'd need to keep my options open. No way would they let me past security with any kind of weapon, let alone a handgun, and I didn't want to have to come back to the wagon if everything went to rat shit.

I let my night vision adjust for another ten minutes and scanned the area for movement. Finally I got out, closed the door and locked it with the key rather than the fob so it didn't bleep and flash its indicators. I felt the threat of rain in the air.

A six- or seven-metre-high berm had been thrown up behind the targets, and the range stretched away from it across a series of sloped firing positions, ending with a covered area fifty metres back. I needed to conceal the pistol somewhere I could identify immediately, even at night and in a hurry, and could reach without having to break cover. The opposite end of the berm from the car park seemed to tick all the boxes.

I moved to the rear of the covered firing position. Keeping between the wall and the trees that separated it from the road, I skirted the far side of the range and tucked my plastic bundle behind a bush three strides in from the forward edge.

I then worked my way round the berm and through the trees that fringed the parking space.

431

Five minutes later a pair of Land Rover beams swept up the road and bounced over the sleeping policeman I'd coasted across when I'd gained entry. I watched it come to a standstill next to Father Gerard's wagon and flash its main beams twice.

Sergeant Mackenzie left the engine running. His interior lights blazed as he exited the Wolf. He obviously didn't share my instinct for caution. Or maybe he was keen to identify himself immediately as the owner of a 4 Rifles uniform, and to reassure me that he'd come alone.

I kept him waiting for a couple of minutes before stepping out across the potholed tarmac. He gripped my hand briefly, admired my new fancy-dress costume, and escorted me to his passenger seat.

The Military Court Centre was a K and a half back down the main that ran through the camp. We didn't say much to each other on the way. He wished me luck with Sam. 'He's obviously one of the good guys. But he keeps his lip zipped, so fuck knows how you're going to deal with that . . .' He asked if I'd like a lift back to my motor when I was done and I said I'd be fine walking.

Arc lights flared across the entrance that led to the detention facility. Mackenzie hung a right and pulled up beside the guard room. A squaddie emerged from where he'd been enjoying a brew and trying to stop his bollocks freezing off. The temperature had dropped steadily since last light.

Mackenzie wound down the window, swapped the usual banter with him and handed over my cover ID. 'Mr Jones is on a prisoner's legal team.

432

Trial's next week. We won't be all night.'

I leaned forward to show my face and nodded.

The sentry glanced at my photograph and poked the ID quickly back through the window as big drops of rain began to splash against the Wolf's windscreen. He raised the barrier and waved us through.

We drove past a row of fighting vehicles — Warriors, Mastiffs and Jackals mostly — and another of five- and ten-ton trucks, but there was hardly a human being in sight.

The Military Court Centre was a brand-new, state-of-the-art set-up that wouldn't have been out of place in an overpriced riverside development. It had been designed to send a very clear signal: this was where justice was done, and seen to be done. Except when there were good reasons to keep the whole process under wraps.

The building that backed onto it was a red-brick fifties block with a recent security upgrade. I handed over my ID again at the front desk to the nearest of the two unsmiling guards. Their expressions didn't even change when Mackenzie tried cracking a funny about my outfit.

The one with my ID looked up and gave me eye to eye. 'Callard case?'

'Yes.' I tapped my slipcase. 'The usual last-minute stuff.'

I glanced at the SIG pistols on their belt kit. I'd have to borrow those weapons — or stay out of their way — at some point if I didn't come out of here on my own. I didn't know how I was going to do that yet, but nobody'd said it would be easy.

5

Mackenzie escorted me through a metal detector and two sets of electronic gates. The second of them opened into a long corridor with doorways either side of it, which was where he said goodbye.

This place hadn't been built for comfort, but the paintwork was clean and the lighting not as unfriendly as some of the prisons I'd spent time in. A third guard was stationed halfway along the right-hand wall, outside a steel door with a wired-glass aperture. He pushed it open as I approached and ushered me inside. It shut with a clunk and I heard the sound of bolts being thrown.

The interview room was like a cell, only larger, and without a crapper. Instead of a bed, it had a brushed-aluminium table bolted to the floor, and a straight-backed plastic chair on each side of it. I took off my very smart overcoat and hung it over the back of the nearest one, then sat down and fished out my yellow lined pad and designer biro.

I'd made a few heavy legal-type notes at the Premier Inn last night, and I added to them now as I waited for Sam to appear through the far door. There were no one-way mirrors or any of that kind of shit, but I still reckoned that scribbling stuff would help our minders take me seriously.

It wasn't long before I heard two more bolts sliding back. My heart never missed a beat, but it came close when Sam Callard came through to join me. It was like Harry had decided not to torch himself at Koureh's house after all, and chosen this moment to reconnect. He grabbed the spare chair a bit more firmly than he needed to and sat down.

He didn't waste time with small-talk. 'Hello, Nick. I want you to know three things. The first is that I'm very grateful you've taken the trouble to see me. The second is that I can't help you any more than I could help Mr Blackwood.'

He reminded me of Harry in more ways than one. His skin was stretched across his forehead and his cheekbones like cling-film. He wore pretty much the same expression that his dad had when all he'd wanted to do was beat Koureh's head to a pulp.

'What's the third?'

'I had another visitor last night.' His jaw clenched. 'They've got Ella.'

'Who has?'

The skin around his temples tightened some more. 'No idea. Grey man. No name given, but enough clout to get in here. He didn't stay long. His job was to tell me that Trev was dead, but they won't hurt her — as long as I don't change my plea. She's their insurance policy.'

'So what happens next?'

'I stick with the negligent-discharge admission and rely on Blackwood to defend me against manslaughter.'

I shook my head. 'No. I mean, what happens

435

to Ella? Whoever has her won't just open the door and wave goodbye as soon as you're banged up.'

I could tell by his expression that this wasn't news to him. But the lad was well and truly caught between a rock and a hard place.

6

I leaned forward and gave him a couple of seconds to start looking me in the eye. 'Sam, your dad always used to say I danced like Virgil Tracy walks, but that's not why I've suddenly become Mr International Rescue.

'Trev was one of my best mates, you know that. Harry too, since way back. And your girlfriend got taken because I fucked up. I thought I was helping to find a way of sorting out this shit and getting you off the hook. I was wrong. I helped whoever lifted Ella to find her hiding place instead.

'Puzzles were always Trev's big thing, not mine. But I've got quite far with this one. I know about Kajaki. I know the mad thing that Guy did to get his VC. To start with, I thought Chris Matlock's death pushed him over the edge. Now I'm ninety-nine per cent sure it was something else. Something else happened between those two actions that none of you guys, or the Head Shed, want to go public.'

He went absolutely still. He looked like I was malleting him with a lump of four by four, and he had no choice but to take the pain. But he didn't disagree.

'I saw Scott Braxton's letter to you. I saw Jack Grant in Cyprus, and I know he was in the Green Dragon the night Scott shot his mouth off. Whatever he overheard, it scared him enough

437

to kill your mate. Then he topped himself because he was a decent guy who'd done a very bad thing in the name of loyalty to some cause. Maybe he tried to put himself in harm's way in Afghan first. Who knows?'

I paused to let this stuff sink in. I couldn't remember the last time I'd made a speech like this, if ever. Maybe my Inner Temple dress-down Sunday kit was to blame.

'So here's where I figure we are, Sam. Jack wasn't the only one who couldn't live with what he'd done. I'm guessing Guy couldn't either. He just chose a different route. So, I need to know what happened out there, after the dam and before the fort, to fuck him up so badly — and fuck you and Scott up too. Because then I'll have a better idea who's got Ella, and we can sort this shit out.'

He didn't say anything at all. He sat there like I'd fixed a red dot on his forehead and all he could do was count the seconds before I pulled the trigger. I wasn't sure whether he'd get up and leave — hoping that his continuing silence would keep Ella safe — or start to realize that we had to grip this thing once and for all before it throttled us.

'It wasn't Kajaki that Guy couldn't handle, was it, Sam?'

He finally straightened his back, found himself a lungful or two of air, planted his forearms on the table and narrowed the gap between us.

'Kajaki was where it began . . .'

His shoulders crumpled for a moment. Then he steadied himself.

438

'After Kajaki . . . I . . . we . . . we would hear Chris's screams and see his tortured body every time we closed our eyes. I'll never forget those things for as long as I live . . . '

He struggled to keep his voice even.

'But you're right. Kajaki wasn't what Guy had to escape from. Kajaki wasn't what Scott couldn't keep quiet about. Kajaki wasn't why I have to keep reaching for the happy pills.'

He raised a hand to cover his eyes and held it there, massaging his temples with thumb and forefinger. When he lowered it to the table again, he was having difficulty blinking back the tears.

'He couldn't live with what happened . . . to the girl . . . The pregnant woman and the girl . . . '

'Koshtay?'

He nodded. 'Koshtay.'

7

To begin with, the story came out in fits and starts, not always making sense. But once he'd hit his stride, there was no stopping him.

The Three Amigos had made their dead mate a promise at Kajaki: however long it took, they would avenge him. They sent out a signal via the few guys they could trust in the Afghan National Army: they needed to know who had been responsible for skinning Chris Matlock alive.

A handful of days later, word came back. Razaq, one of the Taliban players they'd been trying to lift, had given the order to two warriors from his compound. His compound in Koshtay.

Then he had supervised what happened next.

The crucifixion. The flaying. These things were never simple. They couldn't be rushed. Razaq had taken care of the unbeliever's face — and his eyelids — personally.

'We knew immediately what we had to do. I don't think any of us questioned it. It wasn't legal. We didn't kid ourselves about that. But it was just.

'Guy tells the boss we've had a tip-off about one of the players, tells him we're going to check it out. No drama. Only the three of us, on a CTR. If there's any truth in it, we'll come back mob-handed.

'We take a Jackal. Scott drives. Guy's in the passenger seat. I man the GPMG. We somehow dodge the IEDs and get within reach of the compound at last light. We lie up behind the treeline, on some high ground. Not Kajaki-type high ground, just high enough to give us a vantage-point, to get eyes on the enemy through our NVGs.

'We know we're outnumbered, but we have the advantage of surprise.'

He saw the look on my face.

'And, yes, at that moment, as long as we kill those fuckers, none of us really cares if we come out alive.'

They'd pinged seven occupants in the compound, all male, all carrying. Ammunition belts slung across their chests, AK-47s either on their shoulders or close to hand. The Amigos reckoned they were preparing to move out.

'We don't need to take a vote. It's now or never. Immediate Action. We advance through the trees, across a small stretch of open ground. Razaq's place is surrounded by a baked-mud wall, but it's barely above chest height. We vault it and take down three of the enemy with our first burst. They've no idea we're there. Two more appear in the doorway to the living quarters, and we take them down as well.

'Guy's in the lead. It had become a habit of his, since school, probably. Leading was important to him, but winning was everything. That's why he felt he couldn't share the blame . . .'

He was finding it difficult to swallow.

'His blood's up, you see? He disappears inside the building, firing as he goes. Then there's silence.

'Scott and I push back the curtain hanging

441

across the entrance. There are two rooms, lit by candles. The whitewashed wall directly ahead of us is covered with blood. Razaq has been thrown back against it by the force of Guy's blast. The seventh Taliban warrior lies inside the archway to the sleeping area.

'Guy's kneeling beside the body. He raises his head as we follow him in. He's cradling something in his arms. All he can say is 'God forgive me . . . ' over and over again.

'That's when we realize what he's done.'

The seventh body was that of a young, pregnant woman. And the eighth was a child's. Four years old, maybe. Five, max. It was difficult to tell. She'd caught a round that had taken away part of her jaw.

God never did forgive him. Or that's what he thought. Guy Chastain couldn't forgive himself either. By killing the woman and the child, he believed he had become no better than the men who had tortured his friend to death.

8

'It's a thin line, isn't it, Nick? The line that separates the things you can justify to yourself, and the things you can't. And once you've crossed it, there's no going back. I've had plenty of time to think about that, lately. Too much time.'

A small part of me envied his idealism. The rest wondered how he'd got this far without realizing that justice and truth were luxuries most of us couldn't afford. We just did our best to keep ourselves and our mates from sinking too deep into the shit. This boy needed a session or two with Father Mart.

'How much does DSF know about this?'

He raised his hands, palms upwards. 'When we came back from the compound we were so strung out that the slightest glance bored into us. The most routine exchange seemed loaded. And after Guy's citation went public, every single one of Steele's speeches about regimental pride and the need to honour the medal and its traditions sounded like a dire warning.'

'Ella said that Scott was unravelling well before Christmas. She seemed to think the VC ceremony didn't help.'

'That's the understatement of the century. It was mid-November. We were sitting in one of those huge rooms at the Palace, surrounded by *Who's Who* in the military, and Scott started crying like a baby. I managed to shepherd him out to a toilet. I didn't think anyone heard him break down, but I couldn't be sure. It was a total nightmare.'

'DSF there?'

'Sure. The place was heaving with uniforms. That was when I really started shitting myself that the whole Koshtay thing would come out into the open. I knew they'd do pretty much anything to keep the lid on it.

'The last time a VC had to be handed back was in 1908. You can imagine the headlines . . . And you know how the Head Shed have been since Abu Ghraib and Baha Mousa. Like cats on a hot tin roof.'

He wasn't wrong. One minute they awarded a colonel in the Royal Lancashires the DSO for leading from the front during the Basra gangfuck and putting himself in harm's way. The next, they were so badly rattled by an innocent Iraqi being killed in custody by men under his command that they charged him with presiding over war crimes.

'When Scott went into meltdown again at the Green Dragon, I saw the expression on Jack Grant's face. I knew he and the general were close. I don't know who gave the order for Scott to take a round in the head in the CQB Rooms, but when it happened, I figured there was nothing to stop me being next.

'It's why I thought this place would be my safest option, until I had the chance to blow the whistle in the courtroom. But now I've got to get out of here.'

His eyes were burning as brightly as his dad's had when he saw Koureh's happy snap.

I shook my head. 'Staying here is still your safest option, mate. The people behind this might have been able to send in a grey man, but that looks like it's as far as they can go. You haven't been found hanging from your belt strap. You haven't even slipped on a bar of soap. You're still here to tell the tale.'

He bunched his fists so tightly his knuckles whitened. I'd definitely made the right decision. Even if I could get him out of there, the last thing I needed was another member of the Callard family trying to club people to death with a tree branch.

'What about Ella?'

I gave him full eye to eye. 'You're going to have to leave Ella to me.'

9

The rain had eased by the time I went back through the barrier, but it still wasn't the kind of night you wanted to mince around in an overcoat, blazer and chinos. I took a couple of back doubles through the residential area at the northern edge of the camp. The tarmac glistened under the street lamps and TV screens flickered through curtained windows.

When I was confident I had no one on my tail, I headed east into the darkness. I still wanted to stay in cover as I approached the end of the berm where I'd left my weapon.

I crossed the road and pictured the smile on Al's face again as I felt the mud on the tank track ooze over the top of my left deck shoe. I wiped it on a baby's head and moved into the trees. This wasn't great overcoat, blazer and chinos territory either, but at least the canopy kept the rain off.

I reclaimed my package from behind the bush three strides behind the line of targets, and slid the Browning into my waistband, the spare mag into the left pocket of the coat. It wouldn't flick back quite as well as the bomber if I had to draw down, but it'd be better than nothing.

I retraced the route I'd taken earlier, and checked the parking area for movement. There wasn't any. I tucked the slipcase under my arm, gripped the car keys in my left hand, leaving my right free, and crossed the stretch of pitted

446

tarmac. When I had the wagon door half open, three torch beams sparked up at ten-metre intervals along the curve of the treeline and caught me in their glare.

I ducked beneath the cover of the vehicle and spun in the direction of the range. A fourth beam advanced towards me from the covered firing position. It dipped for long enough to show me the pistol in its owner's right hand, then a heavily accented voice instructed me to turn around, put my hands on the roof of my vehicle and spread my legs.

10

I did as I was told. The metal of the Skoda's lid was cold to the touch. Maybe I'd be able to save my weapon for later. If I went for it now the story could have only one ending.

I was facing the wrong way to ping the lad who'd done the talking, but as his three mates got closer, I could see it was just like old times. These guys had all come off the same production line. Zastava EZ9 shorts, jeans, leather jackets, cropped hair and, on the neck of the one I could see most clearly in the torchlight, a rose-coloured tattoo.

The lad who'd come up from the range was now behind me, far enough out of reach to make sure he could put a round in me before I got anywhere near him. The others joined him in a semi-circle, facing the car. Shooting each other wasn't something they wanted to risk.

'Tell your friend to come out now.'

I kept looking straight ahead. The rain was starting to fall more heavily again, and peppered the roof between my fingers. 'I don't have any friends.'

There was a burst of Serbian waffle. This was obviously a bit of a turn-up for them. 'Do not lie to us.'

'I tell you what. Why don't we all come back here tomorrow night? I'll see what I can do for you then.'

That wasn't what he wanted to hear. He took three steps forward and ground the muzzle of his pistol into the back of my head. I guessed it was more out of frustration than anything else. I didn't think he expected my 'friend' to materialize on the strength of it. But the fact that he knew lifting Sam was on the cards told me all I needed to know.

I'd been set up for the Barford mission since my Bermondsey trip. That was why they'd chased me around a lot, but never put a round in me when they'd got the chance. If I'd done my job tonight, these lads would have left our bodies somewhere on the ranges. I'd have taken the blame for springing a plainly guilty man, the court martial would have been avoided, and Sam's secret would have died with him.

The pistol was removed, and as I heard the boss of the Crvena Davo team step back, I realized I'd set myself up for a fall years ago, when I hadn't bothered to become a member of the Good Lads Club.

There'd have been a few questions asked when our bodies were found. But not many. The Head Shed wouldn't broadcast a break-out from the Military Court Centre. And while they might be a bit sad about a heroic young sergeant sliding off the rails, they wouldn't mourn me.

There was another staccato exchange. I could guess what it was about. I hadn't brought them the goods. Maybe they should kill me anyway. Look at the damage I'd done. One of their mates had got a crampon in the head in the Black Mountains. Another had taken a nosedive into a car park on the Tabard Gardens Estate. It was time to stop fucking about.

Two of the team stepped forward and grabbed my wrists. I didn't make it easy for them, so they didn't make it easy for me. They plasticuffed them together so fiercely behind my back that my hands started to throb. One frisked me, top to toe, lifted Sam's Browning and the spare mag, and chucked them into the foliage at the edge of the parking area.

'Come.' The boss barked the instruction. I turned to see him walk back along the path towards the range.

His mates bundled me after him. Their dark hair and stubble shone like crude oil and their skin glistened. They weren't wearing their happy faces, and it wasn't just because the rain had started again. Everything about their body language, the expressions on their faces and the none-too-gentle way they kept me moving said that this wasn't a good day out. I was going to pay for fucking them up. I was going to pay big-time.

I ran through my options. It didn't take more than a nanosecond. All I could do was choose the best moment to leg it and hope for the best — which meant waiting until I was as close as possible to the cover of the treeline before I made my move.

A coil of rope, punctuated at intervals with red and white striped plastic pennants, was looped over a wooden pin on the side of the covered position furthest from the targets. It would have been strung across the entrance when live firing was in progress, but these boys had something else in mind.

The fourth member of the team grabbed it as we passed and began to fashion the trailing end into a noose. He glanced at my neck from time to time, like a tailor gauging his customer's collar size.

An image flashed onto the screen inside my head: maggot-ridden bodies twisting in the wind beneath trees and lamp posts at the Bosnian roadside.

The boss stood in the shadow of a big old beech on the far side of the range. He'd found what he was looking for: a missile-sized branch launching itself out of the trunk about five metres above the ground. It took them a couple of throws to get the tail of the rope over the top of it and a couple of tugs to get the business end at the right height. Then they shoved me forward and raised the noose.

I dipped my head and shoulder-charged the main man, aiming a fraction above his belt buckle. I wasn't wildly optimistic about doing him any serious damage — I just needed a moment of confusion to help get me out of this shit.

I didn't even manage to wing him. He stepped aside as I came through and gave me the good news with his fist on the back of my head. It wasn't a killer blow, but it was enough to make my deck shoes lose their grip on the leaf mould and take me down.

They dragged me to my feet again, forced the noose around my throat and pulled the slip knot so tight it made my eyes water. The boss watched carefully throughout the process. He didn't want me to be in any doubt that they had a few scores to settle, and now was the perfect time to do it. He gave the noose an extra tug, to let me have a taste of what I had in store. Then the three grunts gripped the other end of the rope and began to try to separate my head from my shoulders. I wasn't far from blacking out when the arc lamps at each corner of the range sparked up. As night turned into blindingly bright day, ten lads in combats and cam cream converged on us from all sides, through the trees and across the open ground, SIGs in the aim. One of them barked a set of instructions in warp-speed Serbian.

I was no more fluent now than I had been at the Belgrade Fortress, but I knew Boris's voice when I heard it.

11

It didn't take long for Boris's boys to give the guys in matching leather jackets a set of matching cuffs, and a Mastiff steamed in from the camp to take them off for a sleepover in the detention facility.

I fished the Browning and spare mag out of the undergrowth, then sat and watched from the comfort of Father Gerard's driving seat, trying to get my breath back. I couldn't tell whether the Invisible Man was on the squad. If so, he was in good company.

When the business of the evening was completed, Boris came over and joined me. His hair looked like a freshly forked haystack.

'You're making a bit of a habit of this, Stone.'

I nodded. 'So are you. And I've finally got my head around why.'

Boris seemed quite pleased about that. 'DSF never believed that Sam Callard pulled the trigger in the CQB Rooms. When you bounced into view, he thought you might give us the best chance of finding out what that whole nightmare was all about. Fuck knows why.' He grinned. 'I gather you were never the sharpest knife in the drawer.'

I told him I'd give the general a full report over tea and biscuits when I'd tidied up a few loose ends.

'I'll let him know that.' His eyes glinted as he

treated me to a level stare. 'Just try not to take too long.'

He stood back and let me shut my door, then leaned in through the window, like he'd done outside the Belgrade Zoo. 'And sort your shit out, eh? What *do* you think you look like?'

PART THIRTEEN

1

Allerdale, Cumbria

Monday, 13 February
16.50 hrs

I took Boris's advice about my fancy-dress outfit as soon as I got back to the Premier Inn. It was now in the boot of Father Gerard's Skoda.

The drive from Andover to Bassenthwaite was a good seven hours, but I didn't want to be there until last light, so there was no need to rush it. I treated myself to a couple of caffeine and calorie breaks and beat myself up about the things that should have pointed me towards Chastain instead of the Head Shed while I was playing detective.

They both had a fuck of a lot to lose if the Koshtay incident went public, but I now knew the colonel was staring down the barrel of the bigger gun: the destruction of his son's and his family's very shiny reputation.

I knew he'd served in Bosnia, and Ken Marabula had confirmed it. The Leathermen were on *his* payroll, not Steele's. They must have tracked me from Blackwood's chambers using the Nokia that I should have chucked into the river after I'd called Astra HQ that morning. I hadn't been spotted by one of DSF's helis.

Even when Boris and the Invisible Man had

done their Seventh Cavalry trick at the Belgrade Fortress, I'd assumed that Chastain was busy being my fairy godfather.

I suddenly remembered the colonel's Bermondsey reference during our cosy chat in Guy's boathouse. At the time I'd just assumed he'd pulled it from the depths of his own mental data base — he'd always taken the piss out of my South London accent when I served with him. Now I realized what had brought it to the surface. And that was when he'd seeded the idea of me lifting Sam from Barford.

I caught sight of myself in the rear-view when I got back into the wagon. The bruise from the rope around my neck was developing nicely.

I stopped off at a hardware shop to pick up a roll of gaffer tape. My next target was a biker store. I needed a pair of thin silk gloves and one of those black balaclavas you could fit under a crash hat.

2

Skiddaw ridge dominated the skyline to my right as I drove up the A591, its flanks highlighted by the setting sun. The surface of the lake glistened to my left whenever there was a break in the treeline.

I pulled into the parking area at the back of the Half Moon Inn, two or three miles beyond the end of the wall that enclosed the Ravenhill estate. Knocking on the Chastains' front door was not an option this time around: I wasn't going to be treated to tea and flapjacks. The colonel's foot soldiers would be on high alert, and just pulling up in a neighbouring layby was out of the question.

There weren't a whole lot of other vehicles to hide behind, but enough for the Skoda not to draw too much attention to itself, and the place wasn't awash with Stalag Luft Ill-style arc lamps. I slotted it between a white van and a mud-spattered Volvo with a couple of sit-on-top kayaks strapped to its roof bars. One was a very scary combo of Day-Glo green and yellow and its mate was deep purple and black.

I transferred the Browning from underneath my right thigh to my waistband and zipped up my bomber jacket. The gaffer tape went into my right pocket. The spare thirteen-round mag was in my left.

I exited the Skoda and headed along a lane

459

that Google Maps had told me led to the water. A grass verge lined each side of it, dropping away to a drainage ditch.

Two sets of headlamps bounced up the hill towards me. I slid into the ditch on my left when they were still a hundred and fifty metres away and stayed there until they'd passed — two more estate cars with kayaks on their lids. One turned into the pub car park and the other carried straight on to the main.

I climbed back onto the pitted tarmac and kept on walking. There was a chill breeze from the shore, but the temperature wasn't freezing. I'd be fine as long as I kept moving.

This side of the lake was pretty much all private land, and even the gates into the fields were padlocked. I vaulted the second I came to and slipped on my balaclava and gloves, partly for warmth but mostly so I didn't stand out like a Belisha beacon. I tabbed south along the perimeter of a densely planted evergreen wood for about a mile, then ducked into the cover of the trees.

I moved as quickly as I could through the undergrowth, while there was still enough ambient light to avoid snapping twigs and tripping over fallen branches. The closer I got to the Ravenhill boundary, the more I kept eyes on the shadows gathering ahead and to my right, and the open ground thirty feet to my left.

I stopped a hundred feet short of Chastain's wall, watched and listened. The light was fading fast now and the fir needles rustled in the wind. I stayed stock still, my antennae fully tuned up. A muted cry carried from somewhere across the lake. I hadn't heard that sound in a while. It was an osprey calling to its mate.

I moved closer to the wall, placing each step with absolute care, toe then heel. When I reached it I stopped again, mouth open, ears on stalks.

There was nothing at first, then movement on the far side. Low voices. Footsteps. Two hostiles. Maybe three. The flash of a torch beam. Why would they bother to try to become part of the night? They were guarding the place, not invading it. And I didn't need to clamber up seven feet of strongly mortared stone to put them to the test.

Plan A had hit a rock. But Plan B had already started to take shape in my head.

I melted back into the trees and retraced my route.

3

The car park at the Half Moon had become a lot more crowded by the time I got back to it. Light blazed from the pub windows, and snatches of conversation and the steady beat of the jukebox leaked out into the darkness. It wasn't exactly Saturday-night fever, but if I'd been the landlord I wouldn't have complained.

The white van had gone home for dinner but the Volvo was staying on. The door from the bar opened and closed, and there was a blast of Rihanna's 'You Da One'. I ducked into the shadows while two surfies climbed into a Volkswagen camper van and made for the exit.

The Volvo team had very thoughtfully strapped their paddles onto the roof bars as well as the kayaks. I felt like leaving them a thank-you note. I unfastened the nearest paddle, then liberated the darker of the two craft and swung it down by its grab handle. It was about two and a half metres long, eighty centimetres wide and pretty unwieldy, especially when it caught the breeze, but it wasn't much heavier than one of Anna's suitcases. Someone had spent a lot of quality time painting its name across one side: *Smoke on the Water*. I hoped it wasn't luminous.

I hoicked it to the end of the stretch of gravel that was furthest from the building, then manhandled it over a chain-link fence. Fuck

462

knows what I would have done if the owners had chosen that moment to come out and check their kit, but I made it along the edge of a spiky stubble field and into cover before Rihanna came back for an encore.

A hedgerow skirted the parking area, then paralleled the lane. I kept behind it most of the way to the lake. It took me a good half-hour. No more cars came past, and there were no signs of life in the sailing-club hut or on the hard standing that ran for about fifteen metres along the bank.

I lugged *Smoke* to the slipway, past a line of dinghies on light aluminium launching trolleys. I took several deep breaths then flipped it, hull down, onto the water, soaking my right Timberland in the process.

These craft were built for stability as well as speed through some pretty big waves, so it wasn't too difficult to get my feet and arse into position on its moulded deck without taking another dip.

I made sure the Browning was still tucked securely into the front of my jeans, then gripped the paddle shaft like a punt pole. There was a grinding noise as I levered myself away from the concrete, then I was clear. I flattened the shaft, dug in with one blade then the other, and started to make headway.

The lake ran north/south, and a series of spits and small tree-lined bays fringed this side of it, so I aimed to stay fairly close to the shore for the first part of the journey rather than venture straight into open water. The moon was in its final quarter and the sky was overcast, but there were no islands out there I could use as cover, and I didn't want to announce my presence until I was good and ready.

The osprey gave another cry. Then all I could hear was the water lapping against the hull, and the occasional splash when I misjudged the timing or the angle of a blade as it broke the surface.

I'd done all sorts of insertions and extractions via the ocean over the years, usually in a RIB with a pair of monster outboards on the back, but I'd never spent much of my leisure time with oars or sails. White-water rafting was different: I'd always thought that was more like a combo of freefalling and hand-to-hand combat than messing around in boats. Whatever, I began to get the hang of this, and the kayak glided south, more or less in the direction I wanted.

The cold began eating into my hands. I was only going to use the Browning if everything went to rat shit, but thicker gloves would have made it impossible. My right foot squelched inside its sock every time I pulled the face of my left blade towards me, and that was no fun either. But there was no point in worrying about what I couldn't change.

At least the wind was at my back. It kept my core temperature from dropping too fast and helped push me through the water. The gusts strengthened as I propelled the lump of moulded plastic further away from the shelter of the firs.

After I'd gone a mile or so I began to visualize how I would infiltrate Ravenhill. Cutting away took on a different meaning during this phase of a task. I had to ditch all the irrelevant shit and focus on my priorities. I needed to cruise into Guy Chastain's boathouse without being seen or heard, locate where the Astra muscle was holding Ella, and take it from there.

The only light came from my right, from the headlamps of the wagons cruising along the main on the opposite side of the pond. There was a chance I'd be silhouetted against it before I reached the cover of the jetty, but I hoped anyone watching out for a threat from the water would be dazzled by the glare instead.

4

The closer I got to Ravenhill, the more I had to risk scudding further towards the middle of the lake. I was a long way from Olympic gold, but I didn't want the sound of my paddles to carry too easily to the shore.

When I was still a couple of hundred away I brought the kayak to a standstill. Steadying it from time to time in the water, I scanned the shore. A guard made his way to the end of the jetty and back at roughly fifteen-minute intervals.

There were lights on in the main house and the upper floor of the converted stable block behind and to its left, and shadows fell across their windows. The odd torch beam bounced around in the trees. When I could no longer spot movement in the vicinity of the darkened boathouse, I brought the nose of the kayak round and paddled slowly towards the mandarin temple.

The jetty was mounted on two rows of wooden pillars driven into the lake bed. The crosspieces were horizontal rather than diagonal and about a metre above the surface of the water, so I was going to be able to slide in beneath it.

The wind was now coming in from my left, so I'd have to do my best to stop it blowing me into the superstructure. A big solid clunk would carry

466

through the night air and catapult a reception committee in my direction at warp speed.

I reached out to fend off the second pillar with my right palm and came away with a smear of algae. The lapping of the water against the woodwork echoed across the space below the platform. I passed a slimy metal ladder with a pair of curved handrails and saw another ahead of me, leading up to the sundeck.

A coil of shock cord was secured by a Velcro strap at each end of the kayak. When I was within reach of my target, I looped the bow line around the pillar closest to the wind and let the current rotate the stern towards the one parallel to it.

The kayak would be visible to anyone who got down on his belt buckle and busy with a torch, but I figured that a mooring beneath the jetty, parallel to the shore, was as good as I was going to get.

I turned in the seat, got to my knees and manoeuvred myself as quietly as I could across the rear luggage recess. As I was fastening the second cord I heard footsteps, followed by a dull thud about eighteen inches above my head.

5

I didn't move a muscle for five beats.

Then I loosened my jaw, opened my mouth and, as slowly as possible, lifted the ribbed hem of my bomber jacket with my left hand far enough to allow me to grip the butt of Sam's pistol with my right.

I looked up.

A dark figure began to materialize through the half-centimetre gaps between the ribbed planks. So did the silhouette of a weapon. I eased the Browning out of my waistband and slid my index finger through the trigger guard. I raised the muzzle and applied first pressure.

I had no intention of going the whole way unless whoever was up there decided to draw down on me, but it made me feel like I wasn't completely hopeless.

The wood creaked and the footsteps moved on. An LED torch sparked up at the far end of the jetty and swept the water beyond the temple. I stayed where I was; I needed to remain covert as long as possible.

Eventually the light flicked off and the footsteps made their way back towards me. I listened as they mounted the steps and disappeared up the pathway that ran along the side of the boathouse.

I waited for the silence to return, then thumbed on the Browning's safety catch. I didn't want to blow my bollocks apart as I swung out onto the steps and kitten-crawled across the sundeck.

I slithered up towards the entrance to the boathouse before rising to my feet. I opened my mouth and tuned in to my surroundings. I sensed rather than heard a low moan from somewhere nearby, but maybe it was the woodwork settling down for the night.

I worked my way softly past the windows overlooking the lake. I stopped for a moment when I reached the corner of the building and was about to move on when I became aware of a shadowy presence on the other side of the glass.

Marcia Chastain was standing there in the darkness, no more than two feet away from me. Her face was racked with pain. I couldn't see what filled the frame that she was clutching to her chest, but I knew it had to be Guy's citation and VC.

I waited for the alarm bells to start ringing; there was nothing else I could do.

She looked right through me.

There was no room for anyone else in her world of misery.

I hesitated for a nanosecond, then decided to go and have a little chat with her. I might have to give her a bit of a slap, but I reckoned she could provide my best — and quickest — route to some of the answers I needed.

I only managed to take one step back towards the door before everything changed.

Marcia Chastain's mouth opened. I froze. Any second now she'd be filling her lungs.

469

But she didn't yell for help. She just gave another low moan.

Then I felt a pair of electrodes cold against my neck.

The weapon I'd seen through the planking on the jetty had been a Taser. The lad holding the other end of it murmured in my ear, 'I think she deserves a little bit of peace right now, don't you?'

6

The colonel's foot soldier steered me away from the boathouse entrance. I didn't resist. The last thing I needed right now was fifty thousand volts jumping up and down on my nerve endings. And I was pretty sure he wouldn't want to risk staying this close to me all the way up to the house. Any second now he'd have to push me far enough in front to give himself the space to clip a cartridge onto the business end of the Taser, so he'd be able to control me from a distance. That would be my best time to fuck him up.

Triggered by a compressed gas cartridge, the twin metal barbs could be fired nearly twenty feet. They were designed to leave their housing at an eight-degree angle, each trailing a thin wire and targeting two separate muscle groups. One would make a beeline for my thigh, to stop me doing a runner.

Once embedded in my skin or clothing, the probes could be fed enough current to fuck my motor skills with every squeeze of the trigger. I'd turn into a puppet on a chain. I had to make sure that didn't happen.

Sure enough, as soon as we cleared the corner of the building I felt his left hand press against the middle of my back and the electrodes leave my neck. I swivelled 180 degrees and grabbed his wrist before he'd lifted the hand away and pulled him with me, using his forward

471

momentum to propel us both in the direction we'd been heading.

My arse hit the grass, then my back. I bent my knees, planted both feet in his gut, and straightened them again as I kept on going. He flew straight over my head.

I wanted to mess him up enough to be able to give him the good news with his own cattle prod, but as soon as I'd rolled to one side and sprung back to my feet, I saw that I'd rammed the top of his skull straight into the trunk of the nearest pine. He lay in a heap beneath it.

I hadn't broken his neck, but he'd have a severely sore brain when he woke up. I gaffer-taped his wrists and ankles and stuck another strip over his mouth, then dragged him five metres into the undergrowth. Once in cover, I relieved him of his UHF radio, clipped it to my belt, lifted the right side of my balaclava and shoved in the earpiece.

I straightened the Browning in my waistband and picked up the Taser and spare cartridge. The X26 had a pistol grip and a bulbous nose, a bit like an underwater flash lamp. The Met Police used them to neutralize offenders. Theirs were Day-Glo yellow. I preferred this black version. It wasn't designed to draw attention to itself.

As I took a step back towards the boathouse, a torch beam bounced down onto the sundeck. I stayed where I was, inside the treeline. It stopped halfway along the jetty and traced a slow arc across the water, taking in the mandarin temple and the stretch of bank to my half-right before clicking off.

A match flared and the tip of a cigarette glowed briefly before being cupped in a gloved palm. Elbows rested on the wooden rail and a plume of smoke coiled into the night air. This lad was there to stay.

I turned slowly back towards the big house. Three other beams swept through the darkness up there. One kept close to the stable block and two others patrolled the woods separating it from the road.

If Ella was at Ravenhill, the colonel wouldn't have stuck her in a hole in the ground, but he wouldn't have wanted her down the corridor from Mrs Chastain's bedroom either.

I decided to check the stables first. Apart from anything else, I was familiar with the layout of the place. Unless they'd done a whole lot more than renew the wallpaper since the Sweden briefing, I reckoned I had a better than evens chance of not bumping into any brick walls, and of knowing where the Astra crew might be focusing their energies.

I heeled and toed through the dropped pine needles and bracken, keeping noise to an absolute minimum. When I was still far enough away from my target to be out of earshot, I sparked up the radio and listened in to the traffic between the other members of Chastain's unit. Alpha was on the net, telling Bravo and Charlie to keep eyes on the roadside boundary, and wondering where Delta had disappeared to.

'Alpha, Delta? Alpha, Delta, *check* . . .'

I was pretty sure that Delta wasn't sending because some dick-head had banged him on the head, taped his lips together and nicked his UHF radio. I waited long enough to be certain before thumbing the pressel.

'Alpha, this is Delta. Two bodies making entry on the south side of the compound . . . ' I'd heard only one sentence from Delta, so my impression of him probably sounded more like Jack Bauer. Whatever, the torches ahead of me stopped in their tracks.

'Roger that, Delta. All call signs move to the south side *now*. Acknowledge . . . '

'Bravo . . . '

'Bravo, roger that.'

'Charlie . . . '

Charlie had either switched off, or wasn't playing.

Alpha got back on the net. 'Charlie . . . ' Only one word, but you could tell he wasn't impressed.

'Charlie, acknowledge . . . '

Another couple of seconds of silence, then: 'Charlie, roger that.'

They'd be running through the possibles. Was someone fucking them around? Was it a genuine alert? How quickly would Chastain send them their P45s if they messed up?

All three moved fast to my right, snapping off their torches as they went. I saw dark figures legging it across the driveway and back into the trees on the far side of it. If the lad on the jetty had finished smoking himself to death, maybe he'd crack on over there too.

It wouldn't take them all night to discover that there was nothing going on at the southern boundary, but it might buy me time to poke around.

Keeping the Taser at the ready, I aimed for the far corner of the stable block.

475

7

There were two serious stone buildings in this part of the estate: a long, two-storey affair with bedroom suites where the hay lofts used to be, and a row of designer garages. The cobbled yard between them was accessible at each end via an archway.

The southern arch opened onto a short drive, which linked the guest wing to the big house. I approached from the north, past a random selection of outhouses and through a walled garden. When I'd last been here every spring flower and veggie had been standing to attention like they were Trooping the Colour. Now the bare earth and skeletal branches reminded me of a deserted First World War battlefield.

A cast-iron spiral staircase to my left led to the first floor. The fire door at the top was my first choice of exit, but I didn't bother going up. It had been Harry's favourite place for a smoke twenty years ago, and unless you'd wedged the thing open there was no easy way in.

The yard was empty, apart from a parked-up Defender. Once I'd satisfied myself that no one was inside it, I scanned the top storey. There were six suites up there. Each of them had one bedroom and one bathroom window. Light glowed through the curtains of the four windows closest to me. The other eight gave me a blank stare.

I triggered a motion sensor as I hit the cobbles and filled the space with light, but I couldn't hang around. Thanks to my UHF radio stunt, the clock had started ticking big-time. I moved fast along the stable wall and swerved through the main entrance, pulling off my balaclava as I went and bundling it into my pocket.

A library, a conference room, a twenty-seat home cinema and a recreation room filled the ground floor. Me, Trev and Harry had spent some quality time doing Hurricane Higgins impressions around the full-size snooker table when we'd finished our homework back in 'ninety-two, but a lot of the other toys were new. I guessed that the whole complex saw a fair amount of corporate action, these days, whenever the boss didn't fancy being tied to his desk at Astra's London HQ.

I gave this level a rapid onceover, eavesdropping on Alpha, Bravo and Charlie as I went. They hadn't reached the south wall yet, but were getting increasingly pissed off about Delta's vanishing act. I cleared each room, then powered down the radio and took the stairs two at a time.

I slowed before I reached the top landing, crouched low on the deep-pile oatmeal carpet, breathed deeply, and glanced right and left. The corridor was empty. There were still six entrances leading off the far side of it, three in each direction, and the fire escape at the gable end.

Treading lightly, I angled right, towards the two suites whose lights I'd seen from below. I wasn't assuming that the dark ones were unoccupied, but I'd clear them later if necessary.

477

I ignored the first door I came to. The second opened with a turn of the handle.

Everything inside looked like it had done when I'd camped there. The half-unpacked Bergen beside the bed and the kit strewn across the sofa and floor told me all I needed to know. This was a BG's accommodation. And that meant a VIP close by. Or a prisoner.

I listened for movement in the en-suite bathroom. There was none. I eased the door shut again and took another slow, deep breath.

The last door before the fire escape was five metres away. I moved soundlessly towards it and tilted my left ear towards the upper panel. This time I heard muffled but urgent voices. I gripped the shiny brass knob with my left hand, keeping the Taser at the ready in my right. It didn't shift more than a millimetre.

The latch was designed for privacy, not confinement, and I didn't have time to mince around. I took two steps back and slammed the sole of my Timberland against the point where it met the frame.

8

It burst inwards, wrenching the strike plate from its housing.

This room was bigger than the one I'd just left, and a whole lot tidier. Even the handcuffs attached to the metal bedstead had been neatly arranged.

Ella was sitting opposite me, behind a low, granite-topped table, in a freshly laundered blue dress that fitted OK but didn't look like it belonged to her. She didn't say hello. Most of her attention was focused on the Glock against her temple.

The guy holding it was sitting behind her. He leaned into view, taking care not to make himself an easy target.

I could see cold eyes and thin lips through his balaclava, but I concentrated on his weapon too. I took a step towards them and saw his index finger curl as he applied first pressure on the trigger.

'Move another inch and this won't end well.' The voice was level, with a hint of Jock.

This lad wasn't flapping.

But he *was* bluffing. If he killed Ella, Chastain no longer had a hold on Sam.

The barrel swung in my direction, and stopped when it was pointed at my centre mass.

'Before you do anything stupid, you need to know I won't hurt her. But I don't give a fuck how many rounds I have to put into you.'

The muzzle of the Glock moved fractionally in the direction of the X26 and the lips moved again. 'Drop it.'

When Chastain's Serbian heavies had delivered the girl to the Astra crew, they obviously hadn't warned them about her. He was too busy reading my mind to pay her the attention she deserved. Ella's right arm shot up and smacked his weapon out of his hand.

He tried to get to his feet as she dived to her left and I brought up the Taser. The red dot from its laser pointer zeroed in on his fleece and, before he could count to one, fifty thousand volts surged along the command wires to the barbs that had buried themselves in his chest and leg.

He hit the deck like a felled pine. Nineteen pulses a second had hijacked his muscle control. He couldn't even throw out his hands to stop himself head-butting the granite-topped table between us.

I handed the X26 to Ella and told her to keep her finger on the trigger. While she kept feeding him more current I hauled him across the room and gaffer-taped his wrists and ankles.

Once I'd cuffed him to the bedframe, I grabbed the top of his mask and pulled it off. I'd assumed he was wearing it to prevent Ella from recognizing him, but now wondered if he'd got self-conscious about his hair. It was a peroxide blond mat on the top of an otherwise shaven skull.

He'd severely malleted his nose, and blood and snot bubbled down his chin as he opened his eyes and tried to get some air into his lungs. I wound more tape over his mouth and round the back of his neck. It wasn't going to help his breathing, but I didn't give a shit about that.

I unclipped his UHF radio from his belt and pulled out his earpiece, then sparked up the one I'd borrowed from his mate down by the boathouse. Alpha was on the net, still pissed off with Delta, but ordering Bravo, Charlie and Echo to spread out and trawl through the trees along the southern boundary, all the way to the lake. Echo must have been the smoker on the jetty, which probably made the lad with the stupid hair Foxtrot.

Fucking brilliant. I thought they'd already be on their way back, but now reckoned we'd have a clear half-hour to hotwire the Defender in the yard and get the hell out of here. Things were finally going our way.

To celebrate, I handed Ella a bottle of designer mineral water from the bedside cabinet and treated myself to one too. We rehydrated and I gave Foxtrot another five-second burst through the barbs while she fetched her Puffa jacket. Then we legged it left to the fire escape.

I led. Ella followed.

9

Back in the day, Harry had disabled the motion sensor beside the steel door because he didn't like being dazzled during his cigarette breaks, but some fucker had fixed it. The LED security lights snapped on before we were halfway to the ground.

Chastain and his crew were lined up in the walled garden below us like a firing squad. Alpha, Bravo and Charlie weren't still bumbling around in the woods. They were right here, Glock 17s in the aim.

Before we could even think of scrambling back the way we'd come, Echo appeared on the grating above us. He was in Billy the Kid mode, a Glock in his right hand and an X26 in his left. His job was to encourage us down.

Chastain couldn't bring himself to look me in the eye as we stepped out into the First World War battlefield, but the guy standing beside him didn't even try to camouflage his grin. He had the buttoned-down shirt and buttoned-down hair of an ex-Rupert, so I assumed he was Alpha. He was pretty pleased with himself — and why not? I'd played the bogus radio callout card, and he'd trumped it.

Echo plasticuffed my wrists behind my back and took far longer than necessary to frisk me. I wasn't sure what was on his mind, but he managed to make the whole process intensely personal. Maybe the lad I'd launched into the tree was his brother. He finally unzipped my bomber and reclaimed Delta's radio, then removed Sam's Browning from my waistband and the extra mag from my pocket and handed them both to Chastain.

After frisking Ella, he waved us through the archway and into the courtyard.

10

We were shepherded through the main entrance of the stable block. Echo was sent upstairs to see whether Foxtrot was ready to join the party.

Chastain led the way towards the conference room. I didn't know what version of events he'd given his team, but he instructed them to stay outside in the foyer with Ella while he caught up with me.

He closed the door behind us and steered me towards a seat at the head of the oak table. I'd been right about the flapjacks. They were nowhere to be seen.

He didn't draw down the blinds on the double-glazed panels that now separated us from Ella and the call signs. He obviously didn't want me to forget they were there. Charlie disappeared as Echo and Foxtrot joined the group. The lad with the stupid hair had shed the gaffer tape, but he still wasn't a pretty sight. He glanced in my direction and gave me the strong impression that he'd be rearranging my face too, if he got half a chance.

Chastain thumbed on the Browning's safety catch and put it in the pocket of his Barbour. He remained standing.

One of us had to kick this whole thing off, so I thought it might as well be me.

'I know what happened at the compound in Koshtay. Blackwood has all the details in an envelope. Unless I tell him not to, he'll open it in court . . . ' I glanced up at the row of clocks on the far wall that told me what time it was in London, New York, Bogotá, Baghdad, Beijing and three or four other places, ' . . . in under thirty-six hours.

'And in case you think you might find a way to stop that happening, I have a geeky mate who'll go the Wikileaks route if he doesn't hear from me.' I was talking bollocks, but he wasn't to know that.

He went very still, then sighed deeply. I recognized the signs. Whenever he'd delivered a bollocking back at the Lines he'd liked us to feel it was more in sorrow than in anger.

This time it was a combo of both.

'Have you *any* idea how much damage that will do?'

I shrugged. 'I don't give a shit. All I care about is a lad who doesn't deserve to take the rap for the murder of his best mate.'

'None of this would have happened if those two idiots had managed to button their lips . . . '

His knuckles whitened as he gripped the chair back in front of him. I could see that he was trying to stop himself vibrating with rage.

'I'm pretty sure it was only Scott who forgot to press the mute button, first at the Palace, then when everything got too much for him one Saturday night. And that made Jack Grant think your son's VC was about to go down the plughole. Was the CQB plan your idea?'

Chastain clenched his jaw, then shook his head. 'It was never a plan. Jack was an old friend.

He called me when he left the Green Dragon. I told him to watch and wait. The CQB solution was a spur-of-the-moment thing. He thought the world of those boys. But he believed — as I do — that the institution is more important than the individual.'

'The Regiment or the medal?'

'Both. They stand for something bigger than all of us. Something worth defending. To the death. Imagine the shame for our nation if a VC has to be forfeited now, for the first time in over a century. It won't happen on my watch.

'Don't mistake this for personal vanity. I want to protect my son's reputation, of course. It's all his mother and I have left of him. But in the current climate, now that every single hiccup in the battle space comes under the scrutiny of damned Islington lawyers who don't know one end of an RPG from the other, we must champion greater causes.

'Above all, Queen Victoria's tribute to extreme valour in the face of the enemy must remain unblemished because we can't continue to fight today's dirty little wars if we lose our grip on the moral high ground.'

'Your Serbian mates wouldn't recognize the moral high ground if it bit them on the arse. And what about killing Trev and kidnapping Ella? How the fuck do you defend that?'

'Both those things are extremely regrettable. But, as I'm sure you're now aware, we need the girl to ensure Callard's continuing compliance. Trevor was uncomfortably close to establishing the connection between the Killing House, the

486

events that led up to Guy's VC action, and my attempts to keep the whole situation under some kind of control. He even came up here to confront me.'

'No, he didn't! He came up here to ask for your help! Like me, he wasted a whole lot of time thinking that DSF was the Prince of Darkness, and that you're still the man who was always there for us when everything goes to rat shit.'

'I'm glad you've brought that up, Sergeant bloody perfect Stone, because quite high on that particular list is a certain Swedish task that was *all* about revenge.'

'Shit happens. We all know that. And Grant might have fired the first shot on his own initiative. But Trev was killed on *your* orders, and you only kept me alive so that I could lead Sam into an ambush that would shut us both up permanently.

'And what happens to Ella now? She's pinged the lot of you. You're not going to be able to just wave her goodbye. No matter how you try to dress this up, you're guilty of betrayal, you're guilty of abduction and you're guilty of murder.'

If our eyeballs had been lasers at that moment, we'd both have gone up in smoke. For the first time since I'd known him, he didn't seem to have an immediate answer.

'And *you* may have found a way of justifying all this shit, but what about your wife?'

Chastain erupted big-time. '*Leave her out of this, you little shit. I'm defending the things she holds sacred as well.*'

He thundered down the room towards me.

Fuck knows what he would have done if Alpha hadn't thrown open the door when he was still a couple of metres away.

'Boss, you're needed down at the boathouse. It's urgent.'

He wasn't smiling now.

11

Alpha guided Chastain down the corridor, grabbing Ella as they went. Bravo followed, leaving Echo and Foxtrot to look after me. I guessed that Delta still had his head down in the woods beside the boathouse. Maybe they'd trip over him on the way.

I planted my Timberlands on the carpet and slid back my chair, but didn't get up.

You could have cut through the tension in the air with a knife. And it wasn't just because these two lads hadn't taken a liking to me. Something was happening down by the lakeshore, and I was pretty sure I knew what it was.

Echo stayed by the doorway, Glock in the aim.

Foxtrot circled the table, so that he'd stay out of Echo's line of fire. I kept eyes on him as he came for me. Someone had removed the Taser barbs from his chest and leg and slapped a dressing on his very flat nose, but it hadn't improved his mood.

I filled my lungs, flexed my leg muscles, eased my feet back another eighteen inches so that they were planted beneath my arse, and braced myself for what was about to happen.

He bunched his right fist and drove it into my gut, but he'd wanted so badly to crack it into the middle of my face that he didn't give the blow a hundred per cent. I doubled over to look like I was taking the pain then sprang off my launch pad before he had time to step back. Uncurling as I went, I slammed the back of my skull at warp speed into his chin.

I felt Foxtrot's jaw crack before I heard it and straightened in time to see him stagger backwards, taking out chairs like dominoes. He crumpled beside the table, spat out a couple of blood-stained teeth, brought both hands up to his face and lay there moaning.

He was having the mother of all bad-hair days. And the carpet was going to need some attention too.

I turned slowly back towards the door. I figured that Echo wouldn't kill me until Chastain had decided what to do about the Wikileak challenge, but I thought I might get a round in the thigh for my trouble. I controlled my breathing and kept my weight on my toes. Maybe he'd make the mistake of coming closer as well.

The muzzle of the Glock hadn't moved an inch, and neither had he.

Something was coming in through his earpiece.

He dropped his left hand to the pressel of the radio on his belt. 'Roger that.'

He motioned me to join him in the corridor. Neither of us gave Foxtrot a second glance as we left the room.

12

Lights blazed from the boathouse windows and spilled out across the water. Echo followed me along the path beside it, round the corner and shoved me inside.

The other call signs stood back, doing their best to disappear into the wallpaper. There wasn't a Glock in sight. It wasn't that kind of party.

Guy's VC and citation lay among the wreckage of the frame at the centre of the room. Chastain was kneeling, oblivious, on the shards of glass that were scattered across the polished floor-boards around it, rocking back and forth like Harry had done, back in our Baghdad cell.

He clutched Marcia in his arms.

Two pill bottles and an empty blister pack lay on the low table by the armchair she must have retreated to. Ella stood to one side of them. She'd clearly been in paramedic mode. I glanced down at the dog-eared photo of a small boy in a rowing boat propped against the remains of a half-bottle of Scotch, then up at her.

She shook her head. 'Clomipramine, moclobe-mide and paracetamol. Maybe St John's wort too. Not a cry for help, I'm afraid.'

Marcia didn't deserve this. She'd been knocked sideways by the death of her son. Watching her husband go insane must have tipped her over the edge.

491

For a good five minutes, nobody moved.

Ella put her hands on Chastain's shoulders and murmured in his ear. He had finally joined Marcia's world of pain, but he tuned into whatever message the doc had given him, and allowed her to help him carry his wife's body back to her chair.

He covered Marcia with a blanket. Maybe he couldn't deal with the fact that she looked like she had finally found the peace he couldn't give her.

Then he dusted the fragments of glass off his trousers, apparently puzzled by the flecks of blood that had gathered where they'd pierced the material and his skin, and straightened.

He was back on the parade ground.

I watched his hand dip into his Barbour pocket and reappear with Sam's Browning. He didn't check chamber and flip off the safety catch until he reached the door. Then he turned and looked at Ella.

'Thank you . . . for your grace.'

He paused.

'And though I know this will do little to console you both . . . I'm truly sorry . . . '

He switched his attention to me. 'One request?'

I nodded.

'The Koshtay incident dies with me?'

I gestured towards Ella. 'As long as you tell your foot soldiers to keep away from her. For ever.'

The instruction was given.

Echo stepped aside to let Chastain pass.

We watched him walk to the end of the jetty.

He stood for a moment beneath the cover of the mandarin temple, placed the barrel of Sam Callard's pistol very precisely against the roof of his mouth and squeezed the trigger.

EPILOGUE

EPILOGUE

The King's House, Glencoe

Friday, 6 April
12.30 hrs

Mist clung to one or two of the hilltops that flanked the valley. The bright sunlight made the greens of the grasses and the reds and browns of the heather on the lower slopes come alive, but it was still a lonely place.

I pulled off the main where a three-sided wooden pyramid marked the turning, and cruised towards a herd of Highland deer. One or two of the boys with the big fuck-off antlers looked up as I passed, but soon went back to munching the spring foliage.

I parked the 911 beside the trees and walked into the hotel. I'd picked it up from Father Gerard after the Cheltenham Gold Cup, but said he could have it back for the National next weekend. I'd run the Skoda through a nearby carwash. Amazingly, it didn't have a scratch on it. Maybe his rosary beads worked after all.

A serious selection of single malts was lined up in front of the mirrors behind the King's House bar. I knew I should be toasting Catriona's remission, but I wasn't in the mood. And not just because it was Good Friday. I settled for a bottle of Diet Coke, took it to a table in the corner and pulled out the bench.

I'd slowed my life right down over the last few weeks, partly because I didn't have a clear idea what I was going to do next. I'd driven Ella back to her scented candles and her shepherd's hut, but hadn't seen her since. Neither of us went to the Chastain funeral.

The media reported that the colonel had remained a hero to the last. In the face of his son's selfless sacrifice and his wife's tragic overdose, he had chosen a soldier's death. The congregation sang 'Jerusalem' as their coffins were carried from the local church.

I'd had tea and biscuits with DSF, and let him know that no one would hear the truth about Koshtay and the CQB Rooms from me.

He said that our Serbian friends had been sent back, under escort, to their homeland. The local law-enforcement people had slapped a Red Notice on them: they'd been charged with the murder of a Muslim by a church in the Belgrade Fortress.

I'd found a flat near St Saviour's Dock, but hadn't yet made an offer. If I did, I thought I might drop by and see how life was treating Dave. But right now I had one last piece of unfinished business.

Al threw open the door before I'd had my second swig of Coke. He came straight over and clapped me on the back. 'Great news about Harry's boy!'

His eyes were back on full beam and his beard was totally out of control, but his grin sat very uncomfortably between them.

I gave him a brisk nod. 'No case to answer.'

Jack Grant had left a suicide note. It was one of the things he'd had to sort before I could come back to continue our chat at Bob's apartment.

'DSF has asked him to stay on. I don't know if he will. He might just settle down with his girlfriend and be happy.'

Al frowned at my glass and told me this called for a celebration. I said he should go for it, but that I wouldn't join him. I had a big drive ahead of me.

When he came back from the bar with a man-size Lagavulin, I handed him a piece of paper.

Al gave it no more than a brief glance, then folded it in two and put it in his pocket. It wasn't news to him. He didn't need to read a print-out from the Companies House website, recording the successful acquisition of AGS by a major PMC on Monday, 6 February. A PMC called Astra.

His grin had disappeared. He opened and closed his mouth like a big furry goldfish. No words came out.

'So you're going to be Monarch of the Glen, after all. Hope it's worth it.'

His pain leaked out of every pore. 'It's all about Catriona, Nick. You must believe that . . . '

I did believe it, actually. I was also doing my best to believe Al had had no idea that he and his new best mate at Barford were part of a plan to deliver me and Sam to Chastain's ink-stained reception committee.

I didn't ask. There were still some things I never wanted to know.

'I'm pleased she's on the mend, Al. I really

am. Maybe we'll all be able to raise a glass together another time.'

I pushed back the bench, got up, and headed outside.

Other titles published by Ulverscroft:

FORTRESS

Andy McNab

When SAS trooper Tom Buckingham takes down a renegade Afghan soldier, he's made a scapegoat for the incident and drummed out of the regiment. On his return to Britain, disillusioned and embittered, Tom's unique services are quickly snapped up by charismatic entrepreneur Vernon Rolt, a powerful billionaire with political ambitions and very few scruples. With riots on the country's streets, a government in disarray, and a visit from the American President imminent, there has never been a better time to make a play for power. But, as Tom will soon discover, in the affairs of state hidden forces are always at work. He will have to decide where his loyalties lie and who his real friends are if he is to intervene in a spiralling sequence of events that involve terrorism, insurgency and, ultimately, assassination . . .

RED NOTICE

Andy McNab

Deep beneath the English Channel on a Paris-bound express, a crack team of East European terrorists has taken four hundred hostages at gunpoint — and declared war on a British government with more than its own fair share of secrets to keep. One man stands in their way: Tom Buckingham, an off-duty SAS soldier who is on board. With only a failing mobile to contact the outside world, he must use all his tradecraft and know-how to take out the enemy and secure the train. But the odds are stacked against him — twelve battle-hardened, tooled-up veterans of a bitter civil war to his one, unarmed and injured. And little does he know that someone on his own side is determined that no one will get out of that tunnel alive . . .

SILENCER

Andy McNab

1993: Under deep cover, SAS operative Nick Stone has spent weeks in the jungles of Colombia. His mission: to locate the boss of the world's most murderous drugs cartel — and terminate him. But to get close enough to fire the fatal shot, Nick must reveal his face. It's a risk he's willing to take, since only the man who is about to die will see him. Or so he thinks . . . 2011: Now living in Moscow, Nick has just become a father. When the doctor who has saved his newborn son's life suddenly vanishes, Nick finds himself racing across the globe in a quest to find her before it's too late. The trail leads from Moldova, to Hong Kong, to Mexico, propelling him back into the brutal world he thought he'd left behind . . .

DEAD CENTRE

Andy McNab

Somalia — a lawless, violent land, ignored by the West, ripped apart by civil war and famine, fought over by drug-fuelled, gun-crazy clan fighters. They want the world to sit up and take notice. They have a new and terrifying weapon — pirates. And now, the pirates have in their possession the young son of a Russian oligarch, snatched from a luxury yacht in the Seychelles. His father wants him back, will pay anything, stop at nothing to retrieve his boy. Up to now everything he has tried has failed. He needs the one man with the know-how, the means and the guts to complete the mission: ex-SAS trouble-shooter Nick Stone . . .

ZERO HOUR

Andy McNab

When the daughter of a Moldovan business-man goes missing from her university, British Intelligence want Nick Stone, the only man ruthless enough, to track her down — but this time he doesn't want to play ball . . . FACT: On 5 September, 2007, Israeli jets bombed a suspected nuclear installation in north-eastern Syria — its supposedly state-of-the-art radar failed to provide warning of the attack. FACT: Known only to the Israelis and the radar's manufacturers, the commercial microprocessors within it contained a remotely accessible kill switch. But what is the raid's connection with the missing student? What is the secret to Britain's security to which, unwittingly, she holds the key? And when Stone is tasked to find and abduct her, why is he not on 'receive'?